BETRAYAL OF THE TRUST

BETRAYAL OF THE TRUST

LESLIE ESDAILE-BANKS

Dafina Books

KENSINGTON PUBLISHING CORP.
http://www.kensingtonbooks.com

DAFINA BOOKS are published by

Kensington Publishing Corp.
850 Third Avenue
New York, NY 10022

All Kensington titles, imprints and distributed lines are available at special quantity discounts for bulk purchases for sales promotion, premiums, fund-raising, educational or institutional use.

Special book excerpts or customized printings can also be created to fit specific needs. For details, write or phone the office of the Kensington Special Sales Manager: Kensington Publishing Corp., 850 Third Avenue, New York, NY 10022. Attn. Special Sales Department. Phone: 1-800-221-2647.

First Trade Paperback Printing: November 2004
First Mass Market Paperback Printing: August 2005
10 9 8 7 6 5 4 3 2 1

Printed in the United States of America

This novel is dedicated first and foremost to The Creator, Mother/Father God—who sees all things and whose justice always wins out in the end. It is also dedicated to my parents, two people who lived their lives with many dreams deferred, but who also raised us to have faith, hope, and love for our community. They never gave up, never stopped praying, and never stopped giving. Thank you Mom and Dad for instilling that connection to something larger than myself within me.

However, after working with hundreds of hope-filled entrepreneurs within the social construct of economic development . . . and seeing those grass roots community leaders try to make a way out of seemingly no way for so many with so little resources, and watching the dynamic of social program funding (or the lack thereof), this book is for all those people on the front lines (who also, ironically, work behind the scenes with plenty of guts and no glory). You know who you are—the people who make a positive change, if only in one person's life.

Acknowledgments

I have to acknowledge my agent, Manie Barron, who had the unparalleled vision to allow me to write a sexy female Robin Hood—just so I could get the concept of social justice down on paper; my editor, Karen Thomas, who embraced the project and added her own special panache; and to all my "girls" in the eco-dev world, who stood by me while I gnashed my teeth and became philosophically dramatic: Tina, DL, Darlene, Isabelle, Mo, Iola, Nancy, Carole, Bernadine, Debbie, Linda, Clorise, Asake, Jeanne, Winnie, Asantewaa, Lorene, Pam—hope I didn't miss anybody! Y'all are fabulous, and for every small business you've assisted, you'll find stars in your crown. Bless you!

Chapter 1

The Four Seasons Hotel
Center City, Philadelphia
Present day

"Yeah . . . baby, like that," Darien moaned, his eyes now slits as he watched the top of Najira's head.

She peered up at him as she slowly dragged her tongue the length of his shaft. "You coulda fed a sister first, though," she teased with a devilish grin. "Dag. I thought we were at least gonna get some breakfast in this swank joint."

"I don't have time this morning. Stop playing with it and do it for real. I'll take you somewhere nice later. I promise."

Najira sucked her teeth and offered him a scowl. She couldn't believe how stupid this arrogant bastard was to be getting his swerve on, especially with everything that was blowing up around him. *This* was who was running the major education programs in the city?

"Oh, so I'm not gonna get mine done, *plus* you ain't feeding me? Now, how that sound? My cha-cha needs a little attention; kitty's purring, too, ya know," she said in a huff.

"Baby, come on. I've gotta go meet my attorney and—"

"And I have to go to work, *on time,* or I'll lose my temp agency slot—"

"I promise I'll hook you up. Don't I always? Didn't I get this room for you and your girls last night, and pick up the room service tab—?"

"But you didn't come last night like you said you was. . . ." Najira sat back, pouted, and folded her arms over her chest. "I coulda paid for my own room, but I wanted something more special to show you ain't playing me, and—"

"I'll see if Mike Paxton can take you over at his office on a filing job or something, baby. . . . Now stop playing this morning. I'm already stressed. For real. You're special."

She stared at him hard but loved hearing him beg. Big-money family, phat-paid job, to-die-for house, the car of life, and here this brother was begging to get his dick sucked first thing in the morning by some sister he'd just met a few weeks ago in a club. Pitiful.

"Promises, promises. I ain't playing witchu, Negro," she finally said, her voice going soft as her fingers traced the oozing tip of his member. "But you are kinda fine, and all. Hazel-green eyes, curly hair, tight body, pretty color skin . . . Need to teach your wife how to hit it and quit it in the morning instead of messing with my gig, since she don't have to meet da man. That's the least that spoiled bitch could do."

"Yeah . . . but you know she and I don't roll like that." His voice held a blend of annoyance and a plea. "I told you we don't go there anymore."

"Guess that's why you like me, right?"

"Yeah, Jira . . . you're all that."

She smiled and watched his eyes close again as her mouth replaced her hand. He had some nerve trying to talk street to coax her, like she was stupid. She wasn't one of his social program chicken-heads. He was the fool. Three weeks and he was jonesing like a crack addict. Men were so easy to work, especially the ones with everything to lose.

Najira glimpsed his camera cell phone from the corner of her eye as her head bobbed to the task. Getting him to go to sleep for a few moments might pose a problem, though, she worried. Feeling him shudder, she stopped and kissed his lower belly. She had to be careful, this small-dicked son of a bitch was a lousy shooter—quick on the draw—and could mess up her plan by cumming too fast. Shit.

"You know this sister don't swallow, right?"

"Jesus, Najira . . ."

"Chill, baby. I brought some latex."

He felt her warmth leave him, enjoying how she sashayed over to the dresser with sexy attitude in her stride. Najira Holmes had a nice ass. All ghetto sisters had them—high, round, polished, firm, with thick thighs, tiny waist, and that pretty walnut brown sheen. Yeah. A definite stress reliever. Much better than the athletically slim, high-yellow, high-strung wife that went with his station in life . . . but he hated that dreadlock crap Najira had done with her hair. Mike was never going to go for having *that* in his office, even in the back as a filing clerk. Fuck it, he'd tell Najira whatever and take her to Red Lobster. Why waste another high-priced dinner on around-the-way tail?

But damn, that little skeezer was so slow. All he needed was to get done and get out of there. This trumped-up media bullshit about him taking program money was fucking with his image, and with his head—but with his main man, Mike Paxton, on the case, he was good. Having Paxton on his side was like having Johnny Cochran in his hip pocket. Darien tried to settle back and relax. Yeah. He was cool. That advantage, with all the other serious political favors owed to him in the network, assured this shit would blow over soon. It had to. Najira could suck his dick and relieve some tension before he had to meet up with Mike. No reason to worry.

Najira smiled, watching Darien watch her. "You won't mind if I get a li'l somethin'-somethin', too?" She took her time climbing back on the bed and opening the foil wrapper.

"No," he said, smiling back at her as she swathed him with the barrier and mounted him. "I love the way you get yours."

"Uhmmm, hmmm," she murmured, beginning a slow, pumping, sultry circle with her hips. "I know you do."

It took everything in her not to roll her eyes and say, "Pullease, Negro." But the objective was to rock his world enough to make him doze. His upthrusts were coming faster and harder than she'd expected, and difficult for her to control . . . he was so anxious . . . However, an occasional, seemingly accidental slip-out layered with her vocal drama helped keep him working at his singular goal. Ultimately, it was all good. The harder he worked, the more tired he'd be.

When beads of sweat formed on his brow, she swallowed away a chuckle of satisfaction. She used her voice to give him deeper theater and increased her tempo to harmonize with his moans. Stupid bastard, didn't he know he was only one camera click away from having his whole life blown and not just having his world rocked?

This time when he shuddered, she pulled out all the stops, thrusting her full weight against him and grinding down hard till he cried out. Then she watched him from a very remote place in her mind. He was breathing hard, had his eyes closed, and had slung his arm over his forehead. Very carefully, she climbed down, sure to hold the edge of the condom before removing it from him.

"I'll throw this out for you, baby," she whispered.

His reply was a mere grunt. Perfect.

Slipping from the bed, she leaned down and kissed the tip of his nose, took a tissue and simultaneously palmed his cell phone from the nightstand, then collected her Louis Vuitton purse, and quietly made her way to the bathroom. For effect, she flushed the toilet.

"Hey, girl, you will NOT believe who I did this morning. Darien Price. Will do his best friend, too, soon. Watch me. His wife would have a cow if she thought I did them both.

She might even have to do Paxton herself to make her husband crazy jealous. LOL! I'm out. Will try to send pic of him in bed. TTFN."

Najira stifled a giggle as she entered Darien's wife's telephone number and hit the Send button. This was too smooth. The wife would get the so-called accidental message, thinking it was intended for her husband's lover's girlfriend, all calls would trace back to the husband's cellie, and all hell would break loose. New technology was da bomb! At this rate, every wrongdoing brother in Anytown, USA, oughta be afraid. Najira shook her head. But revenge didn't require slammin' gadgets, just a sistah on a mission. Laura Caldwell, her mentor, had taught her that.

Najira folded the used condom into a tissue, then stashed it in her purse in a Zip-Loc bag. Might come in handy later. A girl could never be overprepared. *Shooot,* after that white girl from Jersey got crazy-paid for doing a president and keeping a stained blue dress in a dry cleaner's bag . . . whateva.

Using the faucet as a sound cover, Najira peeked out the bathroom door to see Darien snoozing. Like clockwork, every man needed a few moments of shut-eye after screwing. She positioned the camera through the cracked door and snapped his picture, then quickly retreated into the bathroom again, clicking the lock. Now all she had to do was send the photo, erase the memory, wash her ass, slip the phone back on the nightstand, and go to work. He would never know what hit him, and his wife would be *off the chain.*

Yeah, like Laura said, to the victor go the spoils. Served his bourgeois ass right for having her father and the rest of her family locked out of all program funding and blackballed in the city behind bullshit. Somebody like Darien was too arrogant to know who she knew, or what last names down the way were connected. . . . Many times it was the same fathers, different mommas, different last names—it was *on.* That oversight was deadly. A brother should never assume and shoulda checked. Darien Price and his crew didn't stand a chance.

Near the Bourse Building
Center City, Philadelphia
Same morning

The blare of KYW news on the car radio sent an electric current of satisfaction through Laura J. Caldwell. Vindicated. For once, justice had been served. Information about the imminent fall of Darien Price III ricocheted through Laura's sleek black Jag XK-3 and entered her nervous system. Behind the drone of the news commentator's monotonous voice, the distinguishable station trademark sound effect—an AP newswire machine—ticked like a time bomb. Yeah, this mutha was gonna blow. She loved it.

Executive director of the prominent Educate America program, Darien Price, is being sought for questioning by police after extreme inconsistencies were found in his educational nonprofit program accounts. Allegedly, Price used seventy-five thousand dollars of program funds, earmarked for community education, for personal credit card expenses, his car note, and other personal expenses. Price has declined comment, pending the investigation. When asked—

She snapped off the radio, pulled her car into her reserved spot in the Bourse Building lot, and got out quickly. Twenty years plus, and that bastard was still trying to wiggle out of the noose. But this time Price was going down. It was personal, not business, especially after what he and his family had done to her father. Ruined a man's life and credibility because her father had started digging . . . all because her father had done what any father had the right to do—protect his daughter's honor. And her mother had died from the stress. Oh, yeah. She'd deliver Darien's head to the media on a silver platter.

New fury shot through Laura with every footfall. Her feet couldn't move fast enough to get her across the concrete divide to the elevators. Adrenaline rushed through her as she impatiently waited for the garage elevator to come. When it finally did arrive, she got in fast and punched the number panel hard, as though slamming the keypad would make the lumbering contraption move faster. The moment the doors opened to the Bourse lobby, she swept past the vendors, who were just opening, and found another set of elevators that would take her to her firm. Pure frustration at having to wait for the laboriously slow elevator to collect her was driving Laura nuts. There was so much to do, and so little time to do it. But, for once, things were working out in her favor.

A phenomenal power shift was in the offing. She could feel it. Laura tightened her grip on her briefcase as she stepped out of the elevator and stared ahead toward the double mahogany doors that led to her consulting firm. Fluorescent light glinted off the large brass name plate. It was good to be the queen.

Her low-heel pumps clicked out a cadence of sheer authority against marble as she crossed the hall. Every single battle she'd waged to ensure Rainmakers, Inc. became one of the top grant fund-raising outfits in Philadelphia had been worth it—from public school to an Ivy League university, to Wall Street, to coming home holding aces. Damned right. She'd worked her ass off and had followed all the rules of the game. Two decades of blood, sweat, and tears, and now only the white males on the affluent Main Line had the edge on her, and not by much.

As she walked, Laura's mind worked on the power grid of wealth she'd have to deal with tonight at yet another fund-raiser event. They were all the same—but were also interestingly unique.

She always tried to tell Najira that the way money was distributed was like a pebble dropped into a seemingly still pond. That was the so-called trickle-down effect. One could almost see the invisible lines as they rippled through every major project and significant piece of legislation in the city.

Laura hesitated, allowing her hand to rest on the door

handle as she summoned a relaxed countenance. She had to distance her emotions from the fact that this game was all orchestrated undercover in private little alliances and secret pacts; the uninitiated never stood a chance. The community was always shit out of luck. It was time to even those odds.

"Respect," Laura whispered as she finally opened her office door.

"G'morning, Ms. Caldwell. You see the papers yet?" Laura's personal assistant asked in a rush, hopping up from her chair and entering the inner office behind Laura.

"Absolutely. Good morning, Najira."

Both women exchanged a sheepish grin. What the hell had Najira been up to that she had to call her by her formal name so loudly? Her cousin was a trip, and she only hoped that Najira wouldn't inadvertently give away their relationship to the other members of the staff one day. Some things were better left unsaid. Especially since the child had bulldozed her way into Laura's covert plan. But it was safer to clue Najira in and keep her close than to allow that kid to do something crazy to jeopardize the bigger picture. Laura studied Najira hard, trying to figure out what new drama the girl had injected into the equation. It was all over Najira's face. What had homegirl done this morning? Hmmm.

Casting her khaki-colored London Fog raincoat on the sofa along with her black Coach barrel purse, Laura never broke her stride. She shook her head at the trappings she had to maintain just to be in the game. One day she'd get out. But she had a lot to accomplish before then: black Rome had to fall.

Deep in thought and not looking at Najira as she'd answered, Laura made her way across the large Oriental rug, collected a stack of incoming mail, glanced at her Movado watch, and dropped her alligator briefcase next to her desk. Seven-thirty a.m., and the whole town was about to go nuts. Excellent. Laura sat down, hit a button on the telephone system console, and punched in her voice-mail code, riffling through her in-box as she multitasked, trying to avoid Najira's wide smile. Oh, yeah, girlfriend had been up to tricks and games. Laura chuckled despite her resolve to remain stoic.

Without waiting for a more engaging response, Najira quickly went to the coffee bar and brought over a fresh-brewed pot. Voice-mail messages droned on as white noise in the background. Offering a coffee fill-up as Laura settled into a sumptuous black leather chair, the young woman pointed to several local rags that she'd laid out in order of circulation dominance for her boss to review, and poured herself a cup.

"Front page, everywhere. This is gonna shake up Philly for serious." Najira adjusted a stray Nubian-twist lock behind her ear, her line of vision fastened on the newspapers, glass coffeepot suspended in midair, as she read along with Laura over her shoulder. "What would make somebody like him take nonprofit program funds to pay credit card bills, his car note, and stupid stuff like that, I wonder?" Her tone was singsong sarcastic, and she fanned her face in mock despair.

Again both women stared at each other, their smiles belying the formal office ruse. Laura cut Najira a warning look that said, *Not here, the office could have ears.* Offices always did.

"I almost can't believe it," Laura replied with false disgust as another staffer passed her office and nodded good morning. Carefully picking up one of the newspapers with one hand, Laura furrowed her brow as though she'd just been clued in, and motioned with her head for Najira to see that they weren't totally free to talk privately yet.

Catching the hint, Najira nodded, feigning the total subordinate-boss role-play as Laura held up her empty porcelain cup for Najira and motioned for her to take a seat in front of her desk. She waited until Najira was settled and had put the pot down on the edge of her desk before saying another word. Both women took a slow, steady sip of coffee, eyeing each other the whole time.

"I have to agree—I can't believe it, either. Then again, yes, I can," Laura added with a wink. "Truth is always stranger than fiction."

"I hear you, but this is absolutely wild." Najira popped up, sloshing the coffee in her mug, hustled past the door to her desk, and snatched up her handbag. When she returned, she shut the door quietly, glancing around first to be sure none of the other staff saw her, and then raced back to Laura's desk. "This morning was off da hook," Najira whispered in triumph.

Laura nodded, chuckled, and glanced up at the young woman hovering nearby. The assignment given to Najira was a simple one, designed to keep the girl from anything too criminal. It wasn't about allowing her cousin to do something that could land that nineteen-year-old kid in jail. Najira was only supposed to keep tabs on Darien's whereabouts—*that was it.* But concern lurched in Laura's stomach as she watched her cousin's eyes sparkle.

"I did him."

"What?" Laura was incredulous.

"You said to keep tabs on him, and I did," Najira said with a chuckle. "Pissed his wife off, too, but that ain't my problem . . . but it does add a little spice."

Laura sighed. Screwing some jerk was not a felony, nor was creating enough static between him and his wife to cause distrust a crime punishable by law. It was done every day—domestic. But no matter what Najira said, Laura wasn't going to let her in on the real action as a potential accessory. She could tell that Najira wanted to get closer to the sting. Laura sipped the dark brew in her cup slowly and then fixed her gaze on the article. "You are so right," she said after a moment. "Must have been all the way live." What else was there to say? Now she had to figure out how to work with this new information and make it work for her. She just hoped that Najira's father, her uncle, wouldn't find out about any of this. . . . Akhan would have a stroke. Laura shook her head.

"Girl . . ."

"Not here," Laura warned with a smile.

"But, boss lady—look." Before Laura could protest, Najira had set down her mug on the edge of Laura's desk and had thrust her hand into her Louis Vuitton, extracting a plastic bag.

"What *the hell* is that?" Laura asked, leaning forward and wrinkling her nose.

"It's DNA evidence, just in case—"

"Don't even begin to tell me about it."

Both women dissolved into hushed laughter behind their hands, straining to keep their voices in check.

"Oh, my God, girl . . ."

"Ya never know when it could come in handy, chile."

"Don't even think about putting it on my desk!" Laura hissed through hearty giggles. "Just stop!"

"And you thought I was an amateur." Najira sucked her teeth and flung the nasty little bag of goo back into her purse with flair.

"My bad," Laura whispered, wiping her eyes. "But that is sooo foul."

"I bet this Darien indictment will be the hush-hush convo of the evening when you go to that Scott-Edward Foundation fund-raiser at the Hyatt. Everybody who is anybody in Philly will be there, along with the media, and I know the who's who will be buzzing about *this* Darien mess. Girl, you're the real pro. I'm just trying to study, okaaay?"

Najira gave Laura a mischievous grin, waiting for a response, and, when she didn't immediately answer, pressed on. "So, how we gonna play this?" Najira laughed hard. "Don't look at me like, *'Moi?'* I know you did it. I just wanna learn how."

"The who's who are my prospects—that's the only reason I'm going to the event tonight. Remember, I have a fund-raising business to run, too. So their speculative conversations are inconsequential, but their money is not," Laura hedged, tempering her emotions and not answering Najira's primary question. "I don't care what they talk about. This guy and his partners are really pissing me off, Jira."

"If it's like that, then why do we have to go through all this slow, double-O-soul shit to bring him down? Why not just have their asses seen?" Najira sighed. "The family tried it the other, legal way, and—"

"It didn't work," Laura replied, her voice tight. This was precisely why she didn't want Najira involved, but she had to keep her cousin close. The last thing she needed was a loose cannon in the family doing something street to upset the applecart. This had to go down smooth to be a total and permanent win.

The two women stared at each other, one formulating a response while the other squirmed in her seat like an excited child. Laura focused on the issues before saying a word. Darien's crew was not her real concern, nor was his attorney. The goal was simply to create enough friction in their camp that they'd begin to tell on each other.

"All right. Sore subject," Najira finally conceded. "We both have that in common, so chill." Najira's shoulders slumped. "What's the politically correct way I'm supposed to respond when people ask me have I heard about this yang?"

"Sorry . . . listen," Laura said slowly, then relaxed. "A lot of times when our people are in power, they become unfair media targets." She winked at Najira and forced another chuckle. "Shame, too, because a physical injury heals, a death leaves a man a martyr, but a media smear with a financial wipeout will leave a man in pain and bleeding forever."

"I can respect that," Najira murmured, taking a sip from her mug and never losing eye contact with Laura. "Which is why you're the boss."

The kid reminded Laura so much of herself: an around-the-way girl trying to make a better life for herself. As the thought crossed her mind, Laura mellowed and smiled at her protégé. "So, we aren't going to talk bad about people without the full story, even though tongues are wagging." Laura motioned with her chin toward the outer office; her meaning directed at Najira was clear: seem shocked and appalled. Play it to the bone around anyone else.

"I hear you. But still . . ." Seeming disappointed that Laura wasn't going to spend a few moments reveling in the latest scoop, Najira finally let out a sigh and nodded in reluctant agreement.

Under the circumstances, Laura didn't want to hear the blow-by-blow details of what Jira had done to get a used condom into her purse. It was up to Najira how far she went in monitoring Darien's movements. But *nooooo,* Najira went in for high drama. Laura almost laughed.

Nervous energy had a stranglehold on her, though. The remaining parts of the plan had to go down without a hitch. Now it was time to go to the ball and work the serious-money angle. All contracts Darien had promised his cronies had to be derailed, and those funds rerouted. His life would be ruined, with no way to rebuild . . . just as her father's life had been trashed.

"You sure you're up to this?" Laura whispered.

"I know what to do—create a diversion so you can work the room before his main money man gets there." Najira shrugged.

"I need to have a clear shot to convince Haines to let me manage who gets those funds, before his attorney, Michael Paxton, blocks my free throw. Understand?"

"All right, all right," Najira agreed, growing testy.

"Be smooth, stay out of sight, and no more drama." Laura looked at Najira hard to be sure the underlying message took root.

"Why not?"

Quiet fell between them for a moment as Najira's eyes continued to sparkle with excitement.

"Because it's too dangerous."

"Like I'm scared of them soft punks." Indignant, Najira sat back in her chair and folded her arms over her chest.

Laura laughed out loud. "I know you're not, and neither am I. But trust me on this. Okay?" She stood and walked to the window.

"All right," Najira said in a weary tone. "Whatever." Najira's face had gone stone serious in the exchange. "Now, I did my part, so while I've got your back, you'll have fifteen minutes to verbally crack that old white boy's safe. You got a small window, Sis, to pick his pocket clean—feel me? Got my mind on the money, and several million on my mind."

Laura let her nod silently answer Najira's challenge. In this faltering economy, every rainmaker in the nation knew that so-called philanthropic campaign giving was at risk. Every firm's clients were on financial life support, and she had a slew of clients to generate substantial funds for, to keep them alive.

What could she say to Najira? Out of the mouths of babes came words of wisdom. Laura went back to her desk and sipped her coffee as she chose her own words carefully, trying to help Najira understand the bigger picture while also fully appreciating where her younger cousin was coming from. But the girl needed to learn how to be strategic in her thinking. All women did. Especially one as bright and altruistic as Najira. This young sister had a chance to make something of herself, if she didn't get wrapped up in the political madness—or in some dumb shit that could land her in prison. At nineteen years old, Najira deserved to have a life. It was not about divulging information that could put Najira in harm's way.

"Let's not lose focus," Laura said after a moment. "Since nine-eleven, all contribution money has been tight. The donors have either diverted funds to where they can recoup their investment with Homeland Security contracts or have lost so much in their Wall Street portfolios that they just don't have it to give. The Price family was always good for an annual fifty thousand in contributions to buy favors around the region—not much, when you really think about it. Their leverage was with the contracts they could influence . . . No doubt Darien has laid out a laundry list of security and education contract favors—I just need to find out who's slated to get them. That's why I have to do the wine-and-cheese circuit to find out. But it looks like the Price family will be spending their grease-the-skids money on legal fees this year." That was all she could give Najira to go on, and she hoped it would satisfy her cousin's thirst for information at this point.

"Embezzlement was brilliant," Najira said fast, appearing revived. "I'll give you that. I just want to know how you pinned it on him." She stood and leaned on the edge of Laura's desk. "They might indict him. Can you believe it? Darien Price? With all the money *they* have?" She laughed, but the sound of it was hollow and brittle. "What would make him do something that crazy as to steal from the city program coffers like that, when his people have all the money in the world? It was a glory position anyway, and he got paid a mint for a salary. I'm loving watching him and his fancy attorney try to scam their way out of that shit."

Najira was talking with her hands now, becoming more animated as the weight of what could befall her enemies took root in her soul. "For chrissakes, Laura, he was only in that job, because his big-time family got him appointed to it, for less than a year!"

"Tragic," Laura said, her tone wry and dismissive. "Money . . . and how much is enough is all relative," Laura added, smiling gently at Najira, although her patience was wearing thin. She'd been up all night, had things to do, and as much as she shared her cousin's savor of comeuppance—as well as her disdain for the rich and foolish—it was time for them both to get to work.

There was a stack of client requests with deadlines in every one of her secretaries' in-bins. Plus, there would be a shift in power, and she needed to devote her mental energy to dissecting where the chips might fall—her goal to grab as much of the realigned contract and grant moneys for organizations that did real work in the community, as opposed to allowing the pretenders to gobble it up before it hit the ground. Then there was the not so small matter of vengeance. Laura scanned the headlines again, mentally checking every variable. But no matter how much Najira cajoled her for a confession, she wasn't telling the girl what she did, or how she'd pulled it off.

Najira shook her head, still in disbelief, lingering despite Laura's growing distraction. "Fine. If you still don't wanna tell me how you did it—because I know you did something—then you *have to* tell me what the insiders are talking about, boss lady, even though I'll be in the hotel, out of sight. I mean, I know you'll hear some real dirt between all the chi-chi discussion and the wine-and-cheese event tonight. I just want to know, just want to see them twist."

"It'll just be idle gossip, but I'll clue you in if I hear anything really juicy. However, I don't expect to." Laura set down the newspaper and flipped open her Palm Pilot. "My main objective for going to that event tonight is to get to a few well-heeled insiders, to make some more rain for our largest-paying clients, with some spillover for the little guys. At the fundraiser I can also find some scraps for the clients we have who simply can't pay our full freight. Balance, Najira. Balance. We take ours off the bottom, not the top, and that keeps the heat off our butts."

Laura sighed and pushed back in her chair. "It's what keeps the lights on in here, too, all of this drama notwithstanding." She studied the young woman with compassion for her point of view. "Remember, even though the Kennedys started with bootleg liquor and mob ties, eventually they had to go legit to keep things smooth. Balance is imperative. Always."

"Yeah," Najira protested, one hand going to her hip, "but it is sure nice to see that sometimes folks like J. Darien Price get theirs."

"No argument here, Sis," Laura murmured, and then focused her attention on the appointments in her electronic calendar as she synched up the handheld device to her desk system Outlook software. "It is pretty bizarre, all things said and done. Cosmic justice."

"You ain't said a word."

"Uhmmm hmmm . . . That's why, this morning, I've got to figure out who'll be left standing when the dust settles, kiddo." Laura peered at the flat, black LCD screen and let out a weary sigh. Mondays were always intense. She never got used to the onslaught that the top of the week insisted on, but she had a grant-developers' meeting and a team that would require close direction in order to pull down a couple hundred thou this morning. By noon, and if the trains held to schedule, she'd be up at the state capitol, in Harrisburg, lobbying with politicians to get her portion of the practically nonexistent state-funded contracts within the Department of Community and Economic Development. This shake-up meant that a few struggling grassroots organizations finally had a shot at some significant resources, that is, if she could use the diffusion of power to her advantage. Shame that Darien had crossed her; his empire would crumble, and he'd never know what hit him. Again Laura glanced at her watch.

Najira pulled away from Laura's desk slowly, catching the hint. Seeing the young woman withdraw with such a dejected look on her face gave Laura a twinge of regret. If she'd had more time, she would have given in to Najira's unspoken request for a little more female coaching interaction—but this morning she couldn't take her cousin under her wing. Her nerves couldn't withstand the "delicious details," as Najira often referred to them, and the full plan was too fragile to give Najira the total play-by-play. As volatile as the girl was, Laura knew that Najira had already risked her entire life by peripherally colluding with her. But, hey, family was family.

The more things changed, the more things stayed the same. The kid just wanted to learn while also serving old-school justice, and she could appreciate that. One day. Laura studied her cousin from a sidelong glance as she walked out of the office, shaking her head in psychic agreement with their private assessment of Philadelphia's black elite.

Laura paused, staring at the attractive young woman, briefly considering the way the deep rust tones on Najira's mud-cloth skirt and matching silk blouse matched her hair, which matched her skin and her suede boots, and the leather on her cowry shell earrings, which matched her bracelet.

Everything that Najira wore closely complemented the natural woods, fibers, tastefully understated furnishings, and African art of Laura's well-appointed, historic Fifth Street, Bourse Building office.

She just wondered how J. Darien Price III would blend into the penal system's basic color of gray.

Laura raked her fingers through her short, naturally curly hair, a new strategy simmering inside her head, her focus returning to how she would approach the targets at the gala later that night. She brushed an invisible fleck of lint off her black and khaki-colored herringbone Chanel jacket sleeve, adjusted her pearls, and made a mental note of each VIP phone call that she needed to return personally.

Needing something in her hands, she reached forward for the red Mont Blanc pen suspended in the crystal ball that sat next to an etched-glass vase of fresh-cut sunflowers, and began jotting down a short list of whom she would approach, and then crumpled up the note in her fist before tossing it in a waste basket. Her mind allowed in a shadow of doubt before she banished it. Her nerves were drawn taut as a wire, making her reach for her briefcase to extract a cell phone, then absently punch in numbers. Irony of ironies, huh.

Laura peered at the newspapers strewn across her wide mahogany desk. God was good.

Not bad for somebody once called a ghetto bitch.

Fury collided with sadness and gave way to the hot tears of defeat. Monica Price sat in the driveway of the Montessori School and held her cell phone, staring at it as though it were some foreign object. How could he? She always knew Darien had a slew of little bitches out in the streets, had known for years. Theirs was an uneasy truce and a marriage totally of convenience. But seeing it was so much different from knowing it. They had children, for God's sake! Little children. Beautiful children. Their children.

A new flood of tears threatened her composure as she

brought her hand to her mouth and swallowed away a sob. This time her husband would pay. The lesson would be visceral and cut his wayward ass to the bone. Her fingers trembled as she punched the number she knew by heart into the cell phone and pressed "Send." Michael Paxton could fix this.

He felt the vibration on his hip and almost ignored it. But at this early hour, and with everything blowing up around Darien's bullshit, instinct made him take the call.

"Give me a minute," Paxton said to Darien. "Could have a bearing on our conversation." He spun around in his chair, gazing out of his Liberty Plaza office window and giving Darien the high back leather to watch instead of his expression.

"Paxton here," he said, thoroughly intrigued that Monica Price's cell number had flashed with a "9-1-1" on his digital display. Obviously, she knew he was in a meeting with her husband—but why wouldn't she have come through his secretary? Anne would have patched her through.

For a moment there was no voice response, just a long sniff. Very interesting. He pressed his ear closer to the small device in his hand.

"Mike . . . can we talk for a moment?" A fragile female voice finally replied. "It's important."

"I'm in a meeting right now, but—"

"Is Darien with you?" Monica immediately shot back.

"Yes." A slow smile dawned on Paxton's face. "But that's all right."

"I know you said to come to you, if ever . . . well . . . I want to send you something that I just received this morning, and I need this to be between you and me until I can figure out what to do about it."

"All right," Paxton said carefully.

"Please, under no circumstances are you to show this to Darien. I've been trying to call that son of a bitch all morning, and he won't return my calls. And I know this puts you in an awkward position, but . . ."

"I understand," Paxton said in a controlled tone. "Go ahead."

"It's awful."

Sobs entered the cell phone, and Paxton glanced at his watch. "It will be all right. Send it."

He waited and stared at his color display and shook his head, bringing the telephone to his ear again after clearing the image. "I understand. I'll deal with it."

Renewed sobs filled his ear, and he waited until they abated. "We should meet about this—this isn't something to deal with on the telephone . . . and as I said, I'm in a meeting right now."

"Okay. Thank you, Mike. Where?"

Paxton spun around and looked at Darien, giving him hand signals to infer that he was trying to get a nuisance client off his phone. When Darien relaxed and nodded, Paxton closed his eyes and leaned his head back. "I have to go to a charity fund-raiser tonight at the Hyatt. After that, perhaps we could meet for a drink?"

"Give me the room number later, okay?" the female voice whispered.

"Will do. I'll leave it on your cell."

"I can't thank you enough, Mike. He's looking at you, isn't he? Staring right down your throat."

"Yeah. That works," Paxton said, doodling on his blotter.

"Good," Monica said crisply. "I'll make the meeting worth your while, as I know your time is valuable."

"Most appreciated," Paxton said, dismissing the call and hanging up without a good-bye. He hooked the cell phone back on his belt and sighed, shaking his head as he picked up the thread of conversation with Darien.

"Guess everybody wants a piece of you today, man," Darien said in a weary voice. "Can't say I blame them—you're the man."

"A pain-in-the-ass corporate client," Paxton replied in a blasé tone. "Had to take that. Sorry. Now, where were we?"

Chapter 2

Laura never looked back as the parking valet gave her a ticket and accepted the keys to her black Jag convertible. Her focus was on the number of media trucks and expensive cars creating a traffic jam on South Broad Street. The hubbub of activity around the Park Hyatt at the Bellevue made the venue seem like it was hosting the Emmy Awards, not a standard five-hundred-dollar-a-plate fund-raising ball for a high-profile charity. Run-of-the-mill war-chest building for operating funds shouldn't be a big media event this evening, with everything else going on regarding the city scandal. So why tonight? Darien wouldn't dare show his face or sully a potential ally by attending and siphoning negative media hype his way.

Her line of vision narrowed as she collected the facts in her mind. The bar at Zanzibar Blue, below the hotel, would no doubt also be loaded with deal maven dignitaries. Given the Darien Price implosion, the media should have been poised to cover more important matters—unless there were key individuals from Price's camp inside the event that they were tracking. Excellent. A possible feeding frenzy. That meant, in the chaos, she'd have access to those key people, as well. Yet, it was up to Najira to give her a little discreet working room.

The cool fall evening bit through Laura's short, black raw silk sash jacket, creating goose bumps on her arms as she alighted on the hotel's wide front stairs and pushed her way through the glass-and-gold-chrome doors. VIPs were straggling in and had begun milling around the huge open atrium lobby. Laura nodded and casually waved to those she recognized, pasting on her best corporate smile.

Her gaze carefully assessed every detail within the huge marble–appointed lobby, its dramatic flower arrangements occasionally blocking her view of the incoming guests until she nonchalantly adjusted herself to peer around the exotic foliage. Oh, yeah. She'd hit the mother lode in here.

"Hey, lady," a short, chubby media photog called out as he sidled up to her with a grin. "Knew you'd be here."

She leaned over and skimmed her favorite newspaper photographer's cheeks with an airy Continental kiss, careful not to smudge her makeup. "Of course. Wouldn't miss it for the world."

"You'll get me next to the right people for a good shot won't you?" The photographer gave Laura a wink and a bright smile.

"Don't I always?"

He laughed, his sweat-dampened brown hair sticking to his flushed face as he jostled his camera into position to take Laura's picture. She couldn't tell if he'd been late and had rushed, which was why his face was reddened, or whether it was Rick's cherublike lack of fitness that added to his exasperated presence. He was one of the special people who transcended race—Rick was just Rick. Her smiled broadened while he fidgeted with his lenses. If only everybody could just be so color-blind and so cool.

As he angled the camera, Laura held up her hand. "You know I always work behind the scenes. Save it for the real news makers."

"Aw, c'mon, lady. You look fabulous tonight. Just one?" He gave her an approving nod. "That little black dress is a killer, and if I wasn't already married, you'd be in trouble. You gotta lemme get a shot of my favorite girl."

"I love you, too, but how about if we go up together and I make sure you get a couple of highfliers for the society pages, instead?" Laura winked at him. "Seems like there's going to be more than the regulars here, given the way your media pals have converged on this hotel . . . hmmm?"

"I'll settle for that," he replied with a wide grin, not responding to her query about the guests and following her toward the main elevators. "So, what do you think about all this stuff? Did Price do it?"

She stifled a chuckle as they waited before the large brass elevator doors and kept their eyes on the descending numbers. She wondered whether Rick had learned evasiveness from all his years as the only white guy shooting for the minority rags around the city, or whether Rick had learned brother-is-too-cool-to-answer-a-sister responses on the streets before he became a photog.

"Who are you shooting for tonight, Rick?"

He hadn't answered her question, so she wasn't about to answer his. It was a cat-and-mouse game they always played with each other and enjoyed.

"Tonight I'm on the *Trib*'s dime, but I might take a few shots for the *Observer,* or the *Sun*—a freelancer's gotta stay loose to make a decent living, ya know."

"And one hand always washes the other." She chuckled with him but made no further comment as they waited for the elevator, noting the intermittent flow of people entering the lobby and breaking off into small, intimate groups of conversation.

Laura's gaze scanned the terrain, and then she glimpsed her watch again. Bright hotel chandeliers caused the light to sparkle in the oval ring of tiny diamonds around its thin platinum-and-onyx face. Yes. She was ready. She knew the drill. She could only hope that Najira's plan had worked and

Paxton had been detained—without any drama. Yeah, after this, Najira's involvement in any of this was over. She just had to figure out a way to extract the girl without any mess.

But inside, she knew there were larger fish to fry. She'd think about her cousin's potential antics later. She glanced at Rick and then at the elevator doors, remembering the basics of how to find her targets and work the room.

The old money would have on conservative Brooks Brothers suits, their wives in understated cocktail-length gowns. The feminists would have on business suits. Black folks trying to make an impression would be overdressed in fancy, full-length ball gowns and tuxedos, the Main Line contingent of white liberals would have on ridiculously expensive custom-tailored suits, and their wives would don cocktail-length designer dresses. The intellectuals would look as if they had just rushed from a campus lecture, their hair rumpled, and appearing as though choking in suits that didn't quite fit, with scuffed shoes; they wouldn't be an issue. They'd spout lofty rhetoric while hovering near other intellectuals and their wives, who'd be wearing pearls and something plain. Laura chuckled. In truth, she liked that grouping best, if one had to choose. At least they passionately believed in something more esoteric than the almighty dollar. But she wouldn't have time tonight to expand her philosophies. She had to corner the money.

To that end, she'd served them all a little basic black dress, a Nicole Miller from the exclusive Manayunk boutique—an elegant sheath that stopped just above the knee to keep things interesting, her bare arms covered by a beaded bolero jacket beneath her lightweight raw silk outer-wrap jacket. It was imperative always to dare to be different even if blending in.

Laura sighed quietly as the elevator took forever to come. She was glad Rick was preoccupied with his lenses and waving to people he knew from where they stood. As nonchalantly as possible, she gave herself the once-over lightly.

Adding a little flavor to her outfit was only a small margin of individuality and control, but it was hers nonetheless. Whatever it took to get her inside long enough to hold the power brokers' attention, she mused, even if it meant exposing one of her best assets—her legs. It was all theater, anyway. The blue bloods always arrived early and would already be positioned in the ballroom. They'd be in pleasant conversation with the corporate types. The old guard was who she had to connect with first. That's who had the real money.

"I thought you might stand me up," Najira said, her smile teasing as she opened the hotel room door. She hated the way the man before her looked at her like she was a speck of dirt that might get on his expensive navy blue suit. But she had to give it to him: he was ragging his ass off. She carefully appraised him. Tall, fine, suited down—*daaayumn*. Yeah, this was Laura's league.

Thoroughly pleased with herself, Najira almost giggled. Her plan to get Paxton's *real* attention had worked. No secretary in her right mind would keep what sounded like a booty call from her boss, especially when a hotel room number had been offered as a meeting place.

"Normally I don't indulge my potential clients like this," Michael Paxton said, his tone arrogant and rushed as he stepped over the threshold and shut the door behind him. "I'm very busy, have other clients waiting downstairs, and I—"

"Don't have time for bullshit," Najira stated flatly. "Neither do I."

Paxton smiled and gave her a brief nod of approval. "All right, then, state your business."

"I wanted a job, but I don't think that's gonna work out."

"Glad we came to terms," he said in a bored voice. But he hadn't moved.

She stared at him, forcing herself to remain calm—but

waited, just like Laura had taught her. The fact that he hadn't moved meant he wanted something. It was more than pussy; it was information.

"So, state *your* business," she snapped after a moment, the stalemate wearing down her nerves.

"Perhaps we began on the wrong note," Paxton said more generously, giving her a sly smile. "You invited me here, correct?"

"I thought you might have a job for me," she lied. "Like I told your secretary on the phone, Darien said I was his favorite woman . . . and we talked about a lot of stuff," she added, baiting Paxton in. "But he never said how fine his attorney was, though."

Paxton chuckled and went over to a chair and sat down. That's when she knew she had him, if only for a few moments. Flattery always worked on arrogant male ego.

"I don't bite, even though I do come off no-nonsense sometimes," he said, coaxing her to relax. "Have a seat. Let's do a politically correct interview, shall we?"

Najira gave him a scowl and took her time finding the edge of the bed to sit down. Every minute she could delay Paxton from going to the ballroom gave Laura a few more minutes to work her thing. She sighed and put on her most dejected expression, making sure her shapely legs were crossed at just the right angle to expose significant thigh beneath her sheer black hose and short, electric-blue skirt.

"Well," she said, her voice quiet and innocent, as she gave him a glimpse of cleavage, "his wife sorta found out about us by accident, and so it got a little crazy, and I need a job. I have an office technologist certificate from American Business Tech—still have ridiculous student loans from that . . . which I defaulted on, so I have to start at Community College from scratch and can't transfer any credits, not that they'd take them, but I'm a damned good secretary. Bottom line is, I need a job so I can get myself together. Like I said, I'm only temping for Laura Caldwell, but I don't think she's gonna hire me permanently."

Paxton rubbed his jaw, his eyes coolly assessing her. "I imagine that Monica took issue with Darien's extramarital relationship, but I'm no judge of what grown people do."

"Yeah," Najira replied on a heavy exhale. "She's so jealous right about now that I know she's looking for ways to hurt him bad. He was even worried that she might make a desperate attempt to do you." Najira suddenly opened her eyes wide and thrust out her hands before her. "But, for real, you didn't hear that from me. Darien would freak if he thought I told anybody some of the stuff we talked about in bed. Okay? Promise me you won't say anything."

"I'm an attorney," Paxton crooned. "I'm used to keeping things confidential. But let's focus on your recent work history for well-established firms, since this is a job interview. Is that fair?"

Gotcha. Najira forced a smile. She'd baited the hook and had let the man know that Monica was vulnerable, a coveted possession of Darien's that Paxton wouldn't be able to resist—and now he was sweating her about Laura. Too perfect. She couldn't wait to clue Laura in. "Thanks a lot, I appreciate that," she murmured as innocently as possible.

"You mentioned that you worked for Laura Caldwell. May I use her as a reference?"

"Yeah, she's real nice and real fair," Najira said brightly. "A classy lady. Although, don't ask Darien about her."

Paxton's smile went to a tight line. "Why not?"

"Well . . . ," Najira said, sighing, "they had some bad blood a long time back. Apparently he wanted to get with her when they were in high school—can you imagine holding a grudge that long?—and she wouldn't, never did, so he doesn't like her much. Go figure."

"Oh," Paxton said, chuckling and seeming relieved. "Is that all? Seems like the lady made a decision and stood by it. We won't count that as a character flaw. She's a good reference for you, though. I'll see what I can do." With that, he stood and offered Najira a dashing smile. "I'll have my HR person call you next week."

Najira was on her feet in seconds and extended her hand while trying to think of a way to further detain him. "Uh, gee, thanks. Uh, but don't you want to hear where else I've worked, or any of the other skills I have? I mean, I'm really good at what I do—irregardless of the thing I had with Darien, for real. I can—"

"A reference from Laura Caldwell's shop is all I need, and don't think twice about your relationship to Darien." Paxton shook her hand, keeping a formal, reserved distance between them. "That has no bearing on my decision. I have to go downstairs to the function that I just spent five hundred dollars on a ticket to attend. You've been remarkably candid, and that's what will count in the ultimate hiring decision. Have a nice evening."

Before Najira could think of anything else to delay him, Michael Paxton Jr. had turned on his heel and was out the door.

"So, Rick . . . ," Laura said after a moment, collecting her thoughts, "what brings all you guys out to this thing tonight?"

He looked at her and tilted his head, then chuckled. "Okay, if you must know, we're hoping to snag some of the political types to get their take on the whole Price fiasco. Word is that his attorney will be here."

Laura glanced around, seeing no sign of Paxton, and said a little prayer. *Just a few more minutes, Najira . . . just a few . . . and please don't do something crazy.*

"Didn't catch his name in the papers," Laura said casually. She knew the name from her grapevine sources and the past. Hell, she and Najira had that in the game plan. But she needed to make sure that Darien's attorney, Michael Paxton, knew hers and would act on the bait. Rick was a good way to ensure that. After all, what were friends for?

"Wasn't in there, because it was just announced," Rick said, coming closer to her. "Heard it was Michael Paxton Jr., though. He asked for a one-day courtesy before it hit ink."

"Oh, is that so? I understand that he normally represents several solid corporations and foundation types as his clientele. He's now doing criminal law?"

"Guess he had to make an exception for his godbrother."

"Interesting . . . and we've never formally met." Laura smiled. Now Rick had her full attention. That piece of information was new to her, and Rick seemed to sense it; it was all in his smile. So Paxton was more than a tight business connection and an old buddy from way back, huh? Very interesting.

"That could be arranged. Like you said, one hand washes the other." Rick studied her with a curious expression as they entered the elevator. "He's single, too."

She laughed. "And?"

"I know, I know. I should mind my business."

"Well said."

"You'll get me next to him for a photo op? He's cagey. Even though I know him, he won't do any easy shot for me unless he sees a direct, personal benefit."

"Why am I not surprised?" Laura sighed. "I might be able to help with that—no promises, though. I'll do what I can if the opportunity arises. Just give me enough time to set up a lunch with him first."

"Done."

They both fell into a companionable private chuckle. Rick was a trip, but a good guy who always helped her find her marks in a room, just like she always helped him get the best position for a cover shot to beat out the larger, majority-owned rags. But they had to work fast.

Soon all the poverty pimps would start to show up—the nonprofit organization executive directors who made six figures while their programs paid lower-level workers peanuts and delivered nothing of substance to the communities they claimed to serve. Then the white female executive directors would flock around the blue bloods, pitching their agendas to keep their salaries above the hundred-thousand-dollar mark, while the people from the community did the real work. The organizations that truly serviced the community wouldn't even be in the house—one dinner like this could probably run their programs for a week. Before the community parasites made their moves and surrounded the VIPs, she had to get upstairs and work the hell out of the ballroom. Everybody was jockeying for position to be on the right team when the money hit the street.

"You know this whole Darien Price thing is gonna blow the doors off and expose a lot of people, if there's any truth to it."

She absorbed Rick's statement and developed a careful reply as she watched the numbers light up above her. "Where there's smoke, there's fire."

"I'll say," he muttered. "If Price goes down, then he's the type that isn't gonna go down alone—if there's more to it than what we've heard so far."

"Uhmmm." Laura allowed the muttered response to stand as her agreement, without saying more. That's why, as soon as the elevator doors opened, she would be about pure motion.

The wait for the elevator to reach their floor was making her claustrophobic. This scandal had put blood in the water, which meant a lot of territory was up for grabs—and just as she was positioning for future contract opportunities, any minute the worried would arrive to descend upon the power brokers, trying to hold on to their prestigious, ineffective jobs.

But as she forced herself to calm down, she also had to remember that the worried blabbered a lot, too. Talking too much was their typical nervous tic. In that regard, they were useful and would be the ones that kept the idle gossip going, and within idle gossip were sometimes gems of information to be scooped up. Those folks carried the underground buzz, regardless of what she'd told Najira about ignoring it. However, she'd have to get to her marks before the competition started their begging pitches for operating-budget funding within new administrations. Then the politicians would come, making bold entrances with an entourage and offering media sound bytes. They represented the third wave of her offensive, aimed at those who knew what legislation was about to happen, and thus gave hints as to where the new currents of contract-funding streams would flow.

A three-pronged banquet strategy was in full effect tonight: first, the blue bloods to lock down the real dollars; then hit the people with the buzz to find out where loose threads dangled; then talk to the politicians to make an assessment of the legislative directions. When Rick nudged Laura with an elbow, she nearly jumped out of her skin. She had almost forgotten that the man was standing beside her.

"So no date tonight? Maybe one of these days you'll let me buy you a drink?"

Rick's comment brought her out of her reverie as the elevator doors opened on their floor. She adjusted her dangling crystal-and-onyx earring and thought of a quick, polite response.

Laura smiled. "You know I always work alone. A date would just slow me down in here."

He nodded with appreciation. "I hear you, lady, but you know I'm living vicariously. Paxton is a possibility, especially since he's linked to some serious money types." He gave her another curious look as they made their way to the coat check. "He's an insider . . . I can't believe you two never met."

"C'mon, Rick," she scoffed with a knowing smile, blowing off his sheepish advance and innuendo as they walked. She wasn't about to give up any of her private knowledge to a soul. "We've got people to see and things to accomplish in here. One day Mr. Right will show up, I suppose, but I'm not holding my breath—or going broke waiting on him. Get me near Paxton so I can chat about opportunities within his portfolio, and I'll buy *you* a drink."

She allowed Rick to help her off with her jacket and ignored his hopeful glances as she accepted the claim ticket from the coat-check girl and placed it in her sleek, black clutch. "You are such a gentleman—I'm glad chivalry is not dead. Keep hope alive." She beamed at Rick in a way that made him laugh as she made a funny face at him.

"You are so cold, love. Just get me a few good shots and I'm out," he said, still laughing and shaking his head, keeping stride with her as they entered the china-and-crystal-laden banquet area.

"Watch me work, baby," she tossed over her shoulder, putting distance between them, glad that he understood. "I'll make eye contact; then the rest is up to you." She winked at him as they parted.

He nodded and then left her, melting into a throng of more important people.

Again she took note of every aspect of the room—the way it was set up; the probable cost of the expensive, exotic orange- and fall-hued flower arrangements; which corporations had brought tables close to the podium and dais panel set for the politicians; the number of white-linen-swathed tables that could seat eight; where several lesser organizations had been scattered toward the back; who was talking to whom—all while making her way toward dignitaries she knew. Set up for two hundred guests. Laura did the math in her head and was galled.

The Scott-Edward Foundation had more than likely spent close to sixty thousand dollars to raise a hundred thousand dollars tonight. In spite of all the money wasted on the extravagances of this affair, the net giving to the needy would only be forty thou—and that was only providing that the whole evening's take would actually go to that cause. Most likely it wouldn't. It rarely ever did. So-called administrative overhead expenses, also known as executives' salaries, would eat up half the remaining forty Gs. Crazy but typical. Events like this were for more than fund-raising. It was all about networking and positioning, and *being seen.* Maybe it would go to pay Paxton's freakin' retainer for one of their fallen brethren. Go figure.

Even though she'd done hundreds of dinners like this on the circuit, her reaction to the opulence was always the same:

pure disgust. The waste of money made her weary. She passed a decked-out table, wondering how much all the crystal, china, and silver on one table alone cost. Probably enough to feed a family of four for a month. Laura steadied herself. Perhaps the thing wearing on her was that it was always the same. She quieted her thoughts so she could get to work.

Spotting a good target, she sauntered toward a huddle of business-suit-wearing men, noting that the primary power broker stood just to the center of it, alongside his wife, with lesser-ranking men hovering in his aura. The game was so predictable. She took in a slow inhale and again steadied her nerves.

"Donald, how are you?" Laura's voice became mellow and ebullient like warm, melted butter, caressing her target as she smoothly sliced through an already formed group and inserted herself into the conversation.

"Good to see you again, Laura." The elderly gentleman smiled brightly and stood a bit taller as Laura addressed him. "And of course you know James Devereaux from the Redevelopment Authority, as well as Mike Polanski, and George Townsend from the Micholi Foundation? Gentlemen, if you haven't met her before, you should: Laura Caldwell, CEO of Rainmakers, Inc. As brilliant as she is beautiful. You also remember my wife, Liz?" He offered her a gracious smile of welcome; then his eyes scanned the group around them, causing each face within it to relax with a nonthreatened smile as his eyes landed back on her face.

The introductions were perfunctory; they all knew Laura well. It was a part of the game; those in authority grounded their position as leader by making unnecessary introductions to the newcomer. But she was in.

"Thank you, Donald. Of course," Laura crooned, shaking the aged, pale hands of the white men that surrounded her, and receiving unspoken permission to be in their midst. Both women exchanged a light peck of recognition on each other's cheeks. She was careful to avoid the glass of Chardonnay that Elizabeth Haines held.

"You look fabulous tonight, Elizabeth," she added as the graying dowager stepped away from her, noting how her porcelain-thin skin showed blue veins beneath it.

"You are too kind, and I am so glad you came," Elizabeth Haines said, beaming. She adjusted her ivory-colored beaded Halston cocktail-length dress, appearing pleased by Laura's compliment. "It would have been so stodgy in here without you. You are sitting at our table, correct?"

"I'll sit right next to you, darling, if you have room."

"Wonderful. Of course we'll always make room for you at our table, right, Donald? We wouldn't have it any other way." Elizabeth Haines hesitated and waited for her husband to nod. When he did, her smile broadened. "Then I'll have someone fun, other than Donald, to talk to," she confirmed in a conspiratorial giggle. "And how are things going at the firm?"

It was the second level in, which Laura had been waiting for. The opportunity to make her subtle pitch for her own clients, couched in elegant small talk. Laura took her time. This had to be a precision strike.

"The firm is going well, but as you know, many of the funding sources have been strained due to the current Wall Street environment. So, we do what we can."

Elizabeth gave Laura a knowing glance and gracefully bowed out of the conversation, seeming satisfied that she had done her wifely and community duty: opening the dialogue for the attractive, educated black woman who fit in, and without words, sanctioning Laura as a visiting insider.

"Your clients are always our favorites, though," Donald Haines said, further opening the door of his wife's discussion trajectory. His tone had become serious, his smile waning, but his eyes held Laura's in what seemed like a telepathic transfer.

"Thank you," she said, never losing eye contact with him. Something was up. "Your support to my client base has always been deeply appreciated." Laura cast a serious glance around the group, allowing her eyes to linger briefly on each power broker before returning it to the main source—Donald Haines.

The other men standing around Donald Haines nodded again. From her peripheral vision she saw people begin to approach and then think better of it. The grave expressions on the faces in the small group that encircled her denoted a warning: *not yet, we're in the middle of something heavy—you'll get your chance in a moment.*

"We've heard a lot of good things about your portfolio," the man identified as Mike Polanski finally said, once Haines had nodded. "I think we'll be able to do something substantial this year."

Laura watched the older white gentlemen around her, noticing the way they had begun to talk to her in code as they tightened the circle around her. She carefully monitored every word they said, as well as the bend of their necks and their steely eyes. Their body language spoke volumes, while their comments became more obscure. It was like listening to people speak another language, yet she was fluent in it. Clues would be in every sentence, directing her toward sources of money.

"Yes, the Redevelopment Authority has been looking for ways to include minority- and women-owned enterprises into our projects, and we understand that your firm has built some very strategic collaborative efforts with the more credible nonprofits in the region." James Devereaux straightened his tie and took a sip from his wineglass.

More credible, huh? Laura smiled, but not too much.

Devereaux smiled, giving her the answer she wanted to hear without words. Then his eyes sought Haines's for approval. Donald Haines casually slipped his hand into his pants pocket and glanced at Laura. Just that fast, the deal had been struck. Good.

"I know that there are some key players within the Governor's Business Action Team, as well as the Philadelphia

Industrial Development Corporation, who might also want to see what you've got," Devereaux offered, and then smiled . . . but not too much.

Bingo.

She nodded without smiling, receiving a slight nod from the others in return. That was all that was needed for a sanctioned money transfer at the state level. It had gone down lovely. Smooth, and just the way she liked it. Had she known, she could have saved herself the ride up to Harrisburg to lobby earlier in the day. But it was all good. The game had definitely kicked up a notch, to go beyond local city dollars. The city was in chaos from the Darien Price fiasco, and the men in this tight circle were shielding her and her portfolio of clients—the question was, why? What was in it for them? And what was the cost of this money? Very interesting.

Intrigued, Laura glanced at Haines, who was now unreadable. She knew instinctively that calls would be made to grease the skids before she ever had to pick up the telephone. That's how it was always done. But why?

When Haines touched her shoulder, and his smile broadened to let her know that he knew she knew, Laura had to bite the inside of her cheeks to keep her own expression serene. She was getting tapped into dollars beyond Devereaux's Redevelopment Authority treasure chest, and it was clear that they'd allow her to build her own war chest of funds from enough sources to keep her firm rolling in green for a long time. Right here on the ballroom floor, they were quietly diversifying her funding portfolio. Excellent. Transfer complete.

"Strong proposals are indeed hard to find these days, as are organizations that deliver true economic impact on our education and job-creation front," George Townsend said slowly as Haines dropped his hand from Laura's shoulder. "We need to employ people in the city—bottom line . . . before things erode any further."

She remained very, very still as Townsend took a deep, labored breath through his thin nose and expelled it through his mouth, his gray eyes nervously glancing around the group as though seeking support for his coming statement. "Given some of the more unfortunate recent events, we do want to align our contract funds with organizations that have sound fiscal checks and balances."

Laura nodded again. *Unfortunate recent events.* If the bluebloods were talking about the Price incident in code, this was serious. Sound checks and balances—she wanted to scream with joy. It didn't get any better than this. No wonder all the press was here. They, too, had to know that a financial hit was about to go down, but just weren't sure where, when, or how. She formulated an answer to let them know she'd heard them.

"Yes," she said, frowning to convey her disapproval about the unmentioned Price incident. If they weren't going to mention the incident by name, neither was she. A bristle was enough to show that she wasn't aligned with the Price camp in any way, formal or otherwise. "It was tragic."

"In this era of tight funding," she began again in a stoic voice, her tone somber, "we cannot have this type of behavior."

She paused, waiting for their eyes to reflect back agreement that it was time for new alliances to be formed. It was financial double-talk, the kind they revered under the cloak-and-dagger circumstances. Her gaze sought theirs, and she waited for what she'd said to register a positive nod from the group. Upon receiving that, Laura pressed on. There were struggling organizations that had integrity and had been the vanguard of doing real work in the community, but never got a dime.

Her brain was on fire when she thought about those people trying to make a way out of no way, banging their heads against one brick wall after another, while the black bourgeoisie consumed nearly everything in their wake for personal gain—gain that never trickled down to the street level. Her sole mission was to force that paradigm to shift on her watch.

Laura stepped in more closely, the slight motion making the men around her move in and give her their undivided attention. "Above all else," she said in a serious tone, truly meaning it, "I always advise my clients to work with each other where they can, especially when they service the same constituency bases—hence, those that fund them can kill many birds with one stone."

"Long overdue, Laura. We should have lunch soon," Donald Haines added. "Do you have anything new and groundbreaking that we should consider?" He glanced around the room, his line of vision settling on a gathering of men by one of the open bars.

"You know I do." Laura's smile widened as he stepped past the others in their small circle and took her by the elbow. She scanned the terrain: no sign of Paxton yet. Good.

"Then perhaps I should also introduce you to some people who might be helpful. Gentleman, Liz, please excuse me while I steal Laura Caldwell for a moment. How about if I get you a drink before dinner?"

Without waiting for a response, he ushered her away from the group and past another high-level knot of people, keeping her close to his side as they walked.

"Laura, this thing with Price is most disturbing, and it has tentacles that may reach further than any of us wants it to." He talked low, his tone threatening, and yet his smile to others they passed as he spoke in her ear was disorienting.

They stopped midroom, in an unoccupied space between the ballroom tables.

"I know. It is totally unacceptable, if not embarrassing, Don. Embezzlement? There are simply no words."

"Correct. Now, I don't want you to take offense at what I'm about to say. I think we've known each other long enough to have a frank conversation."

Laura touched Donald Haines's arm. "Absolutely, Donald. You have *never* heard anything given to me in confidence leak out into the circuit, have you?"

"No. That's what I like so much about you, Laura. You're a team player, and very discreet."

"Then shoot." Her gaze darted around the room and settled back on Donald Haines to give him direct eye contact.

"Price was a fool," he said through his teeth. "We gave him a fucking shoo-in because of the dues his father paid, and the expediency to the social climate in this city. With the jobs drying up, the economy going tilt, and masses threatened with unemployment, it serves no one's purpose to have chaos in the streets. We've got too much invested in the city's infrastructure: buildings, stadiums, plans for university expansion in every corridor. We can't have this crap, or have the community unnecessarily up in arms over bullshit. His role was simple, a cakewalk. Instead, that blithering idiot used visible program money for his own personal use!"

Hell, Haines didn't have to tell her that. She'd read the papers. Darien Price appeared to have run amok using those funds for personal credit card bills, his car payments, personal hotel expenses, a damned brothel of impropriety—electronically, no less. She nodded and looked out toward the filling ballroom floor.

"We have to fix this, Laura. It was too blatant."

"I know," she murmured. *Yeah, and the white boys were coming back to the city to live in it and invest in it . . . suburban sprawl was passé.* Darien Price was the lead dog that was supposed to throw the community a bone—but ate it himself instead. The only thing Donald Haines never understood was that Darien Price was the type of black man who had no intention of using the leverage of his office for *the community,* anyway. That money was already slated for fat contracts going to his friends and family, none of whom were on the financially needy list. The entire point of propping up Darien Price had been moot in the first place. Again she wanted to scream, but this time there was no joy in the sensation.

"What can I do to help?" Laura waited, breathing slowly, every sense keen.

"Keep the elected officials and the community rabble-rousers that are aligned with the old guard Price family off our backs until we can sort this out, simply put."

She looked at Donald Haines hard but tried to keep her eyes from narrowing. As a few stragglers came over, greeted them, and left their side, she kept a frozen smile on her face. God, she needed a drink, but Donald Haines wasn't moving toward a bar. He was apparently on a mission and had her caught between two tables. The bar areas were becoming social watering holes, anyway, with too many distractions and loaded with too many people that neither of them wanted to talk to just yet. His request reverberated through her soul with defiance. Oh, yeah, she spoke Haines's language well. Perhaps too well for her own damned good.

Tension bound them with her temporary silence.

"I'll see what I can do," she finally said in a quiet voice. God, she hated this bullshit.

Donald Haines seemed to relax, and he let his breath out hard and nodded, unchecked. "Good. Because if we pull out our funds from Price's program but do not redirect them to other sound minority programming, then it will become a political nightmare—in a very volatile political climate. That's why you are so pivotal. We need someone on the inside, a neutral person, who can go between both camps . . . the old morass of families and new, to let us know which contenders are on the up and up—and to create a groundbreaking proposal for a new replacement camp where we can filter future contracts."

Now he was straightening his tie. The man was on the ropes, practically strangling from the truth, having said possibly too much. She let him twist for a minute.

"Laura, you understand how delicate this is."

"I do," she said coolly as he jammed his hands in both pants pockets.

"We need something developed that forges many alliances at once and covers all bases in all legislative districts, like Price's educational program was supposed to address. Fast.

The community must be confident that we intend to redirect moneys to the issues they're invested in. We don't need anything to cause a communication disconnect until, as I said, we can sort this all out."

So they needed a pacification, damage control strategy, huh? Laura stared at him, the translation implicit: *We need an African American and a woman to do the power shift so we white men aren't held culpable.* They needed someone to buy time while they wiped their hands clean of Darien Price.

"Understood. Consider it done," she said after a moment, then paused, her stare holding Haines's. She wanted a sure kill—no one blocking her if she took the bait for this mission. Price's camp was going to flatline when they heard about this. But it was about more than Price's stupid ass. It was about having the chance to finally redistribute some wealth.

She let her gaze float out over the milling suits in the room as she spoke. "It's time for a few new players . . . some honest hopefuls that have been locked out . . . time for them to get in on the game. I know where they are, but they could never play before—but they've never stolen a dime, and these people have been on the front lines for the last forty years."

"The community people—the grass roots—thinks highly of them?"

"Indeed." Laura's grip tightened on her purse. The uncertainty in Haines's question almost sounded like a plea. She had him by his hairy blue balls. She squeezed her purse as an alternative.

"I know who they are," she said calmly. "These are the wannabes that spend every dime they get teaching kids in after-school programs without supplies, that feed the hungry without a licensed commercial kitchen, that try to teach people how to become entrepreneurs, even though those entrepreneurs will never get a contract—because, as we know, all the real contracts are locked in by the old-guard families before the bids even go out. . . . They are from your critical mass who work a day job and volunteer at night. Problem is that for all their good work, they've been blocked by their own. People like Darien Price. I'm just as interested in putting an end to that type of waste as you are. If the real squeaky-clean hopefuls get a shot, usually it's for a measly couple thou, never six digits. They never have an opportunity to route contracts to the things the community cares about, either. Might be a prudent move now to make a change, before the dust settles."

Donald Haines sighed. "I just don't want to go too far left. Find me a moderate compromise. If we swing too far in any direction, there will still be issues down the road."

Laura nodded. "I hear you. I have a few in mind, but frankly, I'm amazed that they haven't packed up and called it a day before now."

"So are we." Donald Haines slid his palm across his jawline and let his breath out hard. "We're in this crusade together, then?"

Laura fought not to raise her eyebrow. Her father had always told her that business and politics made strange bedfellows, but damn. With no other option standing between her and 12.5 million dollars of newly available program money, she did what was prudent: she nodded.

"With jobs evaporating, and the belt tightening . . . we can't come up with some flimsy job-and-education program platform hosted by an area corporation. Their operations can't withstand the disruption or absorb the numbers. I don't even want to touch education as a sole platform during this election. The people who run the new nonprofits you're going to direct us toward have to be in synch with our candidate slates. You follow?"

"I understand," was all she would say at the moment.

"You know where these so-called community hopefuls are, and if they'll play?"

Again she stared at him. A man like Donald Haines couldn't even begin to fathom her reality. "Yes. Have all my life."

Donald Haines let his breath out hard again. "Good. Then find them, tidy them up, and find a financial conduit."

"Done."

"I knew we could count on you. Twelve-point-five mil was our collective bargain to keep feathers from getting ruffled in the community. After the school system debacle with the state takeover of that system—and its subsequent delivery into the hands of a private-contracted firm, which was a joke—and the property tax fiasco that's causing another flight pattern to the suburbs, this city could potentially change regimes. We do not need more negative minority-related PR on top of everything else."

Donald Haines ran his palm across his jaw again, tension lacing his movements. "I need not explain that Pennsylvania has a lot of electoral votes riding in the balance, as well as a significant senatorial and congressional bloc that must be preserved in the equation. As you're aware, the city has a nearly fifty-percent African-American base. The others in here from the old African-American families can't be trusted like you," he said in a quiet tone.

She waited. She'd tapped a blue-blood vein, and it was about to geyser black gold. But at what personal price? Half of her was ready for the change, but the other half of her hated the source. Hearing it so neatly laid out by Donald Haines grated on her sensibilities. However, wisdom prevailed. If Donald Haines was going to allow her to be the gatekeeper for moneys that would get redistributed to ailing minority programs that had a little integrity, sans people like Darien Price and his crew, so be it. She had to suck it up and deal.

Haines looked at her hard, searching her face for any pull back, any reticence, waiting for a response once another group of guests that had interrupted them with trite small talk was gone.

"Those old families at the top of the food chain have platform rhetoric that can shift public opinion." He sighed and shook his head. "When we pull their funds, they are going to run directly to the community and cry foul."

She nodded. That was exactly what they'd try to do, and that strategy might even be effective. But the people were starting to get hip to rhetoric and were starting to be wary of African Americans who had abandoned them in times of personal plenty, coming home only to rally support to keep stealing from them once they were busted.

"That was yesteryear, Don," Laura finally said on a forced chuckle. "We are no longer one huge, monolithic group with one or two opinion leaders. The community has seen enough bullshit to make it wary."

He nodded and ran his palm over his chin. "Maybe you're right. Hell, after the Osage Avenue thing . . . It might have been fifteen years ago, but the MOVE incident was a disaster."

She nodded. "You drop a bomb on a residential neighborhood—wipe out eleven women and children like it was a war zone and incinerate sixty-some homes, then have inside contractors skim off the top to rebuild the houses so badly that they have to be immediately condemned—in the name of minority contracts . . . yeah, trust me, the public has had its virginity taken. They've been scammed enough in Philly to at least question this latest one. So, let's do this."

"It's going to be a delicate shift," he said nervously. "Remember, they're all intermarried and have alliances already forged, which trace back to the Scott-Edward people, the Prices, the Paxtons, Crawfords, Thompsons, Ramseys . . . It's a goddamned cesspool, Laura. But, if the grass roots are satisfied . . . This kind of crap threatens federal funding for larger redevelopment projects where real money is vested."

"How well I know."

They briefly stared at each other, allowing the magnitude of what was being offered and accepted to weigh in the silent balance between them. She could see Rick trying to get her attention from across the room. Others were moving in, too. Meeting adjourned. She and Donald Haines had been in their private little midroom session long enough—long enough to start a new buzz. She had to figure out how to play that now, too.

"Your father was one who knew," Donald Haines said slowly. "If the grassroots population is taken care of, then to hell with these pretenders. Good man, and it never set right with us what happened to him. That's why we trust you so much, and why I'm even having this frank conversation with you—we know you would never side with them over what's right."

She felt her body tense but kept her countenance appearing relaxed and intimate. And where were these blue bloods when well-connected black folks falsely indicted her father? Who came to Bill Caldwell's rescue when they snatched his program, his operating budget, his job, and his life? He was filleted in the media, and all the retractions in the world couldn't undo the character assassination. A hit was a hit. Now she was conveniently supposed to be Switzerland, huh? Donald Haines's expression was tight and waiting. Both seemed to sense that the reference to her father had detonated something within her.

But what Donald Haines and his cronies would also never understand was that she didn't give a rat's ass if they all went down—as long as the community benefited in the long run. Who cared if powerful white men wanted to protect the larger five-hundred-million-dollar real estate projects that came from the right candidate getting elected, since Wall Street stocks were going belly-up? The little crumbs that they'd brushed off the table for the black elite, which had always been enough for those greedy, usurious bastards, suddenly were in question because one dog, named Darien Price, didn't mind his manners at the feet of the masters. Pure disdain percolated within her. She fought against displaying an angry smile of triumph at having Donald Haines in a position where he needed to give her the gatekeeper role over 12.5 mil, and she kept her expression appropriately grim. Yeah, she'd won. Now she had to figure out what the interest rate would be on this deal down the road.

Laura finally nodded. "Such are politics in Philly, Donald. There's only so much any of us can do." Any mention of her father was taboo, especially showing this still-raw vulnerability in her to a man like Donald Haines. Although her voice had remained mellow, she could feel the muscles in her entire body wind tight enough to pop.

Donald Haines smiled. "I go way back, remember. I'm one of the old guard who has been around long enough to have a history of the financial body count, and I know where the bones are buried in all these organizations."

"And the Italians?"

"Stay out of that," he shot back quickly. "We've made arrangements to keep everyone happy with the union apportionment and Penn Dot construction contracts once the election is over. The Italians get the highway and building contracts. We diplomatically work out things like this with great care."

Again she nodded. She would gladly stay away from that aspect of any of this. Nobody with any sense in Philadelphia fucked with the Italians. Okay, so, her role was to work the black side of the street and find or make new organizations for Donald Haines to send his money through to wash his conscience clean. Fine. She'd hook up the community orgs; money laundering was money laundering, and God knows they needed it. She'd been working that turf undercover for years, trying to right innumerable wrongs.

But at the moment she wasn't sure who was worse: the white boys who ran everything from the top, the white women who talked a feminist game but had every advantage of white privilege—and used it well, or the black people who espoused African-American solidarity but then bilked the people who believed in them, just to get a nice house and a Lexus. In her mind, it was all fraud. That's why she wasn't on any of their sides. There was only one side: hers and her community, one and the same.

They both looked up as a few gala newcomers made their way toward Donald Haines.

"How about if I let you mix and mingle? We can take this

up further when we do lunch," she said in a controlled tone. "A glass of chardonnay is calling me."

His expression seemed relieved as he nodded and began to move away from her. "Next time, I'll buy you a glass of wine. Soon?"

"Soon," she repeated. "I'll call your office tomorrow to set something up," she added, leaving his side and avoiding a conversation with two executive wannabes that she didn't intend to have right now.

So, the old white guard wanted her to find somewhere to place 12.5 million dollars, in a hurry, to keep the natives from getting restless. After the election, thc Italians would get the construction contracts; the white boys would get the real estate, while blacks, Latinos, Asians, white women, and every other special interest group got to fight each other in the scramble for whatever was left to be slated for community program dollars. The more things changed, the more they stayed the same—crumbs, compared to what the big boys manipulated.

But still not bad for the first twenty minutes working the room.

Chapter 3

He had seen her the moment he'd entered the ballroom, and was impressed by the way she handled herself. Stunning. A real pro. She had picked Donald Haines off from his huddle for a brief one-on-one with ease. A smooth operator, who was now working his libido like she was working the room.

Michael Paxton gave the photog by his side a nod of appreciation, thanking him without words for a confirmation on the name to go with the gorgeous face. All right, he'd give the poor bastard a photo op in trade for the heads-up. Definitely.

He watched her handle her business from a remote position. Long-legged, classy, with velvet jet-black hair worn in short natural curls, a graceful neck, and curves tastefully contained within a raw silk black dress. Nice. He studied her as she cut her way through key conversations like a true predator. He'd always heard the name, knew of the woman who kept a low profile on the circuit but made subtle power moves in the background—yet he had to be sure it was actually she and not just one of her firm's staff before moving in for the kill. It had been a lot of years since he'd seen her. She was never in the newspapers, always seemed to fly in under radar—and he'd always wanted to meet her. Tonight was the time.

Obviously, the white boys had to move their money now that Price had fucked up. Michael Paxton's gaze roved the terrain. The weaker nonprofits didn't stand a chance without a trusted endorsement, given that the old boys were skittish, so the way the wannabes in the room were jockeying for position was ludicrous. A waste of time. They could have saved the five hundred dollars they'd paid for a ticket and spent it on their damned rent. The power brokers were searching for sound investment sources, ones that would be acceptable yet politically viable. That meant they had to find a clean fiscal conduit. Laura Caldwell, now the woman with the Midas touch, made sense.

As he was intermittently stopped along the way toward the bar, he planned his approach, mouthing platitudes and declining press commentary. He kept her in his peripheral vision as he made the necessary and cursory small talk with his larger clients, functioning on two levels of awareness at once. If she was going to structure a new nonprofit conduit, he wanted in on the ground floor. Darien Price might be a client, but he had now become more than a family nuisance—he was fucking up real money. Contracts from fattened programs destined for his shop after the election, and those for the rest of their network, were in jeopardy because a new gatekeeper had more than likely just been named. Damn.

Paxton kept moving, his mind manipulating the options. Getting close to Laura Caldwell presented the perfect way to stem a potential financial hemorrhage. If they were going to come to a financial marriage of convenience, he certainly wouldn't mind any other perks a relationship with her might also hold. It had been too long since any of the females in Philadelphia held his attention like this one did now. This one was a sure business asset, as well as a *fine* trophy. But first, the money. Caldwell was clearly just anointed as the next gatekeeper by Haines, and a cozy business relationship with her could ensure that lucrative consulting contracts for whatever programs she established would come his way. He'd kill two birds with one stone. Excellent.

Paxton took a sip of his drink as he accepted it from the bartender, crushing a dollar bill into the tip glass, his actions leisurely, biding his time. Close to where he was standing, he found a loose gathering of his fellow business competitors and went up to the other attorneys with confidence to begin a little light repartee of wits before dinner, to warm up.

He studied them as he approached. They were all clearly worried about the debacle. It was written all over their faces. Darien Price was a fool, but as his attorney of record, he had to keep the stupid bastard from going to jail. More important, he had to make sure that an unconnected source like Laura Caldwell would not be too narrow in her thinking while the family trust of interconnected firms cleaned up the mess Price had left behind. She could not be allowed to redirect Darien's current program moneys—thus, by extension, his future contract moneys—to outsider firms. It was not about allowing anyone to realign resources in a way that cut out key players in the family. If the white boys were going to give her the nod, then she had to be sure to give the right families the nod, so that everyone's old contracts could be preserved. Smiles dissolved as he came nearer to the group of men. Something was wrong.

"Michael Paxton," a voice from behind him said, "I'm Detective James Carter. Maybe a word, *soon*?"

Paxton turned slowly, taking a sip of Chivas, looking the intruder up and down. So that's what blanched his rivals: a fucking cop. Here, of all places? Unheard of. He reached in his breast pocket and produced a business card with two fingers, which he flipped to Carter. "My office hours are from nine to five, Monday through Friday. Not here, Detective."

"Understood," Carter replied coolly, returning Paxton's glare and allowing it to settle briefly on the other men in the small group. "We were just having difficulty getting our calls returned."

Two bystanders stirred their drinks and quietly melted away from the deadlocked twosome, not even saying good-bye to Paxton as they slipped into another nearby group. Paxton throttled sudden rage as his fellow attorneys got out of Dodge. He hated the smirk Carter offered when they did so. Nobody wanted to be within a hundred yards of the potential fallout with the press in plain view, even though he knew their curiosity was killing them. His friendly competitors had their hands in a part of Darien's cookie jar as a network quid pro quo to keep everyone mollified. Their contracts were now possibly screwed, too. However, a cop in the house, obviously on an official probe, was freaking them out. Tomorrow he'd place a call downtown to stop any future harassment. Paxton's eyes narrowed.

"So, you wanted to make a media statement, then?" Paxton said coolly after a moment. "Tell me, Carter, is your evidence from the investigation so shaky that you need to try a man in the press here instead of in a courtroom, or did I misunderstand your intentions?"

"No, Counselor. If you wanna talk, then—"

Paxton shook his head. "The room is loaded with gossipmongers, and this is not the place or time."

"Then let's do this the old-fashioned way," Carter retorted. "Professional to professional. Return my call, set up a time, and let's talk."

"Done. Now, excuse me."

Paxton brushed past Carter, allowing the rage to recede from the unexpected affront. Fucking dicks were everywhere on this thing. He could wring Price's neck for screwing up so badly. How many damned contracts hung in the balance from this bullshit? It was supposed to be simple; Darien had 12.5 million dollars to be lord over, and every family in the network would have gotten a healthy contract from the catbirdseat once the elections were finished. What was so goddamned hard about moving easy money?

* * *

"Paxton's coming your way," Rick said in a low whisper. "Showtime, baby. I gave him the heads-up that you might be open to a conversation. Now you owe me, love."

Laura gave her photographer buddy a sly smile. "So I do. But who's the guy that pissed him off? The tall hunk in the cheap suit?"

Rick laughed. "A detective that's sweating him on the Price case."

"Very interesting. Name?"

"Carter. James Carter."

"Oh. Hmmm."

"Laura, you never told me you liked the rough-around-the-edges type." Rick chuckled and adjusted his camera lenses. "Gives a guy like me hope—but he'll probably be unemployed by tomorrow afternoon for that stunt. Nobody screws with Mike Paxton, not even the cops."

"Please. I just find it fascinating that a detective would show up here at a five-hundred-dollar-a-plate function. Don't you?"

"Yeah, and so does every media hound in town."

"Well, since you said Mr. Paxton is threading a decisive route my way, why don't I just find out why he and a cop had to meet here, of all places . . . and feed that to ya later?"

"What, and no photo op? Aw, lady, c'mon. Gimme a break." Rick pouted, then laughed, and made her smile wider.

"You know I'll hook you up, Rick—even if I might have to delay on delivering." She glanced at the way key players were positioned in the room. Now was not the time, but she'd definitely make good on her promise. The one thing she'd learned from her father's fall from grace was, stay friendly with the press.

Rick glanced around the room with her, seeming to note the delicate positioning, too. "All right. I'll keep your favor tab running, but if you do hear something, you feed it to me first?"

"Always. How about if I get you a nice shot with Elizabeth Haines and a few topnotchers from the Micholi

Foundation? Plus, the politicians are starting to make their entrances, and I'm sure I could get a few senators to line up next to the Haines group for you. Might make the cover, instead of just the society page?"

"For now, that'll work—big-time. Thanks, Laura. Knew I could count on you."

"Debt paid in full; anything else is extra and off the record by an unknown source." She smiled and kissed Rick's cheek, trying to pacify him. Later she'd get back to him with something truly scandalous. He patted her arm, seeming to know that she would, just like she always did.

"Cool."

"Then, follow me."

Laura intentionally avoided Michael Paxton's oblique approach, ushering Rick toward the huddle of target photographic shots he needed for his quota. Making short work of the introductions, she slid away from that grouping and picked out different clients to chat with along the way as she matched Michael Paxton's rotation around the room.

Each cursory conversation she held kept her senses engaged on two levels: one to seem fully connected to the people she spoke with; the other holding Michael Paxton and Detective Carter in her peripheral vision, noting whom they spoke to and whom they passed up. It was a veritable waltz, a refined movement of chess pieces on a life-size ballroom floor. Pawns, rooks, knights, bishops—all had to be moved and countermoved just so. The same way she'd moved Darien Price into position to take a fall.

"You are a very popular and difficult lady to catch up to," a deep male voice intoned near her ear.

She didn't turn around. She didn't have to. She'd positioned herself close enough to Paxton to know he'd make his way to her or die trying. She knew what he wanted.

"Pleased to meet you, too," she said after a pause, her voice taking a hint of a sensual dip as she turned to shake his hand and to address him formally. She allowed a smile to dawn slowly on her face. "Laura Caldwell." He had hazel eyes, and her negative reaction to them was immediate but well concealed.

"So I'm told. Michael Paxton." He held her hand just a moment longer than a purely professional handshake required, and then withdrew his palm. "We have some mutual clients and, it appears, some potentially mutual sources of funds between us. You know, many of my clients are major corporations, which seek advice about how to direct their charitable giving. You work with some of these firms as well. We should get together sometime."

"Interesting."

"Can we do lunch one day soon to further investigate the possible opportunities within our shared connections?"

"Do you have a card?" She hadn't directly committed and had raised one eyebrow with a circumspect glance, noting how that took him aback slightly. *Perfect. Stay aloof. Draw him out and make him ask for what he wants.*

One-half of his smile gave in to the increasing muscle pull under his skin, creating a lazy, smug expression on his immaculately shaven walnut-toned face. His jet-black, wavy hair was close-cropped, with strands of silver running through it at the temples, giving him a distinguished presence. Several eyes in the room were on the two of them.

Nonetheless, she watched him reach into his navy blue suit and extract a card. Cufflinks, monogrammed cuffs, royal blue shirt, starched white collar, suit obviously from Brooks Brothers and tailored to perfection like a Main Line Mayflower descendent, plus black wingtips that looked like they had a glass finish on them. Height judged to be six-three to six-four. Salt-and-pepper hair. Clean cut. Age: late forties, early fifties. Rolex watch. Lean, black urban professional athletic build, no evidence of unhealthy body fat. She made a quick assessment, leaving no detail out. He hadn't been screwing, either. Cologne was fresh, but he was not too freshly showered. She let out an almost audible sigh of relief for Najira. Approximately size twelve shoes. Oh, yeah, this was a player.

She accepted the business card, glanced at it, and opened her purse to put it away. So this was who was representing Darien Price and wanted a piece of the action. It was time to move away from him. To linger would send the wrong signal to those who had verbally allotted 12.5 million for her to disseminate.

"And you?"

Without glancing up, she produced a card for Paxton from her opened clutch at his request. Talking to him further now, even if to debate giving him the card, would only hurt her position, so she produced the stationery without fanfare.

He accepted it but never looked at it, his eyes on her. "I'll be in touch." As unobtrusively as he'd approached her, Michael Paxton walked away, his gait confident and easy.

Let the games begin. She chuckled to herself as she inconspicuously wound her way over to the tall, good-looking but underdressed man standing alone sipping on what appeared to be a club soda. The bubbles in his glass told her what it was, plus he was a cop and obviously working. Laura fought to keep from smiling. This was so easy.

She'd made enough pit stops that it would appear that she'd happened to be close to him by accident. Finding a group of old colleagues, Laura fell into easy conversation, but her peripheral vision remained trained on her target.

"Terrible, all this . . . mess going on," a lean, brown sister said in a low, nervous tone. "You think the fallout will be far-reaching?"

"One can never tell, Marj," Laura murmured, and then glanced away. "But I think your agency will be safe."

Her friend nodded and let out a breath in relief. "If anyone would know, you would, hon."

"Uhmmm, hmmm," Laura said, her tone distant as she patted the worried woman's arm. "Sit tight and keep your books right. It's all good."

As a few stragglers joined their circle, Laura used the opportunity to thoroughly assess the out-of-place brother who held her interest. His dark eyes were scanning the room as though he were waiting for a bomb to go off in it. Perhaps it had. His thick brows were knit, and his off-the-rack black suit hung just a bit out of alignment, seeming to strain in places against a set of well-defined shoulders. Six-five, if an inch. Needed another shave. Must have been in a rush to get here, or it was a last-minute, unplanned decision. Hmmmm . . . Intense, dark-brown eyes—just like his skin. Black shoes could use a good polish. Oh, yeah, this was an unplanned stop; a guy like this with a nearly military vibe would have shined his shoes and put a razor to his jaw. Timex watch. Civil servant issue. Definitely a cop. Way out of place. Perfect for the job of an insider champion.

"Hello," she said brightly, rummaging in her purse for her business card as she approached him. "Haven't seen you on the charity circuit before. Laura Caldwell . . . and you are?"

As soon as he opened the door to his hotel room, Monica rushed in and pushed it shut behind her. He watched the tears rise in her eyes and simply opened his arms. Immediately, she filled his embrace, clinging to him like a frightened child. By habit he kissed the top of her head—an invitation to take this thing wherever she wanted it to go.

"I know you and Darien and are tight . . . like family," she said on a thick swallow, her cheek crushing his lapel. "But, Mike, you saw the picture! This time he's gone too far."

"I was disgusted by what I saw," Paxton murmured into her auburn hair, stroking her back. "It was not only politically volatile, but it was truly insensitive, if not deplorable . . . given the way you've upheld your end of the marriage with him."

Monica's eyes glistened as she looked up, her gaze searching for understanding and comfort. "I knew you'd understand."

"I do. More than you know." He pushed a stray wisp of her bangs away from her forehead but continued to allow her body to mold against him.

"I know now is not the time to file for divorce, not in the middle of a horrible financial investigation, and not until these silly allegations that were probably trumped up by enemy politicians to smear him are resolved . . . but, Michael, I am just so damned angry. Darien uses everybody, and thinks he can get away with it."

"No," he said, his tone like silk. "You're right. The timing is bad, and filing for divorce now wouldn't be prudent. There are others to consider in the thing, and we do need Darien to be exonerated—so we can squash this scandal as unfounded allegations made by the competition. Right now wouldn't be good to add more fuel to the media fire."

"I just want him to feel what it's like to be betrayed."

Paxton nodded and let out a slow breath, his gaze holding hers. "We have all told him for years that he had to temper his behavior. Discretion is key, especially when you're handling other people's money, and others depend on you. He betrayed us, and now he's betrayed you. We'll fix this."

Monica sniffed and dabbed her nose with the back of her hand. "I want to let him know that he just can't take me for granted, and that . . ." She looked up at him without blinking. "Do you understand?"

For a moment he didn't answer. Monica Scott Price was in his arms, practically begging to be fucked, all so she could cut her husband's heart out. What wasn't there to understand? The question was, didn't she understand how long he'd waited for an opportunity like this? "Ironies of ironies," as Darien's father always said. This was such a wonderful diversion, a nice, unexpected trophy to add to the collection of things to torture Darien's soul with one day. And she was fine, had always walked the straight and narrow for Darien's sorry ass, once she had become his wife.

Paxton allowed his fingers to trace the delicate shape of Monica's face, watching her hazel eyes close slowly as tears spilled over the edges of her lashes. "Oh, baby . . . don't cry. I'll make it all right . . . because I understand more than you'll ever know."

Chapter 4

James Carter manipulated the embossed ivory business card between his fingers as his mind kneaded the puzzle. Who was she? He'd heard the Caldwell name before but just couldn't place why it stood out in his brain. Why would a gorgeous, cinnamon-brown barracuda approach him like that? What was this chick's angle? She didn't seem the type just to roll up on a man for purely hormonal reasons.

"Get anywhere with our man Paxton tonight?"

Carter looked over at his partner, who had flopped down at an adjacent precinct desk.

"No," Carter grumbled. "Arrogant son of a bitch said to see him Monday through Friday, nine to five. His client isn't coming in for questioning without him, and we'll definitely need a warrant if we wanna search and seize anything. They're gonna play hardball. Forget cooperating with the investigation to prove innocence."

"Figured as much," Steve muttered, clearing away a stack of paperwork in front of him so that he could set down his Styrofoam cup of coffee. "So, did the highfalutin' make you pay five C-notes, or did a flash of the shield get you in?"

Carter stashed away the business card in his jacket pocket and shook his head. "The shield got me in, and also made the media swamp me. I told them that I wasn't there on official business, to blow 'em off. Was possibly a dumb idea. Left before they served plates, ya know, so it wasn't like I ripped a charity off for a chicken dinner. I just needed to let Price's crew know that we'd be all over them like flies on shit—regardless of who they're connected to. A bit of psychological theatrics." Carter rubbed his face with both hands, trying to chase away fatigue. "Might have worked. Paxton freaked, in a smooth sorta way. Brother didn't like it at all that I'd publicly come up in his yard. But his client is as guilty as sin. I can feel it."

Steve Sullivan sighed and riffled his fingers through his blond crew cut. "You know . . . we've been partners a long time, and I think you really need to—"

"Oh, don't start that shit, man. Not tonight. Go home and stop burning the midnight oil. I got this."

His partner looked at him with an expression of concern. "Listen, you might not like what this poor white boy from the Northeast, by way of Port Richmond, is telling you, but all I'm saying is that your personal dislike for the elite might cloud your judgment." Sullivan took a slow sip of his brew, making a slurping sound and a grimace as it slid down his throat. "We've gotta stay open. CYA, and cover all bases."

Carter pushed back from his chair and stood, beginning to pace. "It's an open-and-shut case, man. Price is claiming identity theft, which you and I both know is bullshit. What identity thief electronically pulls down money from a restricted source and then goes into your bank account to pay off *your* bills for you, huh? Ever heard such a crock? Gimme a break. Go home. Get some rest. Like I said, I got this."

"I would go home if there was still somebody there to go home to." Steve shrugged and returned his focus to an evidence file. "They're gonna release him on his own recognizance; you know that. Forget a lockup with high bail. He isn't a flight risk, but he is a local dignitary with solid family ties to Philadelphia, and the amount of money he took was peanuts. What's seventy-five thousand dollars in today's economy, as thieves go? So, if your theory proves correct, then the only way to do this is by the numbers. He's got too many people in too many places that just want this thing to disappear. I'm surprised it hasn't already. One slipup, and they'll throw the baby out with the bathwater on a technicality. You hearing me, Jim?"

"Yeah, I hear you," Carter said with disgust, thrusting his hands in his pockets. He hated these people who could steal more than an average man made in a year and get away with it.

Truth was, through their little elite club, over the years they'd stolen more than money—they'd stolen hopes, dreams, and lives. And they'd taken from those who believed they could get a job, or from small businesses hopeful of a contract—innocents who'd pledged their homes to get a tiny business loan only to find out that the doors to access were shut in their faces by the very people they'd believed would hold them open for them. Oh, yeah, Price was going down. Everybody who had an ounce of common sense knew Price was one of the biggest perpetrators of community fraud, claiming he did everything for *the people,* and this time he was busted.

"Good," Steve said, hesitating, apparently unconvinced that Carter had let the situation rest.

Carter rubbed his jaw and glanced down the row of old, dirty metal desks. "But a bastard like Price has also had to make a few enemies—ones that might be too willing to testify to some larger digits he's moved. This thing is probably only the tip of the iceberg."

"You're fishing, Jim. Seventy-five thousand is enough to break Price's back. Hell," Sullivan added with a chuckle, "just knowing that arrogant SOB is gonna have to bend over for the soap in prison would be good enough for me. I don't care if he only does a day; that's long enough to make his life hell forever. His pop put away enough felons to keep him very nervous in the joint."

Carter began walking. He needed space as much as he needed coffee. "It's more than that; it's—"

"Look," Sullivan said quickly, standing. Carter turned now to stare at him. "You've gotta let this thing with your father go." Sullivan rounded his desk and stayed Carter's retreat by the way he dropped his voice. "Let it go, brother," he repeated with more conviction. "Your father got a hero's burial, and all the conspiracy theory in the world never showed up anything more than a convenience store robbery. That's what put a bullet in your old man's chest—not some rich folks with a grudge."

Sullivan neared his partner and blocked Carter's exit from the room. "You cannot start doing a parallel investigation, going back into the past and trying to unearth dead evidence on a closed case while you go after some minor league white-collar, rich-boy bullshit that Price pulled. Not a good career move. You feel me?"

For a moment, neither man spoke. Their eyes met, and a silent understanding bound them.

"I feel you," Carter finally muttered. He broke eye contact with Sullivan and stared out the window for a moment. "You ever run up on a chick named Laura Caldwell? The last name is bugging me." Why would some chick obviously born with a silver spoon in her mouth approach him?

"Caldwell?"

"Yeah," Carter said, walking back toward his abandoned metal chair, feeling more comfortable now that the subject had been changed.

"Why?" Steve moved to sit slowly on the corner of his desk.

"Good-looking, about five-nine, million-dollar smile, legs to stop traffic on Broad Street . . . one of the insiders . . . rolled up on me at the function and gave me her card. Runs a firm called Rainmakers, Inc."

Steve relaxed and laughed. "When's the last time you got some, man? Shit. I'd know what to do with *that* business card. This is the new millennium . . . maybe she got tired of doing soft guys on the circuit and saw your big, burly ass and made a play."

Carter shook his head. "Uh-uh. Not the type. Too refined."

"For chrissake, man. What does that shit mean?" Steve chuckled and reached for his coffee, taking another healthy sip.

"She wanted something."

"So, give it to her—or give me the card, and I'll give it to her. I haven't been laid good since my old lady walked."

"I'ma run a check on the name . . . see what I can find. She might know Price, or owe him a knife in his back. It was the way she approached me. Too friendly." Carter sent his gaze out the window again. Yeah, Laura Caldwell was way too friendly. She wasn't his type, nor was he hers. She came from the kind of people that had probably gotten his father snuffed. The memory ricocheted around in his head; his father had been talking to people downtown, working on something big, before he got shot. Who the hell was Laura Caldwell?

Steve let his breath out hard. "Whatever, man. But I think you might be off base on that one. Stop looking a gift horse in the mouth, would ya? Maybe she was feeling philanthropic. It's not often that guys like us get a little *benefit* from going to a charity fund-raising ball, ya know?"

"Yeah, *I know.* That's why this whole thing just doesn't sit right with me."

"Explain this to me again," Paxton said, losing patience. He hated the way Darien Price sagged in the old Price family living room chair before him, tears in his eyes. The dominant burgundy hues surrounding them seemed to make Darien look even weaker in his dead father's royal living room. He was glad Monica had elected to take a room at her sister's for the night. There were things he needed to say to Darien that no wife should hear. Paxton glared at his client. Big, stupid pussy. No matter what Darien had told him earlier that day, all evidence pointed in his direction. And by the look of things, the new contract gatekeeper was a tad aloof. She'd take time to warm up. Seventy-five grand wasn't worth this crap. For a few luxury items? Credit cards? Plus, sloppily handling some stray ghetto tail so badly that his wife was even sent a phone pic? In the middle of a goddamned investigation? Was he mad?

Pure venom seethed within Paxton as he formulated his statement. "I'm your attorney, and you have to come clean with me, or—"

"You're *family,* man. Not just my attorney. I told you!" Darien yelled. "I've been set up!"

Paxton stood, rounding the coffee table between him and Darien, and came in close to his client. "Don't you ever mention that we are family in public. A godbrother affiliation does not need to be exploited. Understood?"

Darien looked at Paxton with reddened eyes and nodded. Paxton's shoulders relaxed.

"Good," Paxton said carefully, walking away from Darien to pour himself a drink. "You know, this little debacle of yours is shaking up the entire network."

"I didn't do it. I swear."

Paxton watched the amber liquid as it filled a crystal tumbler, keeping his back to Darien. "Do you know how many healthy six-figure and seven-figure consulting contracts were going to get siphoned off of your empire once a new city cabinet is installed? Do you?"

When Darien didn't immediately answer, Paxton swished the Chivas around as he brought the glass to his lips and took a sip. "Ramsey was going to get the board of education contracts. Thompson would have had the city facility contracts. Crawford would have gotten the major city community outreach, media placement, and marketing contract. Scott would have had the food and supplies contract for the convention center. Edward would have had the curriculum development contracts for several job programs. My firm would have had the retainer for fiscal management and legal oversight, audits, etcetera, on these. All you had to do was hold the money, let out small sums until after the elections and our slate was in place. Everything has an educational component and was going to be a conduit through you, as planned."

Darien hung his head as Paxton railed on.

"Your wife would have been fed the advertising portion of city PR dollars at the radio station, so that commissions would route back into your household. You had a nice, cushy job with a decent salary and were jettisoned to a gatekeeper role for one reason: to ensure that everybody's firms got their share, like always. Twelve-point-five million in program funds was a lock for this fiscal year. Once you got in, all you had to do was funnel the additional quietly promised moneys coming from our friends at the state and federal levels to the right places. Then something beyond foolish occurred, and all that got fucked up. Why did that happen on your watch, Darien?"

"I don't know," Darien whimpered. "It wasn't supposed to go down like that. But it wasn't me. I wouldn't jeopardize the trust like that, not for a few measly dollars." He opened his arms wide and spun around. "Look at this place. What do we need? My people left me the house and contents, plus a fat insurance policy . . . Ethan Allen furniture, antiques, the whole nine yards. My sister got the place up in the Vineyard plus a hefty cash-out; my younger brother got a cash knot, was set up to run the magazine that our dad was part owner of down in D.C. I didn't need to do something crazy!"

Darien began pacing as Paxton calmly sipped his drink. Paxton stared at Darien while he walked back and forth like a trapped animal in the middle of his spacious living room floor. Paxton's gaze swept the massive space that was filled with an ivory and burgundy Queen Anne vintage sofa, heavy matching wingback chairs, a taupe leather recliner studded in brass, and custom ivory window treatments of the finest raw silk.

By rights, and as a matter of principle, all that he surveyed within Price's home should have been his. The fact that he could buy everything in the house, along with the property itself, three times over wasn't the point. An old rage quietly kindled within Paxton as he silently appraised the Tiffany and Art Deco lamps, the teakwood table that sat on an expensive Turkish rug, and the luster of the parquet hardwood floors, as well as the eighteenth-century Virginia sugar chest that rested beside the embroidered footstool of the same era. He slowly made his way to stand before a marble fireplace, noting the Ming vase on the mantel, along with the array of original art that graced the walls as though the spectacular home were a gallery. Point taken. The Prices lived well—that he couldn't argue. Had for generations, like his. But Darien was a fool. That was also inarguable.

"Then who would set you up like that?" Paxton finally muttered, taking another liberal sip from his glass, now studying the shimmering liquid as light from the heavy crystal chandelier glistened within it. "You make enemies with the white boys? They're the only ones with the sophistication to do an electronic setup like this—if that's what it is. And then again, what would be their motive? The twelve-five was payoff money to keep the natives from getting restless, and so we wouldn't rally our friendly black elected officials against their larger projects. The couple of legislators in our hip pocket are interested in keeping things smooth in their districts, too, so why would they set you up? Doesn't gel."

"I know. I know," Darien muttered, finding the huge leather wingback chair and flopping into it. He leaned forward with his head in his hands. "I've kept all the old alliances cool. Always have."

"You screw somebody's wife you shouldn't have?"

Darien looked up at Paxton, his eyes searching his face. "Mike, I swear. Okay, so I fucked a lot of dumb broads—but nobody's wife who's important . . ."

"Give me a list of names. In letting the little head do the thinking for the big head, you might have fucked somebody's prized mistress—more important than a man's wife, asshole!"

Darien was on his feet again, gesturing wildly with his hands as he talked. "No, man. Uh-uh. Those bitches weren't connected to anybody. My wife can't find out about that shit, either. Talk about fucking things up. You know who her people are! Her uncle is already stepping back from my program during his campaign. Monica was blowing my phone up all morning, and I thought she was onto some of my shit—then, when I finally called her back, she was cool. She was just worried about me and stressing out. Now ain't a good time for any domestic bullshit. That's not what's up . . . some woman shit. No."

"Yeah. My point. Now isn't a good time for anything to explode on the domestic front, Darien. But do you think your wife might have done you, since you've done half of Philly? Women can be vicious, especially when screwed over."

Both men stared at each other for a moment, the possibility slowly sinking into their awareness.

"Monica would have access to your social security number from your tax records, or wherever."

Paxton went to the window as his mind grappled with the facts. He cast his gaze out of the large Tudor bay window toward the mature trees blackened by shadows. He didn't need Darien's corroboration to know how angry that woman was. "Identity theft is easy. If you have a man's social security number, you can pull his credit report. From his credit report, you can get every conceivable account number for credit cards, a car loan, etcetera. You can make purchases and pay bills electronically, if you know his bank account numbers. You can—"

"But my wife wouldn't do that! We have two little kids . . .

and my wife would die before she'd let the Price family name or her Scott maiden name get—"

"Have you spoken to your damned wife today?"

"No, I mean, just briefly. She'd been sending me nine-one-one pages all fucking morning, and I thought it was about some of her normal silly bullshit, but I couldn't deal with her at that time—I just met you in the morning, hid in the hotel like you told me to, got Don to bring me some clothes while Monica was out. Then, when we did talk, she said she'd been stressed but was dealing with it, and would be at her sister's later because she was tired of the media ringing the telephone off the hook and staking out the house. It's all crashing down, Mike. There's just too much pressure, but Monica wouldn't—"

"Then who else would have access to that kind of information? Wake up, man. Either you are going down for this, unless we can find a plausible substitute, or she is."

"No. There has to be some other way. It's not her. We may have our issues, but she loves me, Mike. She'd never hurt me like that, no matter what she thinks I've done out there . . . She knows the other women never counted. It was just sex. Monica didn't do this . . . maybe one of the broads I slept with got my credit cards, or—"

"But how would they gain access to your program fund bank accounts? How would they know which budget line items had money in them, do the transfer to your personal bank account, and then turn around in one month and pay off all your bills?"

Thoroughly agitated, Paxton turned to face Darien, smoothing his palm across his hair. "You screw anybody on your staff, lately—female or otherwise? Somebody in accounting that cuts checks? Your cushy little city agency was set up to be able to immediately cut checks from your office, without having to go through the whole city system—so *we* could get our contract money faster than normal bureaucratic turnaround. You do somebody over there yet?"

Pure horror filled Darien's eyes. "Jesus . . ."

"Or did you bring your work home at night, in an unlocked briefcase?" Paxton let his breath out in a rush of disgust. "A briefcase filled with your program budgets. Maybe your agency bank statements? Filled with every damning piece of correspondence . . . You ever bring that shit home to your wife after you did lunch at the Pyramid Club, or the Palm, maybe a hideaway like Panorama, and perhaps stopped off for a little afternoon tail at the Four Seasons, brother? Maybe after going to Bluezettes for after-five drinks to pick off one from the herd?"

A sob broke through Darien's lips, and he covered his face with his hands, turning away from Paxton as he sought a chair for refuge.

"If I wanted to divorce a man and take everything he had—because he'd fucked half the city and his staff, and therefore me—I'd do it just like this. Strip his dumb ass of everything, pay off everything, then own everything in the court settlement with full custody of my children . . . all because he was incarcerated."

"I'm not going out like this for that bitch, if she played me!" Darien yelled through a garbled sob, saliva sputtering from his mouth as his terror-stricken eyes held Paxton's cool glare of contempt. "I'm not going to prison behind some bullshit I didn't do. I'll take this whole fucking network down with me, if you all let me go out like this!"

Darien stood, wild-eyed, wiping his flushed face and his running nose with the back of his hands. "Remember," he added, pointing at his chest, "I know *everybody's* dirt, where all the bodies are buried. I know about the contracts that never stood a chance because the decisions had already been made, years in advance. Fuck all that lowest-bidder, highest-quality crap. The Scotts, the Edwards, Ramseys—all of us got to live in Chestnut Hill and West Mount Airy, send our kids to private schools just like our parents did, and live the good life because of the inside track . . . I will sing to the highest heavens about how the black side of this city was carved up into territories since the fucking sixties—you hear me, Mike! I will tell the grand jury about how none of the firms we run delivered squat, and the paperwork was forged to show impact, demonstration; and how none of us gave a shit about *the people*—fuck poor people—I'm not going out like that."

Darien slapped his chest and began walking in a circle. "You want film at eleven, Pax? Oh, yeah, I will give up the tapes to the media and explain how it was always about getting paid off the top, and whatever crumbs fell to the floor is what went to the community. Fuck this shit. I'll do whatever it takes, 'cause I ain't goin' to jail!"

"You need to sit down and get very, very still," Michael Paxton said between his teeth. "I'm glad it's just you and me here, because talk like that could get a man killed. . . . There's no telling what could happen to you if you start threatening to jeopardize some very powerful people's income. Don't go there. Are we clear?" Paxton pointed at Darien, his gaze unwavering. "Sit down."

Taking in huge gulps of air, Darien finally complied, his line of vision never leaving Paxton's, and he flopped into a chair.

"Pull yourself together. I'm not going to allow you to go to prison. However, if you ever threaten me again, I'll let the white boys have you. The Italian white boys. Understood?"

Darien nodded, a new well of tears rising in his eyes.

"Good. Because if you unravel the black trust, it leads to the Main Line—the people who sanction what we get. They broker the allocation of funding between the South Philadelphia Italian contingent and us . . . and I know they won't get their hands dirty. They'll send an Italian sanitation squad for you . . . and your wife—and children. They will make you and all your problems go away. So decide tonight. You or Monica? One of you has to take the weight, if we can't find another source to pin this on."

Darien let his head fall forward into his hands again. "If it comes to that, do my wife. I haven't gotten along with that bitch for years, anyway."

Chapter 5

She sat on the bedroom window seat in her Philly brownstone on Twenty-eighth and Pennsylvania Avenue in the dark, staring out at the mouth of East River Drive as shc waited for the call to connect. Ironic that the street she'd picked to live on had the same name as the major thoroughfare in Washington, D.C.; and as much crap as was going on in Philadelphia, it might as well have been in D.C. anyway. Everything boiled down to politics.

Laura shrugged away the uncomfortable thought. She loved her quiet street, which had the dense foliage of the drive on one side and only a few large houses with garages on the other, like a secret hideaway in plain sight.

The way the wind made the autumn leaves move, and the way the magnificence of the art museum sat on a hill as if it were on the mythical Greek Mount Olympus, made her wonder, *what if?* What if there was something more in the world than what one saw with the naked eye? What if people's spirits did live on and ghosts haunted the planet until wrongs were righted? What if there was a thing called fate?

Her sister's voice broke the spell of her ruminations, and

it took a moment for Laura to mentally come back into her bedroom.

"Hello?" her sister, Nadine, repeated.

"Oh, hey, girl," Laura said with a self-conscious chuckle. "I was just lost in thought while I waited for you to pick up. Almost forgot I was on the phone."

"You all right?"

"I'm fine. Just wanted to hear your voice."

"Yeah, but by your time it's nearly midnight."

"That's why I figured you guys would still be up, since you're a couple hours behind me. How are the kids? How are you?"

Her sister hesitated for a moment. "Well . . . they're taking the move to Chicago as best they can, but given the nasty divorce and the fact that their dad hasn't seen them in years—or paid any support . . ."

"I know." Laura swallowed away her anger and kept her voice upbeat. Every time she and Nadine spoke, her sister recounted the divorce and her ex-brother-in-law's negligence as though it had just happened. What drove her rage was the fact that her sister had been victimized and was still allowing herself to remain stuck in that passive place of pain. Laura steadied herself, forcing her tone to sound positive, wanting so much to heal the terrible wound that a man had inflicted upon someone she loved. "Did you move in somewhere nice?"

"Yeah, hon. Thanks again so much, for all your help, too. I wouldn't have been able to take this nursing position if you hadn't dropped a hefty deposit in my account for the move."

"We're not going to talk about that little subsidy, because that's what sisters are for." If Nadine would just trust her! With all the money she'd squirreled away from her Wall Street days, not to mention her firm, she could afford to help both her sisters out.

"Yeah, but it was so much and—"

"And you know to show it on your taxes as a loan, so the IRS doesn't beat you up for that big deposit, right? One percent interest, just like we signed, with payments not due on it for ten years." Laura made herself laugh to calm Nadine's nerves. "It'll be fine—and you don't ever have to pay me back. The paperwork is for *the man.* Got it?"

"You sure this is gonna work?"

"Rich folks have been doing it for years. Ask me how I know."

Her sister sighed. "But you have to stop spoiling my teenagers, okay. Darrel thinks he's half grown as it is, and Darlene, Lord have mercy, doesn't need another thing to wear. Thanks for the computers and stuff for the kids. Dag, Sis . . . I just needed a little help with back-to-school stuff, not a whole—"

"I'm spoiling yours and Lavern's because I don't have any of my own, and don't plan on ever having any . . . so just let me do my thing as crazy Aunt Laura, okay?"

"Okay." Nadine let her breath out on a hard sigh. "But I wish you wouldn't give up on the whole—"

"We have been down that path before." Laura chuckled, stood up, and walked down the hall into her second-floor home office in search of more coffee. "I don't subscribe to love, marriage, or pushing a baby carriage." She glanced around her sandstone-colored office with its sleek oak furniture and thought about how everything in her home was a light, airy Caribbean color or earth tone, then shook her head. No, her world was definitely not set up for a nursery vibe. The season had passed.

"All right, my bad," her sister finally conceded. "What are you doing? You sound like you're washing dishes."

"Just got in from a political fund-raiser and I'm making a small pot of coffee," Laura said in a distracted tone as she set up the coffeemaker to brew and found her cell phone, switching it on as she spoke. Multitasking, her mind tried to hold on to a conversation with Nadine while she worked. She loved talking to her sisters about everything and nothing, just hearing their voices shut out the world—especially when she had something unpleasant to do.

"Meet anybody exciting?"

"Nope," Laura lied. "Just a bunch of old white men and fronting Negroes." She let her breath out in a long sigh, impatient for the coffee to be ready. She glanced at the e-mail display on the cell phone and waited for the Internet connection.

"Wait till I call Lavern and tell her you are still telling me that same old tired litany about not seeing anyone interesting out on the wine-and-cheese circuit. C'mon, Laura. You have to ease up on a man to meet a nice one. Your standards have always been ridiculously high."

"Both of you-all are divorced," Laura scoffed, circling her desk and sitting down hard in the chair. "Not a good character reference for the species." She stared at the cell phone in her palm and began entering a password.

"But, girl, you should see these fine men in Chi-town. The hospital is loaded with them, too. Lavern met a hunk from Baltimore working the cruise ship junket on her new job with Carnival. I'm glad she got out of Philly and moved to Miami. The change did her good . . . maybe you'll get out of there one day, too?"

"Maybe. But right now I'm working like a Trojan and can't even consider it."

"Girl, you have got to relax and stop working so hard. Have some fun."

They shared laughter, but Laura's mind was drifting a million miles away. Her hands worked on the cell phone buttons. She let her sister carry the weight of the conversation. All she wanted was the sound of home in her ear.

"And speaking of men, what's this mess I hear going on in Philly with Darien Price? You know, Lynda called me—you remember her; we used to work together at Children's Hospital before I left Philly to come here—and she said that the tom-toms were beating in Philadelphia about him stealing money from the city."

"Yeah. Crazy. See, that's why I don't date these Philly men. I think I might—"

"Didn't you used to go out with him, though?"

Laura froze for a moment and then composed herself. She set down the cell phone and ended the transmission. "For two weeks and one prom date; then he dumped me. That doesn't qualify as *going with* somebody."

"I hear you. But why did you guys break up, anyway? I never did get that whole juicy story, 'cause we were little, in grade school, when that happened, right?"

Again her sister's comment sent a chill through her, and she went to the coffeemaker, poured herself a cup and stood by the window. "Because . . . I wasn't giving him any tail that night. You two were too young to hear all that teenage drama." Laura forced herself to laugh.

"Oh. Figures," Nadine said, laughing with her again. "Lynda said he was such a dog, but dag . . . a possible felony charge. You think he did it?"

"I wouldn't know," Laura said after taking a deliberate sip of java. "What I do know is that the pickings are slim here for available men with integrity. So, once my firm is self-sufficient one day, I might just get real wild and crazy and retire to de islands, mon. No worries. Be happy. Find somebody to get me groove back."

Both sisters laughed hard.

"Okay, mind my business; I get the hint," Nadine said through the giggles. "I just want you to be happy."

"Just knowing that you, Lavern, and all my beautiful nieces and nephews are healthy, whole, and safe, I am very happy, Sis."

Quiet settled between them. Laura leaned on the frame of the window. A harvest moon shone back at her.

"Guess we're vicariously living through you, and you're doing the same through us," Nadine said softly. "You ever think about Mom and Dad, and where they are . . . what they might be thinking? I miss Aunt Maude, too."

Out of reflex, Laura nodded, even though her sister couldn't see her. "Don't go getting all weepy and sentimental on me, hon. I love you and will try to get there to see you and the kids for the holidays—I promise."

"Promise?"

"Promise. I know Chicago is a long way from home. Maybe I can send Lavern and her wild bunch a ticket so she can come in from Miami and we can all be together."

"That would be so nice . . ."

Nadine's voice trailed off, and Laura heard her sister sniff.

"I didn't want to fight with Bruce, and I didn't want to get divorced or take the kids through that. Wished Mom was here to tell me what to do."

Again Laura nodded, but this time she shut her eyes. Her sister was caught in an endless cycle. Defeat momentarily claimed Laura as she thought of something to tell Nadinc to help her deal. "Momma would have said, 'Baby, you have to pick your battles.' Then she would have told you to hold your head up high and move forward. You did right to fight him for custody and to get away from him. I'll be there for the holidays."

"I love you."

"I love you, too. Now, go make those teenagers get in bed so they can be ready for school in the morning. I made coffee because my workday isn't done yet."

"All right. And I'll tell Lavern you sent your love. I talk to her every day, nearly. We complain about our kids together . . . and our ex-husbands," Nadine said with a sad chuckle. "But you're the one we talk to when we really want to hear Momma's voice. You're the one, Laura. Don't know what we'd do without you."

It was an honor bestowed on her as the eldest sister. Aunt Maude had told her she had to be the example, and the keeper of the family memories and history when all was lost and gone. She could remember every phrase, every wrinkle in everyone's face, every kindness, and where every important family document was stored. . . . That's when she'd come to realize that her memory was her best asset and worst flaw.

"You two would be fine," Laura said after a moment, fighting back sudden, inexplicable tears. "I'm going to get off the telephone now. Okay? Sweet dreams, honey. Bye."

"Sweet dreams. Bye."

The receiver went dead, and she slowly clicked off the cordless phone. Being the keeper of the memories was nothing she'd ever wanted to be. The words "sweet dreams" had come out of her mouth by rote. It was something her mother had always said to her each night.

She switched off the lamp and set down the phone in the dark, cradling her mug of steaming black coffee in her hands to block another wave of chills. She studied the moonlight and glanced at the cell phone on her desk, remembering how the full moon looked years ago—years before she ever knew she'd be the repository of her mother's wisdom.

Total quiet haunted her. Traffic sounded so far away. But soon the city's urban reality of ever-present harsh music filtered into her consciousness, along with the screeching of car wheels.

Laura stood fast and peered out the window. Najira's car had come to a stop half on the curb, half on the street. As she watched her cousin jump out of the vehicle and bound up her front steps two at a time, Laura could barely catch her breath. Something was wrong, real wrong. She ran to meet Najira, the insistent banging and ringing at the front door matching her heartbeats.

When she flung the door open, Najira was waving her hands, cursing, and had stomped past her so fast that it took a moment for Laura to shut the door.

"I'ma fuck his ass up, girl, hear me!" Najira shouted, walking in a hot circle and breathing hard. "Yeah, that's right. I slashed his motherfuckin' tires. That punk bitch!"

"What!" Laura grabbed Najira by both arms and stopped her dizzying circle.

"That bitch slapped me, Laura! In my damned face, okaaaay? So you know I was about to fuck him up in the room—but the only reason I didn't was, I knew you'd flip. So, I got his ass, though. Sheeit."

"Begin at the beginning," Laura ordered, horrified. Not now. Now was not the time for some around-the-way shit.

"All right," Najira fussed, snatching herself out of Laura's hold. "Darien paged me, nine-one-one. Cool. He was home, had met with his attorney, and said he needed to get some shit straight with me so I wouldn't fuck anything up. I figured I could get some info from the dude. So, I go by the hotel where he's *now* staying, 'cause I figured one more free meal wouldn't hurt a sista—I ain't 'fraid of the big punk, no way. So, he asks me why the fuck his wife was paging him. So, I was like, 'How the fuck I know why the bitch is pagin' you? She ain't *my* wife.' We still just fussing now, so it's cool. Den he says, 'Why was your ass over at the Hyatt?' Like he's my husband, and shit. Said one of his boys had seen me in the lobby when I was leaving, and that made Darien's dumb ass double back and call his wife at her sister's house after his attorney left . . . said something didn't set right with him—he could feel it—some psychobabble shit about instincts and whatnot. They had this big blowup on the telephone, and he wanted to know if I knew anything about what that ho was talking about. So, I was like, 'Motherfucker, who you clockin'? Don't worry about why I decided to go to the Hyatt—ain't your bizness, no way. You don't own me, and since your sorry ass can't even get me a job these days, I was doing my own networking—if it's any of your business!' "

"Oh . . . shit . . ." Laura brought both hands to her skull and began pacing. Najira had delivered her story like a drive-by shooting, not even taking a breath. See, this was *exactly* why you couldn't involve family.

"Yeah, girl," Najira pressed on. "Then that Happy-the-clown bitch slapped me, and it was on. We was scrapping, and I was gonna fuck him up with the lamp, but the hotel people came, and—"

"Oh my, God—tell me this is not happening." Weak, Laura leaned against the wall.

"I'm cool, I'm cool," Najira reassured her quickly, oblivious to any of Laura's alarm about the plan. "I chipped a nail, and now I'ma hafta go get another tip put on—but I got him good before the Four Seasons people pulled me off his burly ass, talking about they was putting me out because I was destroying hotel property—fuck them, this was a domestic dispute, and—"

"You slashed his tires . . ."

"Fuckin-A right, girl—now, you *know* me, right?"

Unable to contain herself, Laura's words and mother-tone flew at Najira, stunning the girl to silence. "Why the *hell* did you answer his page and go over there, Jira? For a dinner! Are you nuts, after what we just pulled? If you wanted a free dinner, I would have . . . Oh, Jesus, Jesus, Lord!"

Najira opened and closed her mouth as hot tears of hurt rose to her eyes. "Oh. So, you don't care about *me,* huh? Don't care that he put his hands on me or slapped me after he screwed me—all you're worried about is some big fucking picture. Fine. I'm done. Since—"

"No. Stop, and hear me out," Laura said more gently. "Take a deep breath, and come into the kitchen with me."

"I'm going home," Najira mumbled, tears now streaming down her face. "I would have been satisfied enough to get his wife mad, make him lose his job, and kick his ass—have him seen for instant satisfaction . . . but, no . . ."

"I know, baby," Laura murmured, putting her arm over her angry cousin's shoulder and guiding her toward the kitchen to a chair.

"See, the problem with you, Laura, is, you ain't never been in no street-level mess, and haven't had a man put his hands on you—that's why you ain't feelin' what I'm telling you."

Laura said nothing for a moment and just handed Najira a tissue. "Sit down while I make some tea."

"Fuck tea—you got any liquor in the house?"

"I'ma make you some tea," Laura repeated in a firm but gentle tone. "Then I'll tell you why I'm gonna make you some tea . . . and I'm gonna tell you something that I only told one other living soul—my mother."

The two women stared at each other, and Najira slowly

sat at the mention of Laura's mother, the family's backbone before it broke.

"Yeah, that's right," Laura said, swallowing hard. "My mother." She let her breath out in small puffs as she spoke, then turned to the task of making tea. The sound of the kitchen clock was the only noise in the room as Laura watched the water boil with her back to Najira.

"I only told you that Darien wanted some, I said no, we hated each other, case closed. Then our fathers got into it, and your father got into it to protect my father. Family. But this all goes waaaay back. This I'm about to tell you went down in nineteen seventy-five. And yes, I do know what it's like to have a man put his hands on you."

Laura turned around to look at Najira, who hadn't blinked. She brought two cups of tea to the table and sat down, and sent her line of vision out the window. "I also know my momma told what was supposed to stay between her and me only, and my daddy confronted Darien's father—who laughed in my dad's face . . . and that started all this shit. Over nothing."

"What?" Najira's voice was a raspy whisper of disbelief.

"I fought him off of me with everything I had, Najira, and walked in a torn-up prom gown halfway down the Drive, until somebody gave me a ride. When I got home, it was after midnight." Laura took a hard swallow of tea, ignoring the sound of Najira's gasp. It was now or never; the kid had to understand just how dangerous these people were. And she had to stop Najira's shenanigans before the girl got hurt.

"I put the key in the door real easy," Laura said, her voice calm, faraway, like her thoughts, as she closed her eyes. "I was praying to God that my father had gone to bed. Mom was the one who did the waiting up, most times. Dad had to rest so he could go to work. His job was no joke; it didn't have regular hours like Mom's job did. Community advocacy was a twenty-four-seven groove. So was supporting black candidates' campaigns. I prayed to God to please let him be asleep. I could break it to Mom, and then Mom could explain to Dad. . . . I was fifteen—shit, you weren't even born—and felt like I needed a defense lawyer but wasn't exactly sure why."

Laura didn't move as a hand covered her own and squeezed it. All she could do was open her eyes and send her gaze out the window again. "Somebody was up, though. The light in the front room was on. I could see that through the window 'cause I stood on the row house porch landing. I was so paranoid and humiliated that I glanced down the wooden porches—you know the ones connected by a three-foot rail between each house that run the length of the block?—just hoping no neighbors would be sitting on plastic chairs or on those rickety metal porch swing-sofas attached to the bricks by a chain." Laura shook her head. "Who would steal stuff like that anyway? I was lucky. Everybody was still out partying, or in bed; nobody was on the stoops for once."

"Oh, baby . . ."

Najira's words offered no comfort as the old wound bled. Just like before, Laura could feel her mind bouncing from thought to thought as dread overtook her. Suddenly she hated her old neighborhood but wasn't sure why.

"The blue flicker from the television coming through the window was unmistakable, though. Girl, I could hear the low conversational tone of a movie or show through the door. The awareness made me go still for a moment. It meant I had to face somebody. Without much choice, I stepped across the threshold. My mother's hand went to her mouth. Mom's eyes said it all: terror, horror, unshed tears—in an instant everything in Mom's eyes made me look away and down to the floor. Sewing fell from Mom's lap, and she unpeeled her body from the plastic slipcovers on that old, blue floral sofa we had. But she stood up slowly, Najira, like I was ghost or something. The sound of plastic separating from flesh made me cringe. I hate plastic to this day because of that."

Laura swallowed hard. "I could still smell dinner in the house; oil from the fried chicken made me want to vomit.

The garlic in the greens, the potato salad: all of it made a slurry in my stomach and threatened to come up my throat." She stared at Najira. "I looked wild in the eye, just like you, when I came in the door—but in seventy-five, things were different. Shame belonged to the girl. And I knew it was real late because Johnny Carson had already gone off."

"But it wasn't your fault; you wasn't wrong . . . what did Aunt—"

"I know," Laura said, cutting her cousin off. "Mom hugged me hard, then pulled back before my arms could respond, and then my mom quickly put her finger to her lips and motioned toward the kitchen. Something in my mother's eyes told me not to utter a word . . . say nothing that could travel up the stairs and be heard by Dad. I followed Mom's lead, like I'm asking you to follow mine now—and to trust me."

"I trust you," Najira whispered, her clasp on Laura's hand tightening.

"Mom held me out from her with two hands on my shoulders as soon as we got into the kitchen." Laura drew a shaky breath and looked away as tears brimmed. "My mother's stricken eyes took in every facet of my disheveled condition. The fluorescent light made the kitchen feel like a hospital emergency room, and my mother was the head doctor. I kept thinking, if Mom would only turn off the lights . . . But I knew what she was looking for—signs of a completed rape—and she had to see for herself. So I stood stock-still without a struggle, without a word, stone faced, allowing my mother's horrified, silent appraisal. I could see her assessing the damage, x-raying, probing in a way that felt like that first, horribly invasive pelvic medical exam you have to have and every woman one day experiences. But it was necessary. We both knew that."

Laura extracted her hand from Najira's grasp. She could feel the tea becoming cool as she rolled the cup between her palms. She had never told a soul. Not for her own sake, but for her mother's. How could she explain that a wife had loved a husband so much that she would protect him even from his own temper? How could she explain that her mother had caved in to her father's questions after months of pressure to tell, or how the man had worried the subject like a dog worried a bone?

Bill Caldwell instinctively knew that something about his baby wasn't right—would always say, "Where's the shine in my child's eyes? Who stole that?" Or how did one explain the simple knowing when a secret had been told? Laura knew it was the day her father walked up to her, hugged her for no reason, and petted her hair, whispering, "Daddy's gonna deal with all of this, I promise." Her mother had betrayed a trust; her father had tried to make it right by confronting another father from a position of principle and honor but had been laughed at—a total betrayal of trust. Honor between men had been breached. Then her father had started digging into things he should have left alone . . . and it buried his reputation and killed her mother from the guilt. Had Mom never told . . . Her mother never forgave herself, and it was all one big circle of horror because of some stupid shit.

Laura straightened her back and looked at Najira. Her tone was no-nonsense. "Let me tell you this, kiddo. Some shit you don't want to know or need to know—but you oughta take family's word to stay out of it. My own father didn't take that advice from my uncle—your father. Okay. I'm not telling you some things, not because I don't trust you, but because I love you; and the bigger the dollars, the longer the time . . . and I'm also asking you to trust that. I'll deal with what they stole from your dad, too; all the contracts he never rightfully got and all the program moneys they stripped from his neighborhood projects . . . with a body to replace it. Darien Price is mine. Got it?"

"You're scaring me, Laura," Najira whispered.

"Good. 'Cause tears filled my mother's eyes that night, just like they're filling yours now, and every night after that. The question contained within them was unspoken but clear: *how bad is it?* Like I asked you when you walked through that door. All the way; a near miss; were you breached?

Three words came to my mind, and I uttered them from a remote place in my throat. *I fought him.* It was like someone else was speaking. *Then* I cried real hard, and Mom held me."

Laura looked out the kitchen window, remembering how her mother hugged her to her breasts and didn't let go . . . missing those arms from a deep reservoir inside; the dam broke internally, but no honest sobs came up to be soothed to stillness by the rock and sway of her mother's body. Warm, calming hands were no longer there to rub her back. She was home. Still, Mom wasn't there stroking it all away. She was alone. Najira was dearly loved but just wasn't her mom.

The young girl seemed to know that—even though not a tear rolled down Laura's cheek. Street wisdom told her that her big cousin was sitting there, breathing in slowly, heavily, sipping in air around the secret flood of unseen tears. They stayed that way for a while, just being with each other, remembering the nourishing link of family, of mother to child, with respect for the elder child who no longer had a mother.

"Najira," Laura finally admitted on a bitter whisper, so quietly that Najira had to strain to hear her. "He thought that I had done it before—just because of where we lived." Laura shut her eyes tight. Old memories made her fingernails sore as she glanced at Najira's ragged manicure. Laura's nails dug into her palms in reflex, and she made fists to keep from wailing. The dripping kitchen faucet made her want to scream.

"It's gonna be all right . . ."

"No, it's not," Laura said fast. "Not till it's done. My mother and father are dead behind this shit. Your father is alive and still has a fighting chance—so do you!"

Laura stared at her cousin now and pulled away from the table and stood. The healing link was broken. Her eyelids felt like sandpaper scratching against her eyeballs each time she blinked. She wiped her nose and cheeks with the backs of her hands. "How could he think that! Why did he think that?" She could feel hysteria bubbling within her, threatening the quiet, sending her voice through the kitchen. "Even so, what would give him the right—" Then she remembered her mother's command and realized that she was talking to Najira, not her mom.

Her mother had said, "Keep your voice down, baby. Sit; I'll make tea." Her mother had fished in her apron and handed her a tissue. *Oh, my God* . . . It was history replaying itself in her own kitchen.

Stunned, she'd watched the vaporous image of her mother wring her hands and pace away from her. Laura sat slowly to keep her legs from giving out from under her and continued to stare at Najira. Her mother had made tea? Her mother had made fucking tea! She'd heard water hit the inside of the aluminum kettle—she hated tea. Why didn't her mother yell and run up the stairs to get her dad? Why didn't her father load bullets into that mythical shotgun he always claimed he had to keep for his daughters? She saw all these same questions flicker and reflect in Najira's eyes, and yet, she still couldn't say the words—*because he couldn't.*

"I'm gonna make some more tea," Najira said in a quiet tone. "I'm a grown woman. When all this shit went down, you were just a baby, Laura, by today's standards. I wasn't no virgin, and I ain't no church girl. What happened to you was beyond fucked up—me and my pop will be all right. Your mom and dad, God rest their souls, paid with their lives. I didn't know all this was goin' on in the family—nobody spoke on it."

Laura played with the sugar bowl and waited for the water to boil, Najira's words becoming farther and farther away. She intently watched the blue flame under the pot on the stove. A dog barked in the alley. She remembered watching her mother begin the laboriously slow process of dipping a bag of Tetley into a small china cup rimmed in gold. She hated slow motion. Momma had pulled out the Thanksgiving wear. Only holidays and funerals brought out those good dishes . . . and it wasn't a holiday . . . so, there you had it.

"Baby," her mother had said quietly after a while, stirring

the tea much longer than warranted and staring down into the dark brew that she summarily lightened with cream, "this was why I wasn't ready for you to go out with a guy his age . . . but you were so adamant about it."

Laura sucked in a deep breath as the bitter memory wafted through her; it was a haunting presence. Her mother had blamed her? The victim? Laura recalled just staring at her mother, holding the cup in midair as she let the warmth from the china seep into her sore palms and radiate through her aching fingers. Her nail beds were cracked and raw and stung as the heat entered where an eerie cold had vacated them, taking up residence in her spirit. Something was not right. Her mother's eyes held a shadow of more than remorse behind them. What was Mom saying?

"It's not your fault, baby. And, I'm just glad that it wasn't worse than it was . . . so sometimes we need to thank our Jesus that He spares children and fools. I should have *never* let you go. You were the child; your father and me were the fools. Never again."

No. Her mother hadn't blamed her; the poor woman had blamed herself. New tears formed and spilled over the edges of Laura's lashes. This time she let them fall without blotting them away. She balled the tissue her cousin had handed her in her fist. She wanted to yell out, "What are you talking about, Momma? 'It could have been worse'? This was as bad as it gets!"

But her mother had looked at her and held her gaze, searching her face. "You fought him, right? Baby, tell me the truth." Her mother did not breathe. Laura held her breath—Najira stopped making tea and stared at her. In Laura's mind she could see her mother release her breath. The hum of the refrigerator was now deafening.

"Hell, yeah, I fought him."

Her mother released her breath. Najira didn't respond.

Rage kindled within Laura and she stood. Staring at nothing, she again saw the strain on her mother's face and really studied it. A silent understanding had passed between mother and daughter way back then. Her mother didn't offer protest about the curse word being tossed out in her kitchen. Something had changed—forever. That was the day she grew up. When she'd announced, "I'm telling Daddy about this right now. He'll have Darien's black butt *seen,*" the words had seethed past Laura's lips, more like a demand to her mom than a threat. Even if her mother was paralyzed to inaction, she sure wasn't.

"Sit. Down," her mother had ordered . . . just like Laura had told Najira.

A hand touched Laura's shoulder. Startled, Laura sat again slowly, confusion clawing her insides. The tone her mother had used that night went beyond any sound she'd ever heard the woman use before. It was quiet, seething, but filled with more than anger—pure terror was at the root of the command.

Laura's palms went to her face, and she spoke quietly, reverently into them, hoping her cousin could understand. "My mother said, 'That is precisely why if nothing terrible happened, your father is not going hear about any of this.' I couldn't believe my ears, Jira. She was scared, and you know that wasn't my mother. She said, 'Leave it be. That boy won't come back here.' Her voice was brittle with a brand of worry that I knew was fear. Then she told me, 'My husband, your father, doesn't need to get himself or any of your uncles messed up or hurt by messing with a well-connected attorney's son.' And I didn't answer her back. I couldn't. It was unthinkable. Mom told me that good, hardworking men don't need to be losing jobs or getting themselves locked up behind something that *almost* happened but didn't on a prom night. Let it alone. You were lucky and got out virtually unscathed. *Baby, you gotta pick your battles.* Consider the bigger picture . . . just like I told you. I'm sorry."

Najira had sat down across from her and was holding two steaming mugs of tea. She slid one across the table to Laura and didn't say a word.

"Mom knew the deal," Laura murmured, taking a sip of

tea as she steadied herself. She could see her mother stand quickly and snatch a dish towel from the hook over the sink and begin wiping down the already sparkling Formica table. "She said, 'That little bastard is the son of a man who is in tight with all the judges, white and black.' Then she paused to let the information sink in, then began furiously cleaning everything that was already clean."

"My mom does the same thing," Najira chuckled sadly. "They're old school: serve tea for problems, discuss nothing, and they clean when they're stressed."

Laura smiled, took a sip of tea, and nodded. "It was probably their way of just trying to bring order where everything had just been blown totally out of order. Momma couldn't fix this. Daddy couldn't fix this. Girl, I had to remember to breathe as my mother half muttered to herself while attempting to explain away that nightmare." She looked up at Najira, who was hanging on every word. "In that moment, I wasn't sure which was worse: what Darien had tried to do, or finding out what my father couldn't do. The latter was worse, truth be told."

Najira shook her head and slurped her tea. "You got anything stronger than this?"

"Yeah, in the other room," Laura said, standing and going to fetch a bottle of Myers dark rum. "Mom said his father is *high up* downtown, and his grandfather is a judge," she called from the next room, returning with a bottle, which she set between them. "Do the honors, Cousin. You buy, I'll fly. But all I can tell you is, my mom crossed her breastbone with the sign of the crucifix as she told me that Darien's father, J. D. Price the Second, had friends that were running for election and would win, which meant he'd rise with them; so would his son someday, taking his place as Darien Price the Third, an heir apparent. That's how it's done, how they do it. Word, then, had it that the guy's father would be the city's managing director, as high as that, if my daddy helped get a black mayor in office—which he did. You understand me?"

"That's some very old and very deep shit, girl." Najira

added a generous splash of rum to their teacups and shook her head. "This is the kinda conspiracy theory mess my father always talked about."

"Girl, you'd better listen to them old folks and get schooled. My mother and father figured that the Prices had raised a gentleman, especially since my father was one of the people who beat the bushes to get the people out to vote for them." Laura sighed with disgust. "Mom knew that something like this would crush my father's soul, since he'd believed so hard in black men getting into positions of power to change things in our community. My dad and your dad worked like dogs for them every campaign. But that son . . . well . . . the fruit don't fall too far from the tree that bears it; that's why I was a fool to go—and my parents blamed themselves for letting me go. Shoulda known."

"It wasn't your fault, or their fault—it was those fucked up bourgie Negroes' fault—shit!" Najira downed her tea and put straight rum in her cup.

"Girl, all I know is, my mother was wiping her eyes with fast, angry strokes as she spoke to the table, then to the sink, then to the cabinets, walking in a perpetual circle in a way that made me remain very still."

"That was Auntie, uh-huh," Najira chuckled. "I can see her now."

"Jira, she was off the hook, as you say, talking about, *'I told your father 'bout those people years ago.* Might as well have dropped my child off on some gang turf corner in North Philly; she would have been in better company. But your daddy is so blind, thinks all men have integrity to go along with their education, nice suits, and the mess they talk on the podium to poor folks—can't blame him; we all marched with Dr. King, Reverend Jackson, and hoped. So, as long as you aren't hurt, and it's just your pride that was damaged, then, then—' "

"Let it rest." Najira sighed and added more rum to Laura's tea. "I've heard that, too . . . people of a certain ilk don't act a certain way. Pulleease."

"My point exactly," Laura agreed, taking a healthy sip of rum-tea. "I could never figure out at first why, if that was *all* he wanted, then why did he ask *me* to go? He said it himself—he could have asked any of those girls up there, and since we're talking real plain here . . . back in the day, they dropped their drawers as fast as white girls. But, see, it wasn't about that. It was about power, conquest, making someone who didn't want to do something have to bow to your will. This is why a strange confluence of events is gonna fuck him good and make him bow to its will—understand?"

"Do him, Laura. Without Vaseline."

Both women clinked their teacups and laughed.

She only wondered when her father had lost his political virginity. Was it that first function, that first high-level black-tie affair where his ticket was free—like a prom? Was it the first appointed post? She knew that they ultimately did her dad like Darien tried to do her: without respect, in the street, without warning, latex keeping the perpetrator clean even though the victim was the one left with the sore ass. When trouble came, alliances like this in the street always broke down . . . and the weaker gang members always got offered up as sacrificial lambs. Something gnawed at her gut. This bullshit definitely wasn't over.

Laura remained still inside while drinking rum with her cousin in the kitchen, laughing about old times . . . and picking her battles very wisely.

Chapter 6

Dawn had not begun to fracture the sky with her teal-blue fingers of light, but Laura was already standing on her bedroom deck, her motions fluid, her skin impervious to the chilly air. A coating of perspiration made her black stretch Danskins cling to her as her muscles moved to the ancient rhythm of tai chi. Her exhales were visible in small, wafting white puffs against the frosted morning.

Pure control threaded its way through her as she took in and released each breath in harmony with her environment. Soon rose-orange-colored tendrils would crack the sky and force the morning's entry. But that, too, was a process of timing. Just like everything else, even the largest star had to adhere to certain standards. There were cosmic rules.

Laura let her breath out again slowly, meditating as she worked. This morning she would feed her impoverished soul.

She fastened her gaze to the horizon and bowed to it in reverence as she completed her daily ritual. Lingering for a moment, she greeted the ancestors with a murmured "Ashé" and left the deck to go take a shower, carefully locking the sliding glass doors behind her.

A hot shower was the answer. Water would be her friend and wash away the sins of the world around her. She moved through her home like a disembodied haint, not turning on any lights, and showered in the dark, using only her senses to guide her. Hearing the water splatter against the tiles, she waited for the temperature in the room to rise as she stripped off her exercise clothes and then stepped into the claw-footed tub, hoping this time the memories wouldn't haunt her—but they always did. A seal of steam and warmth hugged her, and she allowed it to pummel any trace of worry from her. Yet there was a hollow place that still ached within her. A place no one had been able to reach or touch since her parents had died.

But the insistent spray of hot water couldn't make her clean enough. She remembered that feeling, scrubbing her body until her skin was raw—just like her mind had become this morning until it transported her back to a place she dreaded.

Philadelphia
1975

For the first time in her life, she'd gone somewhere really nice with a guy, got dressed up, and didn't have to deal with heat and funk at a blue-light-in-the-basement, possible-shoot-out party. There was no comparison to this. Fifteen and fabulous.

Streetlights glinted off the car windows, their harsh glare softened by the thick canopy of mature suburban trees, as the vehicle hugged the curves of Lincoln Drive. She and Darien practically had the road to themselves, and she could just stare out the window at the pretty green leaves and high rock formations, marveling that people lived in a park by a stream. There weren't even people walking alongside the road. Why would they, up here?

Plus, damn . . . she was actually riding in a *Cadillac*. A

Fleetwood, no less. You could still smell the new-car scent of fine leather upholstery oozing from the white seats and white-on-white interior. The Isley Brothers were crooning "Summer Breeze" from the cassette—it didn't get any better than this.

Laura bit the insides of her platinum-frosted lips to keep from giggling out loud. She had been secretly doodling "J. D. Price III" on her notebook since he'd asked her to go. This was her night. Just like Earth, Wind, and Fire sang in their anthem to the heavens, she was gonna keep her head to the sky. Oh, yeah, he was the one. He had hazel eyes—pretty eyes for a guy—with black, curly lashes around them, and a big 'fro like the guys from the group Black Ivory. Darien wore all the latest rags and had a car—and not some struggle-buggy, either. The green of his tux brought out the green beneath the brown in his eyes. This brother was baaad. She glimpsed her date from a sideways glance as the Isley Brothers' melody took another sensuous dip. He winked at her and gave her a sly smile.

Her body relaxed, but not enough to muss her sea-foam-green prom dress. She'd been the hit of his *senior* prom but still had to look good getting out of the car to go change into yet another dazzling outfit for the after party. Yeah, this was how a sister ought to be treated. No, more like Mom said: this was how a young lady was *supposed* to be treated. Right. Laura played with her wrist corsage, noting that her date had even gone to the trouble to make sure the orchid had been spritzed with pale green dye. Plus, he'd given her *an orchid,* not carnations. Wow. That had to be a sign that this brother was serious. And a guy like Darien Price had given it to her. A guy from a family that weren't even slaves, were "freed blacks," with education . . . all lawyers that went back to when Philadelphia was just started. But he'd still picked *her.* Yeah, this was serious.

When the car slowed down and pulled into the Prices' driveway, Laura turned to her date, all smiles. She still couldn't get used to the mansion he lived in, and, gaping, she allowed her gaze to scan the massive Tudor, with its impressive bay windows, ivory and wood tones, the high stone walls around the circular drive, and the way a profusion of colorful azaleas in pinks, mauves, and yellows bordered it. It was a single house, not connected to anything or anyone else's home like the row house she lived in. Darien seemed as if he'd stepped into her life from a fairy tale.

Every question she'd stored up during the entire night fused with all the excitement within her, making the words rush past her lips in one breathless sentence.

"Okay, so, you want me to go in and wait in the living room while you get changed, and then you'll take me to change, and then—"

She hadn't seen it coming but didn't mind too much. The kiss was sorta exciting, actually, and it left her tingly as she backed him up a bit with her palms resting flat on his chest. If he didn't be careful, he was gonna crush her corsage, and that could *not* happen—because it had to get pressed in her souvenir book as a memento for all time . . . proof that she actually did this, was a princess for one night. She couldn't wait to tell her girlfriends about every detail of this evening, and the flower on her wrist was evidence that she'd been Cinderella. Guys were so dumb.

He kissed her harder, though. That was different. Most guys backed up when you flat-palmed them. It made her heady. Made her bold enough to kiss him back with a little conviction. There was the strong hint of alcohol on his breath, mixed with what smelled like expensive, musky cologne coming from his neckline. His palms were moist against her skin. The slow dances had prepared her for that scent and the way his hands felt, and she kinda liked the way his arms had slid around her shoulders—but brother had to back off the boobs . . . uh-uh. She hadn't gone with him long enough for all of that. Two weeks didn't give him the right to be sliding his hand around the front of her, no matter how good it sorta felt.

She blocked his reach with her forearm, making it seem

like a casual move while still going along with the kiss, but wriggling her body into a semidefensive posture: both knees closed tightly, her handbag now clutched to her chest.

"What? You weren't expecting that?"

For a moment she was too flustered to answer.

"Well, baby, was it worth it?"

His questions made her smile. She tried to pat her hair into place and appear nonchalant. With the windows sealed and closing out the sound of street traffic, and the cool air-conditioning blowing through her carefully coiffed curly Afro, she felt like she was in a royal chariot. Four hours of braiding her wet hair, rolling the plaits onto huge pink curlers with Dippity-Do, sitting under the hood dryer for over an hour, then unbraiding it to be teased and picked out as an urban princess crown, a perfect globe that was twenty-four inches in diameter, held firm and glistening with cherry-scented Afro-Sheen . . . yes . . . it was worth it. Every moment was worth it.

"It was all right. But . . . I don't know." The truth was, she didn't know. Everything was going like a dream, yet something was making her stomach do flip-flops.

He leaned in again for another kiss, which she nervously returned, her mind racing a mile a minute. She wasn't sure why, though. He was an all-right kisser. In fact, maybe a little later she wouldn't feel so uncomfortable. The bitter alcohol taste and the smell that laced his breath didn't bother her too much, like it would have any other time—it was prom night; everybody knew what was up . . . all the brothers had a flask. Another kiss landed on her mouth, prying it open, forcing her tongue into a more urgent dance.

A French kiss? Just like that? It gave her a bit of a rush, releasing butterflies in her belly, making her want to keep it going a little bit longer. But damn. At least the guys around the way gave you fair warning. They started kicking game way long before they got in your face. The whole ride up to his house, Darien hadn't said a word, and the tape was on . . . Isleys were always good for a can-I-get-that-kiss line—or at least something from EWF—before you just pushed up on a sister. You had to have "Reasons" on to get all into it like that. Plus, suave brothers usually stole something from a song and dropped it in your ear before they came in like that—plus . . .

"Dag . . . ," she said fast, avoiding another kiss and turning her head to glance out the window. The bitter taste of liquor covered her tongue. He was smiling as she craned her neck around to see if they'd been caught making out in the car. "Your mom and dad could be looking, boy. Stop. I don't want them thinking wrong about me, and I *definitely* don't want them calling my mom and dad—I was lucky I could even go on your prom." She patted her hair into place, trying to ensure that her perfect Afro globe had no evidence of a depression, and roughly flipped down the visor, intent on repairing her lip gloss as well as on getting him to stop leaning on her.

He finally sat back and shrugged. "If my mother and father were home, they would have long been asleep. They're busy all the time and don't do that wait-up thing. Relax. I told them we'd probably head up to Martha's Vineyard tomorrow, anyway." He moved closer to her and began stroking her bare arm.

"What?" Laura started laughing. "First of all, my parents said I was pushing the limit to stay out this late. The prom was over at eleven; then we were supposed to change, go to the after party for an hour, *maybe* go to I-HOP for breakfast, and then I have to go home. My people ain't hardly letting me go to no out-of-state place, *overnight,* down the shore, with no boy, and your parents ain't lettin' you go with—"

"My parents don't care. Everybody who is anybody is going . . . and you are not talking about going with a boy. You're out with a man. I'm eighteen. Dig?" His voice was low and husky as he'd spoken, and his forefinger was now trailing across her necklace at her collarbone. "So when you're with a man, you need to act like a woman."

She tilted her head to the side, looked at the way the driveway lights hit his Afro, making it frame his face like a halo, and momentarily considered the muttonchop sideburns that connected to his thin mustache and goatee. "Yeah, right. And you need to stop lying . . . like in this lifetime your mom and dad ain't home waiting up for you after a prom, *man*?"

Darien shook his head no and offered her a lazy smile. The car motor was still running, but he'd turned off the headlights. Despite the air-conditioning, the windows were beginning to fog up, and it felt like they were in a private, soundproof room. His alcohol-spiked breath now felt thick on her.

As casually as possible, she glanced at the small lump that had formed in his polyester tuxedo pants. Things had gotten heated, but brother wasn't packing point-of-no-return steel yet. Okay. Enough. She liked him and wasn't trying to dick-tease, but wasn't doing no wild thang, either. And like her parents would let her go all the way to Martha's Vineyard, wherever the hell that was, anyway. Where the heck was Martha's Vineyard—in Jersey? Over a state line?

"C'mon, baby. Ease up."

Laura folded her arms over her chest, no longer worried about the corsage. The change in her posture made Darien remove his hand from her neckline and drape his arm over the wide, sofalike seat. "Boy, pulleeease."

"There's nobody home. We can go inside . . . up to my room, if you want."

She stared at him. Her mouth opened and closed. He laughed.

"They had some political event to go to up in Harrisburg tonight. Most likely they won't be back until Sunday evening. Who cares? The limo came and got them before I left. Trust me."

"But it was your senior prom . . ."

"And?"

She didn't know what to say. Part of her heart broke for him, and another part of her immediately tensed. It was the way he was looking at her. It wasn't that normal, hopeful "I wanna get you to drop your drawers; can I stand a chance, please, baby? I'm begging you" kinda look. It was different, like "You don't know what you've just got yourself into, baby." His look went beyond the normal horny-guy expression. That worried her. Survival instinct coiled within her. She was staying in the car. But that was crazy, didn't make sense. He wasn't some dope fiend or some just-outta-jail dude. At least that's what she kept telling herself as her heartbeat raced.

Laura looked at her date hard and sucked her teeth, feigning ghetto bravado. She glanced at the huge house, hoping for a sign of parental life within it, when he began stroking her arm again.

She shrugged off his touch. "We're gonna be late for the thing . . . at uh, what's the place we're supposed to go to next?—you know, up in Jenkintown, out on route six-eleven, or something? We'd better hurry up. Uhmm. Or was it Elkins Park? I don't know; all I do know is that you should change, then . . ."

He was chuckling low in his throat. Her sentence trailed off, just hearing the tone in it. The sound he made reminded her of a guard dog growling even and slow.

"You're right. I do need to put something else on." Darien licked his lips and sat back. "I definitely don't want to get a sister *like you* in trouble."

Laura let out her breath in relief, not caring that he now knew that she'd been temporarily worried. He needed to stop playing. This wasn't funny anymore.

Without looking at her he reached past her and opened the glove compartment and grabbed a large rectangular object. The light in the compartment flashed for a second, and he shut it quickly. This fool *was not* going to fire up a bong in his daddy's Cadillac and make her smell all reefer-funky with him. This could not be happening.

Laura made herself very small next to the passenger-side door and wrinkled up her nose in pure disgust, noting that the car had automatic locks, which were controlled from

Darien's side of the vehicle. For some odd reason, once she'd noticed that, she felt trapped and began to panic again. Something wasn't right. He was scary calm. In the dark, the slow, romantic music was getting on her nerves.

She heard paper tear but could not make out the markings all the way on the box. The tiny stereo lamp cast a yellow tinge to a flat object he was fumbling with. She didn't smoke that crap that made you act simple, anyway. Not with some guy—some guy who clearly wanted drawers more than he wanted his next breath. What, did she seem crazy?

"Look—I need to go home, if we're not going to the after party," she announced. "Open the door, if you aren't going to take me. I'll walk. I'm not smoking weed and getting in trouble with my parents or yours for nobody—not even on a prom."

"You need to stop playing."

"Playing? What makes you think I'm *playing*?"

"I know you didn't think I asked you to go on my senior prom to act like this. Not when I could have chosen any pick of the litter I wanted. But I have to admit . . . my boys were right. They sure don't make 'em like you up here."

She straightened her spine and thrust her chin up a tad higher. So many emotions were running through her brain at the same time that she was momentarily speechless. Laura scavenged her mind for a razor comeback but came away lacking. Hurt forced her slow retort to sound like a question instead of a zinger.

"Oh, so because I won't get high with you—"

"You don't have to get high; just relax. That's not my issue. Coke is too expensive to waste on somebody fighting against the high. You don't smoke weed, so be it. You don't drink, your loss. If you want a Valium so we can do this, my mom has plenty in the house. If you don't need anything to have a good time, that's cool. I like that in a woman."

He moved closer and traced her cheek with a finger, then slid his hand around to the nape of her neck. She didn't like the way his grip tightened on the base of her skull. She tensed and felt how strong a hold he really had on her. From some reservoir of knowing, she offered a nervous smile and relaxed. This was crazy. He removed his hand and smiled back. But the threat was clear. Now she was beginning to get scared.

"Like I said, Laura, stop playing. I've been waiting for this all night. Let's go inside after round one to christen the Caddy. I know you've been turned out before. You can drop the act, since it's just you and me in here . . . we both know what's up. I won't tell."

"What!"

She wasn't afraid now, just furious. *The nerve.* What a dog!

Her hand flew over her mouth as she looked down and saw that he'd begun to sheath a thumb-sized part of his anatomy with a condom. She didn't know what to do. Plus, she'd never seen one before—an actual penis. One not hidden by madras pants, bell-bottoms, jeans, basketball shorts, or Speedo swim trunks. As she watched him struggle to get on the rubber, ignoring her as he fumbled, she honestly didn't know whether to yell or to slap the bullshit out of him. He'd made a play for her that was so tacky, there were simply no words. She was not giving some rich nigger some tail in his damned driveway in front of his parents' house!

Everything she'd ever heard down the way, every fight she'd ever had, every schoolyard brawl she'd ever seen her cousins conquer, entered her central nervous system and came out of her mouth as an honest threat. "You'd better put that pencil dick of yours away before I kick your ass, motherfucker."

Darien's response seemed like it was happening in slow motion, the way the huge fist came toward her face. She dodged the blow that connected with the headrest, but he still had the reach and weight advantage over her despite her efforts to push him away. Two massive hands encircled her wrists and held them hard against the door. Blanketing her, his weight was so oppressive she couldn't breathe, yet her screams ricocheted within the car. The moment he let one of her wrists go to snatch up the side of her gown, she clawed at his hair only to be immediately stung with a sharp slap.

"Bitch, I will hurt you," he warned, moving his free hand to her throat.

She tasted blood; her nose was numb from the force of the strike, and tears blurred his image, making what was happening all the more surreal. The expression on his face told her all she needed to know: he would definitely hurt her. He already had.

Nearly paralyzed with terror, she felt his hand move away from her neck, then roughly up her leg, gathering her gown, her slip, yanking at panty hose and underwear, which gave way. The sound of the fabric ripping, sweaty hands skin to skin, leaving an awful print of touch against her, a body wedged between her thighs, too heavy to shove off, sobs catching in her throat with a plea to stop—that was summarily ignored with a sneer. Then came the horrible breach as angry fingers scored her flesh and tore at her opening, trying to find her most private place. Pain fused with instant knowing—it was now or never, and she'd die fighting.

He shifted his weight, positioning himself to replace his bloodied fingers, with his peewee appendage left exposed—an error in judgment that meant he was the one now at a serious disadvantage. One of her hands was free, and it went for the vulnerability and yanked, twisted, cut into latex and flesh with nails, trying to wrest the offending body part from its host.

A guttural male yell was followed by a punch solidly delivered to her jaw, but she was already dazed, out of her mind, adrenaline hyped, turning into a sea-foam-green windmill blur of fists, feet bearing four-inch stacked heels, bites, shrieks, language that spiked her blood pressure till her ears rang as she screamed for him to get the hell off her. The rearview mirror broke and fell from the windshield onto her lap, becoming a weapon as her heel crashed the dashboard, got stuck, and broke off in what had been the cassette, fucked up the music; metal sliced the butter-leather interior; he yelled for her to stop damaging his father's car and cut his hand as more mirror glass shattered. Wild, feral, she brandished the rearview like a shank when he tried to punch her again. It was a standoff. The new car was something of value to protect; he had something to lose. He zipped up his pants. A gold Cadillac saved her life.

"Get the fuck out of my car, you stupid Southwest bottom bitch! Get the fuck out before I kill you—fucking up my senior prom weekend with your bullshit when you know you've already probably fucked every ghetto-blaster bastard down the way. And you tell *me* no?" His expression held pure disbelief as he slapped the center of his chest on the word "me," then adjusted the high waistband of his pants, pointed to the door, hit the locks, and bellowed, "Get out, *young* girl! Walk, you ghetto bitch!"

Traumatized, she couldn't even answer him while sucking in huge gulps of air, eyes wild, her once carefully pruned Afro now bansheefied, spaghetti straps broken, tops of breasts showing, ribs sore from body blows in tight confines, fingernails thick with skin beneath them, feeling as though they had been pulled from their nail beds, knees bruised from contact with the steering wheel, dashboard, his groin; beyond modesty trying to hurt him bad by any means necessary, to the point of death struggle; one shoe missing, a loose tooth, cold air sending shards of pain into her gums with each sharp inhale, purse with bloodstains on it—his, not hers; she'd saved her face and saved face—remnants of her corsage flung in the backseat, her jaw throbbing where his punch had landed, her vagina raw and labia scratched from hostile finger entry, but the locks had suddenly popped, and she could get out of the Cadillac that felt as tight as a coffin.

Snatching her split green polyester gown behind her, wrecked white rabbit stole sending plumes of fur floating like dandelion spores exiting the vehicle with her, stumbling to asphalt driveway, bare tiptoes on one side matching the stride of a broken heel on the other, she held her bag tight, ignoring the scattering silver beads from her necklace and bracelet that pelted the ground when she hopped out. All she knew was that she had a second to run, had to flee before he changed his mind, and she began a flat-out dash, then stopped, turned, and glared at him. Something fragile within her snapped. Hands went to her hips in the full moonlight. Oh, hell, no . . .

Fear left her. Insanity, outrage, something ridiculously stupid took its place. Pride. Her back straightened. Her satin purse was thrust under her damp armpit and clamped there. Just like her, it would never be the same—ruined. She'd worked like a mule, doing everything from babysitting to cornrowing hair for money to help her mom pay for the whole ensemble. It had taken days to find the right dye lot to match the satin Baker shoes to the bag, to the dress, to the eye shadow, to the nail polish, to coordinate with his tux. But she and Mom did it.

Now her hands went to her fallen straps and tied them behind her neck in a makeshift halter. She wrapped the remains of her ragged stole around her waist and tied it hard like a kung fu belt, kicked off the one battered shoe, and began taking out her pierced earrings, which had managed to survive the first offensive. She stood wide-legged in a fighter's stance; her chest heaved with a burst of rage that was making her see flickers of light before her . . . then her eyes narrowed, and her gaze locked on the dark car in the driveway.

"You big, lurchy, pussy-assed, motherfucking, low-life, short-dick, not-knowing-how-to-get-some-from-a-woman-if-you-got-paid-to-try, fucked-up, spoiled ho, no-basketball-playing, no-dancing, uncoordinated, no-balls-having, faggot-assed, prep school momma's boy, no-kinda-couth slimeball—get your black punk ass out here and let's dooo this shit the old-fashioned way!"

Snot flung out of her nose, and spittle coagulated in the corners of her mouth as she screamed while walking in a manic circle. The fact that he offered no response made her hear her heart pounding in her ears. Oh . . . hell . . . no! "Who the hell do you think you are? No *real* man would treat a sister like this—*fuck you*! I'm a lady!"

"A lady? A lady! *Irony of ironies*—I go out with a ghetto bitch that only wriggled her way into a stupid little after school clerical internship job for my father, and who sounds like a fucking sailor and—"

"Fuck you, faggot!"

The headlights went on, and it immediately dawned on her that she was standing in the path of someone who was drunk, high, and possibly throw'd off. *Oh, shit.* She heard the engine rev, and she ran to the lawn, choosing a huge maple as her defense.

"Ya pussy motherfucker, I know you ain't crashing your damned drunk-assed daddy's car into no two-hundred-year-old maple tree, so fuck you, trying to act like you gonna run me over, asshole! If you was a *real* man—operative word—you'd get out and we could go right here on the lawn! So get out the car, motherfucker, and I'll show you some real shit you ain't seen up here . . . putting your hands on me like you own me—who in the hell do you think you are? Your dumb ass don't own nobody! Short-dicked son of a bitch!"

In that moment, she loved the power of her own voice. Her anger seemed to reverberate off the trees and echo from the high panes of the azalea-bordered Tudors and sidewalks. Yeah, she was gonna turn this sucker out! Blow the roof off the mother! He'd touched her where no man had been allowed to, and had tried to take it. Her skin crawled at the assault, phantom sensations of violation making her nearly retch.

The neighborhood had once seemed so still and serene until she got there. Now lights were going on, and Darien's head came out of the car window. He looked as worried as he looked enraged.

"Shut up, you dumb bitch! Get in the fucking car so I can drop your ass off back where you belong—the ghetto! I must have been out of my goddamned mind to take someone like you *anywhere*! You may think your high-yella ass is fine, but where your uncivilized ass belongs is in the zoo!"

"Then *kiss* my uncivilized ass, since you can't kick it—punk! I might belong in a zoo, but your stupid black monkey-cuttin' ass ain't getting no tail from me, motherfucker! So molie-olie—your ass is crisp-fried, *burnt* to a crackly crunch—because it ain't *my* prom, okaaaay? And that's right—this ghetto sistah can fight and will fuck you up if you even try to put a hand on me again—who the hell you think you are? Huh! Sheeit, I'll have your ass seen by some people who know some people from the way, okaaaay? Half of my cousins been to jail, punk!"

"I'll run your ass over first, bitch!"

"Try it!"

She spun on her heels, dirt and rocks cutting her stocking feet. All of a sudden, she didn't care if he did run her over. He'd finger-fucked her and almost raped her. Torn skin and aching dampness throbbed between her legs. She wasn't a virgin anymore—it was broken, soiled, penetrated. She felt grimy. Her fifty-dollar Lord and Taylor dress, her shoes, her hair, *her everything*—ruined. What the hell was she gonna tell her momma? That's who she had to deal with, not some asshole having a temper tantrum in his daddy's new car! And her dad . . . Runs popped through the toes of her hose—five-dollar hose, at that. Frosted green toes poked through her expensive silver-sparkle stockings. This was *not* how this night was supposed to go.

After tonight, the snobby girls were never supposed to be able to flip their relaxed hair over their shoulders and give her the "You're an outsider and not as good as we are" look. She had sashayed into that Chestnut Hill Cricket Club like the belle of the ball and had known for a moment what instant fame felt like. She had been pretty, and refined, and accepted—just for a second—and he'd robbed her. After tonight the snobs were supposed to have to give her the "I hate you, bitch, for upstaging me" grit. That was waaaay different and soooo much better, especially at an all-girls' school.

The more she walked, the worse the pain between her legs hurt, and soon it became connected to a large lump within her chest. She was supposed to be able to tell them to eat their hearts out. Darien would probably tell all his pussy-assed boys, too . . . arrogant ass Mike Paxton, and that fucking punk Don Edward, and stupid Martin Ramsey, or loudmouthed Howard Scott, even damned Brad Crawford and Jim Thompson! The whole Mt. Airy crew would know. This was not the way it was supposed to be. But now look what happened. And she had to explain her torn-up condition to her parents, old folks who had resisted letting her go out six months earlier than the no-dating-till-sixteen rule!

Laura groaned. Hot tears soon found their way to her eyes. It was just not supposed to be like this. But then again, it was after midnight . . . Cinderella always got jacked after midnight, when the fairies took all their cool shit back. If they did that to a white girl, then a sister didn't stand a chance.

She could feel her makeup now thick on her face, sweat lifting it, making her skin feel greasy under the foundation—foundation she'd spent her last dollar on at the John Wanamaker's department store Revlon counter, just to look nice for this jerk. Jesus. She knew her mascara was running, her lipstick was either crushed off or cussed off—what did it matter? She was sweating like a prizefighter, and she'd left her home looking like a real lady, a princess, something feminine and dainty, only to break it down to curbside like the Ali-Frazier Rumble in the Jungle. Fucking Don King shoulda sold tickets to this. Suddenly she felt cheap.

Laura's chest heaved with repressed sobs of bitter disappointment as she trudged down the stately tree-lined avenue, ignoring the car that blared its horn beside her. She mentally sent the sound of it far away from her. All she had to do was ignore a huge, buzzing gnat. *Insect.* She replaced Darien's hollering and car horn with remembering all the painstaking attention she'd spent layering on Love's Baby Soft products . . . the bubble bath, the spray, the lotion, the powder, the shimmer sheer—for what? If he had just finessed her, asked her nice . . . dumb bastard. But no. He'd tried to take the panties! Disrespected her by trying to do her in *a driveway*—you didn't do a sister like that for her first time. Not when a brother had resources—or what, he was trying to say she wasn't worth the resources? Oh, right. Fine! Damn.

"Bitch, get in this goddamned car right now! I'm warning your dumb ass!"

She flipped him the bird, didn't answer him, and just kept walking.

Tonight he mighta got some, if he'da acted right. *Act like you know, nigger.* That's what she should have said. Something hip. Fast. Witty. Something like her homegirls would have said. But she was too angry to think of quick, sassy lines. Instead, she had just told that Negro's ass off. *Blatt-ow!* Tore up his tux, too. At least they were even; her dress was damaged beyond repair, but he'd have to pay for the tux. Ha! Her mind screamed everything that her throat was too seized to utter. *How you like me now?* Good thing she'd had cousins and had seen some serious how-to-street-fight shit before now.

"Laura, you'd better get in this fucking car—now!"

Stomping down the road on the safe side of a guardrail, a Cadillac slowly trailing her, she refused to turn around or respond to the fool hollering for her to get back into the car. On Monday at school she would die of humiliation for certain. Over the weekend, he would definitely tell all his buddies, or worse, maybe he'd lie and say they never went to the after-prom parties because he was home getting some from her in his own parents' house. The guys up here were like little bitches and would drop enough hints to their girlfriends to spread the word like the flu. Then girls from Mount Airy would all sit at the table of Girls High's lunchroom, talking about her like a dog, signifying in loud, leering voices of contempt. Jealous whores. One day . . .

From this night forward, Monday would be the most terrible day of the week. Green her most hated color. People like Darien, her enemy. Her reputation was sunk. Either way was bad. They'd more than likely believe his lies that he'd scored, or if he had to explain his black eye, a scratched-up face, and why his daddy's car was in the shop, they'd say she'd gone to Darien Price's *senior prom* and wasn't woman enough or classy enough to just act like she knew, which was why one of them should have gone in her stead.

And the sisters down the way would all be laughing their asses off at her for being the last virgin standing—and for missing probably the best parties around . . . the best food, dancing, and music, to go on some solo adventure with some strange guy from up here, instead of hanging out in a safe group from the neighborhood—why, because he was gonna treat her nicer? Why, because her parents said she was too young to date unless she was going out somewhere that they didn't consider wild? Why, because up here they didn't gang-war? Why, 'cause with a guy from up here her parents thought they could relax? Why? Prep school was supposed to make a guy a better candidate, or more of a gentleman? Shit. All prep school meant was that he couldn't dance or play basketball. Her mother and father were gonna have a fucking conniption. Laura kept walking. She had to get home.

If she could just make it to Gypsy Lane, to where the police had a substation, then she could call her dad. Yeah.

"You wait till *my father* hears about this shit!" she yelled, unable to take Darien's taunts or the sound of his car horn any longer. Her parents were gonna flip, and although she might not ever get to go on another prom in her lifetime, her daddy was gonna fuck one Darien Price up. That was as sure as money; her dad didn't play. Everybody around the way gave him big respect and knew he was a little throw'd off since the war, would step to the hardest of brothers, kept things chilly in the neighborhood, led Towne Watch—that's why he was Cool Bill . . . Still Bill, Mr. B. Yup. Her dad was gonna deal with this shit. Shoot. Her dad might even tell her Uncle Akhan so they could posse up, and then Darien's ass would really be history.

She ignored Darien's increasingly pleading calls out the Cadillac window. Oh, so now the little bastard was whining . . . now that she'd mentioned her daddy, he was saying, "Laura, *please,* get in the car." He sounded like a true bitch.

"Fuck you!" she yelled, and marched on. Punk. The Caldwell clan would posse up and deal with this young boy's ass. She'd seen them do it before, when her eldest cousin got pregnant and the guy was trying to act like the baby wasn't his. Brother got fucked up good. Had to do the right thing, or die.

Right. That's how things were supposed to go. Honor. Some shit just wasn't done. If Darien had asked her nice . . . well . . . maybe. But just to *assume* . . .

Her feet and her feelings hurt so badly that she wanted to weep, but pride kept her marching. Sticks, stones, gravel, tree bark, humiliation cut deep. At least up here there wasn't any trash or broken bottles. At least it was spring and not in the dead of winter. People had yards, and dogs didn't just run loose to poop wherever. But how could he say all those terrible things? Okay, so her family didn't have as much as his, but that didn't give him the right. Before he'd opened his mouth, she'd felt like the most beautiful woman in the world. At least, even though she didn't have much else, she still had some fucking pride!

She needed a new school notebook. Why had she written his name on it in pen?

The substation felt like it was somewhere in California rather than only a mile away. She knew she was close, because the Cadillac finally sped off. The streetlights were oppressive as she looked at her elongated shadow in them, feeling like a beat-up hooker in a torn green gown with smeared makeup. Her mother would die a thousand deaths. No Caldwell woman was ever seen like this. She could not go into a police station with all those white men looking at her in this condition. They would smirk. "Niggers," they'd say under their breaths. Never. Her father would die a million deaths. But that asshole, Darien Price, was dog meat.

Alone, real tears slid down her face, and before long, sobs shook her shoulders as she kept walking with her head now bowed, not even bothering to wipe her eyes. How the hell was she going to get from the drive across the expressway to her side of the universe? There was no walking that.

Loud music, car headlights, and young voices carried on the night air made her stop and cringe. She wanted to disappear. A car was pulling up beside her. God, please, let them pass. If she could just be invisible.

"Yo, sis! You cool?" A male voice hollered, screeching the car to a full stop.

Laura nodded and looked at the beat-up, rust-brown Chevy loaded with kids her age. Three couples, a bottle of champagne brandished by one guy, and Thunderbird held by the driver. The distinctive aroma of weed floated on the air with the music. Six pairs of reddened eyes squinted at her. But they were cool people. They were from around her way. "I'm all right."

"Nah, sis . . . you don't look aw'right at all," a guy from the backseat countered.

The car pulled over closer to the curb, and the driver put on hazard flashers at the stop light. Three girls got out. They looked so pretty in their cream, white, and hot pink after-prom pantsuits that Laura wanted to wail. She should have been in a safe group, a herd, rather than with a wolf in sheep's clothing, all by herself, up here in practically the forest. She cast her gaze toward the creek, staring out into the woodland blackness that followed the road.

"You sho' you all right?" one of the girls asked.

Laura shook her head no, telling the truth for the first time.

"Yo, man—take her to her peeps, yo. This is fucked up, whatever happened to sis."

"I kicked his ass, is what happened," Laura said quietly, not sure why that information was vitally important, but it was.

"Cool," the guy who had been driving said, obviously not knowing what else to say.

"What street you live on?" another one of the girls asked, her voice gentle.

"Warrington. Fifty-six-hundred block." Laura could barely speak. She allowed her gaze to land briefly on the stunned faces before her and then looked away again. The brothers were all done up to the nines in their after-prom gear, platform shoes matching their two-toned pants, matching their dates' outfits, looking like they were having fun . . . the way it was supposed to go down. Yet their eyes held a protective stare, muscles pulsed in their jaws, and she could feel them mentally asking the question: *who did this to you, baby?*

Her parents didn't understand; the brothers around the way had a code of honor. Yet those were the guys she'd been taught to fear: brothers who carried zip guns, shanks, razors, played dice in the alleyways, stumbled from corner bars . . . the guys who shot up parties, created stampedes at dance concerts because they were at the center of the knife fight—that's who you worried about. Not some dude from a neighborhood with manicured lawns.

But her parents weren't hip that these supposedly high-class people up here didn't even come out on their front steps when they heard a young girl screaming her head off. Around the way, the stoops would have been loaded; men like her father would have come off the corners and out of the bars to address something like this. A sob caught in Laura's throat. She would never forgive Darien Price for treating her like a common whore just because of where she lived.

"Where you want us to take you, baby? Home to your people, or to a girlfriend's, so you can clean up 'fore your momma see you like this?" The brother who had spoken had lowered his voice, had infused it with reverence, and was gazing down at his shoes, not staring at her ripped bodice or partially exposed breasts. Respect.

Defeat claimed her, along with fatigue. Laura covered her face with her hands. "I just wanna go home."

* * *

Ending the daymare, Laura shut off the water with conviction, stepped out of the tub, and toweled herself dry—on a mission. Never again would she be powerless; never again would she be poor—both were one and the same. Yeah . . . the old dolls in the family were right. You could definitely show 'em better than you could tell 'em.

Quiet cloaked her as she gathered up her towel and left the bathroom. Light crept upon her in increments, making her eyes adjust to accept it. Now she could make out the sheer Egyptian cotton shower curtain as she looked back at the bathroom, and the pale yellow hucs that surrounded her seemed so far, far away. Her gaze settled on the ferns and candles that had shared the space with her; this morning she took note.

This house was so much larger than where she'd grown up, so much more tastefully designed with the mud cloth fabrics, the natural woods, and elegant muted earth tones inherent in each sleek, modern piece of furniture, African art and natural fibers that she'd surrounded herself with. But there was no running from the past. This place that she'd created was filled with things but was devoid of the wealth of spirit. Her mother and father's tiny home had been rich beyond comparison, which made the violation of what they'd built such a travesty. If only her mother had never told, and if only her father had never started digging into the Prices' business, intent on finding a way to rectify a wrong.

Gathering the thick terry cloth around her, she headed straight for the telephone. Without even looking at the buttons, she punched in the number she knew by heart, and waited.

"Hotep," came the sleepy but familiar male voice on the other end of the line.

Laura closed her eyes. She knew better than to call her uncle by the title of family endearment, especially on the telephone. It was his way of ensuring no electronic eavesdroppers could connect him to any family in any way. She cleared her mind and used the title he preferred. "Good morning, Brother Akhan, it's me, Laura."

"Young sister," the elderly man said, his voice becoming mellow with knowing. "What makes you call this old man so early in the morning?"

She hesitated, not sure where to begin. "I just needed to hear your voice."

"Ahhhh . . . ," he soothed. "How's your morning look?"

"Open, always, for you."

"Then share some libations with me? I'll make us some tea."

"That would be perfect," she murmured, clutching the receiver to her cheek and closing her eyes as she spoke.

"Just come."

"Thank you."

"The fight is getting to you, I can tell," he said, sounding concerned. "We all need respite from the battle."

"I know." Laura sat down on the side of her king-size sleigh bed, staring at the Moroccan rug on the floor, the profusion of cream, teal, gold, and deep blue colors within it becoming blurry from unshed tears.

"Then come on home, young sister-warrior, and rejuvenate your soul."

She nodded even before answering verbally. That was just what she needed to do.

Her gray silk suit duster swished about her steel-gray pants as she walked through the house toward the garage. She didn't even bother to grab her coat; she was on a mission. Needed space.

Talking into her office voice mail from her primary cell phone as she set the alarm, she descended into the garage and got into the car. "Najira, this morning I'll be late. I have something to take care of. I should be in no later than ten a.m."

She slung her barrel purse into the passenger's seat and turned on the ignition, then hit the garage door opener, waiting as the door slowly rose. A blast of bright sunlight greeted her, making her feel as though she were coming out of a cave. Perhaps she was. Engaging the gears, she fidgeted with the radio, setting the station to a local black morning talk show on the AM dial, and listened.

She'd beaten rush hour, and her vehicle leisurely entered the desolate street, yet the loud, contentious voices on the radio pierced her brain. She brought her car to East River Drive, heading toward the north end of the city. Sunlight tried to force its way to the ground through the fall leaves and lost the battle—just as the radio call-ins were losing the verbal battle with the show's host. Madeline Morris was in rare yet predictably disagreeable form. Laura shook her head, wondering how that woman had lasted so long on the airwaves.

Laura's Jaguar navigated the winding curves as though on autopilot. The community folks were calling in and getting a beat-down like she hadn't heard in years. But the conversation was pivotal to understanding what thoughts were simmering at the street level. Laura trained her mind on the blaring discussion as her vision stayed with the road.

"Yeah, but," one man unsuccessfully argued, "why should people be able to get away with stuff like Price did, just because of who they know?"

"I know him *and* knew his people for years!" the show host shrieked. "Y'all just player-hatin' this morning—see, that's black folks' problem," she railed on. "You don't know nothin', and then you want to subscribe to all these conspiracy theories! You should be ashamed of yourself. Next caller."

The host cut off the offending call and took another, her indignation clear in her voice. Laura's palm itched to pick up her cell phone and jump into the fray, but she kept those feelings in check and simply drove.

"How can you say that, Maddie?" another caller said with

force. "For years people like him have been keeping the contracts for their cronies, and—"

"What!" the host argued. "That's a myth. Y'all need to just get your acts together and stop whining about what people didn't do for you or give you. Welfare is over, people. It's dead. Get with the program. That man and his lovely wife worked hard for everything they've got. In fact, they were just at my home not too long ago, and I'ma call his wife this morning to get the record straight, since we have all these nonbelievers out here this morning. And just 'cause they live in a big, pretty house and drive a nice car, *like I do,* doesn't mean that they've done anything wrong. You need to get a job; that's what you need to do. Humph! Trifling."

"That's right," the next caller allowed on the line said, considerably soothing Ms. Morris's ego. "It's good to see our folks, and you, girl, handling yo' business. So, chile, don't you be lettin' playa haters get you all upset this mornin', hear?"

"I won't, doll," Madeline Morris said to the elderly female caller. "I don't pay those folks no mind. Shoot, I remember walking with all the big boys, and lemme just say for the record, all this mess about the Price family, and trying to drag up innuendo about how this was linked to the Officer Carter thing twenty or thirty years ago, is hogwash. You have a nice day, suga."

Laura almost swerved off the road. *Officer Carter?* She turned the volume up and listened hard.

"Naw, naw," a stuttering man said when he was given access to the call-in line. "There was folks who seen what happened—people heard that black cop get shot in the alley, and then they moved his body."

"What in tarnation has that got to do with what we're talking about this morning? Y'all gonna make me lose my religion up in here!"

"Naw, Maddie, for real, sis. Check it out. Word on the street was that he was gonna get put down with some heavy science and was gonna let the people know—then he gets shot. Feel me? The white press suppressed the info, even though the real newspapers down the way tried to keep us informed, and *the man* swept it under the rug, then—"

"See," Madeline contended, cutting off the caller's comments, "this is what I'm talking about this morning. Y'all stand around on corners, talkin' about *the man,* and listen to mess up in the bars like it was gospel, and come up with the wildest accusations—which is why our people can't get ahead. That's the problem. Y'all focus on nonsense. When what you need to focus on is the fact that they're trying to lynch a good African-American family in the press without a fair trail." The show host sucked her teeth so loudly that the sound popped and hissed through the radio. "Get me Michael Paxton Jr. on the line," she bellowed to her producer so the callers could hear her. "Yeah, that's right. Use his private number—I'm one of the *few* people who have his private number; he'll take *my* calls. We need to go to a commercial; then we'll be right back with the real story."

Laura's knuckles had turned white as she'd listened to the diatribe that the host entered into, knowing full well how the conversations from that point would go. Paxton would get on the air with a professional, rehearsed response and would kiss Madeline Morris's ass. Not a single politician or notable could get into office without her. If you wanted to be endorsed, you had to go past Morris, with gifts in hand—only then would you be assured that you wouldn't be verbally dogged on air with the people. They were all afraid of her radio power . . . just as you had to stay in good graces with the major African-American rag in the city, or you were history.

However, the mention of Officer Carter had given her serious pause. She'd never made the link. When it all happened over twenty-some years ago, she'd been a kid in high school. . . . Some of the finer points went to the grave with her aunt and her parents. But she did know that her father had tried to get his information to a source within the police department just before his indictment, but until this moment, she never had a name. Carter. Damn, Philly was small—like an incestuous small southern town. The significant question was, did Officer Carter give his life trying to help her father, or did he double-cross him and simply get whacked because he knew too much? Interesting variable. And here she was sidling up to the son for other reasons, had been trying to get info on the current Price case to ensure that her plan was working. Truly profound.

Remembering her dad's dark, intense eyes or the way he smiled, flashing brilliant white against handsome dark skin, and, his laugh—it boomed in her mind and drowned out the lies being told over the airwaves. To her, in those days, her dad seemed so tall and strong, and smelled so good. Made her feel safe—till they took that all away . . . and eyes that once blazed with confidence never made contact with hers again but instead sought the floor. Arms clung, offering hugs, like a man needing to be saved from himself, not a man with pride, supporting and protecting his daughters from all harm. Her father's daddy smell changed from the clean snap of Old Spice to the dank, pungent aroma of Old Grand Dad. And his dashing streetwise smile lost its megawatt brilliance to a weak, thin line that rarely showed enamel. And now they wanted fairness?

She switched off the radio after Paxton made his pitch for his client's innocence, her senses unable to handle much more, and she turned right onto Huntington Park, deep in thought.

The once vibrant industrial area loomed before her like the giant skeletal remains of dinosaurs, now extinct, lifeless, gutted and hollowed out, burned out in places; humans skittering like vermin between the abandoned carcasses of what was left from an era gone by. Crack addicts shuffled from foot to foot in the cold, the homeless huddled against the stoops of once immaculate, massive brownstones that were now falling down. Yeah, and the white boys wanted this prime real estate back in the worst way . . . and would take it by any means necessary. Why was this her fate, to watch shit like this go down? She was a part of it, couldn't ignore it; and like her father, once grand with dignity, even the old neighborhoods were eroding away to nothingness, before their legacy was stolen.

If only people voted. Laura sighed. Didn't the community understand that folks had died in the picket lines under billy clubs, took the dogs and hoses, for that right? *People had to vote,* had to understand what strings were being pulled behind the curtain—strings that made people puppets, shifted redlined neighborhoods, moved families and jobs to where it was convenient for some and lethal for others. She scanned the streets, her brow knit as she looked at what was transforming into Temple University's expansion in what had been the black zone. But this neighborhood was no different from many others. In Philly there were over twenty-two colleges and universities, all creeping, all expanding, all forcing out native residents.

Her heart broke as she peered at the once gorgeous architecture that was now in ruins as though a war had been fought in the streets. It had. Wrecking balls or time and lack of economic infrastructure had decimated entire blocks. She drove onward, her black Jaguar coupe snaking past it all, but her mind missing none of the dilapidated, barren landscape. This was part of the reason why Price and his type had to be held accountable. With a viable economic base, the people here could have fought encroachment and built up their own homes, saved their own damned neighborhood. This was sacrilege!

She pulled into a narrow street, no sign to tell her where she was; she didn't need one. Although the street was tiny, there was plenty of parking amid the broken-down cars that littered the area. People here were forced to take the bus. A few curious eyes peered out from behind tattered curtains and shut them quickly. For all the residents knew, she was a drug dealer's woman coming to make a pickup—her type of car was not a part of this landscape, unless someone with a Glock nine was about to jump out of it. People shooed their children from the doors and windows when vehicles like this pulled up.

Laura turned off the ignition and got out of her Jag, grabbing her purse, slinging it over her shoulder as she depressed the alarm button while walking. The beep echoed off the bricks and pavement, blending in with the clacking of her short boot heels. When Brother Akhan opened the door, his face lit up, and she went up his white marble front steps in three strides, filling his arms. She could almost feel the neighborhood watchers relax.

"Hotep, my young warrior queen sister. Come in," he said warmly, holding her away from him to inspect her. "Been too long."

She hugged him hard again and simply nodded.

Chapter 7

Laura entered the tiny row home and waited as the elderly man before her managed four dead-bolt locks on the front door behind them. Her eyes took in the stacks of papers and books that covered every tattered chair and the huge yellow floral print sofa, poorly disguised by a long kente cloth swath of material. Oil paintings of Malcolm, Martin, Mandela, and Rosa, with brilliant blue and yellow backgrounds highlighting their brown skins, created by community artists, hung next to worn posters of ancient African kings. The musty smell of the aged and of old cooking oils confronted her.

Warmth settled into her bones as she followed her uncle down the narrow hallway to the kitchen, his purple-toned African agbada robe swishing as his sandal-clad feet softly padded to their destination. He pulled out a chair and, not needing to tell her with words, offered her a seat. Laura glanced around at the disarray. Brother Akhan had turned his kitchen into a combination study and eating space. Textbooks, newspapers, and stacks of files littered every open surface.

The familiarity of it all was comforting, and she hung her purse on the back of a plastic-covered chair and sat quietly, staring at the cluttered kitchen while he brought a steaming Pyrex pot of water to the table and filled two ceramic mugs. Making tea was a part of the process, part of the aged one's way. She now understood all of that much better. So, with deference, she waited as he took down a small brown bag from the rickety, white-painted metal cabinets and began stuffing fresh herbal tea leaves into a bamboo tea diffuser.

The scent of mint filled the air, and Laura waited until her host brought a sticky jar of raw honey to the table and set it between them on the cracked Formica. He then went back to the sink and fetched a small jelly glass and filled it with fresh water. Settling himself with great effort, he reached across the chipped surface and collected her hands within his. Callused warmth radiated up her arms and consumed her with so much familiarity that she had to fight within herself to keep tears from rising in her eyes. She squeezed his leathery palms hard, let her breath out, and relaxed. It had been way too long since she'd come home.

"We will ask the ancestors for permission to proceed." His gaze was tender and yet firm as he waited for her response.

Laura nodded.

His bluish brown eyes peered at her from within a dark, toffee-hued face. Gray stubble covered his jaw, and the flickering fluorescent kitchen light glinted off his clean-shaven head. She studied the lines within her uncle's cheeks, and the creases at the corners of his eyes and those about his forehead, the way each wrinkle made him appear wiser. She wondered how her father would have aged. Her uncle had worn well with time.

He returned Laura's nod, and let her hands go, reaching for the small jelly glass he'd just filled with water. Addressing a brittle potted ivy plant on the table, he spoke slowly, quietly, but with authority.

"For those that have gone before us and have opened the door," he intoned reverently, pouring a small stream of water into the plant's parched dirt upon each sentence. "For those who had endured much and received little; for those who have kept the faith; for those who have died in the struggle. We honor you." He held Laura's gaze as he continued. "We ask your permission to proceed. We ask for wisdom, for guidance, and blessings. Help this young sister, so that she may continue her battle for your people's freedom. Ashé," he murmured, drawing out the last word of a heavy breath to make it sound like "ashaaaaye."

For a moment, neither of them spoke, and Laura waited until Brother Akhan, as he preferred to be called, took a sip of his tea. Only then did she lift her cup to her lips. His eyes held hers as he opened the honey and jabbed at the contents with a bent metal spoon, bringing a glob of sweet bee nectar out with it. He methodically dipped his spoon into his cup, stirring slowly but never losing eye contact with her.

"So," he finally said, taking another sip of his tea and handing her the single spoon between them, "what has a young warrior up so early in the morning, visiting an old man like me?"

Laura accepted the spoon from him and repeated his actions, sweetening her tea, composing her thoughts. Why had she come, other than to be in his healing presence? Her mind could find no refuge, so her mouth offered him the simple truth.

"I'm tired," she murmured, taking a deep sip from her cup. "And I don't know what to do about that."

He nodded and sat back in his chair, his eyes searching her face. "Then you are not alone."

She allowed the warmth of the mug to enter her palms as she cradled the cup. "How did you all do it, without getting co-opted?"

He laughed, but it was a deep chuckle of knowing not aimed at her, but filled with kindness. "Some of us did, young sister."

"I know," she told him honestly, her gaze searching his eyes for answers. "But how did you know where the line was?"

"Depends on your objective."

Laura pushed back in her chair. "That's getting murky, at best."

"Always does when you're close to victory."

She chuckled, enjoying the mental sparring match he employed to make her consciousness grow. "I'm close."

Again he nodded, and sipped his tea. "I know you are." He stared at her briefly, then sent his gaze out the grimy kitchen window, past the iron security bars. "There's going to be a changing of the guard. Are you ready?"

She said nothing, pausing to think about how to respond. "They've asked me to redistribute the funds that had been allotted to Price."

"To be expected. But I will ask you again, are you ready to take the spoils of war once victorious? When our people know better, they do better. You must teach when you take over, so this tragic history doesn't repeat itself."

This time they held each other's line of vision, unwavering. Her uncle pursed his lips, his eyebrow now arched with an unspoken question.

"I'll teach," she finally said with a weary sigh. "Some people have been playing games for years at our people's expense. That can't continue."

"It is one thing to be manipulated without knowing you are being manipulated. . . . Those sisters and brothers must be taught; be gentle with them. Even if they were born with silver spoons in their mouths." He smiled.

"I hear you. But it is quite another thing to willingly go against your people."

Brother Akhan sighed. "Harriet Tubman was quoted to say that if more people had known they were slaves, she could have freed more slaves."

"Girlfriend also carried a gun."

He smiled wider and then chuckled. "Too dramatic an approach for you, young sister. We've lost enough in the struggle. I know you aren't espousing violence."

Laura chuckled with him and shook her head. "No. I'm not crazy."

"Glad to hear that," he said, his easy baritone filling the room and reminding her of her father's. "One must be much more strategic than that."

"Ashé. But as you and I both know, there are many ways to eliminate an infested branch from a tree. As long as the roots are good, the tree can be preserved. Price had to be eliminated, but the money he had to work with is still viable."

Brother Akhan now stared at her, saying nothing for a moment, the mirth gone from his expression.

"I've only got one shot at this, good brother. I need to know where to redirect the money—where it will do the most good. We have to throw a coalition behind a new candidate, then line up a strong slate where his influence will be best felt when he's in a position to direct contracts. He has to have a strong cabinet, whomever we slot in, and we have to be assured that any leverage he has over contracts will go to the people who deserve them, not the old guard. Soon the Price camp will regroup, and things will go back to status quo. You've always been my teacher . . ."

"When the student is ready, a teacher will appear," he murmured in a cryptic tone, now smiling.

"Precisely why I'm here."

His smile widened, giving Laura a glimpse of his misaligned, yellowed teeth.

"After what they did to your father, and you went off to school, then fled to New York, we thought you'd never come back home. It took you two years to visit me, to have this particular conversation."

"I carried home in my heart, though," she countered. "Always." She held his gaze firm. "I wasn't in a position to have this conversation with you before. Now, due to a fortuitous confluence of events, the tide has shifted."

"Like a true warrior," he replied, beaming. "There is an

old Ashanti tale about a princess who was secreted away after invaders killed her parents and plundered her father's kingdom. One day she came back and rose up a mighty army, and built an impenetrable fortress. You remember that story, right?"

Hot tears now stood in Laura's eyes, and she couldn't banish them despite all her efforts. The thought of how she and her little sisters were carted off to community meetings to listen to powerful men speak about the revolution, change, or how her parents would gather with others in basements and in community centers to strategize with the great ones, the uncles and babas, like Brother Akhan . . . and how the children were taught respect for the motherland, the ancestors—culture that had been ripped away was restored by oral history lessons and soul-sustaining food. How could she forget? At the time it had been boring and also oddly exciting to go to those clandestine meetings. Now she just wished she'd paid more attention, hadn't taken the whole village concept for granted . . . especially now that her entire family village had been razed to the ground.

"Where is the best place to send these resources? What can one do to make a permanent change?" she asked, forcing herself to recover.

Seeming pleased, he rubbed his palm over his bald scalp and leaned back in his chair. "This time we must develop self-sustaining enterprises at the community level. Sure, we have some very good legitimate businesses out there, but we need so many more. Jobs are no longer an option for us . . . have always killed our spirits, anyway. The economy has been hard on the people with the least resources. The new candidate's platform needs to deal with wealth building from *within* the community."

She nodded as he went on. This was why she had come to him.

"Dear Laura . . . our people have to be able to manufacture our own goods, then buy those goods from ourselves, distribute those goods to ourselves . . . We must create supply chains for basic products and services, things the everyday person needs—like soap, toilet paper, food, not some esoteric possessions. I'm talking about *the basics,* in this wartime economy, that the average person must have to survive. Our dollars must turn more than once in our community, like other people's do. With enterprises, you have jobs created for us, by us. With jobs, crime goes down, home ownership goes up, and we break a cycle of despair."

Laura raked her fingers through her hair and stared at the old man before her. "Microenterprises, then? Small businesses? Focus there? But that's an old platform that's been done to death, with little sustainable results."

"Yes," he said with conviction. "But there's nothing new under the sun. It's all in one's approach."

She reached around and grabbed a piece of paper and a pen from her purse, which hung on the back of the kitchen chair. "All right. What if old factories in North Philadelphia, like the Botany Five Hundred Building, which is now, oddly enough, going mall-condo, or down in Southwest, like that old Breyer's Ice Cream plant, which a university took over—just pick one of the many abandoned plants still standing in struggling neighborhoods . . . What if there was a way to form a coalition of organizations that taught a manufacturing craft combined with entrepreneurship right here in the city? That would create contracts and opportunities for community-based organizations, as well as create entrepreneurs. That also hits both education and employment creation programming—not too far a diversion from what Price's funds were to do, but with a different spin on it. We could probably rally folks around that to get behind a candidate."

Driven by sheer impulse, she began to scribble furiously on a slip of paper and then turned it around to face her mentor. "I know the concept has been tried before, or at least partially attempted. But if we came up with a comprehensive plan, we'd have an education component, a jobs component—because neighborhood residents could work where they learned, and if we had access to the abandoned storefronts or confiscated vehicles, we could open channels of distribution."

Brother Akhan nodded and took the paper from her. "That has indeed been tried before . . . but—"

"But never on this scale," she said, pushing him to think of the possibilities as her passion built. "We could link into existing, solid black-owned businesses . . . like, like, PNC Wiring up on Lehigh Avenue could set up the facilities, and there's a box manufacturer up there who could use the business—that brother who owns Sperring White can do four-color jobs, and he's hidden in an old supermarket warehouse! And what about all the printers out there who could never get a contract? We could comprehensively develop everything as a learning and business unit—even down to the product packaging."

She was gesturing wildly with her hands, not waiting for Brother Akhan's response; the part of her soul that she'd sublimated was rising within her like a wave of knowledge that would not be denied. "Think of all the struggling black newspapers that could save money by streamlining their processes to share the same presses while teaching real journalism, and the collective of businesses could advertise in those community papers to support them. Think of the computer programs that put out students with nowhere to go. Those students could service small business clients as a collective, especially if we brought those businesses into the new millennium by creating a supply chain bridge on the Internet, too, with computer access within all the community centers and libraries where people have access? What if we could get people computer literate with online, local shopping from local small businesses?"

Brother Akhan stared at her, then made a tent under his chin with his fingers. "That would indeed be profound, and would kill many birds with one stone . . . which I assume is your objective."

"Think about it," she urged. "What if we could link to small, embattled black farmers trying to hold on to their family lands, to bring in fresh produce . . . this could be really big, if we cooperate. There was a time when black businesses thrived in the city, when our newspapers were strong, our media outlets were owned by us, and we owned our own neighborhoods that were not in ruins—because we shopped black, bought black, and purchased from local stores, recycling those dollars internally to our community first."

"I know," he said quietly, his voice distant. "We supported our own doctors, our own shops, our own hair care service providers, our own restaurants, hardware stores . . . You do not have to remind me of that lost renaissance. Desegregation was a double-edged sword."

She reached across the table and clasped his hands briefly, then let them go. "All we need is a realignment and we might even be able to get back a real, black-owned radio station, like we used to have in Philly."

"We might just, indeed," he said slowly, his eyes never leaving the paper that she'd thrust toward him. "But that would require a complete coup over what has crept within our midst." He looked up at her and held her gaze with concern. "That is why I asked you, are you ready?" His gaze went to his spoon, and his thick fingers manipulated the metal utensil like worry beads.

"I'm ready."

The old man picked up the paper with his free hand, looked at it again, set it down carefully beside his spoon, and took up his cup of tea. "You know, when Malcolm and Martin started talking to each other about changing the economics . . . when they started talking about international links, they were assassinated."

"I know." Laura's gaze sought the window. "So was my father."

"I know." Brother Akhan sighed and pushed the paper back across the table to her. His expression was tight with concern. "Your father was going to shake up the power brokers by exposing their dirty deals, was pulling the grassroots community leaders together, and some people objected.

They assassinated him in the media, which was the same as putting a bullet in his head." Brother Akhan took another deliberate sip of his tea. "How much do you have to work with, Laura?"

"Twelve-point-five million worth of Darien's lost program funds, to let the initial contracts that will ensure whichever candidate we back shows some wins under his belt before the election push ends. From there, I don't know."

She looked at her mentor. Brother Akhan's eyes widened; the surprise in them was unmistakable.

"All of it?"

"Yes," she said with triumph. "All of it."

"That's more than I thought you'd ever . . ." His sentence trailed off with awe, and he picked it up at a new entry point. He sat back in his chair and smiled, then gave in to a hearty chuckle. "I thought they'd only give you enough to hang yourself."

Watching him beam with pride made her smile.

"Not bad at all," he finally murmured. "I'm proud of you. Always have been."

"We can do this," she pressed, gaining confidence.

"But that's only enough to start something like this. In the long run, you'll need so much more."

Laura hesitated. What he'd said was true, but she refused to be dissuaded. She was too close to a win.

"I know," she said respectfully. "But it is a start . . . and, once started, with some serious people behind it, the momentum factor must be considered. If I can get the buildings appropriated, with support for some of the renovations, perhaps I can swing the real cash toward program dollars and manufacturing inventory . . . maybe even low-interest, patient capital loans for business start-ups. Those types of buildings are all in Keystone Opportunity and Empowerment Zones—the real value is in the real estate. That's why you see factories being converted by big Main Line real estate companies, within so-called embattled neighborhoods. They're coming back to prime real estate already set up with beneficial business tax structures, and we're being pushed out to reservation lands. Just ask the Native Americans how this works."

"Young sister, I admit that I had no idea how deep inside the belly of the beast you'd gotten. Now I'm worried. What did you have to do to get them to give you the nod?"

"It's a new millennium. I was qualified; Price had burned his bridges . . . sooo . . ."

They both laughed as Laura looked out the window. If her uncle only knew. She prayed that he would never find out the full story of how the power shift came to be, fully cognizant that the old man would have a heart attack if he ever got wind of the crazy stuff his daughter, Najira, had done. But if he ever found out *her* angle in this, he'd go to his grave for sure.

"Uhmm hmmm," Brother Akhan grumbled, sounding unconvinced. "If you say so."

"I say so," she said, still not looking directly at him.

He nodded, his eyes darting between her and the window. "But the more things change, the more they stay the same."

Silence enveloped them.

"A lot of people are going to have to be . . . redirected, in order for this to stand a chance. Price was only one player. There are many people standing in line to snatch up the ball he dropped." His line of vision remained on the window, then went toward the hall, as though he were expecting a SWAT raid at any moment.

The shift in his mood troubled her. They both knew she was treading on thin ice, and this much money being channeled to her would come at a hefty personal price down the road. That was also why Brother Akhan never spoke about things in a direct sense; his statements were always a riddle or parable, lest *the man* overhear him somehow. Years of conditioning and community activism through the fifties and sixties and well into the seventies had probably made him that way—perhaps he had cause. Laura sighed.

"I know," she finally said, her face now rigid with tension.

"I'm working on that as we speak." She had to tell him something to get him to understand that she'd considered the variables.

"How can I help, then?" He'd asked the question slowly, staring at her hard enough to study every pore in her face.

Laura folded the paper that lay on the table. She made careful creases in it, thinking as her fingers pressed it into a neat square.

"When this gets hyped in the media, I'll need to already have quiet alliances formed, people standing ready with their paperwork intact that can accept teaching contracts, build curriculum; suppliers, small enterprises that can bite off a piece of the construction contracts; valid 501c3 organizations that can accept donated buildings from the Redevelopment Authority and the Pennsylvania Industrial Development Corporation . . . but we might have to stand down on allowing the renovations to get done by Italian-owned firms. At most, I may be able to get a split to allow minority subcontractors a shot—but anybody who you anoint has to be squeaky-clean. I also don't want to burn money by reinventing the wheel. So, while in the process, let's strengthen the incubators and other vital programs that are teetering on the brink of extinction. Whoever gets the nod as our candidate has to have an impeccable slate behind him."

"You need me to point out which organizations are worthy versus those who will get greedy and could burn you, and to develop a list of honest community organizations." Brother Akhan nodded. "Understood," he said with a weary sigh. He stood, his knees creaking from the effort as he went to the stove. "Let me ambassador that aspect of things. . . . These are delicate negotiations."

"That's why I came to you," she murmured, addressing his back as he added water to the kettle and switched on the burner.

"You sound just like your father." Brother Akhan turned around and stared at Laura, moisture filling his eyes, his expression suddenly bitter. "He was not only my dear soul brother, but he was also my best student, and almost like a son to me."

She and Brother Akhan allowed the silence to speak, filling in the memory of how the nebulous "they" had cut her father down in the prime of his life, stripped him of credibility, and then worked him like a mule at the gas company, forcing him to walk the streets and check meters in the badlands until his heart gave out. One day she would also ask Brother Akhan how her grandfather had died, but not today. She wasn't even sure if he knew what had happened to her mother when she was younger, and was not about to violate a trust taken to the woman's grave.

As though reading her mind, Brother Akhan whispered a quiet statement that almost sounded like a prayer. "Your mother, the ancestors rest her soul in peace, was a gem."

The twosome remained quiet, locked in their own private thoughts, not needing to rehash how the stress of her father's indictment had given Laura's mother the stroke. But they both knew it was heartbreak that had killed her.

Brother Akhan rubbed his chin, nodding without further comment. What was there left to say, anyway? They both knew what had to be done.

"Najira is lucky to have you as her mentor."

"I'll watch out for her," she promised. "And thank you for your help, as always." Laura bowed to the dignified presence before her great uncle, guilt stabbing at her as she thought about Najira looking up to her. "Ashé." The ancestors had spoken. Let it be done.

"Laura," Najira said fast and low, trying to keep up with Laura's long strides as she passed her and entered her office, "the phones have been ringing off the hook all morning. Everybody in the city, practically, wants to take you to lunch and dinner today—and I do mean *everybody.* I'm sorry I got in a little late, and you and I need to schedule time to talk—soon."

Laura simply nodded, dropping her purse on her desk. She was emotionally wrung out and could only partially filter what Najira was trying to tell her. "Okay. Give all the messages to me in order of importance," she said, riffling through the stack of incoming mail on her desk. "You and I will definitely talk soon, but I've gotta get to these VIPs while the iron is hot.

"I can dig it," Najira said quickly, going through the messages and rattling off the most important ones. "Donald Haines wants a meeting at the Cricket Club at your earliest convenience; Senator Scott also wants to do lunch. Mr. Crawford wants to invite you to a gallery opening tonight, and says there will be media there and it might be a good opportunity for you to be seen with the right people. Mrs. Price wants to know if you're open for coffee late this afternoon."

Both women stared at each other as Laura mouthed, *Oh, shit . . .*

"Yup," Najira said, coolly. "Mr. Thompson asked—"

Laura held up her hand. "Oh, wow . . . I didn't realize there were *that* many." She was still stuck on the Monica Price call, and Najira smiled, confirming that they were on the same wavelength. Haines had called *her* before she'd had a chance to call him, and *Monica Scott Price* wanted to do coffee? This was wild.

"Tell you what—never mind, just give me the messages; I'll sort them all out. I don't even know which ones are most important at this juncture myself, and the phones are indeed ringing off the hook." It wasn't a command, but simpatico, because there was already a line that was beginning to form outside Laura's office, near Najira's desk, of staff members wanting her attention.

Najira nodded, hearing the unspoken request to disperse the other employees. Her eyes were wide with excitement. "But a detective called, too, right after Mr. Paxton called. . . ." Her assistant hovered in front of her desk, expectation winding her so tightly that it appeared as though Najira might spin away like a toy top.

Laura looked up, hesitated, and then went back to the stack of blue and white slips of paper. Finding both messages quickly, Najira separated the two important ones for Laura as she sat down hard in her chair.

"I'll fill you in later, promise," Laura said, dismissing Najira as courteously as she could under pressure. "I just need a little privacy and a moment to pull my head together. Please close my door behind you." They both knew the deal. It wasn't a slight. If the cops were calling, then everything else was on hold.

"Be careful," Najira murmured, and walked toward the door. She watched Laura dial a number then hang up fast.

The phone instantly rang back, and Laura snatched it up quickly.

"Carter," the male voice boomed before Laura could even say hello.

Laura paused and waited for Najira to get out of earshot, closing the door behind her. She quickly glanced at the message from James Carter and then at the number displayed on her office console. She could tell by the digits after the area code that it wasn't an exchange down at the precinct or headquarters. The man had offered up a cell number? Hmmm. "Caldwell," she intoned flatly, extracting the business card that was in her purse, comparing the number on the message pad. No match.

The voice on the other end of the telephone hesitated.

"You called me?" Laura said with sarcasm singeing her voice. "May I help you?"

"How about an off-the-record conversation down at Vietnam—or don't you do Chinatown restaurants?"

She smiled and didn't immediately answer him, imagining an alternative option: Miss Tootsie's small, home-style, low-pressure atmosphere that offered solace to a weary soul. It had been a long time since she had good fried chicken. Maybe thinking of her mother last night had made her hunger for it. "You're asking me to lunch?"

"I'm asking you to talk to me while I eat. If you're hungry, you can do the same. Figured Vietnam was close to the Bourse Building and the Round House, for convenience's sake."

"My phone has been ringing off the hook. I have a slew of requests to respond to today."

Again the male voice hesitated. "I bet you do. Some other time, then."

"You give up too easy." Laura glanced at her watch. "How's eight p.m. at Miss Tootsie's—or don't you do soul food? Or maybe you don't prefer to support emerging black businesses?"

He paused. "That's late."

She smiled. Checkmate. "I'm trying to work with you, but I don't just have wide-open slots in my day on short notice. Unless this is official business and you're hauling me in. Should I contact my attorney?"

"Eight o'clock. Fine."

"Done."

She looked at the receiver as the call disconnected, pleased with herself. As she was about to set the telephone down in the cradle, line two buzzed and Najira's voice filled the room through the intercom. "Mr. Paxton's secretary is asking whether or not you intend to meet him for lunch today? He's made noon reservations at the Garden."

Irritation riddled Laura. His secretary? And already made reservations, too? Fuck him. Presumptuous bastard. Laura steadied her voice. "Tell him I'm booked." She reached for her Palm Pilot and clicked it on. "Wednesday . . . nope. Thursday . . . not even possible. Maybe Friday. Slot him in for Friday at eleven."

"Okay, boss lady, but I don't think they're going to be happy with the delay."

"I've got a senator and a foundation exec way before Paxton on my radar. Slot the senator in at two, at the Omni's Azalea Room, my treat. Be sure to tell him that."

"Okay," Najira repeated, quickly getting off the telephone.

Laura shook her head. In twenty-four hours she was now the most popular woman in the city. Very interesting. Yesterday she'd thought the whole town had gone nuts—correction: *today* the whole town had apparently gone nuts. She began dialing Donald Haines's number when Najira's voice came back on through the intercom.

"Mr. Paxton is now on line one for you. I think he might have recognized my voice, though. What should I do?"

"Play it off like a pro and ask him to please hold; then call back the senator, Mrs. Price—book her to a four-thirty at Rouge on Rittenhouse Square for drinks, and then call every damned body else. Book them in, but savc me open calendar space from eight to eleven tonight. Meanwhile, I'm trying to return Donald Haines's call to set up something with him today from eleven to one, if he's available. Fuck Paxton."

"That Mr. Paxton really has a nasty vibration, Miss Caldwell. Be forewarned," Najira said with a giggle.

"Good, and, oh, I have been forewarned about him. Trust me." Laura chuckled.

"I need to talk to you, lady, *especially* after my visit with that one at the Hyatt. Hear me? Been asking the girls on the secretary grapevine. Need to fill in a few blanks about *that one's* proclivities."

"Then, come talk to me, and definitely put him on hold."

Chapter 8

True to chivalrous form, Donald Haines stood up from a huge burgundy wingback chair studded in brass that faced a massive fireplace, as Laura entered the sunlight-drenched Cricket Club receiving room. He turned, smiled at her, adjusted his red and blue plaid bow tie beneath his white button-down shirt collar, and closed his gray suit jacket, straightening his cuffs in the process.

Soft, moss-green hues graced the walls. Mayflower blue-blood portraits in original oil, framed in gold leaf repose, surrounded her. Eighteenth-century crystal chandeliers dotted the twenty-two-foot ceilings crested in gold-bordered, ornate crown moldings. Custom tapestry drapes were held back from the leaded beveled glass panes by heavy silk ropes. A hint of gentlemen's cigars wafted past her. Laura took it all in and sighed. Some things definitely never changed. She reminded herself that there was a time when she couldn't even have come in the place as a patron, much less through the front door. She wasn't impressed.

As she approached Haines, she could practically see her reflection in the highly polished wood floors where the thick

Oriental rugs allowed it to peek through. Laura pasted on her best smile and acted as though she'd grown up in Donald Haines's understated but elegant world. She had work to do.

"Donald," she purred, "I am so glad we could get together today on such short notice."

"The pleasure is all mine," he said, pecking her cheek and glancing at her with appreciation. "I would have met you downtown at the Union League, closer to your office, but I had a morning golf engagement, and frankly, coming into the city is such a traffic nightmare. I do hope meeting here didn't pose too much of an inconvenience for you?"

"Not at all," she lied.

"Then, shall we?" he asked, smiling as he graciously waved his hand before her to let her walk into the dining room first.

Laura nodded, taking the lead, pausing at the maître d's podium.

"Mr. Haines," the maître d' said warmly, "two?"

"Thank you, Albert," Donald replied, extending his elbow for Laura to accept.

She waited for her chair to be pulled out for her, and set her bag down carefully on the floor as a linen napkin was placed on her lap. After Donald Haines was settled into his chair, she waited for him to begin their verbal dance.

"Hungry?" Donald Haines accepted a leather-bound menu and began perusing the choices.

"I am," she admitted, "but I'm going to behave myself."

"Oh, come, now. The roasted duck is magnificent here. Or might I suggest the grilled salmon?"

"I've been on the circuit," she chuckled, closing her menu. "If I keep eating like that, you won't recognize me one of these days. I'd better stick to a salad."

He closed his menu and scoffed, giving her another appreciative gaze. "Nonsense. I could never imagine you as anything but gorgeous."

"Oh, Donald, you don't know . . . I can put it away."

They both laughed.

"Alas. Women. Well, if a salad is all you'll have, then I guess I'll have to live with that. However, I do believe the salmon and asparagus is beyond my willpower."

"Indulge yourself," she said with a bright smile. "After all, you played a round of golf this morning. I've only been sitting behind a desk."

She watched Donald Haines as he placed their orders and their servers brought crystal glasses of sparkling water with thin rounds of lemons in them. Her synapses fired from one thought to the next, making critical social network connections inside her head while she and Donald Haines leisurely dispensed with the initial formalities of coming together for an early lunch. She wondered how the heads of state did this all day, every day.

Once the large, white china plate rimmed in delicate gold was set before her, Laura chose the outermost silver fork to begin picking at the gourmet mixed greens that had been tossed in a light basalmic-vinaigrette dressing. But she waited, knowing that an offer to taste a bit of Donald's salmon was coming her way. It was part of the ritual to accept a morsel from his plate, which would then open the real dialogue.

That's the way it always went: the gesture meant, *if you can eat from my plate, then you are no threat.* It was a man thing, a power thing. She smiled as he looked up from his plate and pushed it toward her. Had he been angling to be a potential lover, he would have speared a piece of the tender fish with his own fork and offered it to her in that manner. She was glad he'd only nudged his plate in her direction.

"You must taste this," he murmured, closing his eyes.

"May I?" she asked, lacing enough of a sensuous tone in with her question to flatter him appropriately. "Oh, you are making that look so good . . ."

"I told you to live a little," he chuckled, overtly pleased as she took a piece of his fish and brought it to her mouth.

"Oh . . . my . . . ," she murmured, chewing the succulent meat and swallowing it with theatrical flair. She set down her fork, waiting for his next move. This was where one had to make careful, gingerly strategic advances. "Grilled in butter with a bit of pesto . . . If I ate like that every day, I would have to work out for two hours in the gym to get the pounds off of me. How do you keep so fit, Donald, when you're on the circuit more than I?" She just wondered why, when men used these tactics, they were considered charismatic, but there was a different name for women who employed the disarming device called charm.

Donald Haines smiled and retrieved his plate, appearing highly satisfied. "Good genetics," he said, taking a healthy mouthful of food. "But that's what I like about you, Laura. You have discipline."

She took a bite of salad and chewed it slowly. Discipline, huh? He had no idea.

"So, have you had a chance to give any thought to what we discussed at the fund-raiser?" Donald Haines hadn't looked up at her as he'd asked the question, but they were indeed beginning their real conversation.

She nodded and took a sip of water. "I have."

He stared at her, his smile broadening. Taking up his napkin, he wiped his mouth, and then pushed back in his chair.

"Microenterprise," she stated carefully. "I know it has been tried as a basic campaign platform before, but never with the economy in such terrible shape. Before, people from the community had more job options; today they don't. The blighted areas are increasingly vulnerable to rising crime, which, as we've learned, does not stay contained within those areas. It spills over and creates a toxic environment for the entire region."

Donald Haines nodded. "We've known that for a long time. Your plan?"

She studied the sunlight as it bounced off the facets of her glass, and took a sip of effervescent water, then held his gaze. "As we'd discussed, we have to do something that will resonate with the people, and that will also kill many birds with one stone."

He leaned forward, making a tent with his fingers, bringing his lips to them.

"In concert with the current blight-abatement efforts, but taking it to the next level. The voters are already softened up to the concept, so it won't be a hard sell, and time is of the essence. We have to utilize the most logical candidate still in the running, but put a more community-recognized team behind him. Politically it would be wise to take some of the abandoned factories and convert them into manufacturing facilities and/or warehouses for basic household goods. Things like soap, toilet paper . . . and to keep our rural and suburban legislators calm, we can link to local farms to bring in produce, but also teach people in the community basic business skills at the same time."

Laura studied Donald Haines as she spoke. He'd not moved a muscle in his face, so she pressed on. "When we get our man in, we might even induce a few manufacturers to lend money to a few plant managers to help set up operations—and for those things that would be too costly to manufacture, we could work distribution deals for smaller stores to collectively purchase the items they need; then we'd warehouse the bulk order, break it down into individual components, and distribute inventory to the tiny corner stores. . . . This allows small stores to get the economies of scale that only big supermarket chains now enjoy. They wouldn't have to gouge the community to keep their lights on, or sell shoddy goods. Bottom line is, we keep a broad base of the constituency happy in all districts through letting key contracts that would accomplish this aim."

She kept her eyes on Haines's, as well as on his unreadable expression. "Think of it this way. You'll have an educational and apprenticeship component. You'll have a job creation component: manufacturing, or even warehouses and distribution facilities, which require labor, jobs. Plus, you'll have a blight abatement component—without having to tax the corporations to absorb the low-skilled workers that they frankly have no room for at the inns. We clean up some corner storefronts that have been dilapidated and abandoned for years, create more jobs through those healthy enterprises, and absorb all the trucks and vehicles that have been confiscated due to criminal activity. We simply recycle what we already have. The mom-and-pop corner stores get low-interest loans—as long as the owners agree to hire people from, and that *live* within, the community where they have their stores. Add the Internet for free local deliveries on a demand system, and all of a sudden you have a revitalized inner city zone."

Donald Haines's eyes never left her face as he slowly nodded and then abruptly sat back again. "I'm going to play devil's advocate, though."

"Shoot."

"Let's say we were able to get a few buildings donated—I take it that is what you are proposing as a part of the post-election contracts and programs?"

She smiled and began picking at her salad again.

"All right," Haines said, his tone even and noncommittal. "Say we open a specialty manufacturing process or distribution center–warehouse in each one of these reclaimed facilities. Who does student recruitment; who teaches the classes; who develops the curriculum?"

"That's the beauty of this," she said, placing her fork down and dabbing her mouth with her napkin. "Remember, you asked me to deliver the network of groups that have already been working hard in the trenches, correct?"

"Yes . . . ," he said, hesitating.

"The microenterprise community is already a solid but hidden infrastructure in the city. Give them the contracts."

"Then why haven't more viable businesses been formed, if they are, as you say, already solid?"

Bull's-eye. She had him. The energy of a near victory swept through her, but her exterior remained calm. Laura paced herself. "For the same reason we are having lunch right now."

She allowed a well-timed pause to slip between them. He leaned forward. She leaned forward. She pressed on.

"Because of two very important reasons, Donald. One being, once these people are trained in how to start up a business, they cannot get access to the larger contracts that would capitalize and sustain their businesses. They can't get the freaking contracts, because Price's crew gets all the cream off the top. Not to mention, the second reason is, the banks have a horrendous record in lending to inner city, minority small businesses. Most of these folks get taken to the hoop by predatory credit-card-type lenders at three times the prime interest rate—if they can get a loan to start up at all. Those who manage to open, and try to get a decent contract . . . Donald, you and I both know those opportunities are all locked up by a few well-connected people. Therefore, the microbusinesses are always undercapitalized from the door. It's a cyclical problem that leads to bad credit, which makes them unbankable, which means they can't get access to capital, which means they don't fit the parameters to handle larger contracts—then we're back to square one."

"I'm aware of that," he admitted, relaxing and hailing the server for coffee. "But how does what you propose change that aspect? The dilemma would be the same."

"Not necessarily. I'm talking about shared resources."

"Interesting."

"Very," she said, almost unable to contain herself. "Imagine if PIDC or the Redevelopment Authority granted physical plant and equipment to this effort—then smaller manufacturers could rent space from the incubator-type nonprofits to use their manufacturing lines or their warehouse space. No one small business can afford the equipment, the trucks, or the space, but many small businesses could literally time-share. The existing incubators that are begging for dollars could get a cut to have classes in each section of the community—they already have clients, instructors, curriculum, and what they don't have could be developed for them through a portion of the twelve-point-five that had been slated for Darien Price to manage. This hits every neighborhood and would keep multiple constituencies at bay, while rewarding those agencies that have already worked in the trenches for years. Not to mention, the corporations wouldn't have to be pressured to hire people who do not possess the skills. Think massive co-op."

Donald Haines was nodding in earnest now. "That's theoretically brilliant. But the distribution problem—the contracts . . . These small businesses still wouldn't necessarily be in a position to compete for large contracts."

"It's a volume-versus-capacity issue, and not a problem if people are making basic necessities and selling them in their own neighborhoods—that's why I need the boarded-up corner stores . . . at least a critical mass of them. They don't need huge contracts if they can be self-sustaining at the core, neighborhood level. Condemn those rotting storefronts so we can wrest them from absentee landlords, who don't vote in our districts anyway, who aren't even in the state any longer, and then tie the buildings to a very low interest, patient-capital loan program."

"Patient capital? We already have small-business loan programs, don't we?"

"They don't work, Donald." Laura stared at him hard, her voice firm. "And I'm going to tell you why."

He waited, riveted to her every word.

"Because a small business needs six to nine months of amnesty to build a client base—time to work the kinks out of their operations before having to begin loan payments. *That's* patient capital. Plus, people in the most need cannot afford high interest—that's how they get caught up in a web of predatory lending or get shut out. Ten percent interest rates or more in today's banking climate is high. And starting out with bad credit means the likelihood of them getting a loan from a bank, even with a Small Business Administration loan guarantee backing it up, is slim."

Laura opened her hands and held them up on the table, as though about to launch into prayer. "Donald, let me take five million dollars and put it into a patient-capital fund. We'll cherry-pick the agency with a good record to manage the revolving fund. Let me network the existing microenterprise community around a multifaceted, multiproduct manufacturing, distribution, and sales curriculum—a collective purchasing approach. . . . Let me get in *real* curriculum developers instead of bogus ones trying to make a buck on other people's miseducation. Let me turn a few old factories that you guys don't have plans for the next twenty years to utilize, and give me storefronts in neighborhoods where only the fearless tread, and I can guarantee you that every local elected official, every community resident, every so-called grass-roots organizer will stand up and cheer. *That's* what we send our candidate into the streets to tout!"

When he didn't interrupt her, she dipped her voice low, her eyes unblinking, telling him the gospel truth. "We have to do something that will erase this Price travesty from the memories of those affected by it, and we have to do something flashier and bigger than what any current single program is chartered to do."

Donald Haines sent his gaze out the widow, past the expanse of sparscly populated tables in the room. "You think something like this will expunge this recent fiasco?"

Laura waited for his gaze to return to hers, and she held it with a serious expression. "In the face of what is happening with Philadelphia's economic landscape and this Price fiasco, there is no other way. I was up all night with this and made a few grass-roots inquiries—and I can also promise you that Price isn't the only one in his little circle who's dirty. Where there's smoke, there's fire, so make a decision to get your people out of the building now, Donald. The more serious players are gonna get burned, otherwise."

Donald Haines sat back and rubbed his palm over his face and then raked his fingers through his graying blond hair. Laura's fervent plea had been so intense that even the server hesitated until she sat back in her chair before he brought a round of coffee to their table.

"This will turn the city on its head," he said quietly, sipping his coffee from the thin porcelain cup and setting it down very carefully in the saucer. "But it is holistic, integrated, and absolutely brilliant."

"The corporations can no longer be held solely responsible for job creation. One cannot get blood from a stone, and they simply don't have the capacity like they did in the good old days." Laura let the comment weigh in on its own merit for effect, her emphasis on *the good ole days* for Haines's sake. They both understood what she meant.

"Small businesses," she said, resuming her explanation, "especially community-based ones, generally employ people from the neighborhoods. The legislators will love it. The people will love it. The governor will love it. Bottom line is, the community will embrace it—and the existing, real working agencies won't have to battle as hard amongst themselves for funding. Your new candidate will come out smelling like a rose."

She smiled as a wry smile came out on his face to meet hers. What he didn't see was how much it annoyed her that funding of nonprofits was as much about politics as it was about the worthy causes they upheld—and too often those organizations most deserving couldn't sit at a table like this to bargain for a piece of the pie.

"Donald, trust me on this," she said forcefully, refusing to allow her internal outrage to interject itself into the delicate negotiations. Laura sat back and cradled her coffee cup in her hands, peering over the top of it as she took another sip. "C'mon, Don. All I need is a few buildings."

For the first time since she'd begun her intense appeal, he laughed.

"Oh, all you need is a few buildings to go along with twelve and a half mil." He shook his head. "Just like a woman—you want the house, too."

She was in. He'd gotten comfortable enough to be politically incorrect in her presence.

"Just like a woman," she repeated, cooing the phrase while

raising her cup to him to make him know that no offense had been taken and that they were on the same team. "Can you do it?"

He seemed briefly offended by her challenge. It made her chuckle.

"Can I do it? If I couldn't, you and I wouldn't be having lunch."

"Touché," she said, and chuckled more deeply. Laura set her coffee cup down, then glanced up at him. "Well?"

"Anything is possible in America."

"Then?" *Make it so, Number One*, her mind screamed, but she remained cool.

"But, some of those factories are in dire condition, Laura. In fact, many are asbestos laden, aren't up to code, are in brown fields, and would need new equipment—see, hon, it's not just buying the house; it's the maintenance, the retrofitting, the—"

"And wouldn't your friends in construction just love to do the asbestos removal, the retrofitting . . . while, of course, breaking off a little bit of their huge contracts for some up-and-coming minority subcontractors—as, perhaps, mentors? And I'm sure that some of those big, failing corporations would love to have a high-profile project to donate equipment to for immediate tax relief and community goodwill, right? Those buildings are in Keystone Opportunity Zones and Empowerment Zones, if I'm not mistaken. And, without a mortgage or building renovation loan to quibble about paying, the rents from the nonprofits, as well as the manufacturing and warehouse tenants, might just cover maintenance, utilities, upkeep . . . Where there's a will, there's always a way."

"Laura Caldwell, you drive a hard bargain." Donald Haines shook his head and motioned for the check. "I'm watching twelve and a half mil just get expanded to nearly a hundred mil in real estate add-ons, lady. This had better work."

"No pain, no gain."

"Ouch," he said, laughing, signing his club tab. "I definitely feel the pain. We were thinking more like twenty-five to fifty mil, after the election, to bolster Price's program while our candidate lived out his term in office, but . . ."

"Oh, it's not that bad—just a few old buildings. Everybody could win; everybody could play—all except the few annoying individuals who got us here in the first place. Consider it the uplift cost of a total regime change." She'd spoken sweetly, in a way that totally defused Haines and made him laugh harder. They both knew what she was doing.

"They would indeed love it. Let me see what I can do. You're a dangerous woman, Laura Caldwell."

"Absolutely, and I make no apologies."

She was on a roll. Her feet hit the pavement with force as she strode down Fourth and Chestnut Street, her silk duster flapping in the wind behind her. The senator was next.

Laura pushed through the brass-and-glass revolving doors of the Omni Hotel, her heels sending an echo bouncing from the pink and gray marble floors. The hostess simply nodded, because Laura had passed the woman too quickly for her to rattle off a professional greeting spiel.

Forcing herself not to take the taupe-carpeted stairs two at a time, Laura held on to the brass rail of the winding staircase as she made her way to the Azalea Room. At the podium, the maître d' began walking alongside her, ushering her to the waiting dignitary who had obviously left her description.

"Please don't stand up," Laura said breathlessly. "My apologies for being ten minutes late, Senator. I got tied up in traffic on I-76."

"No problem, Ms. Caldwell. I needed to return a few calls and take a moment in my day to catch my breath. Please, relax and have something to drink."

The aged African-American gentleman rose anyway as the maître d' helped Laura into a chair. A broad grin appeared on his handsome mahogany-hued face, and his dashing porcelain smile flashed bright enough to almost make the silver in his dark, wavy hair seem to sparkle. He straightened his red and navy paisley silk tie and opened a button on his immaculately tailored navy blue suit, then extended his hand for her to shake across the table. She took his hand, noting his heavy cufflinks, expensive watch, and tie bar. He certainly wore old black money well.

Wired from too many cups of coffee, she smiled and gave the server an order for iced tea. But her mind raced. If the senator was making a house call, then the elite must really be running scared. Perfect. She wanted to laugh but didn't.

"Have you had lunch?"

The senator's voice sounded so sincere. A true politician always oozed smooth credibility.

"No," she lied. "Just a quick bite this morning."

"Then shall we?" Senator Scott asked, studying her with a warm smile.

"I'd like that," she replied, calming herself and now moving more slowly.

"Their seafood pastas are fabulous," he offered in an eloquent tone.

"I'm going to have to defer to a salad," she said with a wry grin. Lord have mercy! She still had drinks, a gallery opening with food, and a soul food dinner before the day was over. Tomorrow she'd have to begin the whole tour of duty again with the second-tier players.

"I can't tempt you?"

"No," she chuckled, ignoring the innuendo in his statement and hoping to relax him enough to get quickly to the point of the meeting. "But, please, sir, you have to have something more substantial. I'm sure your day is much more rigorous than mine."

"Yes, well, if you insist. But do know that it's not very often that I get to enjoy a hot meal in such lovely company. So I will order, then eat slowly, and digest my food for once . . . savoring my guest in the process."

All the men on the circuit were a trip. Old players, young players, it didn't matter—men at the top had definitely missed the cue to be politically correct. Laura offered him her most engaging smile but declined comment. She waited and made a tent with her fingers as the server took their orders. There would be a different rhythm to this dance. Her head was spinning. As soon as the server left them, Senator Scott leaned forward, causing her to do the same.

"I've heard a lot of good things about you and your firm, the integrity with which you handle all your grant clients—which is why I wanted to personally meet with you."

"Thank you," she said in a quiet voice, looking down at the napkin in her lap. "Senator, I'm honored." Laura let her breath out slowly. What a crock. They both knew who his niece was. Okay, so let the games begin.

"There are unfortunate events that have taken place recently . . . no doubt, you've been following the headlines?"

Laura nodded and kept a poker face. "Very unfortunate."

"But we must not throw the baby out with the bathwater. There are several key players who may have been near the explosion but who shouldn't have to suffer from the blast."

Again she nodded, and dropped her voice discreetly. "Sir, innocent people should never have to suffer. I agree one hundred percent." It was true what she'd said. Innocent people shouldn't have to suffer. Her tone seemed to soothe him, and he nodded, sitting back in his chair. But what she didn't say was that his niece, Monica *Scott* Price, wasn't necessarily innocent, nor was the senator's son, Howard Scott Jr. But it was obvious that he was stepping away from Darien. Excellent.

"Thank you," he murmured, misreading her statement as an endorsement of his niece and son. "I'm glad we understand each other."

Laura looked down as the server set her salad plate before her and attended to the senator. Oh, hell, yes, she understood him.

"If there is a changing of the guard, and if new post-election programming gets put in place . . . it is imperative that we have reputable African-American firms with long-standing history to help shape the future—to ensure that a viable succession plan is cultivated."

Laura absently munched on her salad as he twirled his pasta around his fork. He was now speaking to her in coded legislative double-talk—but she knew that language well, too. She glanced around the lavish hotel dining room, drinking in the muted mauve, gray, and gold tones. The Scott family had been living like this for generations; she was the first in her entire line to get here, and not without an uphill climb. She took a sip of her iced tea, softened her smile, and leaned forward, promising him nothing and everything at the same time.

"Senator, she murmured, "rest assured, if I am asked to assist in the shaping of new programs, I will do everything in my power to keep a historical perspective."

He could take that to the bank.

"Monica, how are you?" Laura asked, clicking off her cell phone and stashing it in her purse while receiving an air kiss from the nervous socialite. She'd returned five calls while walking down Walnut Street and had expected Monica to be late. The fact that she'd been early wasn't lost on Laura. They both knew that if Monica weren't desperate for something, she would have kept Laura waiting.

"I wish I could say fine," Monica replied quietly as they parted from their civil embrace. Darien's wife's expression was strained, and she nervously glanced around at the wrought-iron seating in Rouge's swanky open-air café on Rittenhouse Square. "Even though it's still nice out, mind if we get an inside table?"

"Not at all. In fact, if Rouge is too open, we can walk up the block to the Sheraton, where it's more private. We could even go into the Rittenhouse for tea . . . or maybe over to Opus?"

For a moment Monica Price paused and tossed her long

auburn hair over her shoulder. "No. This is fine, I suppose. It doesn't get really crowded until after five." Then she quickly turned on her heel and ducked inside the restaurant.

Laura followed Monica to the wood-paneled bar area and hailed the hostess for a table close to the back wall, out of street view. Despite the brisk fall day, the fourteen-block walk from the Omni to Rittenhouse Square had warmed her, and she needed to sit down.

Monica immediately sank into a leather chair, the roller balls on it moving as she flopped in it. She set down her Burberry plaid purse and adjusted the jacket of her beige pantsuit that seemed to blend into her caramel skin. Her normally lithe figure was practically swamped in the loose-fitting Ellen Tracy suit; it was obvious that Monica had lost weight due to stress. Tension lines creased the corners of her wide, fawn-colored eyes. All vibrancy that Laura had been accustomed to seeing within the woman was gone.

Waning natural light danced off Monica's heavy tennis bracelet, each diamond reflecting back the orange, gold, and rose colors of the setting sun and the dim lights within the establishment. But a four-karat square-cut engagement ring and wedding band ensemble paled before the exquisite bracelet as well as her alligator-set Lenox watch that matched her outlawed-for-fashion-species boots. Laura watched the woman play with her wedding ring.

Laura put down her purse slowly and stared at the harried but beautiful woman before her. A brief pang of sadness claimed her. If she didn't know better, she'd swear that Monica had just left Toppers Day Spa. Her makeup was flawless, her hair perfect, her teeth made perfect by attention and expensive orthodontic work . . . How many generations of men doing backroom deals had enabled women like Monica to roll like this? Laura wondered. Darien Price had obviously married well. But the look in Monica's eyes said it all. Life with him was a bitch.

"Would you like a cup of coffee?" Laura offered, not sure where to begin.

Monica shook her head and hailed the waitress. "A Dewar's, straight." She glanced at Laura, "C'mon, girl. It's been way too long, and we need to talk."

Laura smiled. "A chardonnay." She shrugged as the waitress left them. "I still have a dinner and an engagement, tonight. Gotta stay sharp." Now they were supposed to be girls, huh? Very deep.

"I hear you," Monica sighed. "But let me get right to the point." She leaned in and glanced around the room at the few early male patrons who'd gathered. Satisfied that they weren't eavesdropping on her conversation, Monica closed her eyes. "Listen, you and I both know that Darien is out of his black mind."

Taken aback, all Laura could do was stare at the woman. She had *not* expected that. She accepted her glass of wine from the waitress without even looking at her; Laura kept her eyes on Monica Price.

"I have two children," Monica said in an urgent tone under her breath. "You and I may have had our philosophical differences in terms of programming and grant money distribution, but woman to woman, however this shakes out, I want to be sure you have room for my media consulting firm at the table after the elections."

Laura took a very careful sip of her wine. Things were definitely getting interesting. It was amazing how becoming the anointed gatekeeper to resources suddenly made everyone your best friend. She and Monica Price only played the circuit together as civil competitors. They'd never been *girls*. It wasn't even like that between them, but then again, desperation changed a lot of things. Laura chose her words with great care.

"If, and I say *if,* these moneys don't get snatched away to vanish into a political black hole again, the table is going to be very large—large enough for a lot of players to sit around it. Why are you worried all of a sudden?" Laura had designed her response to be noncommittal; she wasn't promising any of the old guard anything. All she would guarantee was that she'd hear them out.

Monica glanced around again, leaning closer, and she took a liberal sip of Scotch from her glass, rolling the short crystal tumbler between her palms. "Because Michael Paxton is my husband's attorney."

Laura became very, very still. "I don't understand." But a silent understanding had definitely passed between both women. It was in Monica's eyes; the deep hurt and fear was unmistakable in them. Oddly enough, trust also dawned in them, which made Laura extremely uncomfortable.

"That bastard would do his own mother," Monica hissed, "and I just want to be sure that none of this comes back on me. I could kill Darien for this stupid shit."

Pieces of the puzzle began to fall into place. Both women held each other's line of vision. Something akin to guilt stabbed at Laura. All she'd wanted to do was get the attorney distracted or neutered in order to leave Darien wide open and more vulnerable, but now they were trying to pin the whole scam on the wife? Very fucked up and very male.

"You think he'd try to implicate you to take the heat off of Darien?" Laura was incredulous.

Monica sat back in her chair and let her breath out hard. "In a word, yes."

There was something about the way Monica's gaze suddenly slid away that alerted Laura's senses. This was definitely a high-stakes game of chess, not simple poker, as she'd first imagined. Laura took a risk, pushing a pawn out in the open to be captured by a queen—to expose a hidden but valuable bishop, just to be sure which game was being played. "I take it that the affair ended ugly?"

"Very," Monica said in a quiet voice. "They're brothers . . . and Paxton laughed in my face."

"Godbrothers?"

"No. Half brothers . . . *between me and you.*" Monica

stared at Laura with a plea in her eyes. Monica took a hard sip from her glass. "Darien doesn't even know."

Laura almost spit out her wine. Oh, yeah, this was beyond poker. The plan had definitely worked, but this new tidbit of information dramatically changed the playing field.

Monica's hands shook slightly as she brought the deep amber-colored liquor to her lips again. She swallowed another hard sip of it and set the glass down with precision. "After it was too late . . . I found out Michael only wanted me because his father and Darien's mother . . . It's sick," she murmured into her glass, sounding bitter as she hailed the waitress again for another round. "Old man Price never knew, but Mike did. Has been jealous of Darien, and the attention old man Paxton lavished on my husband, for years. We women have to stick together. I'm not getting eliminated from the game by either one of them. I deserve postelection contracts, just like they do, and I'm not letting whatever happened with Michael and me affect the rest of my life with a shitty divorce settlement or public disgrace."

"But Paxton is your husband's attorney, girl," Laura whispered. "Why him, of all people?" She waited, letting the secret question hover between them as Monica fidgeted with a wisp of hair. It almost seemed criminal to ask, but she had to know how long this had been going on.

"I'd had enough; he's cheated on me for years, and this time I needed to finally let Darien know just how much bullshit like this hurts. I got a nasty little phone-mail gift from one of his hoochies, intended for her girlfriend, sent from his phone yesterday—can you believe it? A fucking photo of him laid up at the Four Seasons."

Laura's eyes widened. That crazy-ass Najira! Oh, my God. Najira's antics had set off a veritable chain reaction. A potentially nuclear one. Problem was, she didn't know how to defuse this bomb.

"I can't even go into how I felt," Monica went on, "But rest assured, when Mike came over to talk to me about everything that was going on after the Hyatt event, I seized the opportunity. I actually thought that maybe there was even a future; Mike isn't attached and . . . forget all that part. It was stupid to even dream that way. I'm just waiting for the right time to cut Darien's heart out with this." She lifted her glass to Laura. "Hell hath no fury like a woman scorned, right, girl?"

Again Laura had to fight to keep from spitting out her wine. *Dayum.* No wonder the good Senator Scott had made a personal appeal. She kept her expression as rigid as stone and only nodded. What was there to say? This was collateral damage, a civilian caught in the conflict. Remorse filled her.

But it was still war.

Chapter 9

By five-thirty p.m., traffic was moving like molasses. Stuck in gridlock, Laura impatiently peered out the window of the yellow cab. She had to rethink her strategy. Even the old Mafia boys had rules; there was a code of honor among thieves. Their new syndicate had changed the way things were handled, the way justice was meted out, just as the new guard did things sloppily. Price and his boys were sloppy. Women and children used to be exempt from the equation, but it was obvious that Price would sacrifice Monica to save his own sorry hide—so would Paxton.

There was no grace, no class, no structure to their hits. The old guard would never have stood for such things. As much as she hated what the old black guard had done to her father, and abhorred the repercussions it had on her mother, still . . . they hadn't directly gone after her mother. That stood for something, as small a thing as it was.

The instant Monica had confessed and asked for absolution, woman to woman, Laura had decided that she was definitely old-school. What the hell. A few crumbs wouldn't kill anybody, and Monica was just a woman with children, caught up in the web of a man's bullshit. Pity. But damn, Paxton was a slimy bastard . . . doing, then setting up, his own brother's wife? She could only shake her head.

Hemmed in by traffic, the cab crept down North Third Street, past trendy boutiques, so slowly that Laura simply thrust money in the driver's hand and got out. Her nerves couldn't take it. The confinement was making her nuts, and she was glad that she'd left her car at the office. If she'd had to drive in this insanity, she would have lost her mind.

Eventually she resigned herself to the fact that she could walk faster than the flow of traffic. Fine. She needed the brisk evening air to slap against her face at this point. Jesus in heaven, what was going on behind closed doors in this town? Darien Price wasn't really a Price but an illegitimate Paxton?

She walked hard, her strides long. After a few blocks, the aerobic action helped dissipate the adrenaline in her system. First thing in the morning, she had to get to the bank. All she had to do was get through small talk at the gallery opening Brad Crawford was hosting, then set up the chessboard with the cop.

Zigzagging past the narrow Quaker-built three-story, red-brick structures that had been turned into eclectic, high-end shops, she headed toward Brad Crawford's chic African-American art gallery located in the Olde City section. Entourage was now the new place to be seen. The wind at her back hurried her along, making it imperative to dodge slower pedestrians. She knew she was getting close as well-dressed couples strolled in the same direction she was walking. A brightly lit plate-glass window was her destination, and it was only a few yards away. Women wearing furs mingled with shivering tie-dyed-shirt-clad artists, vintage-fashion divas, and executives still in their business suits outside the gallery entrance, making her know she'd found the right address.

She spoke pleasantly and gathered her calm about her as she made her way inside the white-walled space and stepped toward the guest book at the front. Impressively framed watercolors splashed the walls flanked by heavy carved sculptures from the motherland. Laura glanced around at the wood floors, exposed brick, wrought-iron spiral staircase, Brie cheese platters overflowing with exotic star fruits, black grapes, white raspberries, strawberries, and kiwi . . . wine, the mellow jazz of Miles Davis—yeah, this was the place.

She briefly paused to sign the guest register, accepting a miniature bottle of spring water from a young woman wearing total black, who by all accounts looked like Morticia from the Addams family. Laura's head hurt.

"Darling, so glad you could make it," Brad Crawford intoned, taking Laura by the elbow. "I know it was short notice, but you had to be here for this media event."

Laura glanced around. No media present yet. Hmmm . . . "Brad, you know I wouldn't have missed this for the world," she said with a pasted-on smile as she gave him an air kiss. If her host were standing still long enough, Brad would have blended right in with the podium-displayed sculptures. "Handsome" did not begin to describe Brad Crawford. Tall, angular, with a ruddy-brown complexion as smooth as a baby's butt, chiseled Ethiopian features with intense black eyes, a shock of silver streaks through his hair.

When he beamed at her, Laura pressed on. "This place is absolutely gorgeous. The pieces you have on display are fabulous, and what you've done with the lighting is sheer genius." That part of what she'd said to him was true. He'd turned a hole-in-the-wall into something spectacular, but having resources to gut the joint had helped.

He preened at her compliment and kissed her cheek. "Everybody who is anybody is here, love. Come meet some of the more important people."

Weary beyond his imagination, Laura made herself ready to cope with another round of social politics as she followed him deeper into the bowels of the establishment, noting the truly exquisite pieces he had on the walls. As they walked, she studied Brad's elegance as though he were a piece of art, framed in a royal blue silk bandit-collar shirt, closed at the throat with an onyx stud, and expensively casual pleated pants, finished off with slip-on crocodile loafers. Laura shook her head as she threaded her way through the gallery behind him. He had an hour and a half, tops, to make his pitch to her, and then she was out.

"There's somebody who's dying to connect with you," Brad said over his shoulder, both he and Laura stopping intermittently along the way to greet people they knew.

Who could be *dying* to meet her that she hadn't already called or returned a phone call to? She stayed in close range to Brad, understanding that there was a back room, a section of the gallery somewhere, that the black power brokers were gathering. They came early and would probably leave before the heavier thicket of after-work crowd and the media arrived. If she was lucky, she might be able to dispense a few platitudes, make a few dates for diplomatically necessary lunches, and then get out of there within an hour—forget an hour *and* a half.

But the moment she entered the open atrium indoor garden, she froze. In the middle of a huddle of dark suits, Michael Paxton stood. Crawford went to him as though fetching him to come out and play. *Oh . . . shit.*

Laura regained her composure, smiled, nodded, and opened her bottle of water. Here we go.

Michael Paxton excused himself from the small circle of guests around him, walking beside Brad Crawford in Laura's direction. She inwardly cringed but kept her facial expression pleasant.

"And so we meet again," she said before he could get off an opening salvo.

He chuckled. Brad Crawford looked confused.

"I thought you two hadn't formally met?" Crawford said in an apologetic tone.

"Oh, we've only met—briefly," Laura corrected, touching Brad's arm to convey that the mistake wasn't a social faux pas.

"She's just a hard lady to pin down," Paxton said, looking her over with amusement in his eyes. "I've been trying to coax her out to a lunch, a brunch, a dinner, drinks, you name it, but her secretary keeps putting me on hold."

Brad held up his hand and laughed. "I'm not in it."

"What are you doing after this event?" Paxton pressed. "Surely you'll allow me to buy you a drink."

"I have a commitment, but thank you just the same."

"Then dinner tomorrow?"

Brad began fidgeting and sent his gaze around the room toward newly arriving guests. Seeing a patron-of-the-arts couple, he begged out of the conversation with grace. "I'll be just a moment. Let me get a few people settled in, and then I'll rejoin you. Pardon." He paced away so fast that he nearly left a blue blur in his wake.

Laura laughed and shook her head no to Paxton's earlier request, mentally riffling through her calendar. "I have a previously arranged dinner engagement tomorrow."

Paxton tilted his head to the side, his smile widening. "I know Jim Thompson won't mind if we switch. Let's walk over and ask him—he's right over there," Paxton said, motioning to a threesome of executives. "Give him my Friday slot at eleven, and let me take you to the Garden tomorrow night."

Laura felt her jaw go slack for a moment. *Brass fucking balls.* But she had to admit that she liked his direct style of open confrontation. He chuckled. She laughed hard now. This day had gone so wild for her that laughter was like opening a pressure valve.

"That won't be necessary," she said, regaining her composure.

"Laura, I can save you two weeks of breakfasts, lunches, dinners, and galas that you don't want to attend, with one pivotal dinner. They're all jockeying for position, but if they know you and I are meeting, they'll trust that their interests will at least be considered."

Although she hadn't stopped smiling, what he'd said to

her was profound. And she'd thought he was a tertiary player—Price being the man on the throne. That changed everything. Laura regrouped quickly, setting a new strategy in motion.

"All right. Sounds like an offer I can't refuse."

"It isn't," Paxton said quietly, moving closer to her.

The look she read in his eyes had nothing to do with business.

"Then you'll have to get Thompson to call and cancel. I generally keep my commitments, unless something truly compelling presents itself." She gave him a sly glance and took a sip from her bottle of water.

Paxton chuckled low in his throat and walked away from her toward Jim Thompson. To her horror, Paxton returned with five men. Five, tall, fine, athletic-looking brothers, each corporate clean-shaven, with practically the same outfit on as though their business suits and silk ties were prep school uniforms, their faces representing every shade of brown from honey-colored to smooth, black ebony. Damn, what a waste of excellent DNA. Too bad they were all game players and not on the up-and-up. Sad. Laura sipped her water, thinking of Najira's preserved specimen from one of them in a Zip-Loc bag.

"Don Edward, from the Scott-Edward Foundation, and CEO of Curriculum Developers, Inc.," Michael Paxton said with a droll smile. "Jim Thompson, who has a conflict tomorrow night but is available to meet with you on Friday at eleven. Jim is the CEO of Urban Facilities Management, Inc. You might already know Martin Ramsey, CEO of Ramsey Consulting, as he does the consulting circuit with you. Howard Scott, son of our own Senator Scott, and CEO of Scott Foods and Beverages, Inc. And you know Brad Crawford, with his tie to the arts and his media firm, Showcasers, Inc.—he and Howard's cousin, Monica, do much of the media placement and events in the city."

"Small world." Laura nodded and shook the hands that thrust out toward hers, heartily shaking them while simmering inside. She knew what Paxton was doing—the introductions were to put her in her place as a rank beneath him and to let her know who would be best suited for whatever access she had to postelection contract moneys. Not to mention she was still salty about the way he'd preempted a dinner on her calendar.

"Definitely," Martin Ramsey said, his unconcealed appraisal of her bordering on being unprofessional.

She smiled. "It is a pleasure to meet you gentlemen in a relaxed, nonbusiness setting. Normally we're all so pressed for time, or mingling with clients, that it's difficult to connect like this." She cut a glance at Paxton, wanting to slap the triumphant expression off his face. "Thank you for the wonderful introductions, Michael," she said as civilly as possible.

"The pleasure is all ours," Jim Thompson said, gaining a cheerful round of agreement from the other men in the huddle.

"We have to get you on a dais panel down at the African American Chamber of Commerce during Minority Enterprise Development Week. It would be good to bring you out then so the players, as well as the community folks, get to know there's a new lady sheriff in town." Don Edward grinned as he glanced at the nodding members of their tight circle.

So now they were gonna put her on the dog-and-pony-show circuit? This was madness, but she smiled and gave them a discreet bow and took on her more professional tone to let Paxton know she was piqued. "Gentlemen, I would be honored to do a panel on minority- and women-owned enterprises."

"I see everyone has met and is comfortable," Brad Crawford crooned, rejoining the group. "Wonderful."

Martin Ramsey shot a careful glance toward Paxton. "So, Ms. Caldwell, Mike tells us that you may be the new gatekeeper."

"Laura," she said, correcting him without answering his question. "Please."

"Laura it is, then," Ramsey said, his smile broadening in

his dark ebony face. "You will definitely have to let me get on your calendar, even though Mike here is bumping appointments to get to you first."

"Done," she remarked coolly, still not answering what he really wanted to know.

Paxton bristled. Good. It didn't matter whether Martin Ramsey's direct question or the insistence on a private meeting had set him off, or whether it was the lustful look Ramsey had given her. Whatever.

"May I steal Laura?" Paxton said, his tone a dismissal, not a request.

"Absolutely," Howard Scott said. "She's in good hands."

Just as quickly as the power circle convened, it leisurely disbanded. Laura watched these masters of illusion melt into the crowd effortlessly, their civil choreography impeccable.

"So, you've formally met everyone and know what their firms have at stake. Are we on for dinner at the Garden tomorrow night at six sharp?"

For a moment she just stared at Paxton. Yeah, she'd briefly met all these guys on the circuit before, one way or another, but they'd never truly acknowledged her until now. But the gall . . .

"You'll get used to it. All of this can be a bit overwhelming at first blush, but we do have a number of realignments to lock down quickly. Business before pleasure."

Again there were no words—at least none acceptable in polite company came to her mind.

"I suppose dinner at six will be fine," she said grudgingly. "But tell me, do you always make such presumptuous moves?"

"When the opportunity allows," he said with a lopsided smile.

"Interesting. I guess I should be honored, as I noticed there weren't any women in your power circle that I needed to meet."

He stepped in closer, the scent of Lagerfeld cologne now wafting toward her. "There's a few still around, and we can discuss the who's who further at dinner."

"But none worth casual mention now, huh?" She needed air and started to walk away. The bullshit in the gallery was too thick around her.

"You remember what happened with First People's Bank?"

Laura went still. Who didn't remember what had happened to Earline Thompson Crawford, the first female CEO of Philadelphia's only black-owned bank?

"She was one of us, by marriage, and got flagrant with her behavior. Certain improprieties happened; she didn't align her politics correctly . . . she couldn't be protected. She had a brief and glorious ascent to the top; now she's back to consulting and scrambling for contracts."

Laura stared at the man before her. Flashes of history etched themselves into her mind. The community came out, rallied, and believed, and put their crumpled-up dollar bills into the first black-owned bank this major city ever knew. The people had been so proud . . . and Earline had gotten carried away, did things that only the white boys could get away with, and she'd been left exposed. Laura knew that a part of it was the sister's own fault—unchecked power could pollute any organism. But she was well aware that another part of the fault lay with the hidden trust; they'd been doing business like that for years. Earline mistakenly thought she could, too. Had hired family that hadn't been properly anointed by the power circle into jobs they hadn't the skills or background for, used operating funds for personal perks—did it all and left no stone unturned. Laura sighed. In the end the people in the community were disappointed, humiliated, and their trust again was betrayed.

"Tragic," she finally muttered, understanding the implicit threat within Paxton's little parable.

"That's why we need to have dinner. You're about to ascend quickly to where the air is rare. If you're not used to the altitude, you could get disoriented and fall fast. Now, *that* would be tragic."

Laura forced a smile. So he was bold enough to threaten her openly. Okay. Then, it was on. New target.

"It would be," she replied in a falsely submissive tone. "I'll see you tomorrow at six." She glanced at her watch. "I will have to excuse myself, though. I have another engagement."

"I'm looking forward to tomorrow night."

Laura couldn't get out of the gallery fast enough. Every time she had to stop and beg off conversation, citing another meeting, she inwardly cringed. There was something about Paxton that made her feel like she'd be going to dinner with the devil. As she moved through the narrow establishment, it felt like his eyes were boring into her. Tragic indeed.

Laura brushed past the thickening crowd, smiled pretty for a media shot, and got out before her photog buddy, Rick, could hem her in. Outrage with Paxton claimed her; she'd connect with Rick another time.

Who the hell did Michael Paxton think he was talking to? What that arrogant SOB didn't know was, the difference between her and Earline Thompson Crawford was that she didn't want *in.* She didn't want to stay. She couldn't care less about the social notoriety. She hated these chi-chi events and didn't need them to bolster her ego. Her nose wasn't pressed to the glass, trying to gain entry into their sick little backstabbing world. And, unlike Earline, who'd also clawed her way to the top from the neighborhood, she had almost seven million dollars from shrewdly watching the white boys on Wall Street—and it was all safely stashed in Swiss numbered accounts.

Laura could feel her breath shortening from rage as she walked. She'd never believed the hype and never depended on a soul but herself. Insider trading? Hell, she'd followed the great white sharks like a tiny, obscure feeder fish, moving her thousands while they moved their millions, until she had millions, too. Fuck scrambling. Never. Martha Stewart got caught, just like Earline did, because she got sloppy and bold with her power. But then again, Martha and Earline were still standing when the dust settled—women on a mission were not to be trifled with. There was a way to do things. Bastard didn't know whom he was talking to. The bourgeois network's house of cards was coming down, and Paxton and his buddies would be the ones left scrambling.

Frigid fall air stung her face as she headed south on Third. In the cold, without a coat, making it to Thirteenth and South was beyond her endurance. Laura rubbed her arms to stave off the cold and hailed a cab, then tossed her water bottle into a corner waste can and jumped into the vehicle that had stopped for her. A blast of heat immediately hit her—thank God an island-born brother had picked her up; they didn't do cold. She began to relax, giving the cabbie her destination: soul food, at Miss Tootsie's, with a Joe-regular-type brother.

When Laura hopped out of the cab, she immediately spotted Carter. He saw her and glanced at his watch. She was ten minutes late but not in the mood for effusive apologies. Detective James Carter would just have to get over it.

She took her time, strolling past Harry's Occult Shop, heading for the tiny restaurant that appeared between that mystical icon whose window looked like something out of Harry Potter, and the Arts Bank, a theaterlike modern building a block up on Broad. Voodoo, soul food, and the fine arts all in a row—only in Philly. Damn, this had been a crazy day. In the last week of the sting, what had she expected, though?

"You know what's deep?" Laura asked, not caring if Carter didn't. "I got in a cab at the corner of Third and Market and went down Second Street."

He shrugged, not greeting her with a hello or anything near civil, his glare on her set hard.

"I'd just left a black gallery opening, very upscale and posh, filled with beautiful people needing to be seen, then rode past the Square and the original courthouse where we used to be auctioned for slave sale. Ironies of ironies, huh?" Laura shook her head. "You ready to eat, or what?" She had no more careful civility left in her. At this point, all she could be was real.

James Carter's body relaxed. He nodded and followed the hard-to-figure-out woman inside the dimly lit establishment. He hadn't been prepared for her straightforward manner. Somehow he'd expected her to start in with a bunch of incessant bourgeois small talk. But she seemed totally disgusted by the people she'd just left. Yeah. Ironic, like she'd said. And he definitely wasn't prepared for how good she looked in a gunmetal-gray pantsuit, a thin silver chain at her throat, with her cheeks flushed from the cold.

He pushed the fact that she was drop-dead fine out of his mind.

"I thought this was a stand-up—that you wouldn't be here."

"Got tied up, but I have better things to do than bullshit other people's time away, or jack with my own." She rubbed the chill from her arms, waiting for the hostess to find them a table in the small, crowded room. "I don't play those kinds of games." The smell of black-eyed peas, greens, sweet potatoes, and ever-present chicken filled her nose. Acute hunger and the need for something regular, comforting, tore at her insides. "If I didn't want to come, I would have had my secretary call you and cancel. Period." She peered toward the open-air kitchen, and her stomach growled.

"That's fair," he muttered.

"I have one for you," the hostess announced, bringing two plastic-covered menus their way. "Follow me."

He was glad to follow the waitress. He needed to keep moving now, and he gestured for Laura Caldwell to go first. After the day he'd had, warmth indoors, the smell of home-cooked food, low lights, mellow sounds, and photos of jazz greats gracing the walls was just what the doctor ordered. If he had to siphon info from some chick who might be on Darien Price's booty-call rotation, what better place to do it? Too bad the joint was BYOB—he needed a shot of Johnny Walker Red in the worst way at the moment. Laura Caldwell had that effect on him, made a brother need something to even out his equilibrium.

James Carter sat down hard in his chair and rubbed his face with both palms before pulling off his black leather bomber jacket. He let his breath out slowly as he turned to hang it on the back of his chair. "You don't mind me packing, do you?"

She ignored the question. He was a cop. Having a gun went with the territory. Whatever.

"You look tired," Laura said, adjusting her purse over the back of her chair.

"I am tired, lady."

She could appreciate that. "So am I, Detective. My cell phone's been vibrating in my purse all day. All of black Philly is trying to realign itself."

He nodded, knowing exactly what she meant, and opened his menu. "Fried chicken, greens, candied yams, macaroni and cheese."

"Hell, make it two—white meat section for me, so I can get a wing . . . and a pineapple iced tea," she said, yawning and not looking at her menu.

He chuckled. This was *definitely* not what he'd expected. "How in the world can a woman your size eat like that?"

She smiled at him. "Brother, I walked about five miles today back and forth downtown and have eaten a half a salad, had about six cups of coffee, some iced tea without sugar, sparkling water, a glass of wine, and listened to enough yang to turn my stomach. I'm hungry. I'm tired. And you're my last stop for the night—so what's on your mind?"

"You get right to the point, don't you?" He looked up at the waitress who'd approached their table and rattled off their order.

Laura waited for the woman who'd taken their order to leave, and picked up the conversation where James Carter had left it dangling. "Why wouldn't I get to the point?"

He shrugged. "Then shoot."

For a moment she said nothing. The way he turned a phrase, his vibe—everything about him seemed comfortably familiar. She shook off the feeling. "What did *you* want to talk about? You called me today, remember?"

"You approached *me* at the fundraiser. Why?"

Laura picked at the tablecloth. Her original thought about using him to get more information about who controlled things was now moot. Paxton was clearly the man. Part of her had also wanted a departmental insider to help her piece together twenty-six years of history—her father had told someone something at the Round House; then all hell had broken loose. But she'd learned in the interim that Carter's father was the cop who took a bullet; was he friend or foe? was the question. Yeah, sitting here before James Carter Jr. was ironic. Until she'd heard the radio discussion on Maddie's show, she was just going to use him to keep track of the finer points of the investigation. Now the stakes were raised. His father might have been a part of the equation from all those years back. Might have been *the* cop. At least she had a handsome face to place with a name.

"I'm still not sure," she murmured honestly after a moment, taking in how good he looked in a simple black turtleneck and a pair of black slacks with a brown leather shoulder holster. She stared at his peacekeeper and smiled.

"If it offends, I'll take it off."

"Don't bother—but do you always eat strapped?"

"When I'm out. The world is a crazy place."

She nodded.

"Most women don't like it. I figured somebody like you might have a serious problem with it."

She raised an eyebrow. "You don't know me."

"I think I'm a pretty good judge of character."

"Really?" She shook her head and chuckled.

"Best of education, silver-spoon upbringing . . . live in the high-rent district over by the art museum."

Laura steepled her fingers in front of her lips. "You've run my tags through DMV, huh? But you still don't know me."

"Enlighten me, then."

They stared at each other. The waitress brought over two iced teas and broke their standoff. Laura picked up her tall glass, marveling at the fresh chunks of pineapple floating in her drink, and took a sip. She closed her eyes and allowed the sweetness to coat her mouth.

"Assumptions and preconceived notions will mess a man up every time, Jim."

"All right," he said, taking a deep swig of his tea. "Talk to me."

"Things are about to get really messy in this town."

"Oh, and you have an inside track?"

"I do."

"What makes you so cooperative?" He looked at her hard.

"A sister is about to get set up, and I know she didn't do it."

"Got a name?"

Laura set her glass down and began pushing the pineapple pieces around in it with her straw. "Monica Price didn't have anything to do with the Darien fiasco. I might not particularly like her, but fair is fair."

James Carter rubbed his jawline in frustration. Here he thought he might have a possible inside lead, and all he'd turned up was a girlfriend of the wife. The only positive thing about the information Laura Caldwell had given him was, if she was lobbying for the wife, chances were great she wasn't one of Darien Price's broads. For some reason, that made a difference to him right now.

"You got any facts to back up your theory, Ms. Caldwell?"

"Female intuition," she said, offering him a wry smile.

"That would never hold up in court, and we can't base an investigation on that."

"I know . . ." Laura glanced up from her iced tea. "But haven't you fellas ever played a hunch?"

"At times," he admitted slowly, carefully watching her

body language. Yet, she didn't tense, her facial expression remained serene, and her hands gracefully moved—she didn't fidget. Nothing about her made him sense a lie. "But we always have to have some facts to back up any gut instinct."

"Then watch the money," she said in an even tone, now holding his stare. "Not the little money that Price allegedly stole—the bigger money. The contract connections."

"Talk to me."

"The first people that were supposed to get paid on the contracts were the curriculum developers and the facility management firm, to ready the materials and space for students in this educational programming bill. From there, outreach, also known as marketing, was to occur to bring in community clients. After that, the consulting firm that provides teachers was to get paid, and the group that supplied foods and beverages to the students would get theirs, and last on the list would be the firm that had administrative oversight to audit the books, keep the accounting on target, and so forth. Follow the money. Each one of Darien Price's friendly associates was to get a piece of the pie. Then, after the elections, more money was to hit the streets."

"So, you're saying one of his boys set him up?"

"Possibly," she hedged. "If they didn't like their cut, that would have been a way to remove Price from the gatekeeper slot. Look at e-mails sent, cell phone transmissions, bank statements . . . I don't have to tell you how to do your job, Detective. But if there was one contracted amount, and then moneys transferred exceeded what was originally won in the bid—call it a transfer of good faith for more moneys to come—that might tell you that there was an internal power struggle going on. Look at who got the biggest chunk of change and who didn't. Might want to look at the books of the big five players in this scene—not just some credit card bills."

Carter sat back in his chair, frowning, becoming wary. He'd originally gotten a tip from a media source about this whole thing, anyhow—which had never sat right with him or his partner, Steve. Yet, sure enough, the source had been right. "Okay, but why are you telling me all this?"

"Because a woman with two kids is about to be implicated in something she didn't do. As per usual, men did this shit. Paxton took advantage of a sexual opportunity. Sister got played by Darien's best friend and attorney when she messed around and slept with him—just to get back at Darien for all his indiscreet affairs, but she didn't do this. The poor woman is freaked out, with just cause. She's not who you want."

"Then who do I want?"

She shrugged.

Laura sat back in her chair as the waitress came to their table with two heaping plates. She paused until the woman sauntered away, and picked up a piece of Miss Tootsie's signature corn bread, breaking off a small piece of it and popping it into her mouth. She closed her eyes as the sinfully rich butter flavor coated her tongue, mixing with the near-erotic soul food scents coming from their table.

"Everybody always wants a little somethin'-somethin' broken off for them every now and again. Some people have discipline and can wait; others just go for broke. The big boys are used to having things their way. I'd look there."

If he didn't know better, Laura Caldwell could have passed for a dressed-up around-the-way sister. He watched her intently, the combination of her and the food and the information she'd just dropped on him working every sense he owned. Damn. This was definitely not what he'd expected.

Chapter 10

First thing the next morning, as soon as the doors opened, Laura entered the bank at the corner of Seventh and Market. Calmly proceeding, she smiled nicely, stated her business, and handed the customer service officer her safety-deposit box key, then followed the woman down the long corridor to the vaults.

"I'll show you to a private room," the bank employee said, inserting Laura's key into a lock and turning it in unison with one she'd selected from a huge ring. With some effort, the woman extracted a long, flat metal box from behind a thick post-office-box-size door and motioned for Laura to follow her. "Take as long as you need."

"Thank you," Laura told her, closing the door once the woman had shown her a room.

Laura stared at the heavy box in her hands and went to the table, setting it down and dropping her purse beside it. She never sat as she opened the safety-deposit box hinge. The glint of her father's revolver held her gaze for a moment, and she touched the barrel of the gun with the tips of her fingers, pulling them away quickly as though it had burned her. She rummaged in her purse and found three cell phones, depositing two of them into the box while extracting another from it, then closed the lid. It had been so easy to get a copy of Darien's credit report, and those of a few of his cronies . . . then to order phones in their names to use against them. Every call logged would come from their phones, showing calls to one another, creating an electronic trail of fraud. The wonders of technology, the Internet, and electronic transfer. Identity theft was the new frontier.

Laura cradled the metal box in her arms, her mind reeling, her soul remembering. How had things gone so wrong? She'd done what her mother had silently begged her to do; she'd talked about the prom in general terms, kept the worst from her dad, and then fast-forwarded to the next day, understanding the need to protect her father—knowing that her mother was telling a truth without words. He could be harmed, badly; the men around Darien Price were stronger than the men around her. And yet, her worst nightmares still happened.

Everything her mother had said had been right. There were implications for the whole family. She'd had two little sisters, and her parents had needed their jobs. Nobody needed to be going to jail for a fight or for making threats against some rich kid. The balance of power was in the Prices' favor. Just like in the streets, where some gangs were notorious and nobody messed with them in their yard. It was better to make peace with them and form an alliance . . . Maybe that's what her dad had ultimately done. She'd watched him do neighborhood coalition building for years . . . it was all the same. That's exactly what he'd done. Formed an alliance. *Oh . . . shit . . .*

The realization broke her heart. Until the family fell apart, her father and her uncles were the baddest mothers in the valley. After that one fateful night, she'd learned that she'd have to fend for herself if she went beyond the small turf her dad ran . . . if she left "The Bottom," her parents couldn't help her. Just like they couldn't help her do what she had to do now.

Laura hugged the safety-deposit box closer to her breasts. Her and her mother's agreement had been sealed years ago, with the dining room clock ticking as witness; her mother's hands then shook on certain days like Mrs. Price's did. Her dad had just gotten a new job five years before that night with the city, and these men her mother had referred to, people in the club with Darien Price's dad, ran the city—just like their sons ran it now. These men also ran the jails. These men also ran the newspapers. These men ran everything black in Philly. It wasn't about a hurtful prom night, some teenage minidrama; it was about the deadly sequence of events that followed it. All because her father had challenged them and couldn't let sleeping dogs lie.

Parts of her brain were startled by the new sensation of hatred, really knowing what screwing and being screwed was all about. Everything else paled in comparison. . . . It wasn't kissing or groping; it was hard down, primal, no illusion when you were getting fucked or fucking. Sweaty, urgent, grunting, ugly, satisfying in the end when you got yours—regardless of whether the other person got theirs or not. And she'd been so naive and foolish at fifteen to wait for love and some romantic way to get broken in . . .

Laura let her breath out hard and set the box down carefully on the desk. Maybe she should have told her homegirls that night after the prom that she definitely wasn't a virgin. That was the stone-cold truth. She should have told everybody who'd listen, "Yeah, y'all, I got fucked real good after the prom." What was the difference? The bastards had taken her father away from her, and her mother had to be the one to tell her.

A hurt so profound that she could barely breathe entered Laura's chest as she thought back on her mother's expression. The poor woman was standing in the middle of the floor after explaining as much as she could, left naked, once it all became clear that her husband couldn't do a thing. It was like watching them pull a train on her whole family. They didn't gang-war in West Mount Airy—they gang-banged.

"Don't worry, Mom. I'm okay," Laura whispered into the empty room as steadily as she could, refusing to cry while tucking a stray wisp of her hair behind her ear. Something inside her shifted. Instinct had told her to protect her mom, her parents, then. She'd played dumb to let her mother off the hook. "By tomorrow morning, me and my girls will be laughing about this." Laura forced a sad smile.

In her mind's eye, Laura could envision her mother nodding, unconvinced in the spirit now, like she'd been in the past, but overtly complicit in Laura's lie, transmitting what they both knew to be true: the trauma of almost being raped, walking barefoot down the street, embarrassed, humiliated, nails bleeding, learning that for something so important your daddy was powerless, when all your life he'd been talking game about protecting that one thing about you—it wasn't a laughing matter. The trauma of learning of your mother's past, and that powerful men had rendered your father a eunuch, was a defining moment.

None of that was a trivial event to be blown off with the girls. Not even twenty-five-plus years later. The girls would never be told the whole thing, or how she'd righted that old wrong, just like Momma would never be told the whole thing. Momma could barely stand to hear the little bit she had . . . because within every woman there is a knowledge that it can always be worse, that one can always die a thousand deaths and still live. These male beings were physically stronger, truth be told, and it was sheer luck, adrenaline, a burst of insanity, a bluff, divine intervention, that there but for the grace of God . . . Yes, it could have been worse that night, but it wasn't. Her mother was right then. Laura could only hope that her mother wasn't right now. Going to prison would be worse than death.

Yet the game of secrets, omissions, was on now, set in

motion years ago by a father who had to be protected from the black overseer on the plantation—the black man who was allowed to be HNIC, high nigger in charge, therefore allowed to carry a whip and ride a horse over those brothers still picking cotton. A mother was saying with her eyes, *Chile, sometimes you gotta take low. Don't make me tell you again. Leave me my dignity by just letting it alone.* That was her mother's survival skill, her way of making a way out of no way, passed down from generation to generation. But Laura wasn't from that generation.

Laura closed her eyes as she thought back on how she'd kissed her mother's cheek, cut off the light, and left her where she was standing . . . in the same spot where too many older black women stood—frightened, worried, hands clasped tightly in a darkened dining room, praying that things would get better by and by.

Laura raked her fingers through her short curls, which for a moment oddly felt like a lopsided Afro. Her nail beds were sore for an instant; then the sensation dissipated. Fuck all this. *The revolution will not be televised,* just like Gil Scott-Heron had said. She had a score to settle.

Philadelphia
1977

"Baby, with your mother so sick and your daddy being away till the lawyers can sort it all out and get his bail straightened out, you and your sisters can't stay in the house. We gonna have to sell it just to pay the lawyers in the end, anyway. Now, I know things will be a little cramped, but we'll make do. Don'chu worry, we'll all pull together to see that there's a roof over your heads and food in your mouths. That's what family is for. I'm just so sorry that this all is happening in your senior year of high school, chile of mine."

Her elderly aunt's voice entered her eardrums and bounced off without comprehension. She was numb, yet her fingertips tingled. Her father had been indicted? The things they said about him in the newspapers just couldn't be true. Her mom had been given a stroke behind this madness . . . How could her mom have taken so many nerve pills? How could she have forgotten she took meds and then have drunk a martini and chased it with Scotch after that? Her mother didn't even drink! What the fuck was going on in her family?

Laura peered up at the aged face as her aunt sat on the bed beside her. Lines as deep as tree-bark grooves were etched in the ebony mask that spoke. Haunted eyes beheld Laura's face, and a callused hand gnarled with arthritis petted her cheek. Her chest hurt so much from hiccup-crying that she couldn't breathe. Never again. Never again. Oh, hell, no, never again. She would have power and money to keep her and her family safe—never again would she find herself here, exposed. Vulnerable. God help her parents and bring her momma out of a coma.

Laura began shaking her head slowly, the motion so subtle that she almost couldn't feel it. But the movement kept the shrieks from erupting inside her and threatening to spill from her mouth.

"Chile, you the smart one in the family . . . got it from your dear momma. She had brains, too, bless her soul. Now, I know you got into that fancy school, but sometimes you might have to take low. You understand what that means, baby?"

Laura watched lightning bugs flash hazard signals beyond the windowsill. Kids were outside in the dusk playing; she could hear them. The streetlights would come on soon. Why was this woman whom she loved talking to her about taking low? She was the eldest Caldwell woman in the family. Surely Auntie knew what to do. And if all she could do was wear a housedress and clean houses, then she would do that, just like her aunt had done for fifty years—but that wasn't taking low.

"Taking low is letting them win," Laura whispered. "I got into Wharton, and that's where I'm going."

"Baby . . . we was all so proud of you when you did . . . but, honey, that school per year costs more than your daddy made every year before taxes. You can't—"

"I can't let them take away from me the one thing he wanted more than anything in the world, more than what Momma wanted for herself . . . She wanted me to have a shot at it. He wants that, too. Now Momma is laying in a coma after a stroke; they got my daddy locked up for something he didn't do!" Laura was on her feet in an instant and had snatched away from her aunt's hand as if it had burned her. "They said he stole money, *and he didn't*—now our whole family is messed up, and you want me to give them my ticket to be able to change all that?"

"Honey, how you gonna pay for—"

"Student loans! Scholarships! A full-time day job! Whatever, but I am *not* going to let them have this back."

Moisture filled the old woman's eyes as she stared at Laura. She lifted her chin and nodded. "I'ma pray on this for you, baby. I'm proud that you got fight in you, but sometimes . . . sometimes, chile, you jus' gotta—"

"Pick your battles? I have! I will never take low," Laura said through her teeth. "Not because they say I have to."

The two women stared at each other for a moment, enough energy passing between them that it nearly made the air pop and crackle.

"Baby, I know that it's had to be hard on you at school . . . 'specially at your age, baby, and all this stuff in the papers . . . If I could wave a magic wand and make it all go away, honey, I would. But I can't. I know it's all hard to accept right now."

"You have no idea," Laura whispered, then swallowed and sent her line of vision back out the window. "I'm going to finish this fight for Mom and Dad, once and for all; that's why I refuse to take low—I can't. I don't even know how to at this point."

"I don't suppose you would." Her aunt closed her eyes and folded her hands in her lap, and let her breath out on a long, weary sigh of resignation. "Baby, you can't go through this life angry at what is just the way of the world. And you can't do nothing to help your parents, but to—"

"Keep their dreams from dying." Laura watched her aunt watching her. It was an eerie out-of-body sensation.

"You gonna have to study harder than the others, be sitting in the front of the class—get there early, leave last, work twice as hard for half the credit . . . gonna have to shun the parties and the fellas, learn how to talk in perfect pitch like them and everything. Gotta speak the Queen's English, sound like them and learn their ways to blend in and not be noticed. Be a good role model for your younger sisters who are too little to understand what's going on. Then guide them, like Sojourner, once you cut an invisible path through those woods none of us ever been through in this family before. You understand?"

Laura's breaths were coming in shallow, sipping inhales, released on short puffs as she nodded. Somehow she knew she was getting through to Maude Caldwell. Her aunt wasn't going to force her just to knuckle under without a fight; Maude was trying to teach her old-school wisdom. She'd at least let her try to best them before reality set in. They both knew that sooner or later the financial weight could break Laura's back, and she'd wind up at Community College with crazy bills—but that wasn't the point.

She was going to march down that aisle at the Academy of Music on graduation day, wearing the traditional Philadelphia High School for Girls white dress and low-heeled shoes. She was going to hear her name called in the top honors category and hear her name echo that she'd been accepted into an Ivy League university. And for every person, every sister, who had been forced to take low, she would hold her head high.

One day, like her grandmother—the wisest woman in the family had said, she would show 'em better than she would tell 'em.

* * *

"Got something that might interest you." Steve Sullivan walked up to his partner and flopped into the Melrose Diner booth with him. "Might take the edge off of the reprimand you got this morning for hassling Paxton at the benefit."

James Carter waited for the waitress to fill Steve's mug with coffee and walk away. Still pissed off, he kept his eyes on the Passyunk Avenue traffic outside.

"Remember you asked me about that chick's name—Caldwell?"

"Yeah," Carter said, jerking his attention back to Steve.

"Did a little more digging than your sorry DMV check. Seems her father's name hit the papers a while back."

Carter stared at his partner hard. "Talk to me."

Steve picked up his mug and slurped his coffee. "Her pop was some kinda community activist, then got domesticated—came inside, took a desk job downtown, to supposedly help shape minority reforms in the city. Something went wrong, or he pissed somebody off real bad. Poor bastard got crucified for stealing money, then exonerated years later, postmortem. But the year he went down, he went down hard."

"What year?" Carter's grip tightened on his mug, and he brought it slowly to his lips.

"Nineteen seventy-seven, dude. Same year your pop got shot."

The day had gone by in a veritable blur of activity. She hadn't been to the office for more than five minutes—long enough to drop off a stack of client grant records, glance at her mail, and dash back out, leaving Najira loose instructions to handle all calls and promising to fill her in as things developed. She needed a clone, somebody to be in multiple places for her at the same time. This was nuts.

She touched up her makeup and spritzed her wrists and throat with the fragrance Red, as she impatiently waited for the cab to make its way to Seventeenth and Spruce. Why did everyone always want to meet during center-city rush hour! She glanced at her watch. Five minutes to six. Fuck it. Paxton would have to wait.

As she exited the cab and collected her receipt, Laura took two cleansing breaths and more calmly ascended the wide, white marble steps to the brownstone converted restaurant. Ornate twentieth-century black wrought iron bordered her, and she looked at the two marble lions frozen in a roar.

The Garden . . . the perfect place to meet a real snake.

She pushed open one of the double glass-paned wood doors and entered the establishment. Quiet classical music greeted her, and she glanced around to get her bearings.

Muted taupe silk-covered walls stared back at her, and the sounds of gurgling fountains fused with Chopin. A tuxedo-wearing maître d' nodded in her direction as her line of vision roved over the neat cobblestone path, hothouse orchids, blooming azaleas, fig trees, lush elephant grasses, ferns, and Spanish moss. It was like standing in the middle of the Garden of Eden, complete with a crackling fireplace, Versailles-era vases, and highly polished mahogany wood moldings that gave way to an expansive, frescoed cathedral ceiling.

Laura breathed in the fragrant scents produced by the plants and what she knew would be exquisite cuisine. She moved closer to the podium and tightened the belt on her raincoat.

"May I help you?" The maître d' asked in a welcoming tone. "You wouldn't happen to be waiting for a gentleman seated for a six o'clock reservation, would you?"

"I am," Laura said, glancing at her watch. Six-fifteen. Good.

"May I take your coat?"

"Thank you," she murmured, obliging the maitre d' as she removed her London Fog and gave it to him.

"Right this way."

Each room she passed was set up like a private dinner party, with a healthy distance between the scattered small tables for seating two and four guests. Sparsely populated, this oasis was tucked away and seemed to cater to couples intent on having a discreet meal. Beautiful couples didn't even look up as she followed the host.

Her target was at a table in the back room. No other tables around him had been occupied yet. Italianate windows framed him. A small tea-light candle floating in a crystal bowl of orchids flickered, firing Paxton's complexion gold. He smiled as she approached, and stood. Oh, yeah, this was definitely Lucifer.

The sight of her made him dismiss her tardiness. She seemed like a doe picking her way nervously through the indoor forest. He watched her with deep appreciation. Her suit jacket stopped just above her knees, her skirt a millimeter below it . . . the same tawny color as her skin. But her long legs held him momentarily for ransom. Wearing the monochrome hue down to her shoes gave her the illusion of sauntering toward him in the nude. He needed to banish the concept. Business first.

"I thought you might have changed your mind," he said, leaning in to give her a professionally platonic peck on the cheek. But doing that had a bit of a destabilizing effect. She smelled so damned good. He lingered in her space longer than was prudent but caught himself and smiled, motioning for her to sit as the host pulled out her chair for her.

"No," she said pleasantly. "Just rush-hour gridlock."

"I'm glad you came."

She said nothing and sat down.

He sat after she'd settled herself. A woman hadn't had this effect on him in some time. He put his napkin in his lap, still wondering how to kill two birds with one stone. Business first, but there was definitely an intriguing secondary option he wanted from her. The question was, how to get her to lower her defenses? He loved the tough challenge she presented.

"Would you care for anything to drink?"

"A glass of chardonnay would be perfect."

He motioned for the server, accepting the wine list. "How about a Mersault Bouchard Pere and Fils, or a Puligny Montrachet?"

"I'd prefer Laboure Roi Pouilly-Fuisse, actually . . . if you don't mind?"

"Then, Pouilly Fuisse it is."

The server nodded and collected the list. Michael Paxton studied his lovely guest. This side of her was disorienting—blowing him away.

"So," she said brightly, "we finally do this."

"You make it sound like a prison sentence." He chuckled and sat back in his chair. "It's not so bad a venue to discuss business, is it?"

"No, it's quite elegant. Where are my manners?"

She'd made him smile . . . easily, without force, and no pretense. Damn, he liked the effect.

"Why don't we have a bit of wine, relax a little, and order before we launch into heavy negotiations?" He sighed. "If your day was anything like mine, a few moments' respite would do us both good."

"I hear you," she said, reclining against the thick, high-backed baron's chair.

"Good," he murmured as the wine server brought over a bottle. "I really don't want to wrangle," he added, truly meaning it. "Maybe we can even get to like each other through all of this."

The smile she allowed to slide out onto her face messed with his head. He loved the way she handled herself.

"Am I really that bad?" he asked, glancing at the bottle and giving the server a gesture to open it.

"Mr. Paxton—"

"Michael, please," he said, interrupting her as he accepted the cork and made short work of okaying the bottle. He swished the small splash of translucent liquid around in his glass and tasted the pale yellow substance, then nodded. "Last night, I do believe you slipped up under duress and called me Michael once or twice at the gallery."

"Michael, you have a notorious reputation for playing hardball and always getting what you want. I may have been stressed, and yes, you are really that bad." She chuckled as her crystal goblet was filled.

"But that's the American way," he countered, needing to talk to break her spell.

He raised his glass to her in a salute and took a sip from it, watching how the moisture from her wine left a damp spot on her lower lip when she tasted it. The matte, fawn-brown lipstick she wore glistened; then the tip of her pretty pink tongue licked the trace of wine away. A slight shudder ran through him. The pursuit of pleasure was threatening to take priority over business.

"Sometimes one can be altruistic—one can do something without a direct and immediate personal benefit, right?"

"Oh, don't tell me you're a closet activist."

She laughed and took a more liberal sip of her wine. "No. Hardly."

"Feminist, then?"

She shook her head and peered at him over the rim of her glass. "Don't lump me in with folks who carried a banner, made a lot of progress, while *we* were the critical mass at the marches but, statistically speaking, as black women, we still have lower-paying jobs, our kids have higher mortality rates, and we die more from diseases and domestic violence."

He laughed. "Land mine. Wow." He took a sip of wine and studied her face. "Decidedly an activist."

"Nope," she said, chuckling and opening her menu while feigning to ignore him. "A realist."

"I like that even better," he said, no pretense in his words. He set down his wine and opened his menu, not really paying attention to the choices. The passion she'd displayed in her little diatribe, though tempered, was stabbing him. A verbal samurai . . . brilliant, articulate, savvy, a competitor wrapped in a stunning physical package that smelled like Red.

"It's hard to decide," she murmured, appearing lost in the menu choices.

"I know it is," he said, not referring to the entrées.

"Sometimes I just want to go rich and sinful; then I have to remember the consequences."

He watched the candlelight shimmer against her skin. "Why not just be decadent tonight?"

"I'm so tempted, I might have to."

He swallowed hard and glanced at the menu. She'd never looked up at him.

"Have you decided?"

"Yes," she replied, closing the thick leather binder. "Roast duckling glazed with chestnuts, trimmed with wild mushrooms and butternut squash."

"I think I'll go with a little wild game, myself . . . the venison with dried cranberry and bread pudding." He closed his menu and held her gaze with his own. "You'll have to try just a taste when our entrées arrive."

"Only if you'll have some of my duck."

"What's good for the goose is good for the gander."

It took every ounce of personal discipline to stop looking at her long enough to give the server their order. "You'll need to save a little room for dessert, though. The crème brûlée, or warm bananas in custard, are fabulous here."

"I might splurge on dessert tonight," she said in a soft tone, holding her wineglass by the stem and staring at the wine as she slowly twirled it. "It's been an awful long time since I've had some."

He could feel his groin thicken; her statement created a dull, central ache. "I might splurge with you. It's been a long time since I've indulged myself, too."

"Then, go for it."

He watched the way her breasts rose and fell beneath her crepe silk jacket, visually tracing her collarbone and the depression in her delicate throat as she swallowed her wine. For a moment, he was at a loss for words, a rare occurrence that thrilled him no end. He just hoped she wasn't fucking with him. But Laura Caldwell seemed a little too direct for a game of cat-and-mouse . . . yet one could never be sure with a woman. When she pushed a stray velvet black curl behind her tender earlobe, that had been his undoing. He could barely breathe now.

"So, we have ordered and are having wine." She set her glass on the table before her and leaned forward. Circling the base of the glass with her fingers, she stared at him, her lush mouth still moist. *"If* I get anointed as the gatekeeper, how should I distribute the funds?"

She'd offered up her power in a husky voice, her eyes half-mast, and had practically slid it across the linen on a silver goddamned platter. His dick was so hard, he almost winced.

"If you keep things the same for at least the first fiscal, people will relax." Beyond his will, his voice had dropped an octave of its own accord, and he found himself leaning in toward her, his elbows on the table, his hands folded under his chin. Her smile was unraveling his patience. He definitely hadn't had a woman with balls like this in years.

"I hear you," she said coolly. "People hate change. Okay."

Her knee bumped his under the table. He fought not to react to the erotic sensation.

"Just like that?"

She sat back in her chair and chuckled. "Everything doesn't have to be a fight, Michael. I just needed to know what you wanted. Now that I'm clear . . ."

He was still leaning forward when their entrées arrived. "But what do *you* want?"

She chuckled more deeply and began picking at her plate with a fork, noting that he was cutting a piece of venison for her to sample. "I haven't decided yet."

"I will not hear of you getting into a cab," he said, handing the valet his ticket. "At least allow me to drive you to your car, Laura."

"Michael, I'll be fine," she argued in a pleasant tone. "I do this by myself every day and night. But thank you for a wonderful dinner—and for a heads-up about how to keep things smooth." She looked away. "I appreciate the inside tip, seriously."

She raised her arm for the cab that was barreling down the street, but Paxton waved the vehicle away. She turned and looked at him. The valet jumped out of a silver Saab 9-5 and handed Paxton the keys.

"Laura, please . . . let me take you?"

"All right," she said in a quiet voice. "Just this once."

He helped her into the passenger's seat, his mind furiously dissecting her tone, her words, every facet of what she'd said to him all night—hoping she could read between the lines. The situation was delicate—high stakes. He hit the automatic locks and shifted into gear. Her scent filled the vehicle, intoxicating him. If he made an aggressive move that she didn't want, and if her responses had been professional submission but not personal submission, then he was screwed. But he'd asked her to let him take her, and she'd said, "just this once." *Please, God.* He tapped the stereo button to engage the CD player, to let Coltrane work out the conundrum in jazz.

"I hope we can do this again," he said after a moment.

"I'm sure we'll see each other a lot on the circuit," she replied, adjusting her purse in her lap.

"I meant . . . not necessarily for business."

She didn't respond.

"What do you like to do when you're not working?"

She chuckled, and he trained his ears to the timbre of it. No hint of tension. Excellent. He relaxed.

"I'm not sure, anymore. I'm always working."

"I hear you. Gets crazy sometimes . . . It's hard to always be on."

"Yup."

"But, if you did have some time when you weren't working, what would you like to do?"

"Hmmm . . . ," she said, sighing, her gaze going out the window. "I'd love to go somewhere that I wouldn't bump into a soul I knew, wouldn't have to paste on a corporate smile, and could just relax."

"You and I would have to go into hiding." He laughed, and her warm laughter threaded through his. "I might know of a little place . . ."

He glimpsed her from his peripheral vision, trying to keep his eyes on the traffic ahead of them, but unable to keep from looking at her.

"That might work."

She still hadn't looked at him, but was smiling. He summoned patience. The perfect place right now would be down by the waterfront, in his warehouse loft, and in his bed. He could just imagine what she'd feel like under him . . .

"You wanna go for a drink somewhere?"

Now she was looking at him.

She couldn't keep herself from smiling and she swallowed away a chuckle. Michael Paxton Jr., Esquire, had lost his command of the Queen's English in her presence? Deep. *Wanna*? Laura bit the insides of her cheeks before speaking. She'd played this hand long enough, and it was time to call it a night. Keep hope alive . . .

"I would love to, really . . . but I have a stack of work facing me tonight, Michael, and—"

"So do I, but I'm not sure I'm ready to switch gears to deal with it yet. I'm only flesh and blood."

Laura's mind snatched at the puzzle Paxton presented, dropping each piece into place. He'd turned to her when the car stopped at the light, his eyes searching her face, the professional restraint wearing thin in his expression. Interesting. Flesh and blood, huh? The real question: was he human? She wondered how long it had been for him since he'd really played hard and for keeps. Monica was no contest. That was just something to do.

She let her silence speak for her and took a risk. The deeper she could get inside his head, the closer she'd be to picking up threads of information about who the original member of the trust was who had set up her father. She was no fool; the only reason Paxton was so hot for her was the strategy he had to end-run Haines. Keep your friends close and your enemies closer . . . Didn't they say that in *The Godfather* or something? Fucking was real close. She was not above it, if she had to go there. But only on her terms. Timing was everything. The light changed.

"I'm not ready to switch gears, either . . . truth be told. But I should," she finally murmured.

"Why is that?"

She watched the muscle pulse in his jaw as his Saab hit the curb and bounced to a stop before the parking garage barrier. He punched the green button and snatched the ticket. She swallowed away another smile. Part of her toyed with the concept—he'd probably do her real good tonight if she'd let him, given all indicators, and it had definitely been a while since she'd indulged herself.

"I'm on the third level," she said, ignoring his question.

She held the door handle when his sedan took the corners sharp as it screeched up the concrete ramps.

"You didn't answer my question."

"I know . . . because I didn't know how to."

He pulled into an empty space on level three and put the vehicle in park. "Why not?"

She closed her eyes for a moment and then glanced down at her hands in her lap. She pushed a theatrically slow stream of air past her lips. "Because I'm afraid."

"Of what?" he asked, his tone gentle. "You don't strike me as a women who is ever at a loss for words, or ever really afraid of anything."

"Compliment accepted, if that's how it was intended . . . but know that I've worked so hard not to get involved with anybody on the circuit . . . and to keep my reputation—to keep myself focused," she stammered intentionally, watching him absorb the information she'd cast out. She hadn't been with any of his boys; he would potentially be the first in the city to win the trophy. It was a critical demarcation for a man like Paxton. She'd also said without words that it had been a very, very long time since she'd been sexually active. He was eating out of her hand. Practically drooling in it.

He leaned in closer, now bold enough to push a stray curl behind her ear. She briefly closed her eyes and allowed him to witness a slight shiver pass through her at his touch, knowing just what that would do to him.

"It's been a really long time for me, too," he murmured, his voice now silken baritone. "You have no idea . . . with the schedule I keep, and the need to separate business from pleasure . . . it's hard to find someone—an equal match, who's discreet. We aren't that different, you and I. We want the same things."

An outright confession baked in with a lie. Her eyes searched his for fraud and found none. Monica really didn't count, even though that was so tacky. She considered the options for a moment. They really weren't that different, all in all—were just playing the game from different sides of the street. She stared at him as he struggled not to move in toward her mouth. She licked her lips. He smelled good; looked good, and was definitely packing.

"Mike, I have to go . . . This could get messy."

"Come back to my place, Laura."

Oh, yeah, his discipline was wavering; he was coming in for the kill—vitally exposed. Near the begging point. She weighed her options again, her discipline intact.

"I can't, because right now," she whispered, "with how I'm feeling . . . I'm too . . . right now . . . we're both going to do something that we'll regret, and we have to work together. Let me think about this . . . It's all happening too fast. I didn't expect this."

"Neither one of us expected this, and neither of us will regret it. I promise you that."

His finger was tracing a line up and down her neck, and his eyes burned with a plea that she'd ignore. But his touch left a trail of heat that made her know he could deliver as promised.

"I haven't let those powerful feelings out in a long time. . . .

I'm almost afraid of how I'd act. I might embarrass myself." She smiled and clasped his hand, taking it from her neck in a gentle sweep. That part of what she'd told him was the truth. "Thank you so much for dinner, and I'll consider the offer."

"It's a standing offer, Laura. You might make me embarrass myself, too . . . so your secret would be safe with me. Attorney-client privilege."

"Please open the door before I change my mind," she said on a husky whisper. "Better stated, before I *lose* my mind."

She watched the way his breathing stopped for a second.

"You said to go for it."

He was almost in the passenger's seat with her.

"Dessert is what I meant."

"But you passed on the crème brûlée."

"I had to . . . I don't think I could have watched you eat it."

His eyes went to half-mast. He couldn't answer.

She hoisted her purse over her shoulder. "Don't get out; my car is right over there," she added, pointing to her black Jag.

He just nodded and hit the locks to open the door, allowing her to flee. "I'll call you tomorrow."

She nodded and escaped.

Defeat claimed him. So close . . . He wouldn't have been able to get out to escort her to her car without humiliation anyway. Just as well. But the things she'd admitted . . . the vulnerability she displayed . . . and the passion that was probably locked away within her for who knows how long. The sound of her voice . . . Damn, this postponement was fucking with him. And all he could do was watch her red taillights go on. Next time, she wasn't getting away.

She didn't relax until she saw the Saab that had been following her head toward the Vine Street expressway. Then she laughed loud and hard, slapping the wheel. "Oh, shit, Laura Caldwell, you crazy bitch!"

Switching on the radio, she punched the dial until mind-jarring music came on, singing the lyrics off-key, jamming in her seat. “Afraid, my ass . . .” She shook her head. “If I go there, brother, I’ll rock your damned world. Pullease!”

Another wave of giggles overcame her as he sped down Spring Garden Street. “Laura, Laura, Laura—that was too fucked up!” She leaned her forehead against the steering wheel when she stopped for the light, and laughed harder. “Oh . . . damn . . .”

Her hand went to her purse, extracted her cell phone, and she hit speed-dial for Najira. As soon as the call connected, Laura screamed. “Girl!”

Najira’s laughter blended into hers. “What did you do, you crazy woman?”

“I got his ass good, girl! Oh, my God! It was awesome. I haven’t done anything like this in years—the thrill of victory, the agony of defeat . . . left him drooling in a damned parking lot, okaaaay?”

“No!”

“Yes, I did.”

“Paxton? Oh . . . shit . . . Laura . . . *him*?”

“I told you I’d deal with that one, right?”

“I know, but daaaaayum.”

“Jira, Jira, Jira . . . the brother is hung; he’s fine; he’s ruthless—what the fuck—I might have to do him before we fix his ass, ya know? A girl’s gotta do what a girl’s gotta do sometimes.”

A sonic boom of laughter filled Laura’s ear, making her howl with her cousin as her car zipped along the streets. This was madness. It was fucking crazy. Worst part of it all was, she had to admit that messing with Paxton like that was more than comeuppance mischief—there was an erotic lure to the danger of it. Possibly sleeping with the enemy had wet her drawers. She was out of her damned mind.

“All right, I’m out,” Laura announced, trying to pull herself together.

“You know what the grapevine said—word is, brother likes it rough. Be careful.”

"Shit," Laura chuckled, wiping at her eyes, "he's the one who'd better be careful. Rough? Pullease, I will serve his ass leather and chains."

She ignored Najira's screams and laughed harder. For a moment she allowed the visual to enter her head as she grasped the steering wheel tighter; riding a thoroughbred racer like that would be worth it. She had to shake it. Damn, she had played herself, and now had to deal with being horny. A power surge always did that to her. But tonight she'd beaten the devil at his own game of seduction and had left him in a parking lot with his dick hard. Laura shrieked, covered her face with her palms, and laughed into them, yanking the phone from her ear, and then gunned the engine when the light turned green.

Rounding the corner, she wiped her eyes, her giggles slowly abating as she pulled her car onto her quiet street.

"Next time, Jira, I'll get his cell phone number and possibly double back at midnight with a breathless I-can't-stand-it booty-call . . . that would definitely stroke his already inflated ego. A couple of those, and I might even be able to get him to tell me some real good info. Whatever. By any means necessary. Paxton was nearly trembling when I left him. They're all going down; no sense in not enjoying the process thoroughly."

"And you told me to stop the drama!" Najira hollered into the phone on a renewed round of laughter.

"Oh, shit . . ." All laughter stopped. Laura froze.

"What's the matter, girl?" Najira said in a whisper for no apparent reason.

"Call you back. A fucking parked, unmarked cop car is blocking my garage door."

Chapter 11

Laura hit the automatic windows and leaned over as her car pulled beside the unmarked car. "You're blocking my driveway."

Carter put his gears in reverse and moved back into a space on the street so she could enter her garage. He waited as the door opened slowly, wondering whether she'd just go inside and lock the door or would stand on the pavement and give him a hassle.

"Is this official business or just a friendly, unannounced pop call?" she asked, coming out of her garage to the curb.

"Maybe a little of both," he muttered, getting out of his vehicle and slamming the door hard.

She looked him up and down and turned away, heading inside the garage. "C'mon. I'll put on a pot of coffee."

He hesitated but followed her. In truth, he wasn't exactly sure what he wanted to say to her. He scanned the neat interior of the garage, noting that she'd blocked his view of the alarm keypad as she punched in her code, then hit the electronic door button to close the garage, sealing them inside it. She said nothing as she walked up the stairs ahead of him, swinging her purse. He kept his eyes on that instead of her lovely ass.

"So, am I going to need an attorney?" she asked casually, walking through her house and taking off her coat and hanging it on a hallway hook without turning around.

"You already have one, it appears."

She stopped walking for a beat but never turned, then resumed walking.

"So now I'm being tailed?"

"No. It's just amazing what information a secretary will give you when you say you're a cop. Dinner at the Garden must have been nice."

"Kitchen's this way." She'd never turned around.

She flipped on a light. No less than what he'd expected, and comparable to what he had seen as he'd passed the other rooms in her house. Granite surfaces, Spanish tile floors, island Jenn-Air range, modern stainless steel appliances, black ladder-back chairs, copper pots hanging from a wrought-iron rack above the counters, expensive African fabric curtains, Varnette Honeywood art, Braun latte and cappuccino machines, funky studio canister lights. The place was museum-display clean—her kitchen alone probably cost more than his Germantown duplex.

She threw her purse on a kitchen chair and went to the cabinets, pulling down two bags of fresh-ground coffee. "Hazelnut or Brazilian roast?" she said, holding up the choices and staring at him hard.

"Whatever." He sat down on a high stool by the center island counter and watched her hum around the kitchen as though he weren't there.

"I did some digging," he said after a moment. He noticed that she hadn't even flinched. The comment had been timed as she poured the water into the coffeemaker. She was either innocent or a smooth criminal.

"Good for you." She fished down two big, black ceramic mugs and hunted in the refrigerator for half-and-half creamer, then went the kitchen table, setting the cream beside a crystal sugar bowl, two napkins, and two spoons. "Care to elaborate?"

"Seems either you're psychic, or there's more to your story."

She smiled and sat down at the table. "Can we stop with the leading half-sentences? I've had a long day and I'm really tired."

"Okay," he said, leaning on the counter, "we started looking at cell phone records, among other things like bank statements and whatnot. Seems the CEOs of the various contracted companies you gave me a heads-up on recently ordered cell phones that were only used to talk to each other—like a little private network. Seems they also used these digital phones to access their e-mail, their bank accounts, and accept money transfers from city accounts . . . all in one month . . . all before the first billing cycle would go down and anyone would find the transmission sources."

She shrugged. "Well, Detective, like I said, follow the money. Works every time."

"Last night I was Jim."

She stood and brought a steaming pot of java to the kitchen table and poured two mugs, then put the pot back on the kitchen counter. "You gonna sit on a stool glaring at me all night, or what?"

"I want to know how you knew to point me towards certain firms—and I'm gonna need a little more than 'feminine intuition' as your reason," he said, making quotes in the air with his fingers.

She smiled as she took a sip of coffee. "You know who I had dinner with tonight."

He did, and it bothered him. He wasn't sure why, but it did. Carter moved to accept a mug of coffee from her as she slid it in his direction across the smooth surface of the oak kitchen table, his eyes never leaving hers.

"That was strictly business," she said, pushing the sugar bowl toward him. "And necessary."

He looked her over carefully. The outfit she had on was

stunning and didn't look like strictly business at all. "Yeah. Whatever. But the point is—"

"The point is, James, he was trying to tell me where to redirect funds . . . should the white boys get nervous. These same firms are the ones I identified for you, because I know where the linkages are. It's very easy math. There isn't a rainmaker in the city who doesn't know how moneys are moved, and by whom. So what's your point?"

He sat down across from her and added sugar to his coffee without looking at her, and stirred it slowly. "I don't expect you'd understand."

"Try me."

He stared at her and took a slow sip from his mug and set it down carefully. "I can't stand those types."

"I hear you, but why not? Specifically."

"Long story. Thanks for the coffee." He stood up.

"You came to my door tonight ready to accuse me of some insider knowledge; now you say, 'my bad,' get up and walk . . . when I just put you down with enough information to get your ass promoted? Well, thank you, too." Now she stood. She'd had enough of his self-righteous bull.

"The kind of people I'm investigating, sis, are the same kind of people that got my father shot. So, thanks for the tip, but you come from their world; your own father was one—"

"Hold it," she quietly through her teeth. "Don't even go there."

There was something in her eyes, the way she'd cut the glance at him that made him stand still and hear her out.

She collected the coffee mugs and set them down hard in the sink, sloshing hot brew along the way. "I grew up at Fifty-sixth and Warrington, *brother*. Whatever half-assed investigating you did on me, know this: my father was set up by these same people, okay? I put myself through school and worked hard just like you had to, to get ahead. So fuck all that silver-spoon rhetoric. I told your big, lurchy ass last night you didn't know me. And now I'm the bad guy, because I see a brother thrown against a case that could end his damned career, looking out of place at a function that is giving him the hives, and I try to do the right thing by pulling his coat—and now I'm wrong? The last word I heard as a kid was that my father was trying to get some info down to a cop at the Round House; then the next thing we know, Dad is going to jail. So, no, I don't like cops and don't trust them in general, but I gave you a break and didn't lump you into the stereotype."

"Listen, Laura—"

"No. *You* listen," she said fast, her neck bobbing as her hands went to her hips. "I grew up in the Rizzo era, where shit happened to *us* in the neighborhoods by unchecked cops riding horses and swinging clubs and riding in *red* squad cars—that was before things were so-called *PC*, and the color changed on the vehicles to serene blue and white, feel me? Just like you probably remember, I was a kid when they pulled Black Panthers out in the street on what was then Columbia Avenue, which is now Cecil B. Moore Avenue, and stripped them naked, and I remember the *first* MOVE incident in Powellton Village—long before six square blocks of West Philly were burned down. No, brother, don't tell me shit about Philadelphia's cops back in the day. As the kids say, they were off the chain!"

He took her blast stoically, but he understood the truth when he heard it—and this was the cold-blooded truth as they both knew it. He'd judged her wrong. Hot tears stood in her eyes, and he remembered what that felt like: the frustration of being caught up in something so wrong there was no way to make it right. He relaxed and stepped toward her. "Laura . . . look . . . I'm sorry. Okay?"

"Kiss my ass and leave my house. I'm *too* through." She'd pointed toward the door, then turned away and wrapped her arms around her waist and drew a deep breath.

"Let's start from square one," he said quietly. "Square one—thank you for the tip and the coffee. Square two—I think we both opened this can of worms between us with a lot of baggage . . . I apologize, I didn't know you and judged you wrong. Three—you aren't a suspect . . . and I haven't even told my partner where I got the word about where to look."

"Fine," she muttered. "Now please leave."

She heard his footfalls get farther and farther away; then the front door opened and shut. She wiped her face and leaned on the edge of the sink with both hands. Too fucking close for comfort, but necessary. She peered over her shoulder at her purse on her chair. It was time to get rid of the cell phones.

What had he just done? Ten o'clock and the city was coming alive again for a second shift. Streetlights cast oppressive shadows on the walking dead. Down the bottom, anything went. Women plied their trade for just one more hit; dealers found new corners despite Operation Safe Streets. A show of force just drove the underground economy into new hideaways. There were still too many cracks and crevices for it to slither into. Toddlers were still on stoops and running down the blocks all hours of the night—where were the moms? Looking for that fast escape in a plastic bag. Young girls looking like women, young brothers on a predatory hunt for trouble. They'd find it.

Carter made his black Crown Victoria sedan straddle trolley tracks, just watching Lancaster Avenue change the farther west he drove. If he went far enough to pass the Overbrook section, the tracks would be gone; so would the druggies. The street would widen. Trees would replace burned-out storefronts. Sidewalks would roll up and disappear at City Line Avenue, and Lancaster Avenue would transform into Route 30, an escape route to a whole different universe—the Main Line. What had he done to the hardworking sister from 'round the way?

He made a left at Fifty-second Street, wound to Haverford Avenue, and found a bar. Johnny Walker Red was calling his name, and he needed some more info on a street warrior named Bill Caldwell.

"Yo, man—long time," the bartender yelled, hailing Carter as he entered the Cozy Nook.

"Whatchu know good, man?" Carter found a stool and sat on it hard. He gave old man Ice a fist pound as classic Temptations hits blared from the ancient jukebox. Heat in the joint was kicking, and only a few patrons were still hanging on, sipping their drinks slowly to stretch a dollar.

"Aw, brotha. Same ol' same-ol'. You on duty, or you drinkin'?"

Ice must have seen the look in his eyes, because he reached for a bottle without waiting for a response. He could always depend on the old man to know things without a lot of words being said.

Carter accepted the short rocks glass and took a sip from it, wincing. "I'm off duty," he lied, "but came here for a history lesson, brother."

"Always got time to school a young buck," Ice said, flashing a snaggletoothed grin. He leaned on his forearms and waited, excitement shining in his eyes.

Carter appraised the gaunt face that was as dark and wrinkled as an old raisin, and took his time. "There was this brother my pop knew, way back. Bill Caldwell."

"Mr. B? Aw, hell, yeah, Jimmy. Dey was thick as thieves. Good peoples. Bof him and your pop. Was a damned shame, dough. *The man* got bof of 'em—dat's ancient history 'round here."

Carter nodded, absorbing what the old man had said. Friends. Deep. "They was tight?"

"Shooooot," Ice said, becoming indignant, pushing away from the edge of the bar. He grabbed a dirty dish towel and slung it over his shoulder, found a glass for himself, and began wiping it out. He poured some J&B in it very slowly and stared at Carter hard. "Was fucked up, is what it was. Dem two was real men. Your pop, him being only one of a few on da force, kept the Italiano cops from coming down here hassling us in the old days—you hearing me? Dat was befo' terrorists made everybody come tagetha, but back in *my* day, man . . ."

"I hear you." Carter sipped his drink. He remembered those days when he was ashamed that his father had become a part of the system. Revolutionary brothers and street brothers from the hood teased him about it, but like Ice said, that was ancient history. So Carter punted the bitter memory, took another swig of Johnny Walker, and listened.

"Mr. B, see, he was on da inside, too. Was downtown, and would put your old man down wif what was about to go down, so a brother on the streets could watch his back and not get accidentally popped—like dey did brothers in Nam. Had ta watch ya back or get capped. Them two was always on the front line, arguin' wif highfalutin black folks 'bout not sellin' out, too. One day, dey bof came in here." Ice pointed to a leaning table and chairs by the back wall.

Carter's line of vision followed the sweaty, frail finger that trembled.

"Was right dere, da two of 'em was talking, and Mr. B gave your pop an envelope. Next day, they pulled yo' pop out a corner store up northside talking 'bout he was shot. Day after dat," he said emphatically, shaking his head, "Mr. B went down on some trumped-up charges." Ice wiped his eyes and took a deep swig of his drink. "Dat po' man's wife had a stroke and lef' three little girls . . . just like yo' po' momma died of a heart attack not long after yo' daddy went down."

Ice unscrewed the liquor bottle and refilled his glass. "See, da people ain't crazy. Us old-heads remember. The real newspapers, the ones we owned—I ain't talking 'bout dat one downtown dat caters to rich black folk—but the *neighborhood* papers run by da brothers from 'round our way, yeah, dey was talkin' conspiracy. Folks seen your pop's car parked out west, heard shots in an alley up 'round Girard Avenue—then it all got squashed and swept under da rug. Said he got shot off duty when he broke up an attempted burglary at some store." He put the cap back on the bottle. "Just like that. Sealed up. Ain't heard tell of it since. People got tired and let it go. Lotsa shit go down like dat . . . people get tired, and gotta let it go so dey can live."

"I knew if anybody knew, it'd be you, Ice." Carter raised his glass in a salute and downed it.

"How come you ain't never asked nobody before, young-blood? I mean about Still Bill? We'da tol' ya."

Carter put a twenty on the bar, shrugged, and stood up, offering the old man another fist pound of respect. "Guess I wasn't ready to deal with it before."

"I can dig it," Ice said to Carter's back as he left.

"Peace."

A hundred thoughts ricocheted inside his head as he walked to his car. The cold was like a knife, cutting his face with thirty-degree winds. When his father had gotten shot, he'd dug into the 'hood, looking for a suspect in North Philly, and never knew Bill Caldwell's name. Odd how Caldwell's name had never come up . . . Maybe it was one of those don't ask, don't tell things that went down on the street level . . . But the one sure thing was, as a cop, his father knew a lot of people . . . knew everybody on the streets real well, except him, his son. And the bullshit between them went both ways. Who was the senior James Carter?

Memories slammed against memories as he drove. He'd never told his father he was proud of him, and hadn't begun to understand the sacrifice the man made, until they were draping a flag over his coffin. No wonder his mother's heart just gave out. She had one son in prison on drug charges, who died in the joint in a yard fight, another one that was supposed to play basketball but had been shot in a gang cross fire, and the only one left was a Cheyney and Temple U cultivated, counterculture revolutionary: him.

Carter swallowed hard as the road became blurry, but anger burned the moisture away from his eyes. The one person aside from Ice who had given him a little insight, had shared the same pain, and had probably gotten him closer to the people who'd done his pop—closer than anyone else alive—he hadn't trusted. Problem was that now he'd spooked her.

He punched the dashboard. Steve had warned him about this shit, not having enough distance. All because he looked at the beautiful surface of Laura Caldwell and made assumptions. All because he didn't do his homework and thought her father was a part of the machine. "Damn!"

Carter looked around, noting that he'd flowed with the traffic from Haverford Avenue over to Powellton and was now on the Spring Garden overpass—all fucking turned around . . . and really close to Laura's house.

When he brought his vehicle to a stop in front of her home, he glanced up to the second floor. No lights on. He knew it was probably a bad idea, but got out of his car anyway and went up her front steps and rang the bell—and waited. Lights slowly went on, and he could hear her footsteps approach the door. She peered out of the glass panes at him and turned the locks.

There was no resistance in her as she opened the door and stepped back, staring at him. Her eyes were red; she looked tired. She closed her ice-blue silk robe over her gown and shivered. He stepped in and closed the door behind him.

"They were friends, Laura . . ."

She looked up at him, her eyes searching his for honesty.

"My pop and your pop." He could see the wheels inside her head turning.

"How do you know that? How do I know you just haven't come back here with some bullshit story to clean up—"

"I went down the way when I left here. My father was your father's inside contact, but it didn't go down like you think. My pop didn't set him up, but he was way over the line as far as his jurisdiction . . . They didn't make us detectives back then. My dad should have stayed in the streets, but whatever his friend gave him must have been enough to make them both take a risk." Carter watched her intently.

Her expression was softening, enough to make him go further.

"Laura, this isn't bullshit. I asked some old brothers who were around in seventy-seven. Your pop gave mine an envelope the night before he got shot. . . . No such envelope or evidence was ever recovered when they found his body. People down the way say he got shot in an alley in West Philly . . . but his personal car and body was found near a store up in North Central. That part I always knew—but that Bill Caldwell, your father, was his friend was a surprise."

Her fingers went to her lips and then slid away. "Whoever set my father up had to have something to do with who shot yours."

He nodded. "I never had a name of who his contact was downtown . . . just went around angry for years at the whole, stinking lot of them. I never trusted anybody on the inside . . . had this feeling in my gut, but had no basis of a lead. I had to let it go."

"And I wouldn't have trusted a cop if I tripped over him . . ." She closed her eyes and leaned against the wall in the dark. Moonlight washed her face in pale gray through the glass panes. "Irony of ironies . . . my father worked for Darien Price the Second. That was the office he'd been working out of. Documents my dad had were probably shredded twenty-six years ago, and I figured if my father had given something to the police, the evidence was made to disappear. I never knew his contact was an honest cop—your dad. Deep."

"Your father worked for the managing director back then, right?"

She nodded, her eyes still closed. "The son must be following in his father's footsteps. And why not? Those families have been running unchecked for years."

Laura sighed and pushed away from the wall and stared at him. "That's how I had a hunch . . . I've lived through this drama before. I know how they operate, but could never prove it."

"Let me and my boys handle that part. We've got the son's ass in a sling, and tomorrow at eleven, once the warrant is processed, we'll be taking Don Edward in . . . From there, we'll be bringing in the rest of them one by one. The only asshole we don't have anything hard on is that slimy bastard Paxton. Thanks for the tip. I owe you one, more than you know."

She came in close to him and touched his chest. "You ever look into the finances of that store?"

"Until this moment, I hadn't even thought about doing that. I was looking for a drug dealer, a street hood either up North or down West . . . or somebody inside the department who didn't like my father's politics. Then I got this crazy idea that the Italian mob did it." Carter let his breath out hard and closed his eyes. "I didn't know what my father was into . . . Maybe that's why I stopped looking. I didn't wanna know if he'd done something that would tarnish his name. I had to let it rest."

"Always follow the money, baby," she whispered. "If they moved your father's body, then the store owner had to get paid to keep the transaction under wraps. That's the capitalist way."

For a moment, he could only stare at her.

"How about the rest of that coffee? Is it still on the counter?"

"I'll make a new pot. Take off your jacket and stay a while."

"I'd appreciate that."

She nodded and walked ahead of him. This time he allowed himself to appreciate her curves and the way the silk brushed them. All the information he needed had been right under his nose the whole time, albeit wrapped in a fantastic package. Two wives, three little girls, and a wayward son . . . the casualties of two men trying to hold the line and not betray the people.

Unlike before, when Laura brought him a cup of coffee, he accepted it without resistance, but put it down. His soul needed so much more than that, and he found his arms wrapping around her on their own volition. It was a natural reflex, and the way she melted against him felt so right. She was from his kind. She'd sustained heavy losses. Her tears were his own. They'd grown up in the same streets. Had listened to the same music. Their fathers had been secret homeboys. He couldn't compartmentalize her away as a lead source, a tip, an information broker. Just like he couldn't keep the softness of her skin, or the way her hands petted the hurt out of his system and cleansed his soul, separate from what was prudent. None of it made sense.

All he knew was that he'd found what he'd been searching for. Twenty-six years of pain collapsed into two hours of frenetic, backbreaking pleasure.

"This wasn't supposed to happen," he murmured, tracing her cheek with his finger.

"I know," she whispered, leaning down to take his mouth again.

"We need to . . ." He couldn't find the words to explain without hurting her.

"We need to keep this between us. It never happened," she said, filling in the blanks and kissing the bridge of his nose.

"But it did." He rolled over, sweeping her beneath him. Her eyes were so beautiful with just the lights from beyond the window making the moisture in them glisten. He cradled her head in his hands and imprinted the silken texture of her hair against his palms, branding the memory of the feel of it into them. Destiny had a wicked sense of humor.

"I should go," he murmured, finding her earlobe.

"Your body says you should stay . . . at least for a little while longer."

There was no denying it, not when her long, gorgeous legs wrapped around his waist. They were as smooth as her white satin sheets. It was hard to argue against the pull of her lush mouth. . . . God, her mouth, and what it had done to his senses. And her voice . . . Jesus. He was gonna lose his job for sure. Could even go to prison for compromising a case. If ever there was an insanity plea, this was it, and he'd claim it. Just like her arch against him now claimed all reason.

His mouth found her neck as his hand slid under the firm, round behind. "Baby, listen . . ."

She reached in the open nightstand drawer and handed him another condom. He forgot what he was going to say. All protest was moot. His vocal cords could only utter a moan as she asked him to stay again with her touch. What could he do? He was held hostage by the trail of kisses she pressed down his chest. Her slender fingers were shredding his common sense . . . just like her body had siphoned away rage and pain and guilt, one agonizing ejaculation at a time.

He looked down at her nude form. She was sipping in air, the dark cinnamon tips of her full breasts pouting in defiance, begging him to taste them one more time. He was supposed to leave. His thighs trembled under his own weight as she stripped him of the past, folded it in a tissue, and cast it into a bedside wastebasket so he could live again. Just one more time, then this never happened. But it did.

His partner had been right; he'd definitely lost perspective.

Chapter 12

Fragments of blue-gray light were cracking the sky, and Laura lay on her side, her back pressed to Carter's warmth as she stared out the bedroom window. Yes. The sky was falling; it wasn't her imagination. Pieces of stability were crumbling away, one tiny chunk at a time . . . and things were getting messy. This wasn't supposed to happen, but it had.

She felt Carter pull back gently and stand, trying not to wake her. She turned over and watched him, admiring how the ancestors had sculpted dark, polished walnut over granite, forging a deep valley along his spine. The effect of looking at his slightly swayed back was mesmerizing. As he bent to find his pants, she watched the pure physics of the way the hard muscles moved within his shoulders and thighs, and his fantastically perfect ass . . . Lord have mercy; this wasn't supposed to happen, but she was only human. And the heavens above had made this living art with such meticulous care—had even given the man a soul. The problem was, she'd probably already lost hers.

"I wasn't trying to wake you," he murmured.

"It's okay. I needed to get up," she said in a low tone, still half drunk from the sound of his mellow voice entering her ears all night. She kept her eyes on his, knowing too well that to let her gaze rake him would start some more mess all over again.

He smiled and turned away and started putting on his clothes, as though reading her mind. "We've both got a lot to do today."

"Want some coffee?"

"That's how this got started in the first place." He chuckled low in his throat and zipped up his pants.

"So it did." She stood with effort, her legs feeling as if jelly had been substituted for her knees, and grabbed her robe from the floor. But she couldn't help watching the thick ropes of muscles in his back and arms work as he pulled his sweater on over his head, disappointed that she hadn't given her eyes one last glimpse of his smooth, broad chest and washboard abs . . . or the way that wicked trail of tight corkscrew curls set a direct path from just under his navel to where he'd been truly blessed and endowed. She sighed.

"I'll call you later on tonight . . . might be a long day," he said in a far-off tone, putting on his shoes.

She just nodded. If he did, he did. If he didn't, he didn't. It was best for her to start making the separation sooner than later. That's how this was supposed to go. So she had to stop looking at his intense, concerned eyes. She would not allow herself to go any further than this. And she had to shake his touch . . . rough-hewn hands that had delicately played over every surface of her. He was gentle, but also aggressive when she needed him to be. Like he knew her. No. She had things to do.

"You okay?" He stood before her, waiting for something, perhaps acknowledgement that this thing had gone down.

She couldn't give that to him, because to admit that meant it did.

"Yeah. You okay?"

He nodded.

"Good," she said, keeping her distance, fighting the urge to go to him.

He put his hands in his pockets and glanced toward the door. That was enough to tell her he was feeling it, too. She walked out of the room so he could. They said nothing as they went down the hall and down the steps and through the foyer, and she opened and closed the door behind him and then locked it. Neither one of them had risked a last kiss.

She moved away from the door as quickly as possible, taking the stairs two at a time. She needed a shower. She had to get back to normal. She had to. There were things to do that just wouldn't allow a judgment lapse. She could still smell his deep, musky, wonderful scent all about her. She could hear his car door slam, then the motor go on. Men weren't allowed to come to her home. She only went to discreet hotels or their place, preferably out of state. Her place was off limits. This was her sanctuary. She had to wash her sheets—his smell was like a damned drug. She would not remember the pair of eyes that could see past all facade, knew where she lived inside, and made her feel like she could spend the rest of her days in a duplex in Germantown. For if she went there, even as a fleeting thought, she might spend the rest of her days in jail.

Laura yanked off her robe and turned the shower on full blast.

"Good morning, Najira. Loaded day today," she said, breezing into her office just as Najira was taking off her coat. "Got a million and one things cooking, so I'm going to talk fast. Try to locate Donald Haines for me, and put him through on line one when you reach him." She turned for a moment, her hand on her office door. "Did I say good morning?"

"Yeah . . . ," her cousin said with a slow grin, keeping her voice a murmur. "And what happened with the cops? They didn't—"

"Oh, there's no problem now. False alarm. Detective Carter and I came to an understanding," Laura said with a bright smile.

Najira covered her mouth with her hand, glanced around, and leaned in close to Laura. "You did *not* do what I think you did."

"I don't know what you're talking about." Laura batted her lashes and fanned her face with her hand.

"Oh, shit . . . you okay? I mean, if you went there, then things must be—"

"Everything is fine. I'm just fine," Laura said fast. "Good. But hold the coffee. I've had too much already."

She escaped from Najira and went into her office and shut the door behind her. Shit. Timing had to be impeccable. She roughly pulled off her coat, flung her purse on her desk, and smoothed her hands over her navy knit dress, checking for undergarment bulges while loosening the dress's heavy vertical brass zipper a little at her throat. Laura glanced down at her knee-high black boots. Possibly over the top, she chuckled inwardly, but what the hell. She didn't even sit as she placed the first call, tapping her foot as she briefly stopped walking with her cell phone in her hand.

"Hello . . . Mr. Paxton, please."

"May I ask who's calling?"

Laura hesitated, using the pause to reset the tone with his gatekeeper. A pause like that from a female meant personal—very personal. "Uh . . . this is, uh, Laura Caldwell . . . and, uh . . . he said to buzz him a little later on his cell, but I can't seem to, uh . . . find . . ."

"Miss Caldwell—*from Rainmakers*?"

"Yes, Anne, and it's a pleasure to meet you by phone," Laura hedged in a gracious tone, feeling her fingertips tingle. She walked to the window as the efficient older woman on the line was stunned to silence. Hell, yeah, she'd done her homework and knew the woman's name from other sources—well aware that knowing the personal secretary's name meant two things: she was really an insider; and if she hadn't called there before for business purposes yet knew the name, this was a lover call worthy of a cell phone number. If Anne didn't give it up, the boss would be embarrassed, and therefore pissed. Laura could only imagine what working for Michael Paxton was like. So she waited while his secretary weighed the odds, and was rewarded with the digits.

"Oh. Well, then. By all means . . . ," his secretary crooned in a much friendlier voice after recovering from shock, "I'm sure Mr. Paxton would want you to have that number. Just a moment."

His secretary was back in a flash, and Laura grabbed the pen from her crystal blotter ball along with a Post-it note, jotting down the number as his personal secretary rattled it off with more information than she'd inquired about.

"He's on the road to meet with a client in Wilmington now, but I can have him call you as soon as he touches base with me. He should be finishing up around ten, and back here no later than eleven . . . but he does have a noon booked. Would you like to leave a number?"

"Oh, no. He has my cell. I'll wait a little bit and personally call him."

The secretary paused. Laura smiled.

"Uh, sure, Miss Caldwell. No problem. You have a nice day."

"You do the same, Anne."

She had to cover her mouth to keep from screaming. This was new info on the circuit that was sure to light up every executive secretary console in the city. She steadied her nerves for the next call and punched in Rick's number.

"Yo, whassup?"

"Rick," she said, dropping her voice and half whispering, "you didn't hear this from me, okay. But I owe you one for the Paxton hookup."

She heard him pause, knowing that he was walking away from earshot of anyone around him. She'd seen him do it when news tip calls came in.

"What's up, love?"

"You clear?" she asked, making her tip sound really intriguing. "Where are you now?"

"Outside the Price house, waiting on a shot of Monica Price. Got a tip that she might be pulled in on the credit card thing."

"That's a bullshit tip. Save your Kodak film and get down to Don Edward's office around eleven—and be discreet."

"What!"

"You heard me. Let the rest of the photogs hound a woman that the police aren't going after. You get the cover shot, ahead of even the TV cameras, for the front page—they'll be hauling his ass downtown sure as rain."

"How do you know—"

"Now, Rick . . ."

"Okay, okay, never ask a source their source. But if you make me miss my shot of Monica, you won't be my favorite girl anymore."

"I'm never wrong, and you'll owe me a very quiet, very discreet drink."

"Damn . . . this must be real, if you're gonna have a drink with me."

"Call my office at exactly eleven—do you understand me?"

"Why?"

"Because, if I'm there, I may have more scoop. If I'm not in, tell Najira to buzz me and find me, okay? Then I'll call you when I'm able to talk. Don't call my cell, whatever you do—you'll only get voice mail. Where I'm going, I'll need to turn it off. She'll be able to find me, though."

"Done."

"Good." Laura sat down at her desk and toyed with the Post-it note that had Paxton's number on it. "And don't you ever give me up as your source. Gotta go."

She hung up and took a deep breath, then hit the intercom. "You got Donald Haines for me yet?"

"Two seconds, boss lady. Was just waiting for your line to

clear. His secretary is waiting for him to get off his current call."

"Good. I'll keep my line open." Laura stood and paced. When the line buzzed, she covered her heart with her hand—her nerves had so much torque. "Donald," she said fast, then dropped her voice. "We need to talk."

"Is everything all right, Laura?" He spoke slowly, apprehension drawing out his words.

"No," she said in a conspiratorial tone. "That thing we talked about needs to get nailed down ASAP. I got a call from a media buddy . . . seems this problem has grown legs and is walking through several houses. Do you understand me?"

"How far is it walking?"

"All the way to Harrisburg and back—starting with the city's *major* curriculum development contractor."

He paused and let out his breath hard. "You have got to be kidding me."

"Nope. But you didn't hear that from me. What I will say is this: watch the noon news. Then we should have a late coffee."

"I'll meet you down at the Union League."

"Very good," she said, her voice made to sound relieved. "I'll work on a succession plan this morning."

"Do it. I have a few calls to make to secure those buildings."

"Donald . . . I'm so sorry to have to have called you first thing this morning with something like this."

"Dear Laura, good thing you're an earlier riser and caught this before the shit hit the fan. See you at four."

She set down the telephone and picked up the Post-it note, then grabbed her coat and her purse and headed out the door.

"Najira, listen—something came up. I need to run to an unscheduled meeting, but I'll be at this number around eleven," she said, thrusting the Post-it note into Najira's hand.

"Before that, I'll be in a closed-door session, but around eleven, if Rick calls, you call me immediately at this number. It's very important. Understood?"

"Right, no problem," Najira replied, putting the number securely in the triangle of her blotter. "You want me to—"

"No," she said fast, knowing where her cousin was leading. "You give *no one* that number. It's a private office. You call me, because I'm the only one authorized to have it, and I'll buzz Rick back. Clear?"

Najira grinned and saluted. "Girl, what are you up to? This is mad-crazy—"

"Paxton," Laura whispered, her stare unblinking. "If you don't call me *exactly* at eleven, it'll cost me—dearly. Help a sister out, and stay true to the game. That's all I can say. Making the rest up as I go."

Najira opened her mouth and then closed it, unable to answer immediately. "Go get 'em, boss," she finally murmured, then winked. "This must be serious money you're huntin' today. Good luck."

"Thanks, kiddo." Laura was out the door.

Her feet were hitting the pavement so hard and so fast, she had to be careful not to bite her tongue. As soon as she jumped into her car, she dialed another number, and wedged the phone between her shoulder and her cheek as she backed out of the space and headed down the parking lot ramp.

"Brother Akhan," she said, cutting off his normal salutation, "I need a word, and I need it fast."

"Go over the Girard Avenue Bridge and meet me at our normal spot in the park. It's a beautiful day—we should talk as we walk and get some air."

"Half hour."

"Ashé."

* * *

She dodged in and out of thick traffic until she could weave her way to I-676 to hit the Art Museum exit and come to the bridge through the neighborhood back door. She'd make her left off Girard and find Brother Akhan chilling on a bench. When he heard certain voice tones, the old dude didn't deal with technology. In his mind, which was probably correct—or at least valid from his previous experience—a phone could be tapped, a house could be jacked, and the old brother had made it this long in the trenches by trusting half of what he saw, and none of what he heard. She could dig it. So, outside walking in the hood and talking in the old patois black code was the only way.

Sure enough, he'd beaten her there and was looking at the colors of the fall leaves and feeding the pigeons bread like he was just a bored retiree. He had on his lint-ridden purple and gold crocheted wool cap, his army fatigue jacket, a gold and red African print dashiki, khaki pants with white socks, and sandals. She smiled, feeling comforted that some things hadn't changed since dirt.

Knowing he hated the conspicuous when he was in one of his on-the-move-to-shake-the-man moods, she hit her car alarm and parked a block away from him and walked toward him, making her footfalls loud enough to forewarn her approach and not to panic him. It never ceased to amaze her how the neighborhoods had changed; on one side of the street stood vacant mansions, their regal park-front, copper-rimmed architecture now home to stray dogs, pigeons, and crackheads who had stolen the marble fireplace mantels and copper pipes for a hit, regardless of the boarded-up windows. She peered at the remains of the eight bedroom castles while blustery winds hurried her along. On the other side of the street, where she'd find her mentor, was once immaculately landscaped real estate. This area had been like Camelot; Philly had a lot of those.

As she came into view for Brother Akhan, he stood and smiled and began walking—as though anyone who spotted them would believe this were a casual, chance meeting. She loved him dearly, so she would not giggle at the concept.

"Hey, brother," she said, hailing him as though surprised.

"Young queen sister," he said as he turned and hugged her, and then walked more slowly beside her.

"Thanks so much, and I didn't mean to start your day off with drama, but there is going to be some drama later today."

"Your voice told me that," he said, deep in thought. "How bad?"

"At least the big five families, not counting Price, who they already have, except Paxton—who doesn't have his hands in that particular till at the moment. He's in it somehow, but I'm not sure to what extent."

"I don't want to even ask you how you know all of this," he muttered.

They said no more as they walked to find a place to sit. Frustration claimed her; all that planning and she'd overlooked Paxton . . . had just thought he was the group's business attorney, hadn't seen any money from them change hands to his, so she'd made a judgment error. Damn. And he'd been the one quietly directing traffic all along, not Darien. But that was okay. It wasn't too late to correct a minor variable. This situation was surely going to have half of Philly's Black Bar Association tied up in litigation teams to keep the big five from going to jail. Paxton couldn't represent all of them—that would present a conflict of interest.

The elderly man scratched his chin as they found a bench and sat. Piles of dead leaves swirled around their feet, and Laura sat beside her mentor, carefully trying to avoid snags in her coat from the juts of broken, grimy wood.

"You need that succession plan yesterday, then?"

She nodded. "But I also wanted to ask you something."

He looked at her squarely and grasped one of her hands. "Anything."

Actually, she had a hundred questions for her beloved mentor, but she could only ask a few of them without getting him too involved for his own good. She took her time as his eyes searched hers with wisdom.

"Ask me the one about the young man first," he said after a moment, smiling.

She chuckled and looked away. "Did my dad ever hang out with a guy named James Carter . . . a cop?"

Brother Akhan squeezed her hand more tightly. "Good man. Good soldier. Died carrying important documents that me and your father collected at my kitchen table . . . but I'd tried to warn your father that the timing . . ." He shook his head and swallowed hard.

"Tell me again, what was in the documents?" She held his hand with both of hers now.

"Like I told you before, child. Copies of bank statements that showed checks cut for work never done, people never employed . . . credit card expense reimbursement for personal junkets—and probably the most damning thing was copies of the contracts to consulting firms that showed gross conflicts of interest." Brother Akhan let his breath out hard.

"But you never told me the cop's name."

He looked away from her. "He was murdered in the community . . . and we didn't want you to ever go snooping anywhere near that. Too dangerous for a sister—and you're so headstrong like your daddy, you would have." He returned a gentle gaze to her and sighed. "Among others, we've lost good warrior Dave Richardson, who fought till his young heart gave out; we've lost good warrior sister Roxanne Jones, whose health got run into the ground—they were young and such good legislators, trying to fight from the inside out, like you. Too many young people were falling, and we didn't want you to be one of them. So I made a decision to leave it rest."

A pang of guilt shot through her, knowing that those named were above reproach and had never done anything like she had to do to even the scales. They'd fought on the up-and-up; she was going guerrilla, inside, and without the checks and balances of the law.

"I know," she finally said. "But I just can't wrap my mind around a part of it." She had relaxed a bit, now that she'd corroborated Carter's story. Yet knowing that James Carter had integrity only made the other things she had to do today all the more difficult. She held her mentor's gaze for a moment and then looked up at the sky, squinting at the sun. "Those docs are long gone, so there'd never be a way to prove it. They could claim records from 1977, or a vital section of it, was lost in computer transitions—whatever."

"Yes. But the ancestors have a way of righting things from the spirit world. You just said a house of cards is coming down—and you have been chosen to build the house back up with a righteous structure that will last. . . . There are certain cosmic laws we cannot ignore or avoid. The truth will always out."

A shiver passed through her. She withdrew her hand from his and wrapped her arms around herself not to sully him. Her hands had been in more shit than the old man could fathom, God bless him, and she could only pray that what he'd said was just superstition.

"Did you know that Darien Price is really Michael Paxton's half brother, not his godbrother?"

Brother Akhan leaned toward her, putting one arm over the back of the bench to steady himself. "What did you say, Laura?"

"Monica Price told me, when she was begging for a seat at the table. She'd slept with Paxton Jr. and somehow found out when he laughed in her face. They may try to pin it on her, but that sister isn't involved in Price's credit card mess—that I can guarantee you."

She watched Brother Akhan close his eyes, sit back slowly, and fold his hands in his lap.

"All this time we thought it was just J. D. the Second . . ."

"What do you mean?"

Brother Akhan opened his eyes and stared out at the birds. "We thought Price did your father and ordered a hit on that black cop, then *the man* got to Price Senior and covered it up—because he was foolish enough to leave them exposed. We thought he'd gotten too big for his britches. Don't you think it's odd that Darien's father died within six months of yours?"

She nodded. This was why she'd come here. "Darien would have just turned twenty-one at the end of seventy-seven. Dad was indicted in late seventy-five . . . two years of that horror, then given a meter-reader job, and Mom died—then his heart gave out. He never even lived to come back from the political ashes. Yeah, seventy-seven. I'll never forget that year."

"Yep," the old man said. "The year of Darien's inheritance. Same year a shrewd attorney husband might want a blood test, if a little bug got in his ear—and in Philly, a little bug always gets in an ear like wax." He paused and leaned back, his expression pained from Laura's recitation of the past. "That's the kind of thing that might make a man lose his cool . . . might make him start throwing around threats about exposing other things he knew in a fit of rage . . . and anger can cloud judgment, can upset an applecart. Maybe *the man* didn't do him, after all. Profound."

"Damn . . ." Laura sat back and stared at the same tree that now held Brother Akhan's attention. "Sorry for the language, but you understand what I'm saying. All this time, I thought one of y'all did Price, truth be told."

He chuckled but shook his head no. "What would make you think that, child?"

"I figured that since he supposedly had a heart attack, brought on by a poor mix of medication and a so-called nightcap, when we all knew the dude was an alcoholic—only black folks in housekeeping positions could have spiked his drink . . . assuming old J. D. didn't die of natural causes. Now I'm inclined to believe that a wife with a baby by another man might have had cause, just like a good buddy would be able to come over, have a drink, and leave a man dying in his own home. Too crazy."

Her mentor chuckled harder. "We thought *the man* poisoned him, and none of us delved into it further, because Price was such a mean bastard and the people hated him." Brother Akhan swallowed away his chuckles and waved his hand over the ground behind the bench. "God rest his soul—when you get to my age, Laura, you don't bait heaven and you don't speak ill of the dead."

"Okay," she said, trying her best not to smile. "Well, we can assume the mob didn't get to him—in Philly, anyway, they do two shots in the back of the head in a parking lot, or throw you off the Camden side of the Ben Franklin Bridge. For them, poisoning a drink is too subtle a method. Main Liners don't care enough about these little peanuts to worry themselves with killing a man—if this was D.C., and international money, then maybe."

"We should have had this conversation a long time ago; then I could have saved several brothers all those nights on my stoop arguing about how this went down."

"Ashé . . . but I didn't know it then." She looked at her mentor until he looked at her. "Darien still doesn't know."

"Ummph, ummph, ummph." Brother Akhan stood and stretched. "The sins of the father shall be visited upon the son. Now I understand how Darien got caught with his hands in the cookie jar. With Mrs. Price deceased, plus old man Paxton dead and buried, Darien's big brother must have laid for him to mess up, knowing a kid like Darien eventually would, and just left him hanging out to dry. This way, he keeps his hands clean and lets that poor, foolish boy tie his own noose—even though he is now professing to be his attorney . . . after having taken his wife, Monica, just like old man Paxton took a best friend's wife, Juanita Price." Brother Akhan leaned forward. "You know, that's old Sicilian law—kill your opponent, and then take his wife and castle. I've seen it all now. Black folks modeling themselves behind the worst of *the devil.* Ummph!"

Laura shook her head, and grudgingly had to admit the brilliance of Michael Paxton Jr.'s plan against Darien. "When did Mrs. Price die?"

Brother Akhan rubbed his chin. "Year after old man Price did . . ."

"Which was?"

They both looked at each other.

"Late seventies—like seventy-eight, or seventy-nine."

"And how did Paxton Senior die?" Laura looked at Brother Akhan hard now. "Heart attack, or stroke?"

"He had a car accident on Lincoln Drive in the winter. They said he was driving drunk, was depressed from losing his wife, Colette Paxton, the month earlier—the roads were treacherous. She'd had a stroke . . . brought on by too many Valiums and too much liquor, just like Juanita Price did. If you ask me, too much money made 'em all crazy."

Laura stood and began walking beside Brother Akhan as they proceeded slowly to her car. "One sounds like a mob hit: the car accident . . . the others, suspicious, at best."

"Laura," the elderly man said, touching her arm and stopping her, "you're still trying to get to the head of the hydra, aren't you?"

"I just wanna know."

"Curiosity killed the cat."

"But satisfaction brought her back. Information is power, Brother Akhan—you taught me that."

"Ashé. But, young warrior sister, please be careful. The old ones are all dead. The universe is efficient. They've all had something tragic happen to them one by one, and now their children are squabbling over the crumbs of their inheritance. Let the ancestors sort out this mess. Just focus on setting up opportunities for the people, with the grace and dignity of a queen."

"But, Brother Akhan, do you know how many opportunities these people have blocked for others, and that their children are still blocking? Have you any idea of just how many lives they've ruined because some people who deserved a chance couldn't get a break? And let's not even talk about the resources they've squandered that were supposed to go to poor people!"

"I know, but don't damage your karma by getting into the muck and mire by doing things like they do. The wrongs have been cosmically corrected—let it be. We cannot start conducting ourselves like *the man,* which is how these errant children got themselves into trouble in the first place. They forgot their basic principles. To be justifiably outraged is one thing; to act in anger for vengeance is another. You will not . . . Promise me?"

For the first time in her life she had to look someone in the eyes whom she loved more than life itself and tell a bold-faced lie. "I promise," she whispered.

"Good."

She felt a piece of her heart rip away from its muscle anchors in her chest as he let out his breath, smiled at her warmly, and relaxed. They resumed walking as the leaves whirled before them in plumes of bright fall colors like African dancers. How could she explain that the opportunities they were now privy to had come from sleight of hand, fast maneuvering, adept schmoozing, and a few other things that she didn't want to name? Couldn't name. Not ever in Brother Akhan's presence. She respected him way too much.

"How did my grandfather die?" she asked out of the blue, making them both stop walking.

Brother Akhan's gaze found the horizon, and he sighed. "I can only assume that you know what happened to your mother when she was a girl . . . if you asked me that. That's why your situation, even though a near miss, wore on her to the point where she had to tell your father about it."

Laura nodded, but his statement struck her.

Her mentor didn't look at her to know that she had responded. He simply replied with a parable. "That wrong got righted long ago. Then your grandfather was lynched down in North Carolina for addressing the problem. I became a warrior from that day forward, and the family moved here. Case closed. So we will let the dead rest, and you will not be a part of history repeating itself." Now he looked at her with a firm stare and waited for Laura's nod before they resumed walking.

She could hear leaves and twigs crack under her heels and his sandals as they walked to her car. It all made sense: why her mother, a Hewitt, feared men in power, why her uncles on both sides addressed issues with sudden force, and why the Caldwell clan banded together so tightly and taught strategy. Her father must have known what had happened to her mother. That piece of the puzzle was now clear. Brother Akhan was a Hewitt before he changed his name and was a master strategist. Made sense—he'd lost his brother, her grandfather, to the sword and had altered his own approach thereafter. Interesting.

Laura kept her gaze on the horizon. Members of both sides of her family were all products of what had been visited upon them in the past. And yet, by an eerie confluence of events, she was involved up to her eyebrows in something that could start the whole cycle of feudal wars and flight all over again.

Brother Akhan hugged her when they came to her car, which only made her feel worse for having to lie to him. How could she just let it go?

"Now, remember," he said firmly, holding her back to stare at her. "A good queen warrior must know where her line is . . . where the point is that she will not allow her integrity to be breached—just like she must know when it is time to retreat to fight another day. We are a people who come from the first people who know about time and patience. There is a saying: 'The ox is slow, but the earth is patient.' So today we will get a list of approved names, and we will let it rest there, Laura. Correct?"

Laura nodded and kissed his cheek, with no intentions of letting it go there. No Scorpio could do that. It just wasn't in her nature.

Chapter 13

She glanced at her watch as she sipped a cup of coffee at the Oregon Avenue Diner. Her mother's words filtered into her mind, drifting like the smell of coffee and the sounds of cheap china clinking within the restaurant.

Laura remembered it like it was yesterday. Her mother had taken her by the hand from the kitchen table. She stood and followed her mother into the dining room. When her mom flipped on the light, Laura squinted and watched her mother come toward her from a faraway place in her mind. Her mother kissed her forehead and turned her around to face the mirror that had once belonged to her grandmother.

"Baby girl," her mother had said gently, "look at you . . ." She brushed back the wild mane of black, bushy hair from Laura's face. "I know you're upset, but before your daddy wakes up and we get him all worked up, you need to understand why now isn't a good time to tell him about this. . . . You have to get this in your head and understand as much as you can—now—not tomorrow morning, not later, but now."

Her mother's expression held a plea for understanding in

it, and she let out her breath slowly, resuming her mother-daughter speech with great effort.

"All your life I've been trying to keep you blind to this so you'd see with your heart . . . and that was my fault. I thought by now we would have moved beyond all this in our community, but some things ain't changed since slavery. They almost ripped out your heart tonight."

Her mother shook her head, and her jaw tensed before she let out a patient breath and began to speak again. Laura just watched the woman slowly pick her words.

"Some men are gonna want you, and some women are gonna hate you, for no other reason than because you're the color of tea in milk, have eyes that are as fiery and wild and black as your hair, which is so silky that you have to *make it* be an Afro style. Some things ain't changed; I don't care what they say about the black power movement, the struggle, or whatever other rhetoric they got to say. Some of your own family got problems with you 'cause of this—the very ones most revolutionary, understand? Top it all off, God gave you a twenty-two-inch waist and legs long enough to shame a thoroughbred racer."

Her mother sighed and lifted Laura's chin with a finger, making her daughter stand taller. "And none of it's your fault, baby. But you've got assets. Don't let carpetbaggers and charlatans ever rob you of that which Father God gave you, or allow them to make you blind to what you have of real value: your integrity. Your good name. Sometimes that's all you got is your good name."

"Assets? We're not rich, Mom," Laura protested. "And our name isn't up on—"

"Fact is, every woman has assets, and in today's environment, you're rich beyond measure. We might be plain folks, but our family name has never been sullied. Women in your generation have options we didn't have in our day. Let the shortsighted be dazzled and blinded by the outside, but always use your brain. That's been a woman's secret weapon in an unfair world since the dawn of time. Been poor black folks' strong suit, too. Hear me? Don't ever lose sight of that. And like you did tonight, fight with everything you have at your disposal to sway the advantage your way, hear? They don't play fair; remember that. Never did. Keep your integrity, but don't let 'em run over you. But pick your battles so you can win."

Laura wasn't totally sure about what-all her mom meant then, or who the invisible "they" was, but she got the basic gist of what had been said, and nodded her head just the same. Back then she'd wondered what her mother was talking about. And her voice had been so hushed and so urgent, and she had spoken so fast, that it was like some secret code that had made her mother sound crazy.

"Your hourglass top and bottom have made grown men turn around since you were twelve and wearing a C cup . . . and that Cherokee in you from your grandmother makes your face look like a piece of chiseled art. That's *why* you. Don't sell yourself short. Understand?"

Laura stared at her reflection in the diner window, remembering too well how she'd stared at her reflection in the dining room mirror. Then she could only seem to make out a torn green gown, a hideous pair of mascara-ringed eyes that looked like they belonged to a raccoon, a wild head of hair sticking up like she was a bat out of hell, and red marks from where all her faux silver jewelry had popped off on the car floor in a Cadillac fight. She shook her head.

She'd told her mother, "He could have picked one of them that wouldn't have fought him. It didn't have to be all of this."

"Baby girl," her mother had said, gathering her into her arms, "understand this now about men, especially powerful men: they always want what they can't have. He underestimated you. They've created myths that beautiful women aren't deadly. Beautiful women won't put up a fight. Beautiful women are stupid, easy, and can be bought like an inexpensive trophy. He thought you were like the others, but didn't have a clue—which gave you the surprise advantage of getting your solid right hook off first."

Her mother had nodded, pulled back a bit, and held Laura's jaw in her hand. "Sometimes it's best not to let them see you coming for them. When you're weaker, you've gotta be smarter, faster, and you have to make the blow count, then get out quick." Her mother nodded again. "Ask me how I know."

Once more, new understanding had happened so fast that it made her head spin. For the first time in her life, Laura had witnessed her mother as a woman beyond the known role of just being her parent. She'd stared in the mirror at the woman whom she was the spitting image of, a younger, genetic carbon copy of . . . only her mother's hair was styled in a short, natural black and silver pageboy that stopped right beneath her earlobes. Instead of a green gown, her mother wore an orange and yellow print sundress and blue apron. The resemblance was eerie. She'd never noticed how much they looked alike before that moment.

The only real difference was that her mother's frame was thicker than hers. But one could make out the once svelte figure her mom had, which was partially hidden by the birth of three little girls, and time. Their coloring was the same; their eyes were the same; only laugh lines, wise eyes, and glasses gave one away as the elder.

It was as though her mother was reading her mind that night. The older woman had smiled sadly and rested her chin on her daughter's shoulder, still staring in the mirror. "I gave you the blue pamphlet that came with the box of Kotex pads when you started your period, and I told you everything about how the body works. I just didn't explain some of the more advanced concepts not in the little blue book that came with the starter kit. Should have bought the 'A' encyclopedia in the supermarket and had you look up the definition for 'ape.' Or maybe 'P' for 'pure *park* ape.' That's how men act when you look like you do."

Her mother had walked to the doorway, giving Laura her

back. She took in a huge breath and closed her eyes as though summoning the strength not to holler. The image of her mother retreating in the diner window made Laura's eyes fill. She didn't want her to leave, wanted the apparition to stay and have coffee and visit a little while longer.

The vision hesitated. "Why you?" her mother said quietly, picking up where her previous sentence had left off. "Because you are fiery, pretty, and smart. He was slumming, or thought he could with you. Wanted what he thought could be had, a replica of what they have in daughters up there, but without any of the social inconveniences of entanglements or respect. You look like them and were tucked away down here, courtesy your father's employment situation. A black man didn't stand a chance in his day—unless he was from connected people . . . old Philadelphia families. Your dad isn't from that stock . . . but I married him over the others because he had a level of integrity that they'll never possess."

Silence shadowed her mother, and Laura watched her play with her wedding band as she appeared lost in thought about what to say next. Her mother had been the one with options, choices, in that day, all because of what she looked like? Her mother could have passed for New Orleans Creole, and that meant she could have married somebody other than Dad? Deep . . . Her mom gave up marrying some rich guy to be with Dad—for love? Like in the movies and whatnot? Oh, my God . . . It was all too heavy in the midst of what she'd just been through that night.

The vision smiled at her. "Laura, close your mouth. That's been going on since we came over here in chains—powerful men go slumming and then marry the girl who is socially acceptable because she comes from their same level in society. First white folks did that to us, and then we learned from them and did that to ourselves. It's called a caste system, baby. And it's alive and well in America. When it's time to go to college, you'll really see it in action. One day I'll tell you how I know . . . and why I didn't go to school and decided to marry your father instead."

"I hate them," Laura murmured, her voice garbled by the thick, salty mucus in her throat.

"Don't," her mother whispered, coming back toward Laura to attempt to hug her injured child. But the glass of the diner window separated them. "It will only harden your heart, make you miserable, and that will affect your life, not theirs. They're pitiful, and they do such things to people that they'll have a lot to answer for come Judgment Day. These people do not live happy lives, Laura."

Laura shrugged out of her mother's visual hold. She remembered telling the woman she loved, "I'm not trying to wait for Judgment Day for everything, Mom. That's why I kicked his natural butt like a man would have. I wasn't letting this soft punk just rob me . . . rape me . . . put his hands on me, Mom." Now only her eyes could communicate that.

"Correct," the vision repeated, just like she'd told Laura twenty-six years ago. "But the best revenge is success, baby. Learn that concept today, tonight, and never, ever forget your mother told you about it—hear?" Her mother waited for a moment, seeming unsure that her lesson was taking root. "Do not focus on him, getting back at him with nasty, petty little digs, or worrying what others like him will think about you. Let go and let God deal with his kind."

Was her mother crazy? Just walk away and act like nothing had happened? Didn't grandma say, "You can show 'em better than you can tell 'em"? In a standoff, the two women stared at each other, one staring into the plate glass diner window, the other a figment of the imagination. Laura softened her mental voice as the old, frightening question formed in her mind again. *This happened to you before, didn't it, Mom?*

The tick of the dining room clock answered the question as her mother's gaze slid away and her voice became very distant within Laura's brain.

"Yes, baby . . . but I wasn't as lucky as you." Her mother swallowed hard. "I told, and it cost your grandfather his life back then. Let it be, Laura. It could've been worse."

Just like her sister Nadine could remember going through a nasty divorce like it was yesterday, she could remember the feeling of helplessness, of victimization, and watching nearly repeated history decimate another woman to the core—her mother.

Never again.

Yet, not a moment went by that she wished she'd never asked her mother that final question, and strangely, not a moment went by when she hadn't wished that she'd asked deeper, more defining questions to understand what her mother had actually been through . . . or who had killed her grandfather. Now it was too late. Her uncle would never divulge it. Secrets, family secrets, haunted them all.

At fifteen, she could not believe her ears, nor could she understand half of what she was hearing then. Laura remembered the look on her mother's face, a woman whom she loved more than life itself. Then new tears had made her mother's image go blurry—just like the street traffic beyond the diner window was going blurry now. A mere question had traumatized them both.

Laura rolled the cool cup of coffee between her palms, fighting the shivers that claimed her spirit. It wouldn't have served any purpose at that point to tell her mom how strange Mrs. Price had seemed, like a woman trapped in her own home and clearly high on something more than the dark liquor she drank. What was there, really, to tell—how the poor woman's hands shook, and how Mrs. Price couldn't look her in the eyes as she kept getting up from the sofa to refill a short, cut-crystal rocks glass from a dining room decanter? No, it wouldn't have been possible to tell her mom what Darien's father had said to her . . . how the old buzzard smelled like a bear when he got up close in her face, supposedly to shake her hand . . . his sweaty palm winding up on her shoulder instead, lingering there, or how that old son of a bitch looked her over with a leer, winked at his son, and told them to have fun at the prom . . . *After the fact, she understood.* But she'd missed her window of opportunity to bring closure to the subject with her mother.

Everything made sense in context, hindsight being twenty-twenty. The real truth was that she had only herself to blame. Fact was, she hadn't told her mother vital pieces of this critical information—which would have probably aborted the entire mission—because she'd wanted to go to this prom so badly that the last thing she was gonna do was cast aspersions on any aspect of the people or the event. When she'd come home from visiting them before the whole prom nightmare, all she'd said was that the Prices were really nice and had a fabulously plush home. Under what circumstances had her mother been placed at risk? she wondered. Did that victim blame herself, too?

But she refused to call herself a victim—she'd fought and prevailed. Always would. That's what she couldn't get her sisters to understand. Suddenly it all made her skin crawl.

Her parents had gone with the info they had to work with. Blame was pointless. Who knew? They were victims themselves. Laura shook her head and brought her hand up to massage her temple. They were all fighting their own demons . . . she'd always wondered if her father ever knew that her mother had been raped as a young girl . . . now Brother Akhan had confirmed that he did. And she also understood the attraction between her father and mother—Dad was safe, was from 'round the way, and was feared enough in those circles to keep a line of respect drawn at her mother's feet.

Looking back, it was pitiful, if not laughable, that she'd actually prayed to God to make her parents relent, to let her go somewhere with Darien Price. Now she was supposed to pray to Him to let her forgive and forget so that she could let it go? Stupid. She shouldn't have gotten God into this mess in the first place.

Her head was pounding. A dagger of pain was stabbing her in the temple. Laura sniffed hard; her nose was running.

She wanted to tell her mom so badly that this wasn't about religion, but too late—her mother was dead. At fifteen she'd learned that it was all about power—who had it and who didn't. It was about trust. Ethics. Integrity. Morals. Maybe religion entered here; she didn't know.

What she did know was that her parents had trusted these muckety-mucks because of the same thing Darien had judged her on: appearances. She'd trusted her own faulty judgment and her mother's supposedly omnipotent powers of perception to keep her safe or get her out of a jam. She'd trusted her date. She'd trusted her daddy always to be there to right a wrong. She'd trusted that if you were black you couldn't get away with stuff like this—a white boy could, yeah, but black people? Didn't we always go to jail?

So, who the hell were these people that got treated like white folks? Who were these new types of Negroes who looked beautifully bourgeois on the outside but were crazy-ghetto trifling on the inside, worse than the people around the way they looked down their noses upon? Now she understood her cousins' street-corner passion and conspiracy theory philosophies. This outrageous shit was mind blowing! Laura could feel her grasp tighten on her cold coffee cup.

"I know it's all a bitter pill to swallow," her mother had finally whispered, coming nearer to Laura and fidgeting with one of the broken straps on her dress, "but in the end, they get theirs. You have to have faith and just move forward—can't look back like Lot's wife. You'll turn into a pillar of salt and won't be able to move forward."

Those broken straps. Damn. A new trickle of hot tears rolled down Laura's cheeks. "Really?" she whispered. In the end these people got theirs? "Yeah, right."

Who created the scales of justice? Who ensured that the bogus did indeed get checked and stopped and outed when they did unthinkable shit to another human being? Huh! Her mind was shouting; she wanted to scream and yell and curse now just like she'd wanted to do then but couldn't, because her mother already seemed worn out—beaten down by just knowing what had almost happened to her daughter, and remembering what did happen to her. Somebody had to deal with idiots like this.

Laura glanced at her watch as she banished the vision. Fuck crying. It was about action. She dabbed her face, careful not to smear her makeup. Ten a.m. She stared at her cell phone resting neatly beside her spoon, drew a deep breath and picked it up, then punched in Paxton's number. She glanced around the nearly empty establishment. On the second ring, he picked up. She let her breath out in a controlled stream through her nose. Lucky break—he could have still been in the middle of his meeting, had it on vibrate, not recognized the number, and ignored it.

"I've made a decision."

"Laura?"

Good. He knew her voice. That meant she had him practically trained. "Yeah, it's me . . . Where are you?"

"Finishing up a meeting at The Hotel Dupont in Wilmington."

His voice had dipped; he was obviously glad she'd called. Very good.

"Can you get clear for eleven this morning?"

"That's kind of tight . . . I have a meeting in Center City scheduled for noon."

"Break it. I've made a decision."

He chuckled low and sexy. She chuckled with him.

"Which decision?"

She could hear him walking. He was on the move.

"The one I couldn't make in the Bourse lot."

He paused.

She lowered her voice and infused a sensual promise in her tone. "My decision is a potentially embarrassing one," she murmured, allowing charged pauses in her statement and delighting in the cold truth in what she'd said. "Unless that doesn't work for you?"

"Where do you want to consummate this transaction?"

She smiled. He was speaking in code, might even be

walking with a client now. This was good, because he hadn't ended the call—which meant she was taking priority over immediate business; therefore he was vulnerable. Excellent. "You previously offered a secluded waterfront venue . . ."

Again he paused.

"If that poses a logistical problem . . ." She let her statement trail off.

"No. I can be there in forty-five minutes—but how did you get my number?"

She paused. "I'm resourceful. I *begged* Anne for it . . . and now you have mine."

This time when he stopped speaking, he swallowed hard. She heard it clear as day.

"You have a pen handy—I'll give you my address."

Ahhh . . . so he was no longer walking in tandem with a client. He wouldn't have gotten that personal and dropped the code.

"I don't need one. I can remember it."

As soon as he'd rattled off the location, she hung up without saying good-bye, and stared out the diner window.

Only twenty-four hours, and he'd won. Paxton watched the front end of his Saab eat up I-95. What a way to start the day: a substantial renewal of his corporate retainer, and now a call like this from Laura Caldwell . . .

Nobody in Philly had even gotten close, and they had *all* tried. Losers. Plus she was opening her 12.5 million-dollar purse for him as well as her long, gorgeous legs? This was a triumph of perfection. Donald Haines was going to shit his pants when he found out . . . and he would indeed find out, when it was most beneficial.

The white lines on the highway whizzed by as Paxton dodged slower-moving vehicles that had been in his way. That voice of hers, too. Man . . . If he was lucky, he could push his noon client back to one and still not miss a beat in his day. *She changed her mind.* Correction: her mind had already been made up at dinner, and it was a question of when, versus if, with a woman like Laura. And if she was half as good as he anticipated she'd be, he might have to keep this going for a while.

He let his mind wander, envisioning what he might do to her, how she'd sound, her texture, her smell, her feel. Like brand-new money—excellent.

When his vehicle came to the bottom of the ramp at the Christopher Columbus Boulevard exit, he had to remind himself to exercise patience. But the light took forever to change. No traffic in sight, no cops to bust his balls—he ran it, heading toward the Northern Liberties end of town.

Trying not to appear eager, he glanced around, but her car was nowhere in sight as he pulled into the private lot. Shit. She should have been early, more anxious. Why were women always late? He revved his engine and brought the vehicle to a halt in his numbered reserved spot. Paxton glanced at his Rolex and got out of the car calmly—quarter to eleven. All right, then. Even better. He had time to get upstairs, make a few calls, and collect himself before Laura Caldwell buzzed his intercom.

Laura shook her head in amazement. Paxton hadn't even seen her sitting across the street in a parked cab. Was he mad—to think she'd drive her identifiable black Jag right up to his door in broad daylight? Men were crazy.

She glanced at her watch. "Five minutes, brother. Let the meter run."

The cabbie nodded and began whistling a tune. That was cool. They'd both obviously done this before. She finally pushed a twenty through the grimy Plexiglas slot and hopped out, not looking back.

She had to get her head together. Had to get into character. Had to get Paxton to trust that she was willing to act upon his sage guidance in the hopes of a permanent seat at their table, rather than the temporary one that Donald Haines had given her this fiscal year.

Laura crossed the wide street, her gaze straight ahead on the huge converted marina warehouse. Yet her focus was singular; she had to make this brother's eyes roll back in their sockets so he'd never believe she'd orchestrated any of what was about to go down. He'd be her alibi to the others, for she'd be in his presence when the bullshit blew. And the more they scrambled as the chips scattered, they'd pull her in deeper, and would have no other choice but to tell her where subcontracts lay, where holding companies held secret holding companies that they owned in other people's names.

That's where she'd find Paxton's stash, which would probably point to his own father's secret coffers—which undoubtedly led to who whacked old man Price and her dad . . . perhaps James Carter's father, too. Price was in it, for sure, but had already been taken care of. The big five families, via Paxton, would have to tell her where to reroute contracts to benefit them, because their first layer of veneer was about to be stripped away at eleven o'clock.

Yeah, Michael Paxton Jr. needed to be anxious for her to get there. She was gonna fuck him good.

He set his cup of coffee down very slowly on the six-foot slave ship replica covered by glass, which served as a coffee table, stared into the open hull of it, and took his time walking over to the intercom. He had to get it together. It wasn't about ever letting a woman see that he wanted her this badly. No, this was as much a transaction as it was a delightful, diversionary tryst.

He glanced at the video monitor, smiled, and just buzzed Laura's entry when she rang his bell, not giving her the satisfaction of his voice confirmation. She looked absolutely undone, standing there fidgeting with her purse as if she was a virgin to afternoon escapades. He'd break her in real good.

Paxton took a seat on the sofa and listened to the elevator motor engage, summoning patience. But damn, she looked awesome . . . was even wearing spike-heeled boots. She'd *have* to keep those on.

When the doors opened, he counted to three and then stood. "Good morning."

"Hi," she said shyly, glancing around like she was lost. "Nice place."

Laura smiled and took her time to let her senses adjust to what had to be no less than four thousand square feet of open space. Okay. It was like that, huh? She'd expected no less. Tiny-paned windows from the floor to the ceiling on three sides, with a Delaware River view. Ridiculously huge, skylight-opened ceiling, black and silver ductwork, recessed and studio custom lights. Enough wood flooring to wipe out a forest. Crazy art from every corner of the globe. A double-wide floating staircase. Oriental rugs, Swedish modern furniture with an eclectic mix of Victorian . . . stovepipe fireplace, a bar bigger than most corner hangouts could boast. Her eyes stopped at the slave ship coffee table—now, *that* was deep. Artistic, and probably cost a mint to have made, but eerie.

Her gaze began moving again as she appraised Paxton's massive black entertainment center with a huge, flat HDTV. Classical jazz was floating in from surround-sound speakers—*sheeit.* Paxton had designed Gotham City.

"You like it?"

She didn't walk over to him; this was the power play part . . . he had to come to her. She nodded and waited. She watched the tension in him as he struggled against the pull of brand-new, hot pussy versus man games. What to do, what to do? He had a noon appointment and had probably pushed it back to one—again, making assumptions. She glanced at her watch and acted as if she might change her mind. Women were known to do that . . . He walked toward her. Good.

"This is very, very nice, Michael."

She used his name, low and deep the way she knew he

wanted her to. She dropped her bag on the floor and took off her coat, leaving it in a pile beside her purse, and watched his eyes. That move had fucked him up. He definitely wasn't expecting it—thought she was gonna play cat-and-mouse. Not today. Power was always an aphrodisiac.

She unzipped her dress at the front, allowing it to fall open without totally taking it off. He stopped walking, like she knew he'd have to. Momma wasn't bullshitting when she'd hooked up her gear. She'd played a hunch and used the information Najira had given her, figured that he'd be the type that liked black leather. It wasn't all that much of a stretch, really—he was a control freak. Bustier with heavy silver metal clasps, garters, leather thong, black silk hose, and boots. Yeah, she was ready. She noticed he still had his cell phone on his belt. Thought she was a rookie. Very good. It vibrated with a call. He glanced down at it but ignored it. Even better.

"I told you I had decided to embarrass myself today," she murmured.

"Damn," he said quietly, his gaze raking over her, "And last night I admitted that I just might embarrass myself."

"Don't worry, if it gets messy, I'll leave my boots on . . ."

He briefly shut his eyes at the suggestion, then closed the short distance between them. The wall clock said three minutes to eleven. He touched her face, his fingers trembling. She knew he didn't know where to begin, so she started the transaction for him.

She grabbed both sides of his face and kissed him hard, biting his lower lip as she pulled away. As soon as she'd done that, it was like he'd mentally snapped. But she had to control this dance. His hands gathered fistfuls of her ass; she bit his neck and he cried out. She pushed him away and roughly opened the knot in his paisley silk tie. He was holding her hard by the upper arms as she ripped the tie through one side of his collar and very slowly wound it around her fists. Tears of anticipation were practically standing in his eyes. He let her go as he closed his lids and leaned his head back. She looped the silk over his neck and pulled him to her once more, biting his right nipple through his shirt until he shuddered and grabbed her again. She felt his cell phone vibrate. He was in no condition to answer it. She chuckled.

Laura heard the arm seams of her knit dress tear as they stumbled against the elevator doors. She glanced at the clock—too early. The calls he'd ignored couldn't have been the one she was waiting for.

His teeth were smooth; his tongue fought with hers. The taste of coffee and Hotel Dupont Danish coated her mouth, Lagerfeld stung her nose, and his deep, guttural moan entered her ear on a hot shaft of breath. His skin had the tart flavor of salt from sweat seeping through his pores on an adrenaline rush. Blanketing her, he roughly brought one of her thighs up hard, caught and trapped it in the bend of his elbow, his pants causing friction burns against her. She let go of his tie, wedged her hand between their bodies, and slid it across his groin, eliciting a harsh sound of approval that came up from the base of his throat. His cell phone was vibrating again.

Rock hard, he'd left a damp spot in his expensive suit, and she yanked down his zipper, her eyes now riveted to the clock over his shoulder as she raked his scalp with her free hand and moaned in his ear. The corset was driving him nuts; nicely designed, he couldn't get it open fast enough—but she might have to do the bastard, after all. Shit. She took him in her hand and squeezed hard.

"Take it out," he said, the words colliding together and spilling against her breasts.

"You got something to cover it?" She licked a trail against the side of his neck.

"Yeah—upstairs."

"Go get it, before I do something really stupid."

"Fuck it, I don't care."

She laughed hot in his ear. "I do. Ten minutes from now so will you."

"You're right, you're right." He tried to back up, but she held him, caressing his shaft. He stared at her.

"Unless you want me to suck it first?"

"Oh, shit, woman . . . what kind of question is that?"

"What's my goddamned name?" She tightened her grip.

"Laura."

"Then say it when you put it in." She let him go and slowly opened his belt, holding eye contact with him as she unfastened the fabric beneath it. She slid down his body; his fingers were splayed against the crown of her head, sending her to her knees. She peered up at him, watching the heavy inhales that he took in through widened nostrils and let out through his mouth. His cell vibrated again, and she glimpsed the tiny panel on it; the caller ID was not a number she could identify. *Najira, Rick, come on!*

She jettisoned what Brother Akhan had said from her mind when it rudely tried to gain entry. Looking at seven and a half inches of corded male member, veins pulsing, tip dripping, had a way of banishing such esoteric thoughts from a girl's conscience. She had work to do, couldn't let that dear man's words mess with her head; this was about business—*old,* unfinished business. A transaction to stamp, "debt paid in full." Then she smiled.

"You're vibrating *again,* and it's not your dick." She masked a sigh of relief with feigned annoyance. She glanced at his cell phone and forced herself not to laugh.

"Fuck the phone, baby," Paxton whispered through his teeth.

She snatched it from his belt before he could. In his condition, he was likely to fling it across the room, for all she knew. "Tell your *other appointment* you're busy. Laura's got you booked."

He grabbed the phone from her, drew back to hurl it, and then double-clutched. "It's *your* office number." He stared at her, his chest heaving.

She stood slowly. Ahhh . . . and he'd memorized her number.

"What? My office? Give me the damned phone, Michael. It was probably my previous call to you that's showing on the display, that's all."

"No. This is new incoming. Call them back—what the hell are people from your office doing calling *my* cell?" Paxton was closing the front of his pants, tucking in his shirt, and walking in an agitated circle as he clipped his cell phone back on his belt. "You didn't tell them you were here, or—"

"Pullease." Laura held up her hand and leaned against the elevator frame, then pushed away from it, seeming indignant. "Are you crazy? There has *got* to be a logical explanation." She walked over to her discarded purse and retrieved her own cell phone, hitting speed-dial to her secretary.

Paxton stood in the middle of the floor, appraising her with fury in his eyes.

"Melanie, it's Laura—did you just call me on that restricted number?" She paused and looked at Paxton, who was still glaring at her. She held the phone close to her ear when Najira laughed and grumbled about Laura giving her a corny false name. Laura chose her words careful to play to both audiences. It was a delicious and intricate verbal dance of answering Najira's questions, yet leaving enough room for Paxton to think a communication snafu had occurred because an unmarked number was left on the boss lady's blotter. Najira rattled on, and it was perfect. Laura watched Paxton lose his erection as the mood shifted and she paced and acted frantic.

"Tear up that number that was on my blotter from this morning. Thanks. I know you were. No. Everything's fine. Don't, under any circumstances, call it again, but I appreciate your trying to find me. You didn't leave a voice mail, though?" Laura's grip tightened on her cell—this part was no act. Then she let her breath out fast with relief. Najira was a pro. "Good. Yes. I'll hit him back now. Thanks."

Laura ended the call, closed her eyes, and held her cell phone to her chest. Paxton stalked away from her over to his bar. She began closing up her dress.

"Oh, Michael . . . damn. My apologies. My assistant is young and eager and prides herself on being so efficient . . .

and I left that number on my blotter when Anne gave it to me this morning, with a note; 'meeting site at eleven,' on it. My media contact just called and said something crazy was jumping off down at Don Edward's office, and my assistant immediately freaked because I had had her working on possible contract proposals for—"

"Back up," Paxton said slowly, holding a bottle of Chivas in midpour. "What is jumping off at Don's office?"

"I don't know," Laura said fast. "Let me give my contact a call."

"Do that," Paxton said, checking his own voice mail as she placed the call. He sat down on a stainless steel bar stool, turning away from her while listening to his cell phone messages and sipping his drink as she punched in another number.

When she got Rick on the line, he was laughing. Laura held the phone close to her cheek so that his voice wouldn't be heard, and began walking farther away from Paxton.

"Lady—oh, shit! I can't talk to you now! I owe you a bottle of Dom! Maybe Cristal! Bye!"

Laura clicked off her cell and stared at the wall-mounted telephone as three lines began ringing in Paxton's condo at once.

"Fuckin' A!" He was walking in circles again with the cordless receiver pressed hard to his ear as he took a landline call, tersely saluted the caller, put it on hold, and picked up the two incoming calls in rapid succession, holding his now vibrating cell phone in the other hand. He answered the cell call, asked his secretary to hold, and hit "Mute" on the wall and cell phones. "Baby, I'm sorry—look. I gotta take these calls. Gimme a minute. Don't go anywhere."

"No problem, handle your business," Laura said calmly, putting on her coat and pressing the elevator button. "We'll take this up later." Technology was grand.

"Yeah. Yeah—maybe that's best. I'll call you and make it up to you, promise," he said, walking away from her. "Wait, wait, Brad—I've got Jim and Martin on the other lines, and my office is trying to get through on cell—Anne has Howard and Darien on two lines over there. Wait. No. Calm down. Let me go to my office upstairs and put you guys on speakerphone. No, two seconds—I'm walking now—what the fuck just blew up in Philly?"

Chapter 14

It was all about motion. Laura exited the marina and headed east, saw a cab, hailed it, and hopped in. Eleven-twenty. The cab made a U-turn in the middle of wide Christopher Columbus Boulevard and sped to where the Olde City Penn's Landing charm began to give way to the more commercial and industrial zone. She had to break away from the school of fish, the mass of humanity that would draw together around this latest media shock wave. She didn't doubt that news crews and aerial choppers would be landing on nearby heliports to get a statement from Michael Paxton Jr.

To that end, it was in her best interest to go underground and swim in the opposite direction from the sharks—in a feeding frenzy, they even cannibalized their own. Right now there was too much blood in the water.

At the Dave & Buster's arcade-restaurant lot, she hopped out of the cab and quickly found her car, leaving the garage practically on two wheels, hitting the asphalt with a bounce, burning rubber. Delaware Avenue widened; the traffic got heavier; soon cargo train tracks separated it, leaving moored tall ships, restaurants, night clubs, docks, and industrial buildings on one side, with her and a series of new town houses, strip malls, and the movie theater on the other.

Damn the traffic. She had twenty minutes to get back to her house, rip off her clothes, and find her navy blue Ellen Tracy banker suit, white blouse, a pair of Kenneth Cole low-heeled, square-toe pumps, flesh-tone stockings, and a strand of pearls—Donald Haines would be moving up their four o'clock, for sure. Couldn't go into the Union League looking like a hooker, even though she was pretty sure many had worked the building. Banker blue was the standard uniform to accept a hundred-million-dollar transaction.

She snaked her way through the parallel backstreets of South Philly using the narrow cement corridors and two-story row houses as camouflage, passing the Italian Market, and careful not to get hemmed into the sluggish flow of vehicles as people stopped, double-parked, and violated every motor vehicle law on the books in order to get dock-fresh produce. That had been the way for a hundred years—she knew better.

University Avenue traffic was bottlenecked, making her panic. With the VA Hospital on one side, the University of Pennsylvania on the other, and a slew of prominent medical arts buildings, the morgue, and the city's largest employer—Penn—within a few blocks of each other, the congestion always made the half-mile stretch impossible to connect easily to West Philly's back door from Grays Ferry Avenue Bridge. But it opened up at Market Street, another transition zone. All she had to do was get past First District Plaza at 3801 Market, then Presbyterian Hospital, and she was home free.

Drexel University still hadn't fully developed the land they'd bought, so it was still simple for her to thread her way over Spring Garden Street, passing through the dilapidated Mantua section neighborhood as the perfect cover. With the Spring Garden Street overpass and the Art Museum in sight, she relaxed. A hundred yards, and the neighborhood switched from winos to ritz.

Nobody needed to see her before it was time. Laura glanced at her watch: fifteen minutes had passed. News crews were most assuredly at Michael Paxton's front door. She wondered how long it had taken them to figure out that he wasn't in his office or anywhere else downtown. She laughed. Bright lights and mics were always an erection killer.

Laura hit her garage door opener and pulled inside and jumped out, dashing through her house. In ten minutes she was in her car again and backing out of her driveway. She glanced at her watch once more—she'd be in her office by twelve-thirty. Her cell phone had been ringing off the hook, rolling over to voice mail. She read the repeated numbers off the lighted digital display and then went into her message box, listening to Najira tell her how many times Donald Haines had tried to reach her.

"Najira," she said fast as her outgoing call connected, dodging slower-moving vehicles, "I'm on my way in. Call Haines and tell him one o'clock is fine. I'll handle the other calls when I'm done with him. And listen, I owe you an apology for the corny name—had a crazy meeting; I thought the number I gave you was a landline; *the client* flipped out on me. It was his cellular. Ditch it. None of us needs that aggravation with everything that's going on today. Sorry I stressed you. See you in ten minutes."

She clicked off the call and pulled into the Bourse lot. Now it was about sonic speed. You only held an information grenade close to you long enough to pull the pin, then you had to get as far away from the blast as possible, lest you blow your own head off. She needed her leather portfolio, not the briefcase. Had to print off a single page with a graphic flow chart of the new world order and a short list of names. That's all she needed. Her credibility was now worth her weight in gold bullion. Donald Haines was coming into the city because the shit was serious—and she'd predicted it for him.

Laura grabbed a bunch of flowers and gave the Bourse

vendor a ten-dollar bill and kept walking. Najira did well today. Had literally saved a sister's ass. Might have to pay off her cousin's student loans with a little somethin'-somethin' from Darien's personal accounts before he went to jail. Laura laughed. If he balked, Najira always had evidence of their very personal relationship wrapped in plastic in the fridge. Plenty of men lost their minds, gave their mistresses huge gifts—didn't make *her* a suspect.

After hitting her office, she'd move up her appointment at Total Serenity Day Spa and hit the bank . . . then would not pass "Go" until she'd collected a hundred mil.

"What, no professional courtesy, Bennett? I'm calling the commissioner on this one!" Michael Paxton leaned forward on his knuckles on Captain Bennett's desk, veins standing in his neck and temple as he yelled, "This is bullshit!"

"Listen, a little after eleven we tried to call your office to give you a discreet heads-up, and Anne patched us through to your cell—we got your busy message and then voice mail."

Paxton pushed away from the desk and raked his fingers through his hair. "You should have called me *way* before eleven. What the hell is going on down in here, and at the DA's office, that I'm getting info after the media? Plus, I was tied up in a meeting at eleven. This was a first-thing-in-the-morning call, Bennett! As soon as you made a decision like this, I should have been notified!"

"My guys had gone for the warrant this morning, but we didn't know if it would go through . . . The info was pretty wild, and I thought the judge would make them go back for more evidence—something slipped through the cracks. What can I say?"

"Aw, shit. We've got a very pissed-off VIP in the house," Sullivan said, motioning toward the captain's office as he and Carter walked down the hall toward it.

"Good," Carter muttered, eyeing Paxton's back. "Let the bastard twist."

"Captain stepped out on a limb and pulled in a few markers for us, dude—probably to make up for kickin' your ass yesterday for Paxton, since he might get dragged into this, too . . . You sure about this Atlanta thing, though?"

"Yeah. What's not to be sure about? You have the files. The cell phones were delivered by the providers to the Peachtree Hotel during the Black Business Conference at the top of the month. Two of our suspects were in attendance, and some temp—probably a hooker one of 'em was doing—picked up the phones from the concierge's desk for them. So we find the phones to go with the phone records. We find the broad who picked up the digital cells and get her testimony that she handed the boxes off to one or both of the guys we nailed."

Sullivan nodded as they walked. "We can probably make it stick, though, just from the telephone records and the other stuff we've already got. But looks like Paxton is giving our boss the blues. No need to have Cap lose a pension if we're wrong."

Carter rubbed his jaw. He kept his eyes on Paxton. "Yeah, that's why I want an airtight case. A technical error could fuck this whole thing up."

As Carter reached for the office door, Paxton turned around and glared at him.

"Detective Carter, Detective Sullivan, Michael Paxton, Esquire—he's—"

"We've met," Carter grumbled.

Paxton narrowed his eyes on Carter, ignoring Sullivan with a dismissive wave of his hand.

"We have," Paxton said. He turned back to the captain. "I want my client out, and the bail hearing set pronto. I'm not having a solid CEO rot in a holding tank with drug dealers and gangbangers while your boys slow-walk my client's paperwork. I want Don Edward out *now*—and get the goddamned media off my steps, you understand me?"

"I'll do what I can, Mike," the captain said, his voice apologetic. "But we don't have much control over the media; you know that."

"You fix it," Paxton said, his tone lethal. He straightened his tie and glared at Carter again as he spoke. "Tonight I have a thousand-dollar-a-plate Republican fund-raiser to do over at the Camden Aquarium. You put your dogs on a short choker chain, Bennett. Especially, if I'm there with a guest." He brushed past Carter and Sullivan, swinging the door open so hard that it banged against the wall.

The miniblinds on Bennett's door swung violently back and forth before coming to a rest, and Paxton's long strides echoed with each angry, black-wingtipped footfall. Curious onlookers within the department stood aside, then peered toward Captain Bennett's office before resuming whatever task they'd been at before the altercation that just took place. For a moment, neither Sullivan, Carter, nor Captain Bennett spoke.

"All right, fellas," Bennett said, looking at Carter and Sullivan, "a lot of feathers way up the food chain have been ruffled. We do everything by the book."

Carter nodded and walked away. Sullivan was right on his heels.

"Yo, man. You and Paxton got something personal between you besides this case—or just general, garden variety hatred?"

Carter didn't look at his partner or answer his question. Mention of a garden fucked with him.

Laura stopped for a moment and composed herself and held on to a fat brass rail, and then headed up the thirty-foot expanse of honey-brown concrete stairs of the Union League. This was the king's palace, the place where the blue-chip deals were closed. The historic portraits and the sheer scale of the twentieth-century monument to WASP power dwarfed the Cricket Club's understated opulence by comparison.

This was Philly's Vatican, the seat of power where all major deals were blessed and anointed. She was early. Donald Haines wasn't even sitting. He was standing in the grand foyer, waiting for her. She drew a breath, extended her hand, and kept her expression appropriately solemn for the occasion. A messy financial hit had definitely gone down. The real estate pope appeared none too pleased at all.

"Donald."

"Laura."

"Lunch?"

"No. Just coffee."

"Good," he said. "I've lost my appetite this afternoon.

"As have I."

"Then let's go in and be brief."

She nodded and followed him.

He waited until she was seated and the server removed himself from their presence.

"What the fuck is happening in this goddamned city, Laura?"

He'd leaned in close, had spoken with such venom that she'd almost pulled away, but didn't. She leaned in closer.

"People had no class and got busted—that's what happened. There's a way to do everything, and they forgot the basics. Just like we're seeing on Wall Street. The CEOs today are flagrant. Tacky, even. This is horrible."

He nodded and sat back. "You've got that right. This new breed . . ." Donald Haines shook his head and rubbed his palm over his hair, smoothing it, then opened the single button on his charcoal-gray suit, releasing his crimson and navy rep tie.

"I have a short list for you, and a diagram of how it can work," she said, not wasting time with chitchat. Laura unzipped her slim black leather portfolio, extracted a sheet of paper, and slid it across the table to Haines.

He picked it up, studied it for a moment, and folded it in thirds, then put it in his inner breast jacket pocket. "I approve."

"The buildings?"

"Done."

"I could kiss you, Donald," she said with a smile.

He relaxed and smiled, and picked up his coffee cup. "One day you might have to. Twelve-point-five just went to a hundred and twenty-two, when we load on the asset valuation, renovations, equipment . . ."

"It'll be worth it," she said, picking up her coffee and sipping it slowly.

"It better be," he said, staring at her hard now, no mirth in his expression.

"It will."

He took a sip of his coffee and then stared down at the cup. "If these guys keep playing around like this, and keep exposing themselves—worse than jail could happen. I would hate to see things get really messy."

Laura went still for a moment, understanding the threat. "We should move quickly, then, to avoid any further unfortunate incidents."

"You'll handle the media timing and positioning?"

"Yes, Donald. I'll handle everything."

He nodded and sat back in his chair, and offered her a tense smile. "Will you be at the Aquarium fund-raiser tonight?"

"Absolutely." She held his gaze, but her expression was stone serious. "However, I'm going to caution you . . ."

His slight smile disappeared behind his sip of coffee, his calculating blue eyes holding hers over the rim of his china cup.

"Donald, while there, believe half of what you see, and none of what you might possibly hear."

He relaxed and smiled, and set down his cup. "That's an old one, darling."

"But old sayings get their longevity from a foundation of truth."

"Ahhh . . . wise beyond your years." He hailed the server and accepted the thin leather binder, signing his tab. "And who might try to make an old man think he's blind in one eye and can't see out of the other?"

"An attorney."

"The pressure's on, then . . . Personal or professional?"

She smiled. "Both . . . And giving false impressions by not-too-subtle innuendo."

Haines chuckled. "Laura, that game is as old as me." He stood, helped her from her chair, pecked her cheek, and walked beside her. "I was born at night, but not last night, honey."

"I'm glad."

Donald Haines briefly touched her elbow, making her stop and look at him. "Do you think, if we thought for a moment you could be so easily compromised, we would have approved this?" he added, his palm stroking his breast pocket.

"No. Thank you for that."

"We've been watching how you operate for years, Laura. It is only good business to see how a young company is performing, using its resources, and building its reputation, before investing in it. Some things are just prudent."

They parted on a handshake followed by a brief hug, but the last part of what Donald Haines had said was chilling nonetheless. Her gait was much slower now as she walked down Broad Street to Walnut.

Cabs passed her. She didn't hail one. She needed the cold air.

"I've got this under control," Paxton said, his gaze landing on each frightened pair of eyes that stared back at him. They all looked like terror-stricken slaves, fucking hostages sitting around his coffee table with no damned balls. "No matter what happens, Laura Caldwell is with us—you can take that to the bank."

Darien Price shot up from the sofa and began pacing in Paxton's large living room area, talking with his hands. "Laura Caldwell has *never* been in our camp, man. Are you nuts? You *can't* take *her* to the bank. Believe me, I tried—years ago."

"Sit your stupid ass down," Paxton growled. "She's all grown up now, and money has a way of smoothing out the rough edges. And for the record, she's *amazingly adept* at what she does."

"Let that bullshit from back in the day go, Price," Howard Scott warned. "If Paxton says he's got it under control, then chill."

"I'm not questioning your judgment, but you're sure you've got it *locked*?" Don Edward asked nervously, shifting to lean forward, his forearms on his knees. " 'Cause after this, we're all gonna have to go on the DL for a while . . . may need a down-low hiatus, and may have to eat while underground."

"I've got it locked and loaded," Paxton confirmed, taking a healthy sip of Chivas from his glass and setting it down hard on the bar. "Right now the main priority is strategically splitting everybody up and getting you all linked with my boys in different law firms, just in case things get worse." He dismissed the nervous glances that passed around the room. "You'll be in good hands; we all went to Harvard Law together; a couple were over at Penn. None of my boys are rookies; like me, they all know the right judges, and have markers they can pull in. But Paxton, McHenry, and Turner can only represent Darien—and now Don, because I had to go in there this morning as his attorney of record to get him released. It's better that way."

Darien Price narrowed his gaze on Paxton. "When did you lock her down, man?"

"Who gives a shit when the man handled his business as long as it's handled?" Martin Ramsey said, standing to go to the bar to freshen his drink. "You've always focused on dumb shit, Price—which is how all our asses got in a sling in the first place. I could kill your stupid ass myself! Damn. Paxton is talking strategy, and you're still caught up in over twenty-year-old bullshit. Let it go."

"Me?" Darien hollered, incredulous. "I'm not the one who got our asses in a sling. . . . I've been set up, and whoever set me up did your fucking asses, too. Take that shit to the bank, motherfucker."

Jim Thompson shot Brad Crawford an uneasy glance. "Why don't we all calm down and stay rational."

"That's our best bet," Crawford confirmed. "We can't start fighting amongst ourselves. That would be a disaster." He looked at Paxton, his expression hopeful. "You're sure you've got this?"

"Positive," Paxton muttered, and swallowed the remainder of his drink.

"The iron's still hot? We can trust this new alliance . . . She hasn't cooled off yet, and everything between you two is—"

"Burning up," Paxton said, cutting off Don Edward's questions and leaving the bar stool he'd occupied. He looked at the assembly of worried faces. He hated how they nervously kept straightening their ties as much as he hated how the currently unemployed one among them, Darien, had come into his home looking like a rapper, wearing a gray velour jogging suit . . . That would be just what the media needed to see. *Fool.*

Paxton steadied himself, responding with control. "She's a pro, but if I know her, she'll be at the Republican campaign event tonight at the Aquarium, just like she'll be at the Democratic fund-raiser two nights from now at the Kimmel Center—playing every position on the board. She's bright, works the circuit with precision, and is *very discreet* . . . but she'll leave a tracer. It's always in the eyes—watch and learn. The sister is poetry in motion."

"Sounds like you're the one who might have gotten worked, man," Darien said, his voice low and his tone bitter. "Haven't ever heard you speak in such glowing terms about a piece of tail."

"It's twelve-point-five-million-dollar tail," Howard Scott

interjected, wiping his face with both palms. "Makes a hell of a difference, man. Chill."

Paxton and Price stared at each other for a moment.

"Break it up," Scott warned. His gaze darted between both standing combatants. "We've got more important things to focus on, like keeping everybody's asses out of prison . . . and making sure the money tap doesn't get turned off. If Paxton can trust her, then we need to start routing her funds allotment to the more discreet holdings we all have. Keep your minds on the contracts, and who the next mayor is gonna be."

"I heard that," Crawford said, standing slowly and approaching the bar. "Fuck all this. My nerves are bad."

"Yeah," Paxton muttered, sliding the bottle toward Crawford, his eyes still on Price. "Fuck all this. Whoever set this foul ball into play is history."

Chapter 15

The moment she crossed the threshold of Total Serenity Day Spa, Laura could feel the tension within her begin to evaporate. Gorgette's ingratiating smile almost brought tears to her eyes as the svelte spa-owner completed her telephone call but nodded for Laura to approach the wide black-lacquer-and-walnut circular receptionist's desk.

Modern electric-blue and pale yellow walls drank her in, and the light citrus scent of natural herbal treatments wafted by her. The aroma was heavenly. Gorgette's hideaway was a lush, feminine contrast to Brad Crawford's starker gallery effect. But the city-block-long brownstone, with its rich wood floors, intricate wrought-iron armoire that housed magic potions for unisex skin transformations, and soft recessed lighting made the bright, airy place a haven. For Laura, today, it was more like a refuge.

Gorgeous antique satin-embroidered seating summoned her to sink against the sumptuous padding, but she stood at the front desk, waiting patiently as Gorgette ended her call.

"Darling," Gorgette crooned, smoothing her perfect ebony

chignon bun and rounding the tall wood structure that separated her from Laura. "I'm sorry," she said, "Janine is on break, and my other girls were busy."

"Don't be silly," Laura replied, going to her fast. "I'm the one who should apologize. I'm the one who's messing up your schedule."

Gorgette opened her arms wide to offer Laura a real hug. "You know I'll always squeeze you in. Where have you been, lady?" Then, looking like a black Paris runway model in her winter-white mohair sheath dress, Gorgette wagged a French-manicured finger at Laura, exposing her flawless teeth in a warm smile. She arched an eyebrow, her expression full of mischief, which made Laura chuckle.

Oh, Gorgette, Gorgette, my sister, if I could only explain . . . Laura cocked her head to the side, absorbing the camaraderie, taking a snapshot of the dark brown beauty in her mind. She was truly going to miss Gorgette, like she'd miss the others. Before she said a word, Laura filled her arms, reveling in the genuine human contact for just a second.

The simple act of female touch reminded her how much she missed her girlfriends; just like she missed her sisters and her true-blue crew that went back to childhood. For a moment Laura couldn't speak. Four days had passed, and she hadn't returned any of her girlfriends' calls or e-mails—there just weren't enough hours in the day. This weekend it was time to rectify that.

"I have been sooo wicked," Laura teased, laughing hard to cover her turmoil but telling the truth. "Now it's catching up to me. Save me, Gorgette—save me from myself."

"Look at you," Gorgette exclaimed, kneading Laura's shoulders as her tongue made little ticking sounds of disapproval. "This is no way to treat yourself. You must behave better than this."

"You know I rip and run like a madwoman all the time," Laura said, still chuckling. "I have to do this fund-raiser tonight, need a new hair thing happening, need you to let

Ivana beat the walnuts out of my back . . . need my feet done, a manicure, a facial . . . oh, girl . . . I am just too weary to pull it all together myself."

"Come on back and put on a robe," Gorgette said, her pleasant voice a balm to Laura's senses. "Let us take care of you for a few hours."

Laura slipped behind the private changing-room door, glanced at the commode and bidet, and kicked off her shoes, her toes reveling in the coolness of the lemon-yellow marble. She hadn't even had time to stop to pee today, it had been so crazy. She forced herself to leisurely strip off everything she wore, making herself slow down, making her heart rate adopt a saner rhythm.

Carefully stashing her clothes in the long matching lockers, she then stared in the mirror as she wrapped her body in a thick, prewarmed white terry cloth robe and slid her feet into flip-flop slippers. She turned the brass knobs and let the cool water from the faucet splash into her palms before she wet her face and began sudsing away her makeup with a fragrant cream rinse. She could do this—the full monte.

Gorgette was personally waiting for her as she left the changing room.

"Rough day, huh?"

Laura smiled. "Girl . . ."

"How about if I prepare some lunch while Ivana beats on you? Fresh shrimp salad on light greens . . . a little chardonnay, followed by some Earl Grey tea and a warm scone—in the private room by the fireplace. You can even take a nap on the sofa after your pedicure."

Laura laughed. "Gorgette, keep this up and I might move in with you. I'll be a squatter, and you'll have to charge me rent."

"And we'd love that . . . come into Ivana's den," she said chuckling. "Then lunch, then the rest of your services. Don't make it so long between visits."

"For two hours, I'm all yours."

* * *

When Ivana kissed her cheek, Laura's body went limp. It was a Pavlovian response. The darkened room, the steamy warmth, the soft strands of Native American flute music, the Italian boudoir appointments, and the table . . . the blessed massage table. All of it felt like she was in a womb, Ivana's hands the umbilical cord to spirit nourishment and repair. Laura groaned without censor or shame, like she was having soul-rending sex, as the woman chastised her in broken English, her Eastern European accent floating into Laura's semiconscious state from a faraway place in Laura's mind.

Drifting to sleep, flashes of images connected in a lazy strand of knowing . . . Boat House Row, permanently lighted year-round and trimmed with pretty Christmas lights, the scullers pulling in unison down the Schuylkill River; summer—sitting on the West River Drive with her family; blankets and picnics; feeding greedy geese, and outdoor concerts at the Dell. When she grew up, Daddy had promised she could go to one of the schools that had a boathouse on the row . . . Times were changing, and her daddy could do anything. He was invincible.

Tears slid down the bridge of her nose as Ivana found another muscle knot in her back and unfurled it with firm attention. The huge entryway marquis to Chinatown was so pretty . . . dragons, another culture, and the streets so lively. Then they'd built the Reading Terminal, and people with old-world Dutch clothes came into the city, sold desserts that melted in your mouth, had the best cheeses and meats—it had been a long time since she'd had a cheese steak. Dad used to bring them home on Fridays when he got paid—she didn't eat them anymore. Another tear slid down Laura's nose, and she sniffed.

"Ivana is too harsh on you?"

"No, Ivana. The world has been too harsh on me," Laura whispered. "This is therapy."

Ivana spread her hands over Laura's naked back, hot from

friction, gliding with rich emollients. Arch Street flickered behind Laura's shut eyelids . . . She remembered when black folks had to march to get included in the new Center City mall, the Gallery—now 90 percent of the population that worked and shopped there was black, and to solve that problem, white folks built a mall to escape to out in King of Prussia. The Civic Center was the convention center, not a film sound stage. The Convention Center was a hole in the street—a huge, gaping, monstrous hole that swallowed up the prostitute district and relocated working girls farther east.

Smut shops had to edge away from the new Marriott's back door; the homeless had to find new places to go. Brothers downtown looked good coming out of the Municipal Services building on JFK Boulevard . . . crossing Love Park, cutting through City Hall's courtyard . . . Zanzibar Blue used to be down on Twelfth Street, when that was the badlands, now the young brothers who owned it had moved it into the belly of the Hyatt on the Avenue of the Arts, with a wood-grain bar—go, boys . . . long way up from their daddy's down-'round-the-way nightclub—the Impulse had go-go dancers in black velvet, silhouette relief on the walls; city worker and Septa worker nights were when ladies got in free. Lew and Chews was still the spot up north end; was Sid Booker's Lounge still there serving shrimp? she wondered.

If she had wings, she'd fly in her dream to double-check that the Holiday Inn City Line Avenue was now the Adam's Mark, and another Holiday Inn was built in its shadow on practically the same lot, but with more functionality than luxury. That's right, it did change. She could see it now. The notables did drinks at the Marker on their way back to West Mount Airy and Chestnut hill—black folks weren't welcome in that section of town that used to be an extension of the Main Line. Deep. Times were changing, indeed. Question was, for the better? A billion dollars in two new stadiums to replace the old Vet, but kids still didn't have books in school . . . Betsy Ross's House still stood in the same place, though. That was cool.

She had an event next week at the Franklin Institute, or was that over at the Rodin Museum? She couldn't remember. Follow the money. The O'Jays had a song about that . . . but James Carter could make love like . . . *damn* . . . the brother was all that and two bags of Georgie Woods chips.

"You ready for me to do your front?"

Ivana's question brought her out of her nap, like a groggy patient coming out of anesthesia. Damn, if she could remember all that she'd dreamed, she had to be getting old.

"Yeah . . . just do me real good."

This time when Laura left the bank, her purse was heavy. Four o'clock . . . forget going back to the office; she'd call Najira and dispense staff instructions from home. Gorgette's team had wiped her out. She only had one hour to change, then a drive during rush hour—yet again—and she'd be on the Jersey side of the bridge . . . walking in early, letting her thousand-dollar plate of pheasant get cold as she worked the room. The cost of entry.

She drove down the Bourse ramp and rattled off instructions for the coming day—Fridays were light; her people had been working hard; the boss lady was running on fumes. Maybe she'd sleep in, depending on what happened tonight, or who she had to bring home or go see—Michael Paxton was still going to present a problem. Brother had issues, but she probably couldn't get away from him twice . . . especially not after a near miss on her knees. But who was she fooling even to tell herself the lie that she could sleep in? She was the boss—the boss never got to sleep in. Had they told her that shit when she was becoming an entrepreneur, she might have taken a government job.

Yeah, right. Laura chuckled and headed down Benjamin Franklin Parkway, her gaze on the Art Museum steps, visible from a mile away, as her Jag passed the Four Seasons and she enjoyed the flag-studded Parkway view.

"You all right, man?" Sullivan asked, flopping down in front of Carter and balancing his foot-long Italian hoagie.

"I'm cool," Carter said, staring down at his cheese steak. At least some things in Philly hadn't changed. They made 'em right up at Delasandro's. Tourists went down on South Street, but you had to go to neighborhood hideaways to get a serious cheese steak that was really righteous.

He didn't want to think about anything else, so he studied the huge chunks of scrambled beef that were sloppily, perfectly set in a foot-long Amorosa roll, fried to perfection with onions, peppers, and mushrooms, and slathered with ketchup and melted provolone cheese. . . . He wondered if Laura had ever checked out this joint.

Maybe he'd bring a sandwich to her house later tonight. Nah. Not without calling first. Then again, she loved soul food at Miss Tootsie's, so she might be down. Then again, she might really like a nice dinner in a posh spot, like they served in Manayunk—deep how if you went down the hill from where he was sitting now, it was regentrified yuppyville, and up the hill it was Roxboro, where a lot of cops and firefighters were mowing postage-stamp-sized lawns . . .

"Earth to Carter, come in."

He looked up at Steve and chuckled. His partner had taken a huge bite of his hoagie, pushing five different kinds of meat, lettuce, tomatoes, and cheese out the back of it. Oil and mayonnaise dribbled down the side of Steve's face. Carter took a swig of his orange soda and popped open his bag of barbecue-flavored chips.

"Got a lot on my mind, man," Carter finally said, digging into his sandwich.

"Lotta crap happening to be on your mind, dude," Steve mumbled through another bite of hoagie. "I just hope you aren't planning on crashing the Aquarium tonight."

"Was thinking about just driving by, to see who was—"

"Look," Steve said, setting his sandwich down and wiping his mouth. "We've got their asses. Now—"

"I know. I know. Was just a thought."

Steve smiled. "Think that Caldwell chick is going?"

"I haven't a clue." Now his partner was getting on his nerves. Carter took a bite of hot cheese steak and focused on getting the doughy bread to slide down his throat with a quarter pound of meat in his mouth.

"Tell you what," Steve said, his eyes crinkling at the edges with mirth, "how about if I be your escort—and to make sure your ass stays in the car, should you, uh, happen to see her with new legal representation?"

"Naw, man. We don't need to stir the pot and get Cap all bent out of shape. There'll be Secret Service for the heavyweights coming up from D.C., and a lot of media, so—"

"Oh, so now you've gone chickenshit on me?"

"Camden is out of our jurisdiction."

"Like that's stopped us before? Professional courtesy; everybody will be cool—especially if we're just parked outside . . . maybe way across the street, just people watching, limousine appreciating, like spectators at an Eagles game; we'll—"

"Eat your food, man."

Carter gave his partner the finger and kept chewing, his eyes fixed to a nondescript point on the red and white walls beyond the industrial-size jars of peppers floating in oil at the front register. He didn't need this bullshit tonight.

"Damn . . . ," Steve whispered. "Looks like the Parade of Stars."

"You know, man . . . this is a bad idea, and doesn't have jack to do with the case."

"Yes, it does," Steve argued. "We know Paxton will be here, and it might help to see who he comes here with, or stops to talk to for more than five seconds. We still have some more collars to make before this is all said and done."

"Yeah, whatever." Carter kept his line of vision moving as valets stripped the beautiful people of their fancy sedans, and limos dumped VIPs at the Aquarium's front door. Two men in dark suits with wires in their ears were walking toward them.

"Okay, dude," Steve said calmly. "We've been made."

Carter hit the automatic windows and eased them down, and held up his shield. "Just adding to the party. Had our eye on somebody, won't make a scene, just clocking whereabouts."

Both men nodded and walked away.

"See, and you thought they wouldn't give you an invitation to the prom."

He ignored Steve and kept his eyes on the building entrance, getting bored.

"Let's blow this place," Carter said after a few minutes.

"We got here early; she's the type that gets to places early, so just be pat—"

"We're looking for Paxton, remember?"

"Yeah, if you say so . . . but, man, oh, man," Steve said, whistling quietly. "If I had money, I'd pay a thousand dollars to go to events like this, just to look at the fall lineup."

He continued to ignore Steve, but when Laura's black Jag pulled up, he didn't have to pretend distraction.

"Damn . . . brother . . ." Steve rubbed his jaw and sat back in the passenger's seat and whistled low again. "We oughta bring her in for murder—she's killin' tonight."

Whatever Steve had to say was temporarily stricken from his mind. He needed every cell in his brain to process what he saw. Laura had stepped out of her Jag, her full-length chestnut-colored sable coat dusting her ankles, rhinestone straps cuffing them and descending down her narrow feet into black-beaded spike heels. Her hair was different, wasn't curly; it was straight with a windblown look that he knew was some New York stylist's intentional creation.

When she turned to give her keys to the valet, light glinted off three-carat teardrop earrings, and her open coat gave a glimpse of her form-fitting black, sheer sheath, a strand of rhinestones holding it up at each shoulder. And she was all legs . . . flashes of them covered in black silk stockings gracefully slid out of the slit of her gown as she moved. He could remember . . . damn . . . He was glad he hadn't been foolish enough to bring her a stupid cheese steak. He'd thought so before, but knew it now for sure—he was out of his league. But a strange sensation of pride also swept through him; she'd done well for herself and deserved it. Baby had come a long way from the hood.

As she hovered by the door, shaking hands and kissing people's cheeks, he couldn't take his eyes off her. Then he noticed the silver Saab 9-5 pull up. Every instinct within him was on high alert. Paxton got out of his vehicle and headed straight for her—what man in his right mind wouldn't?—wearing a black tux, white wing-collar shirt, and bow tie. The motherfucker looked like a black James fucking Bond.

Carter hadn't meant to bristle. Steve was looking at him now. His partner took out a cigarette and lit it; he could see him do it from his peripheral vision, heard him strike the match.

"You want one?" Steve asked with a chuckle.

"Gave it up a long time ago." He kept his line of vision on Paxton's approach to Laura. He gauged Paxton's vibe: his walk was eager, his strides just a little too long to be totally cool, his smile a little too wide, showing teeth like he'd hit the lottery—gave the impression that she was waiting for him, maybe expecting him. She turned and smiled, but not too much. Good. Paxton leaned in and kissed her cheek . . . but had now also marked off his territory by loosely draping his arm over her shoulders. They went in together; she hadn't pulled away or reset Paxton's physical boundaries like she had when other men flanked her. Fuck all that.

Steve tapped the back of his pack of Marlboro Lights, exposing one, and offered it to Carter without a word. Carter accepted it and leaned into the match as Sullivan struck it, making the tip of the cigarette glow orange as he inhaled.

"Stakeouts are always nerve-racking in the cold. I'm glad we ate first," Sullivan said in a sheepish tone, taking another drag on his cigarette as he put the box back in his shirt pocket.

Carter let the smoke come out through his nose in a slow, steady stream. "Me, too. It's gonna be a long night."

Chapter 16

She kept her cool. That was imperative.

Laura glanced around the first floor of the New Jersey State Aquarium as Paxton helped her out of her sable coat and she accepted a numbered chip for it. Pleasant conversation buzzed around her; she kissed cheeks and gave ginger embraces to the women she knew as they met in line. It was all good; she'd never plundered any of their homes—just their husbands' pockets, like they did—so they liked her, trusted her. There was a code. No ethics had been breached.

But even though there were also heavyweight women executives and legislators in her midst, she had to move past the female flock and get to the men. They understood; that's where they were heading, too. So nobody lingered in an all-female group too long, lest they blow their thousand-dollar ticket. "Let's do lunch," and a promise to call soon was enough to acknowledge the connection. This was business.

Her gaze again scanned the first floor, which had been transformed into a Caribbean oasis, where tropical fish tanks had become living wall frescoes, and small round tables draped in sea-blue linen and set with deep blue and purple orchids dotted the marble floors. Butlers in tuxedos glided between guests, offering champagne flutes and exotic hors d'oeuvres. The men huddled around the open shark-petting tank made her smile. Poor fish. Sons of bitches who were gawking at them ought to be a part of the exhibit themselves, she mused, and put her coat-check chip in her purse.

Everybody was in the house; she could see a billion dollars worth of old-world assets milling around casually, making connections—and that was only on the first floor. No business cards were exchanged; they all knew how to get to one another. The grand terrace overlooking the Delaware River was sure to host a few billion more, just as the Greek amphitheater was loaded with men, wives in tow, each with a net worth rivaling the gross national product of small nations. This was money. She had to shake Paxton.

But he was working the room, too. Walking in with him had not been the plan. And it pissed her off no end. Subtle glances went between Paxton and the men—his helping her off with her coat had been a disaster. He knew what he was doing. She'd fix that. He was not going to become a barnacle stuck to her side.

"Let me introduce you to—"

"Oh," she said brightly, walking ahead of him and cutting him off, "we already know each other. That's an old client of mine." She turned and smiled. "I'll be back. I know you have plenty of friends here." Then she was gone.

Laura slipped into a group where she'd spotted a foundation executive, and went up to the old codger and hugged him warmly, then began a conversation with the man's wife, profusely complimenting her gown. Where was Haines? She kept moving. The terrace was her objective. The first floor had local foundation types; the national foundation mavericks would be somewhere off the main drag strip—upstairs.

Each time Paxton got close to her, she made a point to say something breezy and then moved to another group. It thoroughly delighted her that he, too, had to stop, slow his pace, and perform the ritual of meeting and greeting. Distance declared, she made her way to the terrace and found her target.

"Donald, I knew I'd find you up here."

He smiled and then gave her a gracious bow that made her chuckle. "And so I have been located, Ms. Caldwell." He kissed her cheek as Elizabeth Haines beamed. Introducing her to the men around him was a matter of protocol, but she already knew most of them. It was time to pay attention to the wife.

"Elizabeth . . . my goodness, where did you get that dress?" Laura gave Mrs. Haines a sigh of appreciation. The older woman was indeed stunning in her teal-blue, pearl-splashed original.

"You're the one who looks completely stunning, Laura," she said. "You and I *must* do lunch. Come, let me introduce you to a very good friend of mine. Donald, may I steal her?"

"Of course, my dear," he said, but the strain on his face was evident.

Laura quelled her disappointment at being pulled away, but threaded her arm through Elizabeth's and waved politely as they left the power circle of men. What now? Derailed before she even got a shot off. *Patience,* she told herself, *the night is young.*

"We saw you come in with a very handsome and eligible gentleman," Elizabeth said, her eyes glittering with excitement.

How to play this? Perhaps Haines had sent his wife on a fact-finding mission? Be cool.

"We *just* happened to come in together, I assure you. . . . He is trying to be persuasive about a funding possibility that stands between us," she said, laughing.

Elizabeth winked at her. "Let him be as persuasive as he wants to be," she added, her voice dropping as she glanced around, then sent her gaze toward Paxton. "He reminds me so much of his father."

Something in Elizabeth's tone made Laura go very, very

still. Elizabeth Haines's voice had become soft, wistful. Oh, my God . . .

"Noooo . . . ," Laura whispered, needing to draw out this incredible information and be clear.

Elizabeth patted her arm. "Shusshhh . . . ," she giggled. "Just between us girls." Elizabeth Haines looked at Laura; their gazes locked. "Why do you think Donald made Michael Paxton Senior so successful?"

Stunned, all Laura could do was edge in closer and stare at the woman. If Elizabeth was giving up this kind of information, there was an agenda behind it.

"I don't understand," Laura said. Truth was, she didn't understand what had prompted this new level of intimacy coming from Elizabeth Haines, *of all people.* And what the hell would make a woman of her stature tell on herself like this? Uh-uh. Something wasn't right.

"I know that Donald is positioning you, and that you might feel a level of obligation at some point in the future," Elizabcth said coolly. "But trust me, he has a few chinks in his armor—so do not feel obliged to repay him in any more than the rudimentary ways. Understood?"

Oh . . . shit . . .

Laura nodded. The expression on Elizabeth's face was tense, but not sending insecurity messages. It was almost as though the woman was siding with her to undermine her husband. Now, that was deep. She'd been prepared to expect a jealous-wife vibe—she'd dealt with plenty of those before, but that was not what this was.

Elizabeth Haines smiled, but her eyes narrowed. There was an unmistakable bitterness in them. "Donald owed Paxton's elevation to me. He was *very* fond of Colette Paxton . . . Michael Jr.'s mother. Divorce between Donald and me would have been messy." She glanced toward her husband, smiled, and then glanced back to Laura. "Donald, that son of a bitch, is no gentleman. Let him admire you from afar, and block him with someone that'll make him eat his heart out—Michael."

Laura nodded and accepted a champagne flute as a butler passed. They needed to be serving shots of whiskey up in this joint.

"Shocking, I know," Elizabeth said, her voice quiet, her eyes now on Michael Paxton, and her smile one of pure triumph. "I'm living vicariously now, but it is so good to see things come full circle."

Laura almost spit out her sip of champagne.

Elizabeth looked at Laura, her hand resting on Laura's arm with affection. "We liked your father very much . . . and if things are auspicious, Michael Paxton Jr. is a very nice catch. Donald was *fond* of his mother; I was *fond* of his father . . . and after his parents tragically died, each of us, therefore, wanted to help the son of our *close friend*—so we've taken Mike under our wing, as we have you, so to speak. Ironic, isn't it? Mike was the one thing Donald and I shared and could agree about after all that turbulence. But . . . ," she sighed, "that was unpleasant history."

Laura leaned into Elizabeth and kissed her cheek instead of gaping at her. "Thank you, Elizabeth, for being so honest and providing a character reference for Michael. That means so much, coming from you. Perhaps I can relax a bit." She had to give the woman something to feed on, some hope. If Paxton was also the Haineses' golden boy, then she couldn't offend. "He is rather handsome."

The older woman smiled. "Be happy, dear. That's worth more than money." She drew a dignified breath and motioned toward a smiling woman in an off-the-shoulder crimson organza gown across the room. "Let's not dawdle and make the men nervous. We'll keep our little secret. That's Doris Moyer. Her husband, Alan, has been my husband's attorney for years . . . was Michael Paxton Senior's attorney, and all of our sons went to Harvard Law together. That handsome young man talking with Mike is their son, Alan Jr. Oh, you'll get to know some of these people soon—if things go according to Hoyle."

Laura kept her smile from turning into a shriek as she absorbed the information, walking beside Elizabeth toward Doris Moyer. Jesus . . . Elizabeth Haines was old man Paxton's lover? She remained steady as she tagged beside her new best friend. Deep. Wait until Najira heard this one. Donald Haines had been messing with old man Paxton's wife?

Like tumblers in a lock turning and then falling into place, she aligned the facts in her head. . . . If Paxton and Haines had the same attorney, then the son of that attorney, Alan, while clerking for his father, would have had access to old man Paxton's will. And if old man Paxton's son was best buds with Alan, then a leak could have occurred . . . that *had to be* how Michael Paxton found out that he had a half-brother, Darien. It made sense, now, that Paxton would fuck his brother's wife. Old man Paxton probably favored the son of the woman he was sleeping with, Juanita Price, and was moving part of what would have been Michael's inheritance Darien's way, not to the son of his estranged legal wife. Now she understood the bullshit between Paxton and Darien, and Darien didn't even know he was being represented by someone who hated his guts—Michael. Oh, this was too wild. Laura kept walking.

As they made their way to Doris Moyer, it amazed her how intricately woven the trail of intermarriages and liaisons was, no less than it confirmed many of her suspicions. With the right connections, anything was possible—from Harvard Law to not needing contracts to support one's lifestyle. It made sense now why Paxton Jr. never showed up on radar and got his lion's share of clean corporate accounts. Brother didn't have to scramble—that was for the little fish that needed to suck on government handouts like it was welfare. And if Juanita Price had been doing old man Paxton enough for a slipup to occur and a child to be conceived, then it made sense why Darien was put into a power slot—it was bloodline investment protection . . . just like the Haineses ensured that their lovers, Mr. and Mrs. Paxton, respectively, were sufficiently kept. The medieval royal courts of England didn't have nothing on this shit. Dangerous damned liaisons!

Yes, she owed Elizabeth Haines lunch, soon. This juicy tidbit had been a gift. She'd also have to reevaluate her preconceived notions about the value of the female grapevine, black and white.

"If I didn't know better, I'd think you'd been avoiding me all night." Paxton smiled as he dropped the hint over Laura's shoulder.

"No, just being discreet," Laura said carefully, her smile still engaging, as he rounded her.

"I was starting to wonder."

He was standing before her now, slowly sipping his champagne.

"We were both working the room." She cast her gaze away from him and chuckled, staring at the crowd.

"True. It's definitely loaded."

"Uhmmm hmmm."

He relaxed, and his smile became less strained. "Perhaps I was just a bit off-kilter because we had unfinished business to take care of . . . and you look ravishing tonight."

"Oh, I promise you . . . we'll finish that," she murmured, allowing his compliment to pass without further comment.

"Tonight?"

She paused for effect and took another sip of her champagne. "If you'd like?"

He hesitated but his smile broadened. "Is that a rhetorical question?"

"Counselor, you ought to know me better than that."

He chuckled low and put some distance between them, appearing temporarily mollified. "Let's say we work this room for another hour and make a discreet, separate departure."

"That could be arranged." She kept her eyes moving, talking to him without directly looking at him, watching the chess pieces on the board shift as deals were cut and alliances were forged. He was violating the three-minute rule, standing too close to a lone, single female, his proximity telegraphing erroneous messages. She stepped back and caught Donald Haines's eye from the corner of hers. Elizabeth Haines smiled. However, she could use Paxton's ruse against him—later. It would definitely help her with the Haineses.

"But I do need to discuss one point of business with you, too," Paxton said, his voice too even.

Now she looked at Paxton as he glanced away. He kept his eyes on the conversational groupings, patiently watching them the way a cat watches a mouse hole.

"The previous agreement to keep things aligned, the way they have been, may need to be changed, given recent events."

Laura arched an eyebrow, her expression an unspoken question as she sipped her champagne.

"We may need to send funds to some out-of-state, unknown, but credible firms."

"I figured there'd have to be a shift. No problem."

He let his breath out on a controlled exhale and relaxed again. "That's what I wanted to confirm. I took the liberty to draw up a list."

"With contact names and account numbers that will ultimately match what comes in on the sealed bids?"

"Do I strike you as a man who's not thorough, Laura?"

"Not at all." This time her chuckle was an honest one.

"Then I take it, you'll have no problem with my suggestions?"

"Done."

"Then, for the second part of our discussion . . . have you made a decision?"

"Yes. Venue?"

"My place is crawling with media."

She went still. A hotel in Philadelphia was out of the question—especially dressed in a ball gown and coming from this soiree.

"Yours?" he asked quietly, and held her gaze for a moment, then looked away, hailing someone he recognized.

His tone had actually sounded quite nice, if not gentle. *Oh . . . shit . . .*

"Let me think about that," she finally said, moving away from him again. "I need to hit a few legislators." Then she was gone.

It was inappropriate to make a beeline for Haines, so she intermittently stopped, watching Haines position himself strategically so they could chat. She could now appreciate why her encounter with his wife had drained the blood from his face, but the old dude was the epitome of smooth. As they casually bumped into each other, he leaned into her but kept his gaze on other people in the room.

"Laura . . . I will have to ask you to indulge me with the same request you made of me earlier."

"Anything, Donald." Her eyes remained on a distant target in the room.

"Believe half of what you see and *none* of what you hear."

She smiled. "Only if you'll believe none of what you see and half of what you hear."

"That's fair."

"Always." She touched his arm as she moved away.

He nodded. "That's what I like about you, Laura Caldwell. You keep an open mind."

"You sure you wanna do this, man?" Steve said as Carter started the ignition.

"It's all about the case, Sullivan. Why wouldn't I?"

"Because you kept a city-issued car out all night, never clocked out, and looked like you'd run a marathon—even though you'd changed your clothes—and because we've been partners now for like fifteen years . . . and are friends."

Carter ignored Steve's comments. The vehicle had a mind of its own. Perspective was gone. She'd come out of the ball, got her car from the valet, and pulled off—but not before Paxton looked back for just a little too long.

"Let's say we go over there on Pennsylvania Avenue, man," Sullivan said slowly as their vehicle pulled into traffic, "and things aren't cool . . . like are really uncool? Then what? You don't have a shred of police business to cover your ass for why you're going there, and Paxton is a lawyer who is *not* a suspect in any of this yet."

"Don't you think I fucking know that?" Carter kept his eyes on the road.

"Then why are we doing this? I could see being outside the New Jersey State Aquarium for a couple of hours . . . but, dude—"

"I'm playing a hunch." Carter shot a warning glare at Sullivan, then focused on the bridge tolls ahead.

"I'll shoot you myself before I let you go up to her door and make a fool of yourself."

There had been no way of getting around it. If she had bowed out of Paxton's offer at the function, he would have become suspicious—plus he had a short list in his pocket that was worth gold . . . information about the layer beneath the surface, which she had never been able to find out. J. D. Price, Sr. hadn't necessarily been the one pulling strings—old man Paxton had, too.

She kept her back to Paxton as she punched in her alarm code in the garage, and then opened the inner door that led to the house. Just her luck: this guy wasn't only a control freak but an adrenaline junky, too. Figures. It was always a fifty-fifty toss-up; some men went limp when under this kind of pressure and couldn't think, much less do anything else. But the one slowly following her down the hall toward the front staircase thrived on pressure—it seemed to turn him on even more. She just hated that the transaction had to go down under her roof.

Notwithstanding what she'd ultimately have to do to seal their unholy alliance, the brother needed to hand over the goods. Laura dropped her purse on the small crescent table as she passed it, unfastened her coat, and stood before the hall closet. In the dark she could see Paxton's eyes. Moonlight and streetlamp light coming through the glass panels above the door gave his expression an eerie tinge.

"Let me take off my coat. You want a drink?" She'd made her voice soothing and not as seductive as before. She needed to buy a little time.

"Keep it on," he murmured, and then stepped in nearer, pressing her against the closet doors. "I'll have a drink later, when we're done."

She looked up at the ceiling as he nuzzled her neck hard. Well . . . he did smell good, and didn't feel so bad . . . the tux fit him well—he looked great in it, in fact. She brought her hands up his sides under his raincoat and clutched the back of his tuxedo jacket. The action made him release his breath hard against her hairline.

"You have no idea the amount of stress I've been under, baby . . ."

Good, he was talking.

She pulled one hand away from his back to touch his cheek. "I can only imagine."

"This thing is a nightmare," he murmured as his fingers threaded through her hair. He looked at her, his eyes searching hers; then his gaze became almost tender as he caressed her hair. "It's like velvet . . . sable . . . God, you are a beautiful woman. A man could wait a lifetime and never possess a rare woman like you."

A slight tremor of guilt ran through her; maybe he was a little bit human. But she banished the lapse immediately. The last thing she'd ever be was *a possession* of Michael Paxton's.

His mouth claimed hers before she could say anything. He was kissing her so hard that their teeth were in danger of colliding. When he tore his mouth from hers, he sought her throat and bit down hard. It made her cry out, not so much from pleasure as from pain. She held him at the shoulders; that was all she could do at the moment.

Grabbing a section of her gown, his palm had found the slit in it, and he roughly slid his hand up her thigh. Okay, she sighed, so it was going to be one of those types of encounters. Under different circumstances, it might have been fun. However, she needed to slow him down.

"I thought you always said business first."

"Tonight I can't," he admitted, his breathing ragged, his cheek damp against hers. "I just need a release."

Well, on a basic level, the man was honest, she mused, nuzzling his neck. Her hands slid down his back, and she cupped his ass, drawing a shudder and a moan from him. "I understand . . ."

"Have you any idea what's been going down behind the scenes?" He was moving against her as he talked to her, and he dropped his head forward and closed his eyes.

"It's insane," she whispered hard into his ear. "It's dangerous. And it has you living on the edge—strung out."

"Seeing you work that room, *all night,*" he said against her hair, breathing in the scent of it, his hands now covering her breasts, "skillfully avoiding every land mine in the house . . . in that gown . . . that's what has me strung out."

Oh, boy . . . admission of vulnerability from a predator was not good. That was a sure sign the brother was past the point of reason. Also not good. But possibly advantageous. "We could work this thing together, Michael . . . all the way down to the nub. The two of us would be unstoppable—and could go *way* beyond Philly. Just tell me where and how you like it . . . I'll do anything you want. *I've never met a man like you in my life.*"

If she was not mistaken, she could almost believe that she'd felt the man's knees buckle. Very good. It was what they all wanted to hear.

"Don't play with me, Laura," he warned, now holding her by the throat.

She smiled and then closed her eyes. "Do it harder," she murmured. "Power is an aphrodisiac."

"Oh, God, yes . . ."

His mouth had claimed hers again, and she swallowed the whimper of pleasure he'd sent into it. He released her throat, his hands cradling her skull. She unbuttoned his shirt and yanked it from his pants. He rested his forehead against hers, gulping air, waiting for her to open his pants.

"Don't you want to see what I have on under the gown? I gift-wrapped it especially for you."

It gave him pause. He was still breathing hard as he backed up a few inches. Yeah . . . most men liked to watch; Paxton was no exception.

"But put the coat back on," he said on a husky rasp. "When I saw you walk into the ball with it . . ."

"That's why I wore it for you." That was no lie. She had. And it worked. Just like she knew it would. "You like the dress?" she asked, playing to his ego.

He briefly shut his eyes. "You have no idea. I told you, I loved it."

She slipped her coat off and repositioned it on her shoulders like a cape, reaching behind her back underneath it to slowly unzip the gown. He cast his coat off and let it land on the floor, and began loosening his bow tie as he watched her slow, sultry unveiling, one rhinestone dress strap at a time, until the gown was a pool of beaded black silk at her feet.

Breasts exposed, only a black lace thong and lace-rimmed silk stockings on—in an instant, he was on her again. His hands roughly fondled her breasts as his jawline swept across her collarbone, grazed her neck, the side of her face, and his lips drew in her diamond earring and earlobe. She could hear beads from her gown getting crushed under his damned patent leather slip-ons—shit. He captured both her hands above her head and pressed them to the wall hard, deep thrusting against her, only the fabric of his pants now a barrier.

"Tell me you have something in your purse." His voice was urgent, his bites against her becoming more frantic.

"You'll have to let go of me so I can get to it," she said breathlessly for effect, wrapping one leg around his waist.

"Jesus, Laura . . . you make a man want to take a risk."

"Now, didn't we have this conversation before, Michael?" She'd breathed the question in his ear as her French manicure scratched down his shirt.

"Where's your purse, baby?"

He was two inches from her face and had started to unzip his pants.

"It's right over there," she whispered, pointing to the crescent hall secretary. "Let me go get what you need."

He nodded and rolled away from her. She bent to pick up her dress, scowling at its destruction when her back was to him.

The phone rang. She turned and looked at him.

"I *forbid* you to answer it," he said through his teeth. "Not this time—not now."

"Brother, drive away from the house," Sullivan said quietly. "No lights ever went on, and dude's car is in her driveway."

"I'm going in," Carter said, clicking off his cell phone and flinging open the car door.

Sullivan sighed and rubbed his face with both palms. "Partner, give me your gun."

"With all this shit going down, it might have been important," Laura hedged, coming back to Paxton slowly while digging in her purse.

He was ignoring her, had taken off his tux jacket and shirt. They were in a pile on the floor with his coat.

Hmmph, hmmph, hmmph—this was fucked up. A sick part of her wanted to laugh. One day she'd have to tell Najira and her sisters about this bullshit—the edited version, anyway. She found the condom and threw her purse back on the table, tearing the foil as she walked toward him. He was leaning against the wall; his eyes were closed as though he were willing his discipline back to him from outer space. The sound of paper tearing seemed to coincide with his clenching his fists. She put the condom in her mouth, pretty sure that was the way he'd appreciate her sheathing him. The doorbell rang, and she almost choked on the rubber.

Paxton pushed away from the wall like a panther and punched the adjacent one. "Who the fuck is that!" He pointed to the door, then quickly swept up his shirt, jacket, and coat.

She studied him, studied the door, and spit the condom into her hand. He did have a nice chest—very buff body, truth be told. The incessant ringing went to pounding.

"Sounds like the police to me, by the way some fool is banging on my door. Let me go see." She calmly closed her coat and swept her gown off the floor and tossed it on the secretary.

"The police?" Paxton was pulling on his shirt, stuffing it into his pants. "Are you a suspect or some shit? Laura, talk me, goddamn it, and now!"

She placed her finger to her lips and stood in front of him. "They're running around town asking all the lobbyists, grant writers, and campaign fund managers about what was in the contracts—I told them I had never worked with you guys before. But, honey, I'm worried, because on my home office system I had prepared drafts . . . like you told me to, for Haines to bless . . . and if they've come to confiscate—"

"Okay, okay," he said, kissing her forehead as the doorbell resumed ringing. "Close your coat; answer the door. Tell them that they have to have a warrant—"

"What if they already have one?" She glanced at the door, hoping it wouldn't stop sounding.

Paxton hesitated. "Look," he whispered, pulling an envelope out of his jacket breast pocket, handing it to her, "take this list, insert these names and accounts on your home computer. I'll stop a warrant if they haven't gotten one processed yet, but you have to answer the door—my car is out front; they know I'm here. Just tell them I'm your attorney."

She nodded, accepted the envelope, and thrust it in her

coat pocket along with the wet condom. She waited a beat so Paxton could put on his jacket and coat, and she double-checked that her sable was totally clasped. As cool as a spring breeze, she floated to the door and opened it. She bit the insides of her cheeks. Her knight in shining armor was on the steps, puffed up like a damned bulldog. *Men . . .*

"A word, Miss Caldwell," Carter said, peering around her to Paxton.

"Awful late for an investigation, wouldn't you say, Detective?" Paxton glanced at his Rolex and held Carter in a lethal stare.

"Awful late to be coaching a client, wouldn't you say, Counselor—unless that client has something to hide?"

"Would you care to step in for some coffee?" she offered, unable to suppress the sly smile that Paxton couldn't see.

"Some other time," Carter shot back, his gaze raking over her disheveled condition.

Aw, Jim . . . Baby, it ain't like that. This was business. Laura sighed. Too bad the man wasn't psychic. All she could do was give James Carter a hard look, one that said, *If you've got any sense at all, you'll double back.*

Paxton smiled. "You're not talking to *my* client, or coming into her home without a warrant."

Carter never looked at her; his stare was in a deadlock with Paxton's. "I'll be back in the morning with a warrant, Miss Caldwell."

"Good. I'll put on coffee."

Chapter 17

"*God Damn!*" Paxton walked back and forth, intermittently punching the wall in her foyer. "I will have that bastard's *badge* in the morning!"

Laura took a dejected pose against the stairway newel post, casting her gaze down, summoning tears, occasionally sighing to add to her look of fear and disappointment. "I guess you have to leave . . . damn."

"Yeah," Paxton muttered. "This is too fucking crazy. They may have pulled back from your front door, but I guarantee that they aren't far away. My car sitting here much longer wouldn't be appropriate, even if I did claim to be here coaching you . . . then what? They'll harass you for sure and wanna know why. Now the shit between me and Carter is *really* personal." He fished in his pocket for his car keys and punched the wall again.

"I'll go upstairs and get right on changing those names on my system," she murmured, going to Paxton and touching his arm.

He cupped her cheek and kissed her wet lashes. "Baby, listen . . . it's going to be all right. I won't let you get caught up in this madness. I promise." He kissed her forehead and then drew her into his arms. "I'm not going to let anything happen to you," he whispered, stroking her hair. "Not you."

For a moment, she had to have a brief conversation with the Almighty about original sin. She'd found the man's soul and was about to hurt him *real* bad . . . and a tiny part of her remembered what her mother had taught her about right and wrong. But the memory of her mother and her pain was also the thing that allowed her to pull back, kiss the man who now held her in his arms, without a shred of remorse. Then she thought of Monica—a mother, too, whom the bastard had no qualms about sacrificing for profit. It made it easy to look Paxton in the eyes without a flicker of deceit in them—and lie.

"Mike . . . when this all blows over, we'll have a chance to finish what got started." *That* she'd promise him, even on her deathbed, if need be.

"We'll get together before that," he said, placing a soft kiss along the bridge of her nose.

His voice was so gentle that she could swear the man was falling in love. She nodded, touched the center of his chest, and he clasped her hand, pressing a kiss into the middle of it. Oh, shit . . . maybe he was. Oh, well.

"I'll call you tomorrow. My day will be nuts, with them still digging up evidence . . . but I'll do what I can to get together." He shook his head with disgust and drew away from her. "I'll make this up to you."

"Okay," she whispered, touching his back as he slipped out the door.

She stood behind it and waited until she heard his Saab pull off. As soon as it did, she ran through the house like a banshee, snatching her gown, grabbing her clutch, and running upstairs. She thrust her hand in her fur coat, drew out the envelope Paxton had given her, and kissed it, and then ran down the hall to her office.

Laura clicked on her tube, working in her coat, no bra, wearing only a thong, stockings, and heels. It was about motion. She got the information loaded into her computer within five minutes, printed off a copy of it, and reached for the telephone.

Paxton snatched his cell phone off his waist. If it was Laura, he knew he didn't have the discipline not to go back to her house. Anticipation shot through him. He could still smell her sweet pussy on his fingers. Maybe she could meet him somewhere secluded. But the sight of Darien's number pissed him off. He slammed the cell phone into the hands-free unit.

"What, man?" Paxton grumbled, keeping his eyes on the road.

"We're supposed to be fucking family!" Darien hollered. "I'll kill you!"

A slow, burning hatred awakened inside Paxton, but he kept his voice even. "What are you talking about?"

"You know what I'm talking about," Darien yelled. "Our fathers were best friends! Our mothers played bridge together. You and I got the best money seats in the network—and you're even my damned attorney, motherfucker! That's what I'm talking about!"

"I know all that," Paxton said, letting his breath out in a controlled stream through his nose. "But you still haven't told me why you are on my goddamned cell phone sounding like a madman."

"Oh, you fuck my wife and don't know why I have a problem with that?"

Silence crackled on the line. Paxton could hear Darien breathing hard in what he knew was blind rage.

"Is that what she told you?"

"Fucking-A right," Darien shot back.

"I take it, then, that you confronted her about setting you up?"

"That's right! I told that bitch I wasn't going down for her, especially if her bullshit was pulling in the rest of our network. Don Edward just went down; who's next? I told her—"

"You told her what I told *you* to never discuss with her, namely, the intricacies of your case—but, as always, Darien, you have no self-control." Paxton could feel his voice escalating as his fury built. "So of course she'd tell you anything that would cast aspersions on the *only* person who can help you—your fucking attorney!"

For a moment Darien said nothing. Paxton jumped in before Darien could think about it too hard.

"I suppose she made all sorts of wild allegations about your family, and I would figure that she had you all confused, all fucked up, and—once again—acting stupid." Paxton paused. He was so angry that he could barely speak. He gripped the leather-covered steering wheel and counted to ten, then pressed on. "How many times have we all told you to stop thinking with your dick? Stop letting that woman play you."

He could hear Darien swallow hard.

"She and I have a lot of shit between us, Mike . . . I might have messed around, but, man, that's still *my wife*—the mother of my children. Crazy as it sounds, I love her, man. Thinking she was with somebody else . . . one of my boys, my best friend . . ."

"Do you hear yourself?" Paxton said coolly.

"Yeah, but, Mike," Darien cut in, his voice quavering, "she said all this wild shit about my father . . . said your dad and my mom—"

"Darien. Be logical. You know the relationship our parents had with each other. Does this sound like a woman who cares about you or has your best interest at heart, to make you question something as solid as that?"

Again there was silence on the line. Paxton used it to his advantage. He hadn't planned on a wifely "true confession" from Monica. Variables.

"Darien, I hate to be the one who tells you this . . . but the best way to tell a lie is to lace it with the truth. Women are very skillful at that, especially women like Monica."

More silence.

"I *know* Monica was messing around," Paxton said in a soothing tone. "That's why I had no compunction about going after her on your behalf. And, *it is* one of your boys . . . I just don't know which one. That's how this whole thing got out of hand—somebody wants a higher position in the inner circle and got greedy."

Sobs replaced silence. Michael Paxton drove.

"I'll kill her, man," Darien said thickly.

Paxton sighed. "As her husband, I can understand your position. But as your attorney, I'd have to advise against that course of action. You can divorce her. Do what you must to wipe the image of her lying naked in another man's arms—a friend—out of your mind."

"Who was it, Mike?"

"I don't know," Paxton replied, his tone ultracalm. "But, if you'd like, I can call for a paternity test on your children."

"What!"

"Again, as your attorney, and your best friend and god-brother, I have to watch your back."

Darien's breaths came in heavy bursts through the phone. "Oh, shit . . . oh, shit, Mike. No, man. Fuck it. My kids? That bitch!"

"I'm sorry, Darien . . . brother, this is—"

"Then you know what?" Darien shouted. "I'm blowing up this whole network. Fuck it. I'm outing everybody. This goes beyond money, man. It's a matter of principle!"

"Listen, man . . . don't go back there and start some shit. Promise me."

Carter didn't look at his partner as Steve moved to get out of his car and go collect his own. When Carter's cell phone rang on his hip, Steve held the passenger door open for a moment, then shook his head and slammed it.

That bitch had to be out of her fucking mind! No, correction, he was the one who'd left his partner in a parking lot and was driving back to her house—he was the one who was crazy. His vehicle swerved into Laura's driveway landing and came to a skid, almost going through the garage door. He swung the car door open so hard that it swung back and almost hit him. Four good paces and he was up her steps, and she had the nerve to open the door, all changed into stretch pants and a sweater. There were simply no words for a woman like this.

He headed for the kitchen, brushing past her, furious. He could smell that she'd made coffee, saw two mugs on the table—like that shit was gonna explain anything. It burned him up, too, that she knew he would come back.

"What the fuck was that shit, Laura?" He was walking in a tight line back and forth between the counter and the sink.

She was leaning on the door frame, all casual. He wanted to slap her.

"It was business, baby."

He pointed at her as he spoke. "No, that shit I just saw was *not* business!"

She brushed past him and sucked her teeth, appearing unfazed.

"While I don't *have* to explain, I will—since we're partners." She sat down and leisurely sipped her coffee.

"Partners? Partners!" He was so angry, he was almost stuttering.

"Haven't you ever been undercover working an angle, and had to go in a little deeper than you perhaps wanted to . . . but got what you needed?"

He didn't answer for a moment. That was not the point. "Oh, so what—now you're a cop?"

"No. But I'm a damned good investigator."

"I'm listening," he said, half meaning it, but needing to—he hoped she'd tell him something he could live with. This shit was crazy; she wasn't his woman.

She let her breath out hard. He kept his vision focused on the cabinets behind her, fuming.

"Paxton has been trying to get next to me—"

"That much I've gathered." Carter sat down hard on a counter stool away from her.

"He only wants one thing."

"So far I'm not being enlightened."

"He wants more than a quick roll in the hay."

Now he looked at her.

"Finally. Progress." She sipped her coffee and then set it down. "He knows I've been given the nod to move whatever funding, twelve-point-five mil, that Haines blessed for Darien Price and his slate, as the new gatekeeper. At first, he thought things would be business as usual; then the Don Edward thing blew up."

"Keep talking." Carter moved to the table, picked up a cup, and went back to the counter to pour himself coffee.

"But with the police going after everybody in the big five families, and Darien's butt in a sling, they couldn't do business as usual. They needed to route the money through other holding firms they have outside of Pennsylvania . . . firms in Atlanta, Chicago, New York, D.C., Baltimore, New Orleans—understand? No matter who gets put into office, they want to make sure they get the contracts that come after the elections. Very simply put."

He nodded, sipped his coffee, and slowly came to the table. He pulled out a kitchen chair, turned it around backward, and begrudgingly straddled it.

"I have never slept with any of the crew in Philly. Paxton wanted to be the first—that's his ego making him blind. He wanted to start more than business, because he needed to be able to trust me to do his business like someone who was his woman would—loyally—so he asked me if he could stop by for a cup of coffee after the gala, to discuss business, and to try to put a firm down payment on my loyalty with his dick. Pullease."

Carter practically spit out the coffee in his mouth. "Don't play me, Laura."

"You saved my ass, literally. Thanks."

He looked at her hard now.

"You spooked him. He thought I was interested but that fate had conspired against anything more going down . . . and he gave me a list of names and accounts on his way out the door—you want it?"

Carter let his breath out slowly; he didn't like it but had to admit that her methods had been effective. "He gave you the list . . . just like that?"

"You really wanna know?"

He looked away again and stood, leaving his coffee.

"He gave me the list—just like that, then."

"Good," he muttered after a while.

"I didn't do him," she murmured. "If that's important for you to know."

He found a spot on the wall and kept his gaze attached to it. Fuck it. She was grown. It was a one-night stand . . . that never happened, anyway.

"I have it all on disk, and a list in his own handwriting."

Her comment made him glance at her, and when he did, he had to keep his line of vision glued to her eyes.

"I want to find out who set up my father, as much as you do . . . things got heated in here, got out of control, and that frightened me."

He kept looking at her, trying to detect fraud. She was at the table wearing all black, like a black widow spider. A soft knit sweater covered her shapely torso—no bra, au naturel. She wore stretch pants that left nothing to the imagination, and she gazed at him, her dark eyes innocent-looking, her mussed hair making him wonder.

"I'll give you the list," she said in a weary tone that irked him, "because I know that at the bottom of all of this, we'll be able to figure out who stood to gain what—these companies were established in the seventies . . . when everything else went down."

He could feel the muscles in his shoulders begin to relax. "If I hadn't knocked on your door, then what?"

As soon as the words had come out of his mouth, the tension was back. He hated that he'd asked that question. The fact that she took her time to answer grated on him even more. He hated that he'd gone to her door like a lover and not a cop. He could have put his own nine to his skull. How in the hell had he gotten himself to where he was, allowing a woman to make him act stupid? He'd been around the block so many times it wasn't funny. Tail was tail, not some new invention. So how in only twenty-four fucking hours, just from good sex, was he losing all perspective?

Carter looked down at his cup, wondering if she had worked roots on him, or something—that would have been a better and more rational explanation than anything else that came to mind.

She sighed and picked up her cup of coffee. "I would have been in here with an animal . . . and I would have had to use all the self-defense training I'd ever taken and hope a daily morning ritual of tai chi would have saved my ass."

Guilt sliced at him. Damn . . . the sister had put her body on the line trying to get information they both needed, and could have been jacked. He walked over to the table and sat down, turning the chair around to face her.

"Look . . . Laura, I'm sorry. I've . . . my judgment has been a little . . ."

"Off?" She sent her gaze out the window.

"Yeah," he murmured.

"Still don't trust me, do you?"

He couldn't answer her. "Baby . . . I'm sorry." He had to stop calling her baby, and needed to do a pulse check when he got close to her.

"Guess it doesn't matter what I try to do for you, then, does it?" She stood and went to the sink and dumped out her coffee, and then fished around in the refrigerator and extracted a bottle of wine. "You still think I'm one of them."

He watched her methodically open a bottle of wine and pull down a crystal glass. Damn . . . under different circumstances, this could have been the one. This could have been a woman to go listen to jazz with at the Keswick, or over the bridge at the Tweeter Center—somebody to share his vacant life. Yet, a fantasy like that was dangerous; he was a confirmed solo artist, a bachelor till the end of time. He must be getting old . . . Still, something about Laura Caldwell took him back to the old days, before life got ridiculous. Beneath all her polish that she'd earned from pure sweat equity, she was old-school Philly, as well as something else he dared not consider.

"Want one?' she offered. "Where are my manners?"

"It's cool," he said quietly. He slipped off his leather bomber jacket and hung it on the back of her kitchen chair.

"No," she said fast, "it's not cool." She came over to him and pulled down her sweater collar, showing him red marks around her neck. "It is *not* cool. It was not pleasant. It was one of the hardest fucking things I had to do in my life, but a man will never understand something like this."

For a moment he was frozen as he looked at the red and now darkening bruises on her throat. He reached to touch the soft skin that had been violated, but she slapped his hand away, tears rising in her eyes. She wiped her eyes with the back of her fists, lifted her chin, and strutted over to the counter.

"You sure you won't have some wine? Or I might even have something stronger in the dining room." Her tone was sarcastic; she hadn't looked at him when she'd spoken. She poured her wine and took a healthy swallow of it, and then refilled her glass.

"If you've got something stronger, that could work." He just stared at her. What she'd just shown him made him sick.

"Name your poison."

"Johnny Walker—if you've got it?"

"Black. In the house." She strode out of the room and came back with a short rocks glass. She thrust the bottle and tumbler at him and went back to the sink to lean against it, glaring at him.

He poured his drink slowly, watching the dark liquor fill the glass, knocked back a shot, then set the glass down hard on the table. "And I started to come by here with a cheese steak under my arm," he said, chuckling in an angry, far-off tone.

"Why didn't you?" She sipped her wine with a hard swig, but her voice was gentle.

"Because I was foolish . . . thought you wouldn't want it."

She sighed loudly, allowing the sound to be her answer.

"Then I saw you walk into that ball, wearing full-length sable . . ."

"So, you're following me again?" She peered into her glass and twirled it by the stem.

"No. We were following Paxton," he lied. "Wanted to see if there were any connections he'd make that might help us."

"Hmmm . . . out of your jurisdiction, though, Detective."

"There's a lot of that going around."

She finally smiled. "Touché. All right."

He relaxed. She came to the table and sat with him. He stared at her; he'd kill Paxton if he ever laid a hand on her again.

"You looked so beautiful tonight . . . and I sorta lost it when Paxton's car was in your driveway."

"I know," she chuckled. "But I'm glad you did. Shoulda brought me that cheese steak, too. I never get to really eat at those functions—too busy working the room."

Her admission coated him, rubbing salve on his flayed nervous system. He'd make this up to her. He reached across the table and let his finger trace her cheek. This time she didn't pull away. His eyes followed a path to her throat. "What did he do to you?" He'd asked the question through his teeth.

She looked down at the table. "He put his hand around my throat and told me not to fucking play with him." She drew a deep breath. "I told him that he needed to give me the list so we could do the transaction—but if he wanted more than that tonight, I wasn't the one."

She looked at him hard now. "That's about the time my spine got pressed to the wall and my skull collided with it

. . . and then the doorbell rang. 'Nough said. I got the list and a warning, and took a hot shower to get the creepy imprint off me. Like I said, thanks."

Laura stood to take her wineglass for a refill, but he captured her hand, gently pulling her into his lap.

"I will kill that motherfucker—do you understand me?" he whispered, trying to touch her bruises softly, placing a kiss where his finger had landed. "You don't have to be afraid of him, and you stay away from him." He took her glass from her and set it on the table. "Promise me."

"I'm not scared of him," she murmured, touching the side of Carter's face, kissing his forehead. That was the truth. She wasn't scared of Paxton; reality dictated that she had to interact with him. "But I might have to at least be civil, have some meetings with him to get deeper—"

"No," Carter said, his tone firm. "Too—"

"He's not going to kill me. He'll try me, but he won't kill me. . . . The man isn't crazy—just a man."

"Well, as a man," Carter murmured, his fingers lacing themselves in her hair, "lemme tell you that unplanned things can happen in a one-on-one situation . . . bad things, Laura, that can leave a woman scarred for life. And a lot of it doesn't get reported. I don't want to ever see you in that situation. Maybe because I'm a cop, and I see so *much* shit, I'm paranoid . . . like you wouldn't believe. His kind can wriggle out of incidents, then blame the woman, and discredit her—"

She put her finger to his lips and looked at the man who'd barreled through her door, old-school-style indignant, all puffed up in a black bomber jacket, gray turtleneck, black Hugo Boss slacks, and black slip-on shoes, wearing a gun—chivalry was not dead.

Her eyes drank his in; she indulged herself for a moment. The fantasy was so fleeting but felt so good. God, if only he'd been the kind of man she'd met before. Where was this gentleman, this rough-around-the-edges homeboy, when she was fifteen? Maybe he was in a car somewhere with two buddies and their girls . . . like the kind of boys who were real men, back then, who would have enough decency to drive her safely, unmolested, to her momma's door.

She closed her eyes and kissed him softly, with care, so he wouldn't disappear. He would have definitely been her first, had she met him way back then, not some fool in college who did the same thing to her that Darien had tried, only worse—when she gave herself willingly and then her first lover, a spoiled Ivy League brat, abused her heart . . . like the one after him, and the one after him, and the countless others that followed. Then she'd sifted through the homeboys, looking for a real man, and came away wanting. Thcy hadn't been much better. A man like James Carter should have been first.

"Laura, listen . . . I had no right to come to your door like I did. I just thought . . ."

Her kiss tried to eclipse the memories as her mouth covered his. Her tongue tangled with his as an unspoken reply: *Don't speak; don't go there, baby. Just love me in the moment and let it be. No promises; I'm not the one.*

Didn't James Carter understand that she couldn't go out like her mom, so in love with a man that when life took him away, she'd taken her own life? One call from lockup—she could only imagine what her father had said was happening to him, an honest man in the joint with criminals . . . It had to have been horrible enough to irreparably break her mother's heart. Enough to make a woman lose perspective, to make her forget that she had three little girls who needed her. She would never be that out of control.

His slow, tender kiss slid through her bloodstream, though. Perhaps, had things been different, James Carter would have been able to get her to drop her vengeance mission, might have seduced her to get a job and have babies, maybe . . . but at forty-three, she'd robbed herself. Time waited for no man, and it certainly didn't give the sisters a break.

Tears spilled from the corners of Laura's eyes as he nuzzled her so gently she thought she'd melt away. This man's touch, his taste, his earthy scent, made her remember the old

Philly, before the destruction of all she'd known. Double Dutch rope in the streets, mega five-act concerts at high school auditoriums for only a few bucks . . . water ice, the fireplug opened, moms hollering for kids to come in before street lights went on, the Mr. Softie ice-cream truck bell in the distance ruining dinners, dirty mustard pretzels that tasted so good, nickel bags of barbecue chips, an orange soda for a quarter . . . neighborhood block parties with the street roped off to cars, and neighbors who knew your name plus all your business with it—because they cared.

"James, stop . . . I can't take it right now."

She'd meant to pull away, but a sob caught in her throat as James Carter stopped kissing her, though never stopped petting away a hurt so deep within her. He could never be allowed to understand. His earnest expression when he'd tried to warn her about Paxton had opened a dangerous fissure in her. It was cracking her foundation, threatening to give James Carter a peek too close to the truth. He'd broken through the firewall around 1975—she already knew how dangerous being alone in a disrespectful man's company truly was; didn't he know?

But as his hands soothed her back, and his mouth joined with hers again so tenderly, she tried to let him know that had things been different, he could have been *the one.*

It was the way he kissed her eyelids, then looked into her eyes, seeing way down to her soul. It was the way he paid reverent homage to her skin, as though she were glass, something of value worth cherishing and not to be handled like raw meat. It was the way that he whispered to her, "Baby, it's gonna be all right," and his voice, its tone contained a promise of protection with it . . . like the man would take a bullet for her. Almost the same tone her father once used when he was strong and she was very small, making her feel safe in a very unsafe world . . . but different from Dad's—more permanent, more sure. And James's voice also contained so many more things that she dared not wrap her mind around too tightly or get too used to.

But the way he picked her up and carried her into the living room as if she were a baby, his baby, and deposited her on the sofa and then stared down at her like God had granted his prayers—that also had a lot to do with it. Perhaps the fact that he'd dropped to his knees and pulled her forward to kiss him, rather than just blanketing her for his own desire . . . mindful of her bruises . . . yeah . . . that had an awful lot to do with it. That was everything.

"I don't want to hurt you," he whispered, harsh against her cheek, his hands trembling at her shoulders with the repressed need to hold her harder.

She wanted to sob. Her mind screamed out, *I don't want to hurt you, either . . . but in the long run, I probably will.* "James . . ." She swallowed hard. *This was not supposed to happen.* "You are such a decent man." Laura blinked back tears. That was the raw truth, and all she could say to him right now.

She pulled her sweater over her head and she watched his eyes linger on her bruises, the red streaks that she knew had been another man's passion bites, not brutality—and yet, Carter's eyes never left those marks.

Other men would have been distracted by her naked breasts. *Oh, James . . .* She couldn't do this to him. When he leaned in to kiss the marred surfaces of her skin, she had to stop him. God in heaven, what was happening to her?

She covered her face with her hands. This man had somehow gotten on the other side of her secret wall, because in this moment, she did give a damn. He'd made her find an internal line that she couldn't afford to have right now. Brother Akhan's words beat her conscience's ass, while a tender touch from James felt like a lickin' switch.

"Baby, I'm sorry."

She rocked, because he was apologizing. He was on his knees in the middle of her living room floor, in front of the couch, apologizing for hurting her, when he hadn't done anything wrong. *Oh, God . . . make him stop.*

She sucked in hard and pulled herself together. She

chuckled a sad, honest, self-deprecating chuckle, her hand cupping his cheek. She closed her eyes when he kissed the center of it in the same spot Paxton just had. "Where have you been all my life?"

Her corny, yesteryear line was supposed to make him smile, was supposed to lighten the mood, was her way of giving him props—letting him know he was all that . . . but not now. She was not prepared for his response to be serious. She was not prepared for him to trace her eyebrows with his thumbs and then hold her face. She was not ready for him to look at her long and hard, and for unshed tears to make his eyes shine in the darkness . . . or for him to ask her on a thick swallow, "No, baby, tell me where you've been all mine."

He was scaring her more than Paxton ever could. James Carter was scaring her to death as he showed restraint, didn't touch her, because he thought he might hurt her. Through those deep, intense eyes of his, she could see his mind fighting his body's natural impulses. But the more she looked at him—and it was all in his eyes—something much deeper within him than his mind kept his body in check. That scared the bullshit out of her. She could not allow that to happen.

She took his wrists and placed his hands on her breasts, then leaned against them, and kissed him hard. "You can't hurt me; I'm all right," she said into his mouth.

"You sure?" His question was strangled by her tongue.

She slid against him and began working on his holster, trying to free him from the leather bindings and the weapon. He helped her and slid his gun across the floor, then pulled off his sweater. She unfastened his belt and pushed him to lie back on the rug.

It all happened so fast—wasn't supposed to go down like this. The night before there had at least been a little sense to what was already too crazy. But when she came off the sofa to join him on the floor, somehow she wasn't thinking of much more than he was when she stripped off her stretch pants. And he definitely wasn't thinking about much more than her when he allowed her to straddle him without a condom.

Hot, wet fusion, sensation not felt since the eighties, made her whimper. Pleasure so profound made him forget about her bruises. Her name came up from way down in his chest upon entry . . . Nobody was thinking. It all happened so fast.

Her back suddenly hit the floor hard when he flipped her to gain leverage, and she wasn't making any sense when she wrapped her legs around his waist. In her heart she knew the man couldn't pull out if he wanted to. Then she tried to get rational for about two seconds past too late, but all that came out of her mouth was a half-uttered sentence that made him crazier, like her.

"Oh, God, James . . . please . . ."

He couldn't pull out of her curves; he was driving too fast—and the road was real wet. It had been too long since he'd experienced that. His mind told him to ease on the breaks, pump with control, don't skid. Then she'd told him not to stop . . . Jesus, he was only flesh and blood. All he could do was wrap his arms around her waist, drive faster, harder, and brace for impact.

This was definitely madness—crazy, risky, ridiculous madness that he couldn't explain, not even to himself, much less to her. His vocal cords had seized; rational thought was blocked from access to his brain; shudders wrapping around his spine choked it. Heat like molten lava created pressure, filled his shaft. Sensations he hadn't felt in years: wet, no latex; oh . . . damn . . . it was so good between her silk-smooth legs, planted deep in the thick, swollen, center of the God-damned universe—Lord . . .

His eyes were shut so tight, he was seeing colors behind his lids; then she messed around, arched hard against him, and called him by name.

The spasm tore through his groin so quickly, pressure released, pleasure so good it hurt—snapped and contracted stomach muscles, a long holler sent from up from nowhere, charley horse–creating thigh tremors, fast-gathered Oriental rug nap under his nails threatening to make them bleed—hold on. Her voice making it worse. Making it better. Her nails cutting his shoulder blades—she could have it all . . . just take it. Colors expanding, pushing hot tears from his eyes . . . can't get enough air—gonna suffocate and die cumming. He hadn't meant to cuss, but when a man is dying, sweet . . . *shit* . . .

For what seemed like a long time, they just lay there on the floor, still fused. He could tell she was now starting to think about things, just like he was starting to think about things, and as they both lay there, breathing hard, basting in warm juices that weren't supposed to be exchanged on a casual basis—forbidden, hot primordial soup—to speak would mean that it had happened. And it wasn't casual. *Oh . . . shit . . .*

His cell phone was ringing. At this hour, it had to be Steve. He was paralyzed and couldn't reach it. His partner hadn't lied; he was all fuckin' compromised. The woman under him was still trembling. Jesus, it was so good with her . . . He could still feel her contractions, her body slick with sudden sweat like his. The phone stopped ringing, and then it started ringing again.

He tried to lift himself up enough to give her some air, wasn't trying to suffocate her. But it felt like four-hundred-pound weights were on his shoulders; his arms shook when he tried to push his hands against the floor. She wasn't helping matters when she pulled him back to her, closing off the stab of cool air that hit his belly. His pants were tangled around his ankles with his boxers. Damn. He hadn't even gotten his shoes off. But the incessant phone was like a reality check. He opened his eyes. *This* was *not* supposed to happen.

"Oh, shit . . . ," she finally whispered.

All he could do at first was nod. Aftershocks were still hitting him. He couldn't catch his breath, much less reach for the phone and talk. He peered at his holstered gun, which was several inches away from his head on the floor, the barrel end pointing in their direction, then closed his eyes. "Oh . . . shit . . . Laura."

Chapter 18

His back was against the couch, but he was still sitting on the floor, pants around his ankles, breathing hard, when he clicked on his cell phone. "Yo, man," Carter answered in staccato. "What's up?" If Steve would just chill . . .

His partner paused.

"You called me, man," Carter said, dropping his head back and trying to breathe through his nose. He did not need this shit right now. He glanced at Laura. She was lying on her side, staring at him, picking at the rug.

"No judgment, brother," Steve said slowly, judgment clearly in his voice. "Get dressed. Darien Price just wigged out—shot his wife and put a gun to his temple."

"What?" Carter got to his feet and pulled up his pants, moving fast as he found his sweater and his gun. "What time?"

"Sometime just before midnight." Steve hesitated again. "Bodies are still warm, and there's blood everywhere in the Prices' bedroom. Meet me and the forensics squad up at their house." There was another pause. "Unless you need me to pick you up—you do have enough energy left to drive, right?"

"I'll meet you there," Carter said, clicking off the cell phone, becoming annoyed. He didn't like his partner's tone at all. Fuck it. He looked at Laura, who was now standing and getting dressed. "I'm gonna have a squad car sorta hang out in front of your house for a while. I don't want you to worry, but—"

"Wait a minute," she said, standing before him and holding up her hand. "What just happened?"

God, he hated to blow the groove like this. "Darien Price freaked, blew his wife away in their bedroom, and then put a bullet in his head—we think. But until we sweep the site, run forensics . . ."

"Oh, my God . . ."

He watched Laura's hand slowly come to her mouth. Her eyes held a stricken expression that he never wanted them to hold ever again. Seeing the blood drain from her face reminded him of his mother's face, all those years ago. Just like now, he'd gotten off the telephone and had to deliver the bad news that his father had been shot—DOA.

In reflex, Carter ran his palm over his hair and searched the floor for the rest of his clothes and his gun. It was now beyond some credit card bullshit, or money. Bodies were dropping. This was no longer, so-called clean, white-collar crime. Homicide Division would be all over this, too, blurring the departmental lines. Whatever Laura was near, or had found out, made her a possible target—if this wasn't a crime of passion. For her sake, he could only pray that it was.

Carter tightened the strap on his shoulder holster as he put on his gun. Damn Steve Sullivan for being right; he'd just made love, with no condom, to a material witness. Yeah, this was over the line.

"Look," she said slowly, "I'll be all right. I don't need—"

"Two things," he said, his voice serious. "One, this has now kicked up a notch. And you're a possible material witness—if—"

"Me! Why?"

She was walking in circles, and he watched her.

"Because you told me that Darien and Paxton shared the same woman—"

"But—"

"No buts." He stared at her hard. She didn't move. "A man finds out that his best friend is screwing his wife. That's enough to create a Greek tragedy—yes, even in the new millennium, Laura. Then let's add the fact that Paxton, a very well connected attorney with solid corporate clients, number two, fucked his criminal defense client's wife while representing the man, which I'd call a conflict of interest. That might be enough to have the man severely reprimanded, if not disbarred. Even though all this was hearsay, we can establish a motive from your testimony about her mood, her statements to you about her marriage, then find the backup evidence with enough digging, I'm sure. And in the meantime, Paxton's reputation, his client base—"

"Okay. I got it," she said in a weary tone, and then flopped down on the couch. She held her head in her hands as she spoke. "I told a detective that the man's wife came to me and confessed an affair. I got it."

She was numb when James kissed her good-bye and told her to be safe and to lock her doors. Jesus H. Christ, what had she done? This was not supposed to happen. The man blew away his wife. Took his own life. It wasn't supposed to go down like this.

It was all supposed to be clean, albeit an-eye-for-an-eye justice. Getting the cell phones had been so simple—all she had to do was order them like a secretary would for the boss, provide the business credit card information, have the providers express-overnight–deliver the units to the hotel where there was a business conference. Atlanta, Chicago, New Orleans—it didn't matter; these brothers did the circuit.

She'd just had to pick the phones up posing as the secretary during a business conference. There was nothing hard about wearing her hair different, sporting a wig, doing the pickup at an hour when the concierge's desk was clear—

worst case, seeming like a lover running an errand for her man. Then it was a cakewalk: watch men who weren't where they were supposed to be.

No, no, no, no, no. People weren't supposed to *die.* This was a white-collar job of opening her pocketbook and calling herself while in the company of people who could provide her with an alibi if necessary—she would always be able to say that she was with clients or friends . . . people who never saw a cell phone against her ear at the appointed time of the alleged calls and transfers.

But in her big barrel purse, each phone set on vibrate to establish a connection between the target men, clocked minutes between cells to link all the men involved with a time-date stamp. Calls would triangulate in the hotel; voices would register from the general bar or restaurant hubbub . . . like a secret conversation was going on. Then all she had to do was go to the ladies' room with a girlfriend, go into a stall and keep talking to her friends, move stolen money into the target males' accounts; make it look like they'd discussed the transaction first.

From there all she'd had to do was click off the phones when the boys were on the move. The whole thing was simple: watch the men at conferences room-hop, not wanting to give up the truth about who they were with to an attorney or a wife. Stand in a noisy club, looking at them work a bar from a discreet table, while she talked with clients, electronic minutes passing phone to phone inside her purse. Transfer money and pay off all their bills while she knew they were getting laid. All she had to do was be patient and watch them work the rooms. Or do the transaction while she was on the landline phone talking to her sister, or on the office console phone talking to someone at work, always when she was sure these men were where they weren't supposed to be. Then it was easy to feed a tip to the cops through a media insider source, stand back, and wait for the whole thing to blow. It was Sweet. Smooth. And very, very clean. But not this.

Laura sat on the hallway stairs, looking out at nothing. It didn't take a rocket scientist to figure out what had gone down with Darien and his wife. Paxton was going to set Monica up; that much was certain. Other members of the hidden trust were getting indicted. She'd probably panicked. Monica did what any rational female in her position would do—she'd made a decision to save her children from having their mother go to prison. Divorce was a better option. She had to be trying to build an alliance with Darien, banking on old love, using the children as human bartering chips. She wasn't thinking clearly when trying to warn her husband not to trust the man who'd be representing their lives in front of a judge. But she'd miscalculated one thing. Tears rose to Laura's eyes. For all of Darien's philandering ways, he was desperately insecure . . . That's probably why he did it. His parents had covered up his violent outbursts against women—his wife didn't know how off the hook he could be. She was from a stratum that his dirty little secret was hidden from. But sisters like Laura and Najira had witnessed Darien's rages firsthand. Oh, shit . . . this unwise sister didn't know men well enough.

Laura's elbows found her knees, and she held her head in her hands. *Oh, God . . . Najira will freak.* She'd implicated a nineteen-year old kid in these war games. Not even the strongest of the men she'd ever dealt with, white or black, could cope with having a wife throw his best friend in his face—a best friend who had bested him at everything in life . . . who had about four inches of wood on him, a sore point for Darien that *she knew* had to have been said when Darien refused to be Monica's ally. Of course she'd fight back, using her tongue as a blade to stab him. She'd set it up that way but didn't know Darien was close enough to the edge to go ballistic. Damn. Manhood was the weakest chink in Price's armor—his dick.

When crossed, a woman *always* went for the verbal jugular. Laura shook her head with her eyes closed, just thinking about what the woman could have said. . . . Shit, describing

Paxton's moves to Darien. Suicide-homicide—there was never a justification, but it all made sense. Then to have his children's paternity flung in his face, too? That crazy woman . . . that dangerously off-the-hook woman, who let spite blind her, had to say things that took him over the edge.

Unless . . .

Another shiver ran through her as she stood. Laura walked to the hallway closet and opened it. She stood on her tiptoes and retrieved the hatbox on the shelf. It was heavy with metal. She went to the kitchen table and set the box down carefully, then lifted the lid. She extracted her father's .357 Magnum, and began loading it.

Fuck vulnerability. If one of the fellas was getting nervous, was thinking about coming her way . . . if somehow she'd been suspected, she knew how to fire Daddy's peacekeeper. She didn't need a cop to keep her safe. She couldn't only hope that Monica hadn't been *real* crazy, hadn't said some in-your-face mess about her to Darien, or to Paxton. Shit like "Yeah, Darien, and I went to your old girlfriend, who now holds the keys to your stupid fucking kingdom, and I cut my own deal, motherfucker." A woman's tongue could be vicious when she'd been scorned.

Or what if Monica had gone to Paxton with "Yeah, you bastard, I know you think you could move me out of the way, but I cut a woman-to-woman deal with Laura to keep my money flowing"? That would be nuts. Laura's gaze went to her gun. But knowing Paxton, if Monica had done that, the arrogant SOB would have laughed in her face, telling Monica they were lovers—a lie that would have freaked the sister out . . . maybe freaked her out enough to make her fall on her sword and go to her husband to cut a deal. What if there was another variable?

Laura sat down at the kitchen table, her mind working like a Pentium chip. In only fourteen hours, the cell phones in her briefcase were now a problem. Before, her plan was to go to a few unknown people's funerals—people who were going to be cremated—wear a black hat with a veil, lean in and kiss the deceased, and slide away, leaving a cell phone in a man's funeral suit pocket to burn to ash after the family viewing. She'd contemplated making a few charitable visits to hospitals, and discreetly dropping a phone wrapped in red plastic into a biohazard box destined for an incinerator—nobody would open that these days.

Or she could have easily scammed a way into the number 2 Streets Department plant, over in the Bridesburg section at Delaware Avenue and Wheatsheaf Lane, to have the cells incinerated, or come up with some community service yang to have her payload dropped in with a neighborhood project—one call to the recycling coordinator in Camden, New Jersey, would have sealed that lovely.

Forensic science was too advanced these days not to track down a cell . . . find a trace of makeup on it, perspiration, a loose eyelash, whatever. She should have gotten rid of the phones first thing this morning. But now there was a problem; she was being watched for her own protection. All because she'd taken a little detour in the middle of her living room floor.

Laura sighed. At least she was in good company and had an alibi—James. This was messy, not clean and neat at all. But if she went to jail, it wouldn't be for murder . . . maybe. That was the one line she hoped she wouldn't have to cross, since she'd tap-danced on all the other lines between right and wrong. She held the gun, feeling its weight. A man had killed his wife and blown out his own brains . . . perhaps, unless someone else had.

In the last twenty-four hours, it seemed that detours had screwed a lot of people around. Her mind created a chronology file: Old man Paxton did Darien's mother, Juanita Price, making a son. That would mean old man Price was in the way of their union, if divorce presented a problem somehow. Interesting that Paxton Senior had risen to power by doing the wife of a powerful man, Haines. Then Paxton's wife, Colette, betrayed him in what had to be vengeful tit-for-tat, by doing Haines. Or vice versa. It didn't matter. Either way,

Colette Paxton had died under suspicious circumstances, too.

She just wondered how Donald Haines had reacted when he found out, in that era, that a brother had tagged his wife. Hmmm . . . not good. A potentially lethal combination, knowledge and power . . . Car accidents were very lethal; Donald Haines was very powerful. Elizabeth had said he owed her. And how would an arrogant, power-drunk black man react to finding out that his wife had been with a powerful white man beyond his reach, a man who had made him successful just to keep his wife, Colette, nearby? Ugly. But probably not half as bad as the man who'd learned somehow that his son, Darien, wasn't his—Juanita Price had to be one lie-living, scared bitch. No wonder the woman's hands used to shake.

Laura sat down slowly, dazed as she thought about the magnitude of it all. There was one fact that would eradicate all this hypocrisy: power brokers ultimately controlled the resources people needed to survive. Therefore, murder was not out of the question—especially if passions got added to the equation.

And in the middle of this whole incestuous drama, that left two warring sons, one of whom was now dead—the one who was blind to the front line of the conflict. The sins of the father—history repeated itself: Paxton Jr. took his best friend's wife; now that friend and wife were dead. Yet it still didn't explain who set up her father and shot a cop.

Laura pushed herself up from the table and poured a glass of wine. Damn. None of this was supposed to happen. She had to rethink everything—not from a strategic position this time but from a place in her soul. These had been human beings. Parents. How many people had she possibly judged without thinking of the ramifications? A spirit could be fragile, just as a mind could be.

She studied the liquid in her glass. Perhaps it was all poetic justice. Perhaps other factors had contributed to this beyond her tampering hand. Yes, she'd been the catalyst, but the way they were all living their lives had imploded, too. Maybe she wasn't supposed to start any of this madness.

Then again, Brother Akhan had said the universe was always efficient.

By the time he got there, media was nearly blocking the road. Carter let his gaze scan the scene as he walked past patrol cars and the coroner's wagon and stepped beyond the line of yellow crime scene tape. Crossing the line, he paused in the Price driveway. Black Cadillac Escalade parked slanted, skid marks—Darien must have been in a hurry to get home. A cream-colored Lexus ES 300 sedan parked normally, as if the wife had already been inside.

His partner met him at the door, and they only exchanged a nod as he followed Steve. Teams of his brethren in blue were combing the house for evidence. Carter allowed his eyes to scan the terrain. The expanse of the well-appointed home wasn't lost on him. Damn, everything in the world at your feet and it still wasn't enough? He shook his head and followed Steve upstairs. The first floor showed no signs of a struggle. No broken lamps, no overturned tables. This was a walk-in, hi-honey-I'm-home blindside.

When Carter entered the bedroom, the scene that greeted him was too grisly to believe. Although he'd witnessed a hundred like this before if he'd witnessed one, it still took him a moment to process the sight of a killing in a home like this. And it was the sort of thing that had made him move from Homicide Division over to Fraud . . . he didn't have it in him to deal with this kinda shit anymore.

In a heap on the floor on one side of the bed, Monica's bullet-riddled body lay crumpled. Carter glanced down at her—the woman's once beautiful face was partially blown away. One third of it was gone, from her left eye and forehead up . . . as though her husband had literally been trying to blow her brains out. Carter shook his head, hoping that the coroner would later tell them that this had been the first shot.

Steve glanced at him. "Yeah, I hear you," he murmured. "I hope so, too, man. At least she wouldn'ta had to suffer."

Carter nodded as he neared the female victim's body. Her chest and abdomen had taken practically a full clip. Her blood had splattered from exit wounds, making the silk Laura Ashley wallpaper host a new, noncatalog design. High-velocity blood spatter also stained the goose-down comforter on the four-poster Rice bed. "Jesus Christ, this motherfucker totally flipped, Sullivan."

"Yeah, partner," Steve muttered, pointing across the room. "You wanna walk this out?"

"Yeah," Carter said, going across the room. "Price entered here; path of destruction leads there . . . the bed is between them; they argue."

Sullivan nodded as Carter went to what had obviously been a Tiffany bedside lamp, which was now in shards across the room, next to Darien's body. All the crystal bottles and atomizers, a silver comb and brush set, children's framed photos, were also on the floor, the vanity swept clean.

Carter's mind drew the mental picture reconstructing the probable events—argument upon husband's entry to the room. Steve looked at the door with Carter, both detectives silently counting the footsteps it would take to put the bed between the dead husband and wife.

Carter stood still, his mind assessing the damage. Husband, enraged, hurls accusations, trashes wife's vanity. Carter looked at the children's photos on the floor again, bile rising in his throat, the stench of blood and perfume so rank he wanted to vomit. "Husband stomps the children's photos, before or after he or the wife says something about them. Wife reacts and hurls a vicious verbal response, then throws the lamp."

"That was the point when Darien Price pulls his gun; she backs up against the wall, pleading." Steve reenacted the gruesome event next to where the female victim lay on the floor. "He unloads half a clip. Realizes what he's done."

"Looks down at the children's smiles on the floor," Carter muttered. "Puts the gun to his head and pulls the trigger."

Both Carter's and Sullivan's focus went to a meaty, dripping pulp of flesh. Half of Darien's skull was now in a clump of grotesque jelly on the other side of the room.

Carter walked over to the lifeless male body and stooped with Steve at his side. He sighed again. This was such a waste, even if Darien was a worthless SOB . . . there was a line—never women and kids. A forensic tech handed each detective a pair of rubber gloves. Carter put his pair on slowly, hating his job.

"Where are the kids?" Carter asked, his focus still on Darien Price's body.

"They're at a neighbor's. The wife's family is on the way to get 'em. The live-in nanny called nine-one-one during the argument and had rushed the children next door. They heard the shots from across the street." Steve shook his head. "This was a crime of passion . . . I mean, it looks pretty obvious that we can rule out an intruder. This was domestic."

Carter nodded, looking down into Darien's vacant expression. A photo that contained Darien and his wife and children was near his body, as though he'd been holding it when he dropped. "The question is, however, what set him off? He'd been running for years; his wife wasn't a saint . . . Something had to take him over the edge." He wanted Steve to draw his own conclusions. For some odd reason, he didn't want to have to tell Steve about Paxton with Laura as a witness. If he had to, he would. But this shit was so convoluted . . .

"Yeah . . . Maybe it was the stress of getting caught with his hands in the City Hall cookie jar. Add an affair or some shit like that—go figure." Steve raked his clean, rubber-clad fingers through his hair. "Or, you know how this goes, Jim. Sometimes it's just one last wrong look, one last argument that breaks the camel's back. Dude was under serious stress. Might be an open-and-shut case."

"Maybe. But I'd like to ask one person in particular what might have touched off an explosion."

"Paxton?"

Carter nodded.

Steve looked at the dead man on the floor. "He had tears in his eyes," Steve muttered. "Can still see salt lines on his face."

Carter stood. "They always do, when it goes down like this."

"So, tell me why you gentlemen are standing in my living room at this hour, with media swamping the parking lot? I imagine you have a boatload of paperwork to file, or something else constructive to do?" Paxton paced away from them and went to his bar to fix a drink. He took his time and sat down on a stool far away from them.

"We just want to ask you a few questions, since you were his—"

"Two points of order," Paxton said, cutting Steve Sullivan off and glaring at Carter. Paxton then directed his comments toward the detective who hadn't spoken: Carter. "One: if I'm some kind of suspect, then you know I have nothing to say unless my attorney is present. Don't be foolish. Two: anything discussed between Darien Price and me falls within attorney-client privilege. That makes what we have to discuss very limited—and the only reason I allowed you up here is that I didn't want that basic lesson to Philadelphia's finest broadcast on a news sound bite."

"Okay," Steve said, throwing up his hands. "This was a waste of time."

Carter stared at Paxton, and his gaze narrowed on him. "Yeah, partner. It was a waste. We'll have to come back later after we interview Monica's girlfriend. The one she confided in about her affair with her husband's attorney, and everything that she told—"

"That bullshit is hearsay, and you know it!" Paxton stood quickly and went to the elevator, slamming his palm against the button. "It is also slander, unless you can prove it has merit on the case, and you have ironclad evidence that anything like that went down. Step wrong, and I will own the

Roundhouse in a defamation and damages suit. Don't fuck with me, Carter. Get out of my house."

"Cool," Carter said, his expression nonplussed. "But you wouldn't have happened to talk to Darien tonight at all?"

Paxton returned a sinister smile as all three men listened to the elevator motor. "You know where I was, and who I was with, right, Carter? Maybe you should ask Laura Caldwell if I had time to call Price, or if I seemed like a man with the inclination to do so." He chuckled when Carter bristled. "Nooo . . . calling my client Darien was the last thing on my mind. He called me later while I was driving home, and our call was brief—because, frankly, I was too exhausted to hold a long discourse with him at that point."

The elevator doors opened, and both Carter and Sullivan stepped in, hit the button, and left without a word. Steve looked at his partner, monitoring the muscle working in his jaw. They said nothing to each other as they crossed the lot and pushed microphones out of their faces.

"No, Michael Paxton is not a suspect," Steve said with irritation to the dozens of reporters gathered and blocking their path. "He was Darien Price's attorney, and we just wanted to know if Michael Paxton Jr. might have any information that he could share that might help us understand what went wrong to create a tragedy at the Prices' home. No. No further statements while we're working the case tonight. Statements in the morning—call the captain; you know the drill."

Once inside the car, they'd created a barrier to the media. Steve drove. Carter looked out the window. Except for light traffic, Delaware Avenue was fairly desolate at that hour. Every instinct within Carter told him that Paxton was guilty—just not of a direct hit.

"The bastard bristled," Carter finally said.

For a moment, Steve didn't answer. "Shit, so did you."

"There's more to this."

"The money part, yes. The murders, no. The man shot his wife, dude. Her old man finds out she's fucking his best friend and attorney, the man representing him to keep his ass out of prison—hell, yeah, I'd freak, too. Darien wigged. Period. Close this end of the investigation. Tomorrow we pick up a few more white-collar types, hope they get better lawyers and don't go home buggin' to their wives, feel me? But, if you don't want to get your girl Laura in the middle of a media gangbang, you're gonna have to get one of the inner-circle dudes to say something about Paxton and Monica. Eventually, we're gonna have to make a statement about what might have made Darien Price flip . . . and we'll have to have evidence to back it up, or we'll all be in big—"

"Yeah. I hear you. If possible, I'd like to leave her out of it."

Steve pulled over and looked at his partner hard. "Man, you're in too deep. Your ass is fully compromised. And you'd better leave sleeping dogs lie—and stop fucking with Paxton 'cause you've got an ax to grind. *That* is what you'd better hear."

Carter made no comment. What was there to say? He looked straight ahead as Steve pulled back into traffic again, heading for the Oregon Avenue Diner. But his mind kept worrying the jigsaw puzzle like a dog worrying a bone. Then the dispatch radio popped and hissed, and the dispatcher's voice came on.

"Yo, Steve, Jim—we've got a Martin Ramsey on a line, sounding hysterical, talking about he wants immunity for some info. You boys are shaking up the town—better get some coffee. Got another black professional teetering on a ledge."

Chapter 19

"Oh, my God!" Lavern shouted, her voice shrill in the receiver as Laura pulled it away from her ear. "You knew those people. You're in the same circles—something could have happened to you. Laura, you could have been there when that man went off and killed his wife!"

There was no getting a word in edgewise as her sister's breathless diatribe knifed guilt into Laura's conscience. "I wasn't that close . . . and it was obviously some sort of domestic problem." Her cell phone was ringing, and without checking the ID, she knew it was either her other sister, Nadine, or her cousin, Najira. Then the two-way calling clicked again on the house line. "Lavern, let me get this call. It's probably Nadine."

"Put her on three-way, then," Lavern said fast. "We have to know you're all right!"

Laura swallowed hard, fighting back inexplicable tears as she answered the second line. It was too late for tears now. The damage had been done. She should have let the cosmos run its course and deliver its own brand of justice.

"Hello," Laura said quietly, only to be greeted by Nadine's hysterical sonic boom.

"They're crazy," Nadine hollered. "Where are you?"

Laura paused. "I'm at home. You called me, remember?"

"Right. Right. But we just saw it on the news! Lavern is—"

"On the other line."

"Put her on three-way, then!"

"All right. Both of you-all just calm down. Philly is—"

"Sick!" Lavern yelled as her side of the conversation was conferenced in.

"I know. I know," Laura said as calmly as possible, but then she froze as the doorbell sounded. "Somebody's at my door," she said slowly.

"Oh, my God! Call the police!" Nadine shouted, her voice cracking. "It could be an accomplice—or a serial killer. Maybe one of his boys are in on this whole thing, too, just like you see on TV. Who knows? Remember what Mom always said about those folks—crazy. Sick. Ya need to leave them alone and stay outta their way."

"That's right," Lavern chimed in. "Girl, don't be no fool and answer that door."

Her sisters were over the top, and yet were so right, while also being so unaware of just how enmeshed she was in the Prices' lives, that it sent a chill through her. Ignoring them, Laura walked to the door with the cordless receiver in one hand, clutching her cell phone in the other, with her finger hovering over the speed-dial button on it to connect her to 911, just in case. Seeing Najira, her shoulders slumped in relief. "It's just Jira," she said quickly, turning the locks. "She probably came to check on me. Relax."

"Put her on the phone," Nadine ordered. "Don't you hang up this telephone till we speak to her and your door is locked again."

"All right, all right," Laura said, growing impatient. "Let me open the door."

Najira didn't say a word as Laura cracked open the front door. She simply burst through it, barreled into Laura's arms, and began sobbing.

Laura held her hard and instantly put the cordless unit on mute. "Listen to me," she said fast. "Lavern and Nadine are on the telephone and are worried sick. They want to be sure that neither one of us is near this whole group of people. They do not know about what happened in the past, so don't go there." She made Najira look at her. "You have to tell them you were just shaken and came to check on me, but that we're fine. Got it?"

Najira rapidly shook her head no. "I can't. Oh, Laura . . . the man died and killed his wife. It wasn't supposed to—"

"It wasn't your fault." Laura held her harder. She understood Najira's pain, as well as the guilt wound in her cousin's soul, but now was not the time. "He ran with a lot of women," she added, trying to soothe Najira. Laura allowed her voice to drop to a soft but firm whisper to calm the distraught woman in her arms. "You and I both know that he was already crazy. Plus, he was bound to get caught doing dirt sooner or later." As Najira's sobs abated, Laura staved off the pang her own words caused. In her heart she knew the truth: that it might never have gone this far. Najira probably knew that, too, but needed someone to give her absolution. So Laura pressed on, attempting to purge herself in the process.

"Besides, if you didn't tell his wife, one of his other women would have. You didn't have anything to do with this—now you have *got* to get on the phone."

Drawing several shaky breaths, Najira looked up and accepted the telephone from Laura as she eased out of Laura's embrace.

"Hey, y'all," she said in a falsely upbeat tone. "Laura scared the mess out of me . . . I couldn't get her by telephone and knew she used to travel in those circles. I just busted out in tears when I saw her . . . you know how crazy I am."

Nervous laughter filled the receiver, and Najira closed her eyes, two big tears rolling down her cheeks in the process.

"Yeah. I know. I'll keep an eye on her . . . but she hasn't really hung with them in a long time, so you guys stop being such mother hens, okay? And yeah, we love y'all, too."

Najira thrust the phone at Laura and wrapped her arms around herself. She waited until Laura ended the call, both women staring at each other for a moment.

"This is why I didn't want you up close to any of this," Laura said in a gentle tone. "In war . . . sometimes it gets ugly . . . and—"

"I know we're right and they're wrong . . . and they did some horrible things to our family. But . . . Laura," her cousin said so quietly that Laura had to strain to hear her, "just answer me one question."

Laura touched Najira's cheek and pulled her into another hug. "Yeah, baby. What?"

"How you sleep at night after something like this?"

Sleep deprivation was kicking his ass, but adrenaline was running through Carter like crank, keeping him alert. He trained his focus on the precinct office door just ahead of him. Steve yawned, walking beside him like a zombie. Captain Bennett was rubbing his face with both hands as though trying to wipe the fatigue away with each palm pass.

As they entered the captain's office, Carter's attention went to the two men facing Bennett: one preppie-looking white dude wearing a navy Polo shirt and khakis with penny loafers, and a corporate-tense brother in a burgundy velour sweatsuit and Nike sneakers. Carter sized them up quickly. The stressed-looking brother had to be Martin Ramsey. The white guy with the briefcase on the floor beside him was obviously his attorney.

The two visitors stood. Captain Bennett took a sip of his coffee.

"Detective Carter, Detective Sullivan, Martin Ramsey and his attorney, Alan Moyer, from Moyer, Burrell, and Strauss." Bennett simply waved from his seated position, motioning for Carter and Sullivan to sit down as perfunctory handshakes were exchanged.

"Normally, I would have advised my client to wait until a decent hour, and until a DA could be present, to have this meeting. But under the circumstances, my client was anxious to be cooperative—as quickly as possible," Alan Moyer said. "He'd placed the call to you before I'd had an opportunity to advise him otherwise," he added, cutting a glance filled with irritation toward Martin Ramsey. "So here we are. Gentlemen, let's talk."

"All right," Carter said, finding an empty chair by the window in the captain's office. He glanced at Steve, who was now sitting across from him in the tight confines.

The attorney nodded to Martin Ramsey.

"Look, I wanted to make sure I'm not implicated in *any* of this," Martin said, leaning forward on his forearms, his eyes nervously searching the faces in the room. "I want full immunity for cooperation."

"We might be able to work something out," Sullivan hedged. "But that depends on the quality of the information—and if the DA thinks it's worth it."

"No deal on maybes and ifs," Alan Moyer said, his gaze roving the faces before him. "My client has valuable information and hasn't done anything wrong. This is a professional courtesy call—especially at this hour of the night."

"We can't necessarily cut deals directly," Steve hedged, glancing at his partners. "The DA has to do that. But if there's something really worth listening to, then I'm sure the DA might be persuaded to remain open to the possibilities."

Carter rubbed his jaw. "If you came down here at this hour, then that means one of two things: either your client has a lot of involvement and you're nervous about that, or you're very nervous about—"

"I thought we'd get your full cooperation, Captain." Alan Moyer was on his feet, his briefcase in his hand.

"Sit down. Let's everybody relax. It's been a long day,"

Bennett said, soothing the attorney. "We'll take a risk, given the unprecedented nature of this cooperative visit." He gave Carter and Sullivan a warning glare and then returned his attention to Moyer, who slowly sat.

"All right. All right," Carter said begrudgingly. "Talk to us."

"Okay," Martin stammered. "Look. Like I said, I want to cooperate. But I want to be sure that I'm protected."

"We got that part," Sullivan grumbled.

"You-all don't know. Paxton is a crazy son of a bitch."

"So far your information isn't opening our eyes, Ramsey." Carter leaned back in his chair. Pure exhaustion was making him irritable.

"I know," Martin said fast. "But this thing with Darien and his wife was way over the top." Ramsey's eyes searched the faces of the men in the room.

Carter and Sullivan nodded and became more interested in what Ramsey had to say.

"Darien was the baby in our crew; he looked up to Mike—didn't know what was going on with Paxton and Monica. Me and Brad Crawford were the only ones who knew—Howard Scott, her cousin, would have flipped. Howard loved Monica like a little sister. Jim Thompson and Don Edward didn't even know."

Carter stood and paced to the window. His body hurt; he needed to stretch and had to keep moving. This whole thing was giving him the heebie-jeebies. But Ramsey's story did do one thing: it got Laura Caldwell possibly off the hook as a star witness in the domestic case. He didn't even want to look at Steve, knowing what his eyes would tell him. "That's all well and fine, but I still don't see what that has to do with the charges you're up against, brother."

"Let me finish," Martin shot back. "It has everything to do with it."

"Give the guy a chance to tell his side of it, Carter," Captain Bennett warned. "We should really have homicide squad in here . . . and I'm taking a few liberties only because this has so much to do with the fraud and embezzlement cases."

Carter nodded and returned to his seat with a thud. "My bad—go 'head."

"All right," Martin said, now on his feet and pacing. "See, Paxton always wanted everything Darien had—and it made no sense. It went as far back as I can remember." He shook his head and raked his fingers through his hair. "Me and Don and Jim are only a few years older than D.; Howard grew up with Darien—they're the same age, which is how he wound up married to Howard's cousin. Paxton is the eldest in the group and, so to speak, the head of the business network we're sorta in."

"All right, so we've got the family tree, and know the oldest member in your little club had a problem with the group's baby brother. But I'm not following how this—"

"Hear me out," Ramsey said, his tone brittle. "Like, even when Darien was a kid . . . we were all in college, up at Martha's Vineyard on spring break, Darien came up there trying to impress Paxton, a guy ten years his senior, about some bullshit date-rape thing he did to some girl on a prom. Me and the fellas were like, 'Yeah, in your dreams,' and we laughed it off. But Paxton started grilling D. . . . until Darien whipped out a home Polaroid picture of him and Laura Caldwell—"

"Laura Caldwell?" Steve shot a glance at Carter.

Carter could feel every muscle in his body turn to steel cable and begin tying into knots. Now Ramsey had his undivided attention.

"Yeah," Ramsey pressed on, oblivious to Carter's mood shift. "Said he'd taken some ghetto sister to his senior prom, did her in his daddy's Cadillac and left her on the side of the road to walk home—like that was something to be bragging about. The rest of us were like, 'What, man? Your ass is stupid. Why'd you do a sister like that?' But we let it go and kept partying. But us ignoring D. just made him go on and on about how she fought him, and he was showing off his black eye and scratches on his face like a badge of honor. But Paxton kept digging and digging into Darien's ass—wouldn't let it rest. Was almost hanging on Darien's every word about the specifics of what he did to her, and how she'd fought him—disgusting shit like that. Twenty-five-some-odd years later, Paxton, like he did everything else of Darien's, tagged Darien's wife and went back to tag Laura Caldwell."

Carter inhaled slowly, his gaze never leaving Ramsey's eyes. He'd kill that bastard . . . but first he needed to have a serious conversation with Laura.

"Okay, so we've established that there's bad blood between—"

"No, you don't get it," Ramsey said, cutting off Steve's comment.

Steve glanced at Carter, who never returned the eye contact.

"We had a meeting at Paxton's place right before the Aquarium fund-raiser," Martin interjected. He began walking back and forth again, causing the others in the room to follow him with their eyes. "Darien and Paxton went at it about the chick that, ironically enough, had been the one Darien supposedly date-raped. Paxton said he'd hit it—you know what I mean? All of us could tell it fucked with Darien—that poor fool still kept the professional prom picture hidden in his wallet underneath his kids' baby pictures. Do you believe that?"

"Yeah, I do," Carter said slowly, every instinct in him coiled tight, ready to spring.

"Me and him went to Zanzibar's for a drink after the meeting—"

"Him who?" Carter held Ramsey in a cool stare.

"Me and Darien," Ramsey said, letting his breath out hard and taking a seat again. "Darien whipped out this old photo and was talking about how he thought Paxton was lying. The brother got drunk and sloppy and started talking about how Paxton was always busting his balls . . . but how he loved him like a brother. Poor bastard looked up to Mike like he was his idol." Ramsey rubbed his face and let his breath out hard again. "Darien was scared. Thought Laura Caldwell would screw him out of his allotment, but was glad Mike had his back—even though Mike was fucking some broad Darien had always had a thing for. Darien never knew how much Mike couldn't stand him. None of us could figure out why the chemistry was so foul."

Carter chose his words very, very carefully. "What makes you so cooperative, though? And how could she do that? Unless her business—"

"She's been given the nod to move the money to a safe haven—the money in Darien's city fund—because with all the bullshit, the foundations are pulling out." Ramsey glanced at his attorney, who nodded but didn't say a word. "Paxton said he had her locked down. He and Darien had a standoff, and things got heated. I made a comment in anger in front of the group. . . . I said I could kill Darien myself, and I know Paxton will try to use that against me. But I can prove that I was nowhere near the bullshit, or had anything to do with what went down between him and his wife."

"The thing looks like a standard domestic tragedy," Sullivan said, his voice slow and even. He glanced at the other cops in the room. "Doesn't seem like Ramsey pulled the trigger. So?"

"So," Alan Moyer said, his dark brown eyes moving around the faces in the room, his expression guarded. "Paxton will probably have a media block on his involvement with Monica Scott Price. I'm sure the good Senator Scott is very upset, as is the family, and won't want her name sullied with an extramarital affair coming to light. However, anyone in that meeting bearing a grudge against Darien might be made to take the weight in the press—and my client has too sterling a reputation to protect, as well as his marriage. Do we understand each other?"

Captain Bennett nodded and sent a hard glance toward Sullivan and Carter.

"My consulting firm was going to provide instructors for Darien's program," Ramsey said quietly. "And I know the money would have been rerouted to another firm I have based in Atlanta . . . but I would not tell a man something to make him blow his wife away and then blow his own head off. There are limits—there's a line."

Ramsey's gaze went out the window, his expression pained and his voice distant and rambling. "Darien was just a kid to us. Like an annoying little brother that we all indulged. But he had a soft heart; that's what Mike could never understand. And Monica, God rest her soul, might have run on Darien to get back at him, but she was as naive as the day is long. . . . Their children are all fucked up now." He shook his head and paused as his voice cracked. "I know Paxton told Darien some crazy shit, because Darien called every one of us—you pull the cell phone records. He called me, hollering about doing his wife, called Don, Brad, Jim—all of us, except Howard. Said he couldn't get the image out of his mind, and that Paxton had told him it was one of us. *That's* why I'm here. Fuck all this madness."

Ramsey stood again and paced to the wall, his back to the group as he wiped his eyes. Alan Moyer stood, causing the others in the room to stand.

"The only one in the network that hasn't had money routed to him—yet—is Paxton." Ramsey's comment had been said low and quietly. His back was still turned to the group as he spoke. "Mike is picking us off one by one . . . and when the dust settles, because he's got Laura Caldwell as his woman, watch how the money flows. Mike has companies in D.C., Baltimore, Chicago, and New York that can deliver services that our firms would have provided. All of us will be discredited, her transfer legal and sweet. Darien blew his own head off; any involvement with Monica will be squashed as a courtesy to the senator. I'm not going down like that—not without a fight. I'll tell you anything I can to stop this travesty. And I didn't steal any money; I don't care what trumped-up evidence you guys find."

Ramsey's tone had been weary, defeated, no anger left in his spirit as took his leather coat down from the rack by the door. He stared at the men in the room. He held Carter's eyes in a private brother-to-brother attempt at psychic connection. His eyes transmitted a message: *Brother, you know I'm telling the truth. Don't let me go down like this—I have a family.* Carter nodded. He could dig it.

"I always knew Paxton was a ruthless bastard," Ramsey said, putting on his coat. "Now I've seen everything. Never thought he'd do family, though. He said something to D. to take him over the edge—I know it."

As the men moved to leave Captain Bennett's office, Alan Moyer paused.

"Martin, why don't you meet me in the car?" He waited for Ramsey to nod and walk out, then turned and looked at Bennett, Sullivan, and Carter. "Gentlemen, may I have a word?"

They all nodded, and Alan Moyer closed the door.

"What I'm about to do could have me disbarred, but this is personal."

The detectives glanced at each other as the tension in the group strangled them.

"I have a copy of Michael Paxton Senior's original will. I acquired it years ago for his son, who used to be one of my closest friends." Alan Moyer opened his briefcase and extracted a document, carefully sliding it across the captain's desk. "Darien Price was the elder Paxton's son." The attorney waited and let the information implode silently as Captain Bennett gathered up the papers in his hands. "I cannot see an innocent man like Martin Ramsey get taken out on some crap like this."

Carter stared at Alan Moyer. "You said it was personal. Paxton *used* to be your friend. Help me?"

Alan Moyer raked his fingers though his brunette hair, his gaze tight as it sought the window to escape the eyes of the other men. "Mike wanted the will. If you read it closely, you'll see why old man Paxton had to pull out of the firm that was then Haines, Breckinridge, Lockhart, and Paxton." Bitterness filled Moyer's voice. "My father was Haines and Paxton's attorney. I was clerking for my father, then. We'd all just left Harvard Law. We were kids. I saw no harm in letting my close friend see what he'd get if his old man kicked the bucket—there was never any love lost between Mike and his dad . . . just like there wasn't much love lost between me and mine. Mike and I bonded on the concept. Then, Mike's father did something unspeakable to my best friend's father. Don Jr. has never been quite the same, but we all keep up civilities for business purposes."

"You'll have to *really* help me," Carter murmured, his eyes never leaving Alan Moyer's profile as Sullivan and Bennett looked at the document and shrugged.

"Darien Price was Paxton Senior's son."

For a moment, none of the men in the room spoke.

"Yeah, you told us that. And Michael Paxton Jr. knew this for at least twenty-five years." Steve just shook his head. "Damn . . ."

Alan Moyer nodded, answering Steve's disgust without words.

"Darien never knew." Alan began pulling on his London Fog.

Captain Bennett simply whistled and sat down hard behind his desk.

"Yeah . . . okay," Carter said, his line of vision still on Moyer. "But how does that make it personal between you and Paxton?"

Alan Moyer looked at James Carter hard now. "Old man Paxton did my best friend's mother, Elizabeth Haines. Made a fool of that woman."

No one spoke as Alan Moyer's quiet truth permeated the room. His voice was so strained that it seemed he'd swallowed hard not to lose it. "Paxton Senior rode Donald Haines Senior's coattails to the top, had an affair with his wife right under his nose—while also siring a son by the real woman he wanted, Juanita Price."

Alan Moyer shook his head. "Michael Paxton Jr. was under a . . . for lack of a better term, under a protective order and still is, because of Elizabeth's threats to divorce her husband—who'd become fond of Colette Paxton." He looked at the detectives now, his eyes seeking understanding. "Don Jr.'s father started this. He was crazy about Colette. Would give her anything, would even elevate her husband to ensure that his mistress lived in luxury. I guess Colette Paxton's husband found out and went after Haines's wife, Elizabeth, for man-to-man justice . . . and then his friend J. D. Price's wife, Juanita—just because. Who knows? But old man Paxton had left everything to Darien—he loathed his first wife, and any fruit of her womb, that is, Michael Jr. *That's* why Mike hated Darien's guts."

"But wait," Carter said, his voice controlled, staying the attorney's move to leave. "The Haineses' marital problems and their son being your best friend notwithstanding . . . what broke up your friendship with Paxton Jr.? Surely you can't hold a man responsible for something his parents did? I don't follow." Carter picked up the documents from the captain's desk and sat on the edge of it. "You and Don must be pretty tight to risk your law license on some old family drama."

Alan Moyer returned a laser glare to Carter. Sullivan and Bennett fell mute. Nobody moved.

"Donny and I are *close,* and have been since college." Alan Moyer allowed the import of what he'd said to sink in. "Seems another mutual friend of ours brought us a piece of information . . . right about the time all this crap with the city case began."

"Which was?" Captain Bennett cast a nervous glance between Sullivan and Carter, his gaze returning to Moyer's after a moment.

Alan Moyer sighed. "Seems like Mike wanted to shore up his old affiliation with the Haineses to cover his odds. Elizabeth recently wound up on his female hit list—Donny can *never* learn that. For him, history would be repeating itself. He'd commit suicide if he found out his mother had stooped to . . . if Mike had . . . I can't let that happen." Moyer's eyes filled with angry tears. "You fix this, gentlemen, and keep it out of the press. I want Martin Ramsey bypassed, as a favor. Period. I'm calling in a marker. Or I will bring down such wrath upon this department with every resource at my disposal, that you'll . . . Just fix it."

Alan Moyer brushed past them, leaving the miniblinds swinging against the door. Carter and Sullivan trained their stares behind him. Captain Bennett held his head in his hands. Steve closed the door slowly, shock making him move with methodical precision.

Carter was like a piece of stone until he and his fellow officers sighed in unison. Clearly none of them worried about the idle threat, even though Moyer could probably deliver enough heat to make all their jobs uncomfortable for a while. It was the freakin' media that would surround the case, along with the damned layers of paperwork, technicalities, and related drama within this wild soap opera. How did people sleep at night?

"Oh . . . shit . . . ," Captain Bennett whispered.

Steve shook his head, "Oh . . . shit . . ."

"Captain," Carter murmured, "you ain't said a mumblin' word."

Chapter 20

Her cell phone was ringing in concert with the telephone on her nightstand. She just prayed that it wasn't Najira on the line again. She wasn't ready to fix her mouth to discuss with her cousin that a man and his wife had died . . . all because they'd set some funky wheel in motion. Not now. Not twice in one night.

Laura dashed out of the bathroom dripping wet, clutching the towel wrapped around her body. She glanced at the cell phone, recognized Paxton's number, and ignored it, choosing the phone by her nightstand instead. A number appeared in the LCD panel that she didn't know by heart. She snatched up the receiver fast before the call rolled over to voice mail.

"Hello?"

"Laura?" a tired male voice said.

She didn't recognize it immediately. "Yes?"

"Good, honey. This is Howard Scott Senior."

She hesitated. "Senator Scott . . . I . . ."

"Let me talk. Please. I know it's late, and this is your private home number—I've had it for a while but had never—"

"You don't have to explain, sir," she said, sitting slowly

on the side of the bed before her knees gave out. "Please go on."

"There's been a tragedy in our family. If you've been asleep, you may not have heard."

She listened to him pause, swallow, and breathe hard to steady his voice. She could find no words to answer him immediately.

"My niece . . . oh, God. Something went wrong between Monica and Darien, and he shot her and then shot himself. Laura, they're both gone."

"Oh, dear Lord," she whispered, guilt still lacerating her. This time it wasn't feigned concern. She closed her eyes, the sound of the old man's voice on the line haunting her conscience.

"I know, Laura. My sister is catatonic. They had to sedate her. But I'm going to ask you a favor, and I need you to trust me without questioning what I'm about to say."

"Whatever I can do," she murmured again, truly meaning it. Two lives were not supposed to be taken, especially not the wife's. Children weren't supposed to be orphaned and traumatized or scarred for life. When this all began, she didn't care if Darien went to jail, and all his cronies along with him. But this was over the top.

"Any contract funds you were going to send to Monica's firm, my son's, or to Michael Paxton's, I'll ask you not to do that . . . not right now. Please just take care of Edward, Ramsey, Thompson, and Crawford—if you can . . . and only if they're not indicted. Otherwise, I just don't know." The old man paused and drew a ragged breath. "Laura, what's happening to our children these days?"

"I don't know, sir," she whispered, her mind drifting as she answered his rhetorical question.

"Things were supposed to happen differently." He paused again as his voice quavered. "We all started out with the best of intentions . . . We all wanted to make a difference and make a better way for our families, for the ones coming behind us . . . and somewhere in the transition, the end didn't justify the means. Something got lost. Perhaps *we* got lost."

What could she say to him? She let her silence agree with him. In that moment a new awareness began to wash over her. Perhaps she'd lost her way, too.

"I know you have to do what you have to do . . . just like we all must," he said in a quiet tone. "Just be as gentle as you can with your decisions. Can you do that for me as a favor?"

"I'll do that, Senator," she murmured. Yeah . . . she would. Enough was enough.

"I know that Monica trusted you. She told Howard that you'd been good to her, had met her after our little discussion and were trying to help her."

"I'll fix it as best I can, Senator. Count on that." Laura's gaze went out the window. God forgive her.

He let his breath out slowly, the weary sound of it filling the receiver. "Oh, Laura. I'm an old man, and I'm so tired of this."

She nodded, even though he couldn't see her.

"Your father was a good man."

She went still. She couldn't speak.

"J. D. and Pax should have never hurt him the way they did. I can't imagine the way your family suffered . . . Maybe I'm only beginning to fully understand that now. And, yet, irony of ironies, you were good to my family, even though . . ." The old man drew another ragged breath and continued, his voice becoming nearly inaudible as his veiled confession took shape. "I know you don't understand what I'm talking about . . . You were just a child then. But after all this blows over, we'll do lunch and have a frank discussion. This is beyond money. It's a matter of principle. God struck my family down, and it's time for things to be set aright."

Again she nodded, her fingers clasping the receiver so tightly, her knuckles went white. "Senator, I'd like that. I know there are things I don't understand, but I have blind faith in you." While it was not completely true, she knew that something in him had surrendered. Although she needed to forge the alliance with him and seal it tightly, and although whatever else was going on had to be known, there was a line of honor . . . even among thieves.

"And I you, sweetheart," he said after a moment, his voice thick with emotion. The tone of it contained such hurt, such remorse, that his words fractured as he spoke them.

It was as though he was trying to rinse his soul clean by talking to her. She heard a father's pain, a parent's anguish, in the broken voice of an old man. He was not a senator, then, not a figurehead, not a pack leader, not even an enemy—just a tired old man . . . a human being who'd obviously lost his way, had been blinded by power and office, had done things that would shame his spirit when he went to his grave; and it opened a sliver of forgiveness within hers.

Perhaps Brother Akhan had been right: she should have let this be, should have let a greater authority handle all this ugly affair. But the die had been cast: she'd sewn the dragon's teeth; an army of skeletons had been raised from the dead, bearing arms; and now things had been set in motion that were way beyond her control. Laura sighed and shut her eyes.

"I'm going to say something else to you, Laura. Then I must hang up and attend to my family."

"Go ahead," she said, her tone soft as he swallowed hard again. "I'm listening."

"At the Aquarium . . . Mike made it seem as though . . ."

"No. Senator, I assure you."

"Good."

"Things can always look one way on the surface and be another way under it, true?"

Although she'd answered Senator Scott, she was also talking to herself. Things could indeed look one way on the surface but have a completely different reality behind closed doors. She could hear him draw a long, ragged breath, emotion filling in the spaces of his pause, creating a vacuum that drew her thoughts and her conscience into it.

Perhaps she had misjudged the quality and quantity of

people's lives in a quest for vengeance. She wondered if she had become like those she most despised, looking at people from the outside, thinking in gross generalities and stereotypes instead of seeing the intrinsic value of an individual. How ironic indeed that she had looked down her nose at the same people who had looked down their noses at her . . . and their victimization, caused by her unseen power over their lives, was such a hollow victory that it was pathetic.

Her mother's words riddled her spirit and numbed her vocal cords. What could she say to this man? Yeah, maybe she should have left vengeance to God and just lived her life the best she could. These people, for all they had and all the power they possessed, didn't live half the quality of life she had as a child . . . and yet she'd robbed herself of years of happiness, too. Her mission had been flawed by an investment in blind hatred. Laura shut her eyes tighter.

"Okay, then," the senator said after the brief pause needed to gather himself, his words coming out on a rush of air. "Stay away from him on a personal level. Do not be compromised. There's too much at stake; he is very persuasive, and my niece just took several bullets for him. Understand?"

"I understand," Laura whispered, standing as her cell phone began ringing again. She quickly switched it to "Vibrate" in order not to alarm the senator because someone else was trying to reach her this late. Yet his admission chilled her. Several bullets? And the senator had dropped his guard enough to allude to the affair? Jesus . . .

"Laura, it's goddamned history repeating itself." His voice was now tense, angry, too controlled.

Laura steadied herself. She'd been where the good senator was, so filled with fury that at times her hands shook. And his rage was making his words come out in a rush of truth when he'd glossed over the past. But he'd confessed nonetheless. She kept her voice gentle, needing to convey sorrow as well as empathy, despite her own private demons. "Senator, I hear you . . . and please give my deepest condolences to your family." She meant that.

"I will. We're trying to get Monica's body released as soon as possible for a proper funeral service. My sister is so upset; she wants to cremate. We might have to. However, I am going to insist on an intimate viewing, even if my dear sister does take that drastic step to turn my niece to ash. I'll have you added to the private family viewing list. Be well, and take care of yourself."

"I will, Senator. You, too. Good-bye."

"Good-bye, Laura." He paused, let out another long sigh, and was gone.

Laura looked at thc receiver and gently returned it to the cradle. She reached for her cell phone and saw that Paxton had called four times. It was not supposed to go down like this, nor was she supposed to have to feel this level of remorse. These people, all of them, from Haines on down, were becoming humans, vulnerable beings of the larger human family. The distinction between black and white, rich and poor, was becoming blurred by the thin red line of blood. There was so much deception, so much betrayal. No one was exempt, and everyone was complicit. It was all so tragic, and her hand had started the ball rolling.

Punching in her voice-mail code, she listened to Paxton's increasingly urgent messages. Banging at her front door made her look up.

Laura Caldwell had a lot of questions to answer. Carter nodded to the patrol car and dismissed it as he stood on her front steps, peering up at the darkened windows of her home. He watched the car pull away, not knowing whether he'd stay or storm out, or even whether he still cared that she was protected.

Carter rang the bell. God help him if he'd been played. If this sister had a closer alignment to these people than she'd explained, she was going under the jail. She knew too much, was too on-point, and had been too precise.

Coincidences now converged to a setup in his mind.

Everything Monica Price had said, Ramsey had said, and Moyer had said confirmed everything that she supposedly knew from psychic ability. He hated games and lies. Yet he also knew that these people had injured her, too. What was Laura Caldwell's deal? His mind tried to process every angle as she took her time to open up and let him in.

When she reached for him, he shrugged away and brushed past her, headed toward the kitchen. He could hear her managing the locks behind him and walking without hurry to where he'd fled. She stopped in the archway and leaned against it. Her feet were bare, and she was still damp from an apparent shower, her ice-blue silk robe clinging to her.

"You never told me you actually went out with Darien Price before. Did you know he still carried around your prom picture hidden in his wallet?"

Her expression hadn't changed. "It wasn't important, to answer your first question, and no, to answer the second one."

"Why not?"

"Because that was more than twenty-five years ago, and the experience wasn't pleasant."

Her expression was cold. He leaned against the counter, watching her for a lie. He could understand that she might not want to relive the incident, but all this time they'd been talking about Price and the others, some inkling that she'd known him more personally should have come up. Something about it all just didn't sit right with him.

"I can dig it that you didn't want to tell me about the date rape, but—"

"I didn't tell you that, because I wasn't raped, *Detective.*" Fire glittered in her eyes, and she pushed herself away from the wall, finding wine in the refrigerator. "I kicked his ass," she said, reaching for a glass in the sink. "Why? What did his boys tell you? I shot him and his wife because of some bullshit that went down when we were kids?"

"No, and that wasn't even where I was going, Laura."

"Then where were you going?" she said, her voice tight, her eyes raking his face with fury.

"I thought you would have brought up the fact that because you two had gone out, that added to Paxton's interest in you—interest in forming a more permanent alliance than a business pact. Is that why the man put his hands around your throat?"

When she didn't immediately answer him, he could feel his own palms tingle with the urge to do the same thing to her. Instead, he crossed his arms over his chest and glared at her.

"What'd you do, Laura? Play both of these brothers for some old-time female revenge?" He dropped his arms, shaking his head as he now walked in a circle. "You should have seen that bedroom, sis. Blood everywhere. Brains on the floor . . . kids' pictures splattered. You can't go fucking with people's minds, Laura, no matter who they are! So, be straight up with me. What's your angle?"

"We've been over that before, and it's not police business—*or yours.*" She turned away and filled her glass, then went to the table to sit and stare out the window. "They gave me the nod; Paxton wanted to ensure that he'd get his cut, and his boys would be taken care of. They probably discussed me because they knew I had some bad blood with Price a long time ago, but then they thought better of letting something so trite stand in the way of access to twelve-point-five million dollars. What about this don't you understand—not that I have to justify shit to you?"

He didn't move. Her logic was beginning to poke holes in his. Her tone was slicing his pride, but he tried to be cool. The wound was too raw to admit the truth. But it was also too raw a gash to stop it from bleeding all over her kitchen floor. "His boys said Paxton had you *locked down.* They were certain of that." He looked at her hard.

"And what the fuck is that supposed to mean?" She hadn't looked at him as he'd asked the question and she answered him. She sipped her wine and kept her gaze on nothing outside her window.

She was making this hard for him. Too many emotions

were woven together to sort out what he really wanted her to tell him. He shoved his hands deep into his pockets, finding nothing in the room to look at with her. He studied the pebbles within the granite counter. "Did you *do him* to get inside, Laura? Did that add to Price's stress level . . . knowing Paxton had tagged both his wife and an old flame?" There. He'd said it.

"Do you have attention deficit syndrome, James?"

"No. My full faculties are with me—now."

"Good," she said, standing. "Because you're gonna need 'em."

"Where are you going?"

"To get you that piece of paper you wanted so badly—the one you forgot to take with you when this conversation got derailed a coupla hours ago." She'd brushed past him and was heading upstairs.

He followed her and stopped at the foot of the stairs, watching her disappear.

For a moment he said nothing as she stomped up the stairs and vanished. When she returned, she flung a sheet of paper at him and marched into the kitchen. He followed her, reading the list slowly as he walked, and then folded the paper and tucked it away into his jacket pocket.

"All right. I'm sorry," he said after a while. "You got the goods, like you'd said. But this is just a list of legitimate enterprises, assuming none of them has received an illegal transfer of city funds." Watching her angrily glare at him was messing with his head.

"It's a *bid list,*" she said coolly, staring down into her glass of wine. "It's a list of winners' names, account numbers—out-of-state businesses that would have received contracts no matter who sent in proposals on the supposedly *sealed* bids that would come in on the city's requests for proposals for program funding—for programs that would have been established after the election." She let her breath out hard, her impatience clear. "It's also a list of firms where your ass could start digging to find out where, years ago, payoffs might have occurred to get your father shot, my father derailed, and to pay off a shaky store owner who looked the other way. Not that something like this is worth anything to you. My bad."

Her statement gave him pause. "I'm sorry," he grumbled after taking a moment to digest everything she'd just said.

"So am I," she finally muttered. She stared at him hard. "You've got what you wanted—on both counts. You can leave now. And you can also get that squad car off my block. Neighbors are beginning to talk. I don't need that aggravation."

"It wasn't like that, and you know it."

"Wasn't like what?" she scoffed, shaking her head and looking away from him. "Nothing happened, not that I recall, Detective."

Her comment stabbed him again, but he shrugged it off. She had a right to be pissed. It bothered him that he'd taken her there again. He looked at her bruised throat and then thought about what Ramsey had said. Something fragile inside him began to give way as he tried to imagine what she'd been through.

"How old were you?"

"What does it matter?" she spat, her tone defiant. "You've already made up your mind."

"How old were you?"

"Fifteen." She looked out the window and sighed, then took a deep swallow of wine and sat down hard in a kitchen chair.

"Darien Price was six-six."

"I know. But I could fight. Still can." She brought her hard gaze to challenge his.

Shame swept through him. Why had he barged into this woman's house and taken her back to an almost thirty-year-old nightmare? What was wrong with him? In his mind he could see a triumphant young punk, laughing with his friends, older brothers blowing him off, telling the traumatized girl's business, just laughing . . . and Paxton's sick curiosity with the resistance she'd shown when violated. Darien Price was insane; so was Paxton—she didn't have a hand in that.

"Damn . . . and he made you walk home." He was talking to the floor, and more to himself, but the comment was too loud in his mind and had pushed itself out of his mouth.

"Yeah," she whispered, her voice so bitter it was chilling. "I'd lost my shoes, my dress was ragged, I was crying my eyes out, and all I could think about was, I had to get home to my momma." She peered up at him from where she sat. "The only thing I hadn't lost was my virginity—for what that was worth," she said in a cold tone, and swallowed more wine.

He knew better than to move toward her, although his arms ached to hug her.

"You have no idea, James." She glanced away again. Then she chuckled in a distant voice. "My poor mother . . . I wasn't allowed to tell my father, so he wouldn't lose his job. Then one day she finally broke down and told him, and he confronted Darien's father, then started digging into things he should've left alone when Darien's father didn't give him—or me—any respect. Ironic, isn't it? Dad lost his job anyway, so he should have just kicked Darien's ass right then and gotten the worst of it over with. He went to jail for a while anyway, so what the hell?" She returned her gaze to his. "You don't know what it's like to lose a father like that, or a mother."

"I lost my dad, too, baby . . . I know what—"

"You *don't* know!" She'd pushed up from the table and had come close, to stand before him.

Her eyes held a level of hatred that he couldn't fathom.

"Laura—"

"Your father died quick, tragic though it may have been. Somebody, one of them, somehow put a bullet in his chest. But he died a hero, and your mother was probably given a widow's pension. You and your siblings never got put out of your home, saw everything your parents had built auctioned, separated, sold off, taken for legal fees to defend your father for something he never did. Your father's name was *never* tarnished. And trust me, you never watched him die a slow, agonizing death by becoming a broken man—a shadow of who he was, ashamed to hold his head up in public as people whispered when he went by."

She slapped his hand away as he foolishly reached for her. "You never saw a grown man cry quietly at the kitchen table. You never saw your father's friends get scarce and disappear like your father had the plague. People he'd helped vanished, got real invisible—ghosts. And you never saw a funeral so empty, so unpopulated, for a man who'd been the unofficial neighborhood people's mayor. My father didn't get out of his bed for three months after my mother tried to take her life, but she miscalculated the dosage of Valiums and booze, and had a stroke . . . and died slowly, too. No, James Carter—you do not know *anything* about this pain. Even a heart attack is quick—even your mother went fast, as you told me two nights ago, when we were supposedly telling all secrets and heartbreaks in bed!"

Her chest was heaving, and unshed tears glittered in her eyes. He reached for her cheek, and her palm connected with his hard enough to slap the spit out of his mouth.

"And you come in here to ask me if I fucked Michael Paxton, one of Darien's boys? His mentor! The one who probably showed him how to attempt some shit like he pulled on me? Then you want to know if I was still dealing with Price? Check your damned male ego at my front door and *get out*!"

She paced away, her robe billowing behind her as she went to get her wineglass. He rubbed his jaw as he watched her grip on the crystal tighten.

"After what they did to my family, do you honestly believe that I would side with any of them?"

It took him a moment to answer. Her rage gave him serious pause on a lot of levels. His gut instinct was sending alarm signals to his brain, but his heart was canceling them out one by one.

"No," he finally murmured. "I don't. But a man and wife died in a way that isn't supposed to happen—"

"You're right. *None of this was supposed to happen.* In fact, I'm sorry Darien Price died—that punk took the easy way out. He should have lived a *long* and miserable life, and done a turn in prison along with it . . . and had his manhood taken in a laundry room somewhere, watched his friends disappear, his money dry up, and his kids be ashamed of their family's last name. *That's* what the fuck was supposed to happen. God bless Monica, and may her soul rest in peace—but he could kiss my natural ass."

She flung the glass she'd been holding into the sink, shards of it littering the stainless steel basin. Laura wrapped her arms around her waist and drew several deep, shaky breaths as she gave him her back to consider. "I thought, of all people, *you* would understand."

What had he just done . . . and whom had he been sleeping with . . . ?

For a while he said nothing, just watched her breathe hard, attempting to stabilize her emotions. The depth of her anger paralyzed him as he stared at the way her supple back expanded and contracted with sudden inhales and exhales of pure rage. *Hell hath no fury* . . . The magnitude of what he was witnessing kept him rooted to the floor where he stood, guarded, waiting for the silent storm in her to pass.

"Did you know back then that Paxton was Darien's half-brother?" he asked quietly as she seemed to begin to calm down. It was important to know how close she was to the situation; that way he could assess her possible risk—or involvement. From all accounts, she was close enough to get splattered by the media and legal muck that would soon fly. He couldn't let that happen. She'd already been through enough. And he didn't want to think of any other possibilities beyond that.

"No," she said evenly, her breaths becoming steadier now.

"I don't want you anywhere near this, Laura. Especially near Paxton. He plays very rough, from what I understand."

"He's been blowing up my cell phone since he left here, but don't worry. I'm not dealing with his ass tonight—not after what just went down over at the Prices'. I'll find out what cut he wants tomorrow." She shook her head with disgust. "Poor Monica. The bastard probably won't even go to her funeral."

"I'm worried," Carter said in total honesty. "I'm worried that he called, and I'm worried that you're even considering having a conversation with him about cuts, and—"

"Don't worry." She repeated, holding him in a hard stare and then laughing coldly. "I've got diplomatic immunity. He fucked himself good this time. Senator Scott called here earlier and wanted to be sure that I sent nothing Paxton's way. He's lost favor with the families, because this shit with Monica and Darien was never supposed to happen like this. I'm sure the only reason he'll have a brief media pardon is for Monica's sake."

James let his breath out hard. The niece's body wasn't even autopsied, wasn't even cold, and the business transactions were shifting. Damn. Sharks were circling already in the bloodied water. It was too crazy.

"We're going to pass over one of their guys who's cooperating, and bring everybody else in that's directly involved on the city case—just so you know." He didn't know what else to say to her.

"Martin Ramsey was always a good guy," she murmured, her gaze drifting to the window once more. "Wasn't as bad as the others, but he still had his shit with him. You probably won't find much on him, just small improprieties that will get him an embarrassing slap on the wrist, but not more than that. He won't get hurt too badly, I'm sure."

He walked toward Laura and turned her around gently by her shoulders, now extremely concerned. "How'd you know Ramsey came to us?"

She sighed. "Feminine intuition."

"Don't play, Laura. I'm serious."

"He was the man with the most to lose. It makes sense, James. Some things just make sense, so let it be."

"I don't follow." He stared at her hard.

"Of all of them, Martin Ramsey is a good father and *really* loves his wife."

Chapter 21

Steve took one and a half steps for every one of Carter's to keep pace with his long strides as they left the district attorney's office. Huffs of steam created small white clouds that dissolved quickly in front of his face as they hurried to their car.

"You ready to round 'em up this morning, partner?"

"Let's do it," Carter said, sliding into the driver's seat. He turned the ignition on and pulled out into traffic, his nerves carved to shreds by the events of the last twenty-four hours, and from having met Laura Caldwell. Something just wasn't right.

"Okay," Steve said, tapping the breast pocket on his black wool coat. "We pick up everybody but Paxton—who we don't have anything on except the fact that he's a piece of work—and we deal with Howard Scott after his cousin's funeral, as a courtesy to the senator." Steve sat back and stared out the windshield. "That's cool, I suppose. Scott isn't a flight risk per se. But sure must be nice to get all these little professional courtesies, yo?"

"Yeah," Carter muttered. "Must be nice."

"Yeah, well, where I come from, if your ass does a crime, you get hauled away and do the time. There ain't no such thing as a courtesy, I don't care if your momma is on life support."

"You sound like you're from another country, Steve, with that 'where I come from' yang. I hear you, though." Carter chuckled and shook his head.

"Well, the great Northeast Philly is another country, brotha." Steve laughed. "We tried to defect from Philly to at least be our own county, but got sucked back into the black hole." Steve gave Carter a sheepish glance from the corner of his eye when Carter's chuckle deepened.

"Glad to see you in good spirits again, though. Was getting worried about you, man."

Carter shrugged off Steve's attempt to pry. "I'm cool."

"I know you're cool—James Carter is always cool . . . that is, er, uh, except for when Ramsey started running his mouth about one Laura Caldwell being locked down by Paxton." Steve grinned at him.

Carter ignored his partner and kept driving.

"See, there you go again. One mention of that chick's name, and I get the steel jaw. Whassup with you, man? This thing out here is heating up, like Cap said—and judging by all these collars we have to do today, it's gonna be hot for a while. So chill. You gonna fuck around and lose your pension behind that woman."

Carter kept his eyes on the road. "I am chillin', man. Nothin' ever happened."

The flicker from her computer screen was the only light on in her home office other than daylight. She was in way too deep to pull out now. So okay, fine, she owed James Carter something and would give him something back. She just wasn't sure why she felt that way. Truth was, too much was now making her feel, which wasn't supposed to happen. After this, it was time to get out.

Laura's fingers worked the keys as her eyes scanned the Lexis database, looking for the news article that she knew would be there. She had a cop's name; all she had to do was find the date he was shot in 1977, where they'd found his body, at which store a supposed burglary had occurred—then she'd have an address.

Bingo. "Ain't technology grand," she whispered, memorizing the number, grabbing her purse, and then heading out the door.

By the time she crossed City Hall's scaffolding-blocked courtyard, it was already dense with people milling through the center of the city's nervous system. Four arches, facing in the cardinal directions, created a foursquare block intersection designed by the old Masonic orders over two hundred years ago. Now renovations, construction crews, and wire fences to keep pedestrians safe hid the majestic antiquity. But like all things, in time, those barricades would be removed.

All she had to do was either find Gladys in the prothonotary's office or find Maxine in the Department of Records office. She decided to hit Maxie first. Maxie was good for insider tips—she'd tell her who had owned that North Philly property.

Within the bowels of the hall of records lay the truth. There were documents in City Hall that had probably been drafted by William Penn himself. The only thing you had to do was know what you were looking for, which had been her problem all this time. She hadn't known exactly where to look, until James Carter came along. Yeah. She owed him.

Nervous energy coursed through her as Laura lost patience and passed the crowd of leisurely strolling people in her way. She hurried through the Market Street doors, careful not to lose her footing on the slippery marble floor as she paced to the Department of Records in search of Maxine.

Jockeying for position between lawyers, law clerks, interns running errands, and realtors, Laura wedged herself into the throng waiting for service.

Maxine spotted her and gave her a wink of recognition. Laura smiled as the sister adjusted her minibraids over her shoulder and hailed her. She ignored the scowls that came from those who'd been waiting before her. They knew the deal—if you knew somebody on the inside, you got a leg up. They did it; why not her? That was the way of the world.

Sisters and brothers were thick in City Hall, and those city employees took no small measure of satisfaction in making a nasty, harried lawyer with an attitude wait. The nastier the lawyer got, and the more indignant they became, the slower the people serving them moved. It might have been the only shred of power city employees had, but the sistahs worked it well.

Laura chuckled as Maxine rounded the desk and then held her away from her breasts with both hands.

"Oh, so today we servin' rust suede from head to foot—and gimme dem boots, girl," Maxine said with a laugh, cocking her head to the side. "How you gwan come up in here, looking all cute wit a full-length suede coat, plus suede pantsuit and boots ta match, and not give Maxine a hug right off? How you seem? You gwan to Paris, or you gwan to work?"

She had to laugh as she filled Maxine's arms. Her friend's thick, warm arms and pretty, dark skin and perfect teeth, along with the island lilt, made Laura long to run away to St. Lucia.

"You look good; you crazy, chile," Laura said, giggling. "I'm working. Need a quickie, though."

Maxine sucked her teeth and held out her hand for the slip of paper with the address on it. "See how she do me, y'all?" Maxine fussed to another worker behind the desk, who smiled. "Come flouncin' in here wit demands. Yeah, you workin'; question is, who dis time?"

"Me?" Laura said, hitching her purse up on her shoulder as she followed Maxine into the restricted area for employees only, ignoring the grumbles from waiting customers behind them.

"Uhmmm hmmm," Maxine giggled, searching for the address ownership listing. "Heard tell from some people who know some people dat you got a cell numba dat every single woman in Philadelphia would love to have—at least for an hour. You bad girl, you. And you come in here wit'out even calling Maxine wit de lowdown."

Laura covered her face with her hands and laughed into them hard. Lord have mercy . . . she'd forgotten about Anne, Paxton's secretary. Too much was going on at the same time. But the more she laughed, the faster Maxine worked on finding the address.

"Tell me dis, girl," Maxine said, dropping her voice and holding up her hand to stop a question from an impatient person trying to hail her over the counter. She gave the would-be customer her back. "Was it *all that*?"

Laura sent her gaze to a rickety gray metal file cabinet that was taller and older than she. "Girrrrrlllll . . . I can't even talk about it."

Maxine slapped her arm. "Lordy. See. Why can't good tings like dat happen to Maxine?" She sighed and flipped the huge binder open for Laura to inspect. "Was for some reason condemned in 1977, went into the sheriff sale reclamation to be turned into a dollah property—then de current owner acquired it. Afta dat, to find out what happen you have to go to—"

"Thanks, Max. I know where to go from here. Gimme a hug, and don't tell nobody about my mischief. *Promise me.*" Laura giggled with her again as they rounded the desk, and Maxine went back to work.

"Oh, your secret's safe wit me, chile. *Uhmph.*"

Laura walked fast, but she could hear Maxine's sharp, sarcastic responses to information seekers echoing off the marble floors behind her. It was as though, for that brief moment while she and Maxine were together, everybody in the poorly lighted, gray space became sunshine and perked up.

In that environment, they were like plants in dire need of a good spring rain. The ladies and a couple of the men were laughing and joking and all in her business with wide grins and sly looks.

She just wondered why people had to be pigeonholed into jobs that underappreciated their creativity, if not their humanity. Didn't seem right that only a small sliver of the population should be able to breeze into work, enjoy what they did, and be financially prosperous to go along with it. Why, because of slot of birth? That was insane.

That was also why people who had the power to offer individuals like Maxine an opportunity to thrive should be horsewhipped, she told herself. What right did they have to block access when they had all the access in the world? Made sense that J. D. Price II had owned the building with old man Paxton, then routed it through the subway system of heavy paperwork to get it out of their names and transferred to Juan Esposito for a dollar. Motherfuckers.

She had to remember why she'd undertaken this whole mission in the first place. Last night she'd started going soft. Not today. Cold air stung her cheeks as she pushed through the doors, desperately needing escape.

Jumping into a cab on the JFK Boulevard side of City Hall, she took a detour to South Street. Why not? She'd detoured her entire plan messing with James Carter. She chuckled to herself, knowing that a detour on a morning like this was crazy. Friday morning, and Philly's core black elite was under siege. She just needed a break before answering ringing phones, Najira's excited queries, or figuring out her next move. Right now she was living in the moment, and when the cab came to a halt, she gave him a twenty-dollar bill, telling him to keep the change.

She needed space—her head was about to explode, and as she peered into the window of Pearl of Africa, she sighed. Maybe one day she would just pull up stakes and make a run for it. Who knew? She didn't. Her sister worked for Carnival Cruise Lines, which debarked from Philly now. If she asked

Lavern nicely, she could take a short junket to the Bahamas . . . and drop the phones offshore in very deep international waters. Hmmm . . . Maybe she'd go as far as St. Lucia, or go check on a couple million she had stashed in the Caymans. Switzerland was too far and too cold, and the critical mass of her Wall Street–wrested fortune was safe there. Maybe she'd just disappear and never come back. However, a short family cruise could work; she'd promised that they'd all be together for the holidays. But booking that might take weeks if she waited for Lavern to get around to it. Time was of the essence.

Everything was tumbling around in her mind at once. She could feel her position deconstructing, shifting, and she didn't like the uncertainty one bit. She had to maintain control.

Centering herself, Laura window-shopped for a moment to regain a sense of peace, taking in the eclectic mix of Bob Marley CDs and posters, incense and oils, and beautiful African cotton prints. A pair of amber and silver earrings caught her eye, and she went into the shop to claim them. Najira would like those; she loved amber and deserved to have them. The heady scent of frankincense and myrrh oil made her think of church.

Church. She hadn't been inside a church since her aunt Maude passed, except for the occasional perfunctory appearance at a wedding, funeral, or christening. That was for the living, her friends, or business. She and God hadn't been on real speaking terms since the seventies. Laura sighed and made her purchase, then went out into the fresh air.

To hell with James Carter. She couldn't afford that drama in her life. The world was full of fine, sexy men. She shook his haunting as she walked down South Street's tightly packed corridor of interesting stores, cupping her hands to the windows as she peeked inside.

Yeah . . . the world was full of alternatives. Island men were *fabulous* . . . their voices and their natural funk were unparalleled . . . just like they made sensuous, dripping, spicy food a part of the whole orgasmic experience—sensualists, that's what they were . . . as were the brothers from Brazil, with those eyes and capoeira-refined bodies, and she had to give props to the Greek gods in the Mediterranean, and Latino men—*ummph.* Have mercy. *No más, por favor.* She couldn't take it, they were so hot. Italian men, like Latino brothers, were worth all the chauvinistic rhetoric just to hear one say, "Bella, oh, bella," in bed. She laughed out loud as she carried on, thinking of running away from home for good. Almost ten million in hidden accounts could keep a girl living well for a very long time.

But as she stopped to peer into another window, she had to give the brothers from the motherland their props, yes indeed, much respect, circumcised or not . . . those fine, suave, embassy-working, five-language-speaking, black as asphalt creations of pure wonder. Maybe she'd go to Africa for a few years and call it a day. But Europe was also an option, and it was where the major stash was located. The British weren't as uptight as folks were led to believe, she giggled to herself. The French, *au* . . . and an occasional man schooled in the *Kama Sutra,* from the Asiatic part of the world, could work wonders when inspired. And men from the stock used to keeping harems in check, well . . . shit . . . what could she say? They had stamina. She shivered and began walking. The world was abundant; sisters just had to think outside the box. She was not about to invest in Philadelphia's finest.

So why had she allowed one Joe-regular brother from the hood—in Philly, no less—to get her all turned around? Crazy! Not today. But *damn,* there was something about James.

"Okay, okay, okay, get a grip," she said, calming herself, though talking out loud. She didn't care. People talked to themselves all the time in the streets. Madness was rampant. Nobody paid her any mind. She laughed and walked faster. *Think outside the box, Laura.* Her mind briefly went to Rick. She'd buy him a bottle of Dom and a magnum of Cristal that he could share with his wife. She'd send it by courier with a gift basket, too. It was all good. Then she was out. She just had to think outside the box.

Laura kept walking. Then she went still before an antique shop that had a gorgeous tiny, gilded white music box, about seven inches long and four inches deep, made circa the Victorian era.

"Good morning, Ms. Caldwell," Najira said fast, rounding her desk as soon as Laura walked through the door. "Me and the team were beginning to worry . . . so much is going on; you never called in; your phones are blowing up," she said, her eyes darting between the ringing console and Laura.

"Thought I might have gotten arrested, did you?" Laura said, forcing a chuckle to keep her own nerves from snapping, and then dug into her huge barrel purse, pulled out a small parcel, and pushed it into Najira's hand when the girl blanched. "I shouldn't joke around, I know. What's happening is tragic." She leveled her gaze at Najira. "But it wasn't *your* fault."

"I know . . . I guess," Najira said quickly, grabbing a line that was ringing and putting the caller on hold. "What's this?" she asked, looking at the tiny bag Laura had given her. "We need to *seriously* talk—you know that, right?"

"Just something to let you know how much I appreciate you working here, kiddo." Laura sighed, expecting an insane pile of messages to be awaiting her. "Just hand me the stack, and I'll deal with them one by one."

She hadn't even taken off her coat, and Najira was back in her office, fidgeting with one of her Nubian locks.

"What the fuck, Laura," she whispered through her teeth. "The man—"

"We've been through it once, so let it rest in peace." Laura stared at her cousin hard, sending both a warning and a bolt of strength. "Wasn't your fault. He was grown. His wife was grown. They made choices—insane ones at that."

Najira just stared at her for a moment.

"It's all right. Don't start panicking on me, now. Keep your head." Laura's gaze was steady, paralyzing, and she didn't blink until Najira nodded. "Like I said before, that's why I didn't tell you everything . . . in case it got messy."

"It's messy for a motherfucker now, girl."

Laura nodded. "And that's why I need you to revert to being blind, deaf and dumb, and out of the equation—simply acting as my very efficient assistant for the time being. It ain't 'cause I don't love you, but because I do. Understand? And I need my messages, every single piece of correspondence that hits this office, ASAP, because it could be mission critical."

Again Najira nodded slowly, producing the stack of messages for Laura. "Mr. Paxton has called here for the fourth time this morning—*he* called, not his secretary. . . . should I, uh—"

"Patch him through," Laura said on a heavy exhale as she plopped down in her chair. "I'm gonna have to deal with him sooner or later, I suppose."

She waited for Najira to shut her door, and then she picked up the receiver. "Well, good morning."

"Where were you?"

She looked at the telephone and brought it back to her ear, not liking his tone at all.

"I was asleep last night, took a sleeping pill to calm my nerves, then had a meeting first thing, Michael. I haven't even checked my voice mail yet."

"Well, have you been watching the goddamned news, Laura?"

She paused and smiled. "Yes. Terrible."

"And, you didn't call me?"

She allowed her voice to become as smooth as silk. "Baby," she said quietly, "of course not. I knew you'd have to be swamped, and you said you'd call me when you could, right? I respect what you do; your job is so stressful—I didn't want to add to it in any way."

She heard him breathe out sharply with impatience.

"You're right . . . yes, I did say that. I don't like you going off radar, though. Not with everything that's happening."

"Okay. It won't happen again. But, are you all right?"

"Yes, and no. I'm surviving today."

"I am soooo sorry to hear about what happened with Darien and Monica."

"I know. Tragic. That's all I can say about it right now. I'm too stunned by the whole sordid incident."

"What can I do, Michael? I know this has to be eating you alive." She doodled on a notepad as she talked to him, sorting messages that she needed to return.

"I just want you to be there when it becomes a media travesty." His voice had gone soft, beckoning for her allegiance. "And don't believe *anything* that anyone might tell you, without checking with me first. You'll be in my corner, right?"

"You know I will."

He paused and then spoke slowly. "Are you going to Monica's funeral?"

"I think so . . . but I haven't decided yet. Are you?"

"I don't know if I can handle that right now . . . but maybe we can go together."

Again she pulled the phone away from her face to glance at it before putting it next to her ear. Was he *insane*? He was going to try to bring her out on his arm in front of Monica's grieving parents and family—at a funeral, no less! *Oh, shit . . . Think fast, Laura.*

She drew a deep breath. "I lost both my parents when I was very, very young, Michael." She strung out her breaths between the words. "Funerals . . . they just . . . I don't know. I can't commit."

"I understand," he said in a gentle voice. "I lost my parents early, too. But if you decide to go, let me know. We also have that Democratic fund-raiser at the Kimmel Center on Saturday night, right?"

We? What's up with this "we" shit? It irked her no end, and she'd truthfully forgotten about it—but had to recover fast.

"Oh, Lord, yes. With everything that's been going on, I completely forgot."

"I hear you. The chess pieces are moving so fast on the board, it's ridiculous. Listen, I'll call you tonight. I don't think I can get away. I need to have a strategy session about what's happening in the network. Why don't I pick you up on Saturday for the event?"

She could feel her nerves stretch and pop under the surface of her skin. "Why don't we play that by ear?" she said, her voice submissive. "Who knows what might go down, and you may have to hang loose to address it."

"That's what I admire so much about you, sweetheart. Plan on going with me, but if something comes up, I'll meet you there. I have to run. Bye."

Sweetheart? Laura set the telephone receiver in the cradle and wrinkled her nose. See, this was the problem with men. One shot—or a near shot, she chuckled inwardly—and they thought they'd planted a flag, marked you off as their sovereign territory, and owned you. Then again, that was indeed the power of the pussy. She shook her head and dialed another number.

"James," she said quickly when he answered.

"Yeah, but I can't talk."

"I know you're in the midst of arresting bad guys, but—"

"Yeah. And I can't talk."

"I've got a tip. The store was transferred to Juan Esposito in 'seventy-seven, via sheriff sale reclaim for a dollar, but used to be co-owned by old man Price and old man Paxton. While you're in the street, ya might wanna drop by and check the current owner out. Bye."

She clicked off the telephone, but before she could make another call, Najira's voice came through the intercom. "Mr. Haines, line one, says it's urgent. Shall I—"

"Put him through." Laura stood and paced behind her desk as Donald Haines's voice filled her ear.

"Laura, have you seen the news?"

"Yes, Donald."

"A travesty."

"There are no words."

"Do the press drop ASAP."

She paused. "Before the funerals, sir?"

He paused. "I guess that would be callous."

"Yes, sir. They'll do the funerals at the top of the week, more than likely. After the ceremonies, we can alert the press. . . . That would be much cleaner."

"All right. Since it's only Friday—but the moment the services are over, I want the new slate of organizations announced."

"Done."

"Good. I'll see you at the Kimmel. Good-bye, Laura."

"Good-bye, Donald."

She hung up, closed her eyes, and let out a slow stream of breath. Jesus H. Christ. A near miss. If she made the announcement for the new program slate before all the family tentacles were stopped, and before she had time to dig into this co-owned building, Paxton would pull up, become her instant enemy, and then it would be on. She wasn't crazy; she could tell he was definitely not the type to take a double-cross well. By the time he figured out what happened, she'd have Donald Haines as a shield and could say he disapproved the proposed slate—because of the arrests and media heat—or she'd be out of the country.

"Let me get this right, Mr. Thompson," Steve said, ignoring the man's attorney. "You are alleging that you had to go along with whatever Michael Paxton dictated, because he had some information in a file about all of your families?"

"Yes," Donald Haines Jr. said firmly, speaking for his client. "My partners and I at Haines, Breckinridge, and Lockhart have developed a full statement that our client—"

"Hold up," Carter said, walking around the men seated at the interrogation room table. "Have you seen these documents? Can you prove that they exist? Because if not, and if this is all collusion by a group of very scared guys who cooked up a tale to bring down a prominent attorney because they don't like him . . . hey." Carter shrugged. "We can add perjury, and I'm sure Paxton will sue for—"

"I saw it, Detective. Mike showed each of us pieces of it," Thompson said quickly, then began rocking in his chair.

"Talk to me." Carter rubbed his jaw, monitoring the man's anxiety to keep from feeling his own. Laura had said there were papers. Old man Ice had said there were papers. He was so close to the truth he could taste it. He just hoped that the captain and the DA behind the two-way mirror were soaking it all in.

Jim Thompson's attorney sat back in his chair, and Sullivan stood to take a position at the edge of the table.

"The only reason I'm allowing my client to be here," Donald Haines Jr. warned, "is because a legal colleague of mine said that you gentlemen were fair, had integrity, and wanted to get to the bottom of this—not to convict the lesser-involved parties, if they were cooperative."

Carter and Sullivan let out their breath in unison and glanced at each other, both understanding the motivation coming from this unnamed legal-colleague source—Alan Moyer.

"We're listening," Carter muttered. "And we hear you."

Donald Haines Jr. nodded toward his client, and Jim Thompson took a steadying breath before speaking.

"Each of us . . . a long time ago, had a private meeting with Mike." Jim Thompson's eyes darted nervously between the detectives and his attorney. "He showed us just our section of the records that pointed to some less than aboveboard business practices our fathers were involved in."

"Like what?" Carter folded his arms over his chest and waited, but his mind was racing a mile a minute.

"Like copies of check transactions—payments for goods never supplied and services never rendered. Expenses reimbursed that shouldn't have been. Payoffs made by contracts given to out-of-state holdings our fathers owned. And he's held that over our heads for years."

"Extortion, sounds like to me, partner." Steve cast a quick glance at Carter, who nodded.

"Our fathers are old or dead," Thompson said slowly. "All their assets that we used to build up could be snatched, companies we inherited shut down, if anyone were to ever open that can of worms. So, I admit, I went along with the group and kept things quiet . . ."

"Yeah," Carter grumbled. "I hear you. But you didn't have a problem spending Daddy's dirty money, or living in the house that Jack built, or profiting from old alliances made—wasn't a problem until now. Why?"

"Because nobody was doing anything stupid!" Thompson banged on the table and glanced around the group. "Nobody, currently, in this era, was doing anything illegal per se. Everybody was legit—okay, insider assistance to get a few nice contracts, but that's the capitalist way. *That's not illegal.*"

"If you're slanting closed state and city bids, it is." Steve shook his head and sighed.

Carter stood and walked to the far wall and leaned against it. Disgust filled him. "You guys have been rolling unchecked for so damned long that you seem to have forgotten some of the finer points of—"

"My client is trying to be forthright, Detectives. If you're going to be hard-asses and not—"

"Okay, okay," Sullivan said. "Talk to us."

"This generation was legit," Thompson argued, folding and unfolding his hands at the table. "Darien messed up. That made people start digging. Somehow—and I know it wasn't me—stolen funds got transferred into all our companies except Mike's. Now, that's odd. And that's what made me start thinking . . . he's got a voracious appetite for power. There is never enough, never a line—just look at what happened to Darien, poor bastard."

"Literally," Carter muttered, and ignored Steve's warning

glance. He continued on a different path when the color drained from Donald Jr.'s face.

"But you do have a point," Carter said, self-checking his previous statement. "That is mighty peculiar that one man in your group has had nothing transferred to him."

Steve looked at Carter hard. "To play devil's advocate for just a moment, however: what if the reason only one man has no transfers is because one man in this entire cesspool is clean? Not liking the son of a bitch doesn't mean he's guilty of anything *we* can prosecute."

Carter pushed away from the wall, rubbing his chin, pissed at Steve's comment, true as it was. "All right," he finally said, "if you saw these papers, how do you know they're originals, something we could—"

"Because they had blood on them," Thompson said, now standing and walking back and forth near the wall.

Both Carter and Sullivan glanced at each other, then focused on Thompson.

"The docs I saw had my father's signature on them, in original blue ink—not Xeroxed. . . . Our firm does facilities maintenance, and he'd invoiced the city for shit we never did, supplies we never purchased. Paxton has stuff like that on all of us."

Thompson looked up toward the ceiling as tears rose to his eyes. "And nobody had the balls to just whack that bastard—"

"Jim, that's enough," his attorney shouted, becoming alarmed.

"No, fuck it, Don. We didn't and wouldn't go there because we didn't know where the papers would turn up; not even our fathers would go there—nobody was trying to do time for murder."

"Sit down," Carter ordered. "You need to really talk to me now."

Chapter 22

"Okay," Steve said with a smile, glancing at Carter as he drove, "now, you know how when you go 'round the way, as you call it, you always leave me in the car 'cause the people you wanna have a conversation with won't talk easy around a white boy?"

Carter chuckled. "Yeah. Port Richmond section is your old part of town." He glanced up at the I-95 overpass, listening to the highway traffic thump above him, the shadow of it eclipsing the sun but not the litter and blight.

"Exactly," Steve said after a moment, bringing the vehicle to a stop. "This is like Kensington around here—worse than where I moved to in the Northeast. I'll hit your cell when I need a pickup. You might wanna keep moving; take a ride up north end to check out that info Caldwell dropped on you about the store. We ain't in a squad car, and somebody might not understand, at first sight, that you're a cop."

Carter nodded as his partner got out of the vehicle. He wasn't offended; this was reality. Sections of Philly were as bad as the backroads of the Deep South, always had been. It was all good, though. Steve had stopped near an ethnic transition zone, an invisible borderline between Polish Americans, Irish Americans, Italian Americans, and, oddly, Puerto Ricans—one block that was the weigh station between worlds, and a long way from the black enclaves in town. His partner was telling the truth. Here, a black man sitting outside a crossroads bar, alone, was due for a hassle.

He watched Steve's back as his partner entered the corner establishment, painted white with the mortar between the bricks painted red—the only building in sight with no graffiti on the walls. He didn't have to be told that it was a power hangout marked off-limits territory to the neighborhood punks. Carter chuckled to himself, noting the Eagles and Flyers team emblems in the window, then drove away.

Steve glanced around and made his way to the bar. A beer was pushed to him before he even sat down. The bartender's smile broadened.

"Yo, Sullivan—long time no see. They still got you shackin' wit dat black cop, or they give you a break yet?"

"Hey . . . what can I say?" Steve shrugged, accepting the mug and taking a healthy slug. "Affirmative action."

The old man shook his head. "Whatchu gonna do?"

Steve shrugged again, his gaze roving through the bar. "Well, at least we finally got a football team that's kickin' some ass."

"Now you're talkin'." The old man began cleaning a glass. "So, who'd you come down to see today?"

"Was, uh, hopin' to have a conversation with Caluzo."

The old man nodded, his white hair plastered to his skull from sweat and pomade that gave it a yellowish tinge. He motioned with his chin. "Joey's back there eatin'. You want somethin' from the kitchen?"

"Nah. I'm good. Thanks, though, Louie. Next time."

"Always on the house," the barkeep said, and began watching the huge overhead television.

Steve collected his beer and went to where a plump man

sat. He was hunched over a plate, devouring a meatball sandwich. He looked up as Steve approached, and smiled, red sauce staining the corners of his mouth.

"Sullivan—long time no see," he said, accepting a quick embrace from Steve without standing up. "You on official business, or just a social call?"

"Maybe a little bit of both," Steve said, sitting across from him in the wooden chair. He set his mug down in front of him on the plastic red-and-white-checkered tablecloth.

"You eatin'?" Before Steve could answer, Joey Caluzo hailed the barkeep. "Yo, Louie—fix the man a plate."

"I'm good," Steve protested, although he knew that eating was part of the ritual.

"Okay. So it's a business call." Caluzo smiled, waved the barkeep back, and began eating again. "So what can I do for you?"

"You been watching the news?"

Caluzo chuckled. "Who hasn't? Fuckin' moolies have really gotten themselves fucked up this time."

"Yeah," Steve said, taking a slow sip of his beer. "Problem is, they're dropping in my yard, and I need to wrap this shit up fast. I hate paperwork."

Caluzo nodded without looking at him. "Like I said, what can I do for you?"

Steve let his breath out slowly, watching the top of Caluzo's balding head as his information source dug into his sandwich. He waited until Caluzo sat back, noticing the heavy gold chain around his neck, and the fact that he was packing heat.

"Long time ago, a cop got shot—a black cop."

Caluzo smiled and started eating again. "Damn shame," he mumbled through swallows. "Shit happens. Affirmative action."

"Yeah," Steve said, bile building in his stomach. "Well, they happened to find his body near a joint up in North Philly—a joint that had been owned by a couple of high-powered black guys: a judge and an attorney, Paxton and Price."

"You need to leave that nigger bullshit that happened in North Philly alone, Sullivan. That was ancient history. Nobody is left from that era. They're all dead."

Sullivan rubbed his hands over his face. "See, Joey, that's just it. I can't leave it alone."

Caluzo let his breath out hard. "Why not?"

"Because I'm trying to put their sons behind bars, and I need— "

A friendly punch on his shoulder stopped Sullivan's words. Joey Caluzo leaned in, his eyes merry.

"Then why didn't you say so, Sulli? It was fucked up. Crazy." Caluzo laughed and shook his head, pushing his plate away. "I knew you was a good guy. Yeah. Put their bastard sons away."

"How?"

Caluzo dropped his voice and leaned closer, but his expression held unconcealed excitement. "See, you didn't hear this from me, and I'll put a bullet in your head myself if I ever hear my name. But I'ma tell you, for old time's sake, since we go way back to Catholic school togetha. And since it looks like the powers that be are shifting, I assume there'll be no repercussions . . . so, you'll owe me a pass on some shit you might hear about in the future. Deal?"

"Yo, man, have I ever given you up?" Steve allowed his gaze to remain steady, never agreeing to the free pass, although it was implied.

"Nah, you're cool. I trust you."

"All right, then, talk to me."

Caluzo nodded, glanced around the near-empty establishment, and smiled. "This was Peyton Place at its best. Motherfuckin' black judge was doing his best friend's wife. They even had property all tied up together; the attorney friend was in the managing director's slot, so they had a section of Philly locked up. Then this hero, some dumb black community activist bastard, decides he's got a conscience—takes some papers. Is gonna blow the whistle on the nice little setup they've got going on—you following?"

Steve nodded, and sipped his beer very slowly, his eyes never leaving Caluzo's.

"So, this asshole gives the papers to a cop, another dumb fuck with a conscience." Caluzo shook his head. "I told the boys to never take a job order from the moolies, but money is money."

"Yeah. Money is money," Steve said in a quiet voice.

"Right," Caluzo said, hailing the bartender for another beer. "So the judge and his friend order the job. It was supposed to be easy; knock off the cop and get the papers off him in West Philly. Then do the whistle-blower."

Caluzo accepted a beer and waited until the bartender had moved away, and then laughed. "It was the craziest shit I'd ever heard. My boys said they'd gone in like planned, were ready to do the cop bastard in an alley out west, but then somebody started shooting at the goddamned jobber! In the chaos, the cop went down, but it wasn't our bullet. The jobber never even got the papers off the body. Then what was supposed to be our first fuckin' job turns up in North Philly—nowhere near where the job was supposed to be done."

Caluzo sat back, ran his fingers through his sweaty hair, and took a gulp of beer. "I told 'em it was dangerous territory over there fuckin' wit niggers. Probably had the Black Panthers or some shit watchin' the black cop, with their own ax to grind. So the jobber had to leave the body. It wasn't worth it. It was getting sloppy." Caluzo shook his head in disgust. "Then the sons of bitches didn't want to pay the other half of the job delivery money, 'cause we didn't have the papers. Can you believe that? Motherfucker was dead, so what'd they want? It was our job. So, rightfully, we said fuck you—we ain't doin' the second job. Can you believe their balls?"

"No," Steve said in an even tone. "What has the world come to?"

"My point exactly," Caluzo said, shaking his head. "There has to be a code, you know? You do a job, you get paid. Simple. But them damned moolies . . . well, whateva. Point is, we was gonna whack the judge and his friend for nonpayment on the first job, but then we get this call from the Main Line to do the judge instead. We ask why—just for curiosity sake—and get the word that this new job was ordered because the freakin' black judge knocked off his own wife so he could marry his best friend's wife. Beyond that, we don't ask no more questions. If a Main Liner has a thing for some black pussy and is pissed off because she got herself poisoned by her husband, hey. We ain't in the marriage-counselin' business. Next thing we know, the whistle-blower is goin' down on some trumped-up shit, because those punk-assed bastards can't do a hit themselves and can't find a reliable black jobber. We wasn't gonna hit the whistle-blower, since we hadn't been paid. Who the hell knows who got him?"

"Get the fuck outta here." Steve sat back in his chair, incredulous.

"No shit, Sulli. The judge poisoned the bitch—his own wife. The Main Liner was *real* pissed off behind Colette Paxton taking a long nap. Paid us for the job that was left unfinished—sorta like a good-faith down payment, like respectable business should be done—*plus,* paid us for what would have been the standard invoice on a car job for the judge and his friend. We couldn't pass that up, especially since we was gonna whack the judge and his buddy anyway."

"A two-for-one sale, huh?"

"Yeah. Sorta like a freebie. But it gets crazier," Caluzo said, laughing hard.

"How crazy?" Steve ran his finger through his hair and took a sip of beer to fight the nausea.

Caluzo leaned forward on his elbows, still chuckling, and fingered his gold cross, which was dangling from a thick chain. "Before we got to the judge, who had a little traffic accident later himself, the other bastard, the managing director, has a fuckin' heart attack. Word is, the judge had somebody working over in the guy's house drop some shit in his drink. Go figure. But dat wasn't our business. We got paid for both jobs as ordered, the way clean business is supposed to be done—that's why the Main Liners are all right with us: they pay well. The whistle-blower wasn't our concern anymore. So we let the poor bastard live. There wasn't no paying purchase order on him, anyway. You know what I mean? We never got the skinny on who did old man Price; it was out of our hands, and business is business—you don't get personal wit da shit."

"Yeah," Steve sighed, finishing his beer. "Business is business."

"It always is. But, it's ancient history—we just laugh about it from time to time."

Carter leaned against the register until the store was empty, looking at Esposito real hard. "Tony, man, you don't want none of this. Your pop is long buried, and I ain't coming to take your store."

Esposito glanced around and narrowed his gaze on Carter. "Look, you've been coming around here annually for the last how many years? Ain't nothin' changed since the last fifty times you asked me. Why you sweatin' me, Jimmy? You and every other cop in Philly been over here when it all went down. My pop heard somebody breakin' into his store, went downstairs, and your pop, who was off duty, chased whoever shot him into the alley, and—"

"I know the party line, dude. Save it." Carter pushed away from the counter and came closer to Esposito. "But if you haven't been watching the news, let me hip you to something: the power bases are shifting fast—like sand. The people who might have been in this, made the transfer happen so your pop could get this store for a dollar with no mortgage, are going down."

Carter hesitated, watching the new information sink in. Every time he'd been here to press Esposito, it had been to ask about the invisible running man in the alley—never about the sheriff's sale. God bless Laura. She was a genius.

"If you get real smart and real cooperative, you keep the store . . . and since you were a kid twenty-six years ago and had nothing to do with it, just like your momma didn't, then everything stays smooth. All I want is a name. Or a face. Take your pick." Carter watched Esposito squirm with the decision. Fuck all this; he'd shoot the bastard himself if he didn't talk.

"I can't testify against these guys and—"

"The store transfer was legal; that can't be reversed. This wasn't a mob hit. It was black-on-black crime. The people involved have lost their power and can't touch you. You were a minor, and just a witness. Now, talk to me."

Esposito rubbed his hands over his face and glanced out the door as he spoke. "Look, I was in high school, feel me?"

"Yeah. Talk to me."

"This young dude, like late twenty-somethin' or so, hooked my pop up. I was in the back and never saw him," he added, motioning with his head toward the storeroom. "I only heard his voice, but could tell he was young, and from the conversation knew the dude was a lawyer. Said he managed the property for his pop, and had something that would make his pop sign over the store with no problem . . . had connections to make sure my pop got the store. It was supposed to be easy. Clean. Said all my pop had to do was look the other way . . . If the cops asked him what was up, all he had to tell them was, he heard somebody trying to break into his store, came downstairs from the apartment above it to deal with it, and then heard footsteps running, a shot fired—and say that he was afraid, so he went inside to call the police, without seeing anything."

Esposito glanced around nervously and then held Carter's eyes with a furtive stare. "Listen . . . all my pop did was look the other way. They were breakin' our backs with the rent; my folks worked like dogs and couldn't get ahead. If my pop went along with it, he'd have his dream to finally own something of his own. He didn't shoot no cop. And I'm really sorry somebody did your old man. But all mine did was look the other way."

"Yeah," Carter muttered, brushing past Esposito, "all he did was look the other way."

"I can't get away tonight," Paxton said, his voice weary. "There's just too much going on, and I'm wrung out."

Laura held the telephone to her cheek and relaxed on her sofa. "I figured as much," she said in a quiet voice. "It's been crazy for me, too. I'm exhausted. My telephones were ringing off the hook in the office all day. I'm getting backed up on grant proposal deadlines. Why don't we both get some sleep tonight?"

"Yeah, baby. Thanks for understanding. I'll see you at the event tomorrow—will try to pick you up. But I can't promise. I need to meet with my attorney."

"Okay," she murmured. "Sweet dreams."

"I'll make it up to you tomorrow. Bye."

As soon as the call disconnected, she stood and glanced around the house. The natural laws of acceleration were in full effect; once a ball got rolling down a steep incline, it would continue its forward motion, picking up speed until it hit a solid block—she needed to match that quickness, or hit a wall herself. *That* couldn't happen.

Yet all of this was moving too fast and was way out of control. Bodies dropping, people getting murdered—that was not in the script. Sudden personal impact was never a part of her plan.

She went to the closet and moved the hatbox to the secretary in the hall, and then went up to her office to collect the music box. A parcel filled with electronic gadgetry sat on the floor, and she glimpsed it and smiled. Yeah . . . it was also time for a little redecorating.

* * *

He was so tired that he could barely hold his head up, but he now had a target to focus on after nearly thirty years of wondering. What Steve had uncovered would never let him rest until he played out the entire hand on this one.

Carter sat with the one thing that didn't go back into the evidence room, manipulating the wallet-size prom picture of Laura and Darien between his fingers, his nerves beyond the breaking point. "She'd been right all along, Steve." It was still tearing him up . . . she looked so young, and so innocent. He couldn't get the image of what she must have dealt with that night out of his mind. Then to lose her parents, one after the other. There was no justice.

His partner nodded and yawned into his cup of coffee, glancing around the Roxboro Diner. "The whole thing is fucking incredible, man."

"I know." Carter gave in to a yawn.

"First Colette Paxton sleeps with Haines to get her husband, Michael Paxton Senior, elevated to judge status. Paxton brings his own crew along and up with him, making his best friend, J. D. Price, the city's managing director. Then Paxton, who now hates Colette and doesn't trust his own son's paternity, connects with Juanita Price, the wife of his best friend, Managing Director J. D. Price the Second—probably in some kinda warped debt-payment thing in his own mind, given the way these guys operate. Paxton and Price's wife have a little thing, and those two sire an heir: our one and only Darien Price. In the middle of this little cesspool, some spouses get anxious." Steve shook his head.

"Paxton kills his wife, Colette, to make way for a marriage to Juanita . . . old man Price was probably no problem, and would consent to a divorce if Juanita walked without assets. But the hit on Colette pisses off Donald Haines, who sees to it that, by way of our South Philly friends, Paxton has a car accident—but not before Paxton probably did away with his best friend, J. D., if there was any divorce holdup. Then somebody whacks the grieving Juanita. Or some shit like that." Steve riffled his finger through his hair. "This crazy shit is too confusing."

"I knew it was bad, but just hearing you tell me is turning my stomach, man." Carter cast his line of vision out the window. "And somewhere in all of this, Laura's father and my father knew too much, and both of them got killed: one on paper—Laura's dad—and mine, literally."

"It was fucked up," Steve muttered through a slurp of coffee. "But it's old history. All the players are dead. We have to focus on the present case. The only thing we do know is, these guys' sons have no real love lost between 'em."

Carter nodded. "No doubt."

"You gonna tell Laura that all roads lead to Rome . . . unravel this sordid shit so that woman can get some closure, maybe a little peace?" Steve sat back, spinning his coffee mug around on the Formica table.

"Yeah. I owe her that much." Carter tucked the photo into his bomber jacket pocket. "Maybe then she can let some of the bitterness go so she can try to have a life . . . they're all dead, and their sons are all going down. What the hell, man."

Steve nodded. "All the old guys are dead, so it's time for you to let sleeping dogs lie, too, Jim. Give your soul a little peace. Everybody who did anybody got offed by somebody else—that's some crazy shit. Rest assured, one of them did your dad . . . and it's practically moot now, because all the bodies are buried."

"Tell me about it," Carter said, letting his breath out hard. "Then why do I still feel so goddamned hollow?"

"Because you never got a shot off and there's nobody living to bring down, to get it out of your system—but you're gonna have to deal with that. This time, the universe brought justice, not us. The shit happens like that sometimes."

Carter grudgingly nodded and slurped his coffee. That reality was kicking his ass.

"Listen to me, Jim," Steve warned. "While we're pretty sure that Haines hit the dirty judge and the managing director—killers themselves, who offed their own wives and tried to put a hit on two innocent men: your dad and Laura's—I don't see any reason to unearth that particular can of worms. Haines didn't do your father or Laura's, okay. Capeesh? So we might have to look the other way about his deliverance of justice on two very foul motherfuckers. That's out of our jurisdiction, and had been tied up in a neat bow a long time ago. Ancient history."

"I hear you," Carter said, sipping his coffee slowly. Defeat claimed him. He'd smacked a twenty-six-year-old brick wall. "No sense in going after a case that's been closed for years without ironclad evidence," he added, trying to convince himself to drop what was futile as much as he was trying to make his partner believe that he would—both knowing there was no way in hell he could. "For what?" Carter pressed on, almost talking to himself as he stared out the diner window. "The collars we did today didn't do it; their asses were away in college. The blue bloods didn't do our fathers. Your mob contacts didn't do my pop or Laura's."

Steve nodded and took a sip of coffee, staring at Carter as he did so.

"Thing that fucks me up, though, Steve, is, old man Paxton or old man Price could have had another contract out on the street; then one of their sons paid off the store owner to look the other way. Or somebody else diverted the mob hit from the inside—somebody shrewd, who knew what was about to go down and didn't care what happened to either old man Price or old man Paxton."

"I hear you, and I know where you're going, partner, but—"

"You and I are both pretty sure who did my father in an alley—and that SOB still has the envelope of evidence my father was carrying when he was shot. Remember what Thompson said? That's fucking with me real bad."

"Like I said, I hear you . . . Problem is this: Esposito was a kid, never saw a face, and anybody working for old man Paxton could have had evidence to blackmail the judge to do the transfer. Don't forget, Darien's so-called father, J. D. Price, was the co-owner of the building; and those two, old man Paxton and old man Price, had reason to hate each other—a damned wife stood between them . . . and Darien wasn't J. D.'s son."

Carter glanced at his partner and then held his head in his hands. "I know. I know, man. This shit is too twisted."

Steve nodded. "Crazy, complex bullshit. Plus, if Paxton Jr. has the evidence now, that still doesn't mean he shot your father. Darien, who looked up to him like he was an idol, might have given it to Paxton under persuasion. Don't forget, Darien didn't know Mike Paxton was his half-brother, or that old man Paxton was really his dad."

Steve sighed when Carter didn't interject. "Or, as smooth as Paxton is, he might have had Monica Price, Darien's wife, steal it from her husband and give it to him. . . . That might have been part of why Darien blew her brains out, then his own. We may never get to the bottom of that. The only thing we could definitely pin Paxton on—and that's *only* if we find the original evidence he used to kept the families in check—is maybe extortion, gross conflicts of interest, shit like that. But not murder, or moving a body. So, you're gonna have to let this rest, Jim. For real, for real. Everybody is dead. Got that?"

"Esposito said the building owner's *son* did the deal with his pop." Carter looked up and held Steve's gaze locked within his own.

"There were two sons, though, brother. Remember? One of whom blew his own head off. The other is still walking around. But the one who's dead, his father was the managing director—the office that Bill Caldwell stole the evidence from—so, more than likely, crazy-ass Darien Price did this. Why would Paxton Jr. put a Harvard Law degree and a ticket to the good life on the line?"

Carter sat back and rubbed his chin. He didn't have an answer for Steve. Why did anybody do crazy shit? He pursued the question like a bloodhound, unable to shake the info. He had to. The scent was locked too deep within his nose.

"But check it out, Steve. Esposito said the guy who spoke to his pop about the transaction sounded to be in his mid- to late twenties. Darien Price would have been younger."

"He never saw a face, so you know that won't hold up . . . and a memory from almost thirty years back? C'mon, Jim. They'll sweep this under the rug and pin it on the man in the coffin. I'm sure whoever did the transfer, if he had something to blackmail the building owner—or *owners*—with, didn't do the transfer himself. Smart guy like that would have made one or both of the building owners do it themselves to keep his name off any records. Plus, the blue bloods will make this go away, because to unravel this complicated ball of yarn exposes too many people. Fuck with their part of the story, and you and I could both wind up in the Delaware River."

Carter nodded, knowing his partner was telling him the truth.

"Get some rest; call Laura tomorrow after you get your head together about this. We'll dig a little more on Paxton, and if we can't get him on business corruption and fraud, you'll have to let the other shit walk . . . and just hope that Darien was the one who did your pop." Steve's expression was serious but also held empathy within it. "Yo, man, at least you finally know what went down."

Chapter 23

Donald Haines walked slowly, his charcoal-gray Chesterfield swishing against his pants legs. He brushed a fleck off his velvet collar and made sure his footfalls were loud enough to be heard from a distance. That was always the way Mr. Akhan insisted on being greeted. He could respect that. It was wise. When Akhan saw him, he stood but kept their eyes from meeting, and began walking, his hands behind his back.

Finally side by side with Akhan, Donald Haines put his hands behind his back. "Beautiful fall day."

"Ashé."

He glimpsed Mr. Akhan, appreciating his consistency. He still wore the same army fatigue jacket from a time gone by. It was comforting in an odd way. Haines put his hands behind him, matching Akhan's strides.

"Mr. Akhan, you and I go way back."

Akhan smiled. "We are both old soldiers, of sorts."

"Yes," Donald Haines said. "It is time for me to settle up with you, though."

"I'm a patient man."

"That is what I like about you."

They walked for a little longer, until Akhan found a place he wanted to stop and rest.

"Do you know how she did it, Mr. Akhan?"

Akhan chuckled and sighed. "No . . . but she's brilliant."

Donald Haines nodded with deep respect. "I want her to be safe—she's like a daughter. I owe her father." He stared at a tree. "It was regrettable that I couldn't intervene in his behalf."

"We share that, then," Akhan said quietly. "The debt to Bill, and our concern for Laura." His gaze found a pile of swirling leaves. He chuckled sadly. "I knew she'd go after them . . . I just wished I knew how she did it."

"Good friend," Donald chuckled, "there are some things one must allow to rest easy." He rubbed his jaw and thrust his hands into his coat pockets. "Until Laura brought me a proposal, I wasn't sure how best to repay your invaluable information about Paxton . . . and Elizabeth." Haines looked up at the sky.

"One hundred and twenty-two million for my people is a debt between us paid in full, old soldier." Akhan took a deep breath and sighed. "And I must thank you for the prescriptions—and for allowing us to handle J. D. Price Senior. There are some things we must handle internally. That wrong was ours to correct."

"I can appreciate that," Donald Haines said, his gaze never meeting Akhan's. "But . . . some curiosity between old friends. Did you also deal with Juanita? That seemed harsh—although I'm sure you had your reasons. I am in no position to cast judgment."

Now their eyes met for the first time since they'd been walking.

"No," Akhan said firmly. "Not a woman. This was business between men. What Price did to the people, and then Brother Bill, who'd tried to redress his actions, was inexcusable."

Haines nodded. "Patience is a virtue, and war is the business of men."

Brother Akhan nodded, satisfied. "Juanita Price was a bystander and should have never been involved. We only let you handle the Paxton problem—which also addressed justice for Carter and Caldwell—because your issue was much more personal. We would have ultimately dealt with Paxton, too, if you hadn't. But that's another matter. But never a woman. Not Juanita."

"Then who?" Donald Haines raked his hair. "That, I assure you, was not our doing—not even to rip out Paxton's heart with the loss of his favorite woman."

"I know," Akhan sighed.

Donald chuckled. "You didn't trust me not to go overboard? You watched me?"

Akhan chuckled with him. "For a while."

"Am I still under surveillance?" Haines's smile broadened.

"From time to time. But not often. Don't you know our people are invisible to you while in service positions, Donald? You've been around long enough to know that."

"But also discreet . . . and very, very fair."

They began walking again.

"I'm glad we understand each other," Akhan said after a while.

"We've always understood each other, Mr. Akhan . . . your people and mine." Donald Haines stopped walking and turned to the man before him. "This young girl is at risk, then, if neither of us sanctioned Juanita's demise. I can only assume that either Price Senior or Paxton Senior was responsible for the police officer, but whoever eliminated Juanita from the equation is still unknown—so I worry about Laura in the midst of all of this."

Akhan nodded. "She's just like her father. I told her to let it be, but I know she won't. She can't. That worries me about her, too."

"Did you have a hand in positioning her with Carter's son? That was most—"

"Noooo," Akhan chuckled deeply. "That is the efficiency

of the universe." He looked at Haines, his mirth slowly dissolving into seriousness. "We are a very spiritual people, and there are certain cosmic laws of reciprocity. You and I have seen much—and have much to atone for, by the by. However, the innocent are always guarded from the other side—both of those children were innocents when this all began."

"So, old friend, we shall indeed meet in hell."

Both men chuckled.

"Did you position her with young Paxton?" Akhan stared at him and raised an eyebrow.

"Spit out your teeth, Mr. Akhan. If anyone did that, it would be Elizabeth."

"Then," Akhan said, his voice filled with pride, "she's working him to get to the truth. I can feel it. Unfortunately, maybe she's working both of them, not sure of which one to trust—or perhaps has herself in a position where she cannot allow that—but this is a part of what she will not share with even me. She can't let it go." His gaze found a point in the sky as heavy cumulus clouds passed and cast a shadow. "I'm like a father to her, and she has been brought up in the old way of respect. Donald, I don't know what she's done to have these gentlemen acting this way . . . but I can tell you, she will *never* tell me."

"I'm a father, too. You might not want to know when it comes to a daughter."

"Ashé. So, I don't ask questions to which I do not want an honest answer."

"But if all the old men are dead, then why can't she be satisfied with that and let it be?"

Donald Haines stood quietly, patiently, waiting for an explanation. Mr. Akhan put his hands behind his back, and a slow, sly smile crept out on his face.

"There is an old folk tale, Donald, a parable perhaps, where a scorpion is drowning, and she begs a frog for a ride across the lake. The frog tells her he's afraid of her venom. But she pleads, explaining to him that it would be in her own best interest, just this once, to behave nicely. So, the frog agrees, fool for her that he is." Akhan winked. "Halfway across the water, the frog feels a sting and begins dying. In his last breath he asks her why she'd stung him, because now they'll both drown. The scorpion shrugs and shakes her head sadly, explaining to him as they both die that she couldn't help herself—it was simply in her nature. Laura Caldwell is a Scorpio woman, Donald. They made her that way. We all did."

Akhan and Haines resumed walking. A profound silence became their intimate companion. At the edge of the park, Donald Haines stopped.

"Which frog will die and which frog will turn into a prince, Mr. Akhan? Young Paxton or young Carter?"

Akhan chuckled and shook his head, his gaze far off. "Odds are, she'll sting them both."

He'd slept like a dead man. Carter slowly sat up, panicked for a moment as he saw the digital display on his clock radio, and then relaxed. Saturday. Cool. He looked down at the tent in the covers and groaned. This didn't make any sense. Here he was, only awake for two minutes, and he was saluting this woman? He had to get Laura Caldwell out of his head.

He stood and grabbed his gray sweatpants. One day off—he had to chill. The week had been ridiculous. Relax. He hadn't called her once he'd left the diner. His head was too messed up. Needed to talk to her when he'd sorted it all out himself. Later. Yeah. Later in the afternoon, maybe he'd stop by with that cheese steak she said she wanted; they could talk then—just talk. He'd drop the info on her. She'd probably react like he had and be numb. Then he'd leave her alone to process what she'd been told. Maybe try to rent a movie for her, or something . . . Sunday—maybe grab something at a diner . . . just relax, slow it down. Yeah. Like his partner had said—before he lost all perspective.

He was brushing his teeth when her call changed his

plans. He had promised himself he'd wait, but Laura always had a way of making a man change his mind. He wasn't sure how he wound up on her front steps carrying a cheese steak in the middle of the afternoon, but he did. Just like he was gonna wait to tell her all he knew. But at her kitchen table, it almost felt like home. Then he showed her the prom picture, and her eyes filled up with tears. Those big, beautiful, dark, intense eyes hadn't changed—only the expression in them had, given the last twenty or so years. He'd put it away, hugged her, and told her everything he knew. After they'd talked—just talked, much to his disappointment, although he could understand why—she'd stood on her landing, looking dazed. He'd told her he'd come by on Sunday. She'd nodded and said she needed some space.

That he could definitely understand. Events had taken an unforseen turn.

When the telephone rang for the fifth time in a row, she shook her head, glancing at Paxton's number, then at her watch. No way in the world was she walking into that event on his arm. Never. And there was no time to meet with Najira, to really talk face to face, since the telephones were out of the question now. There was simply too much heat in the system. This was a conversation to be had later, maybe even in the park.

Laura kept applying her makeup and tussled her hair back into style, adding a bit of mousse. She'd tell him she was at the beauty salon, missed his calls, and assumed he simply had to meet her there, not wanting to be late. For a significant part of the morning, she'd spent valuable time on the telephone, trying to catch up with girlfriends who had waited four days for her to slow down. Although she'd been multitasking as she talked, and while she loved them dearly, the calls right now were a major distraction. Her call to her sister Lavern, to get her cruise booked, had been a real time bandit . . . but then James came by; she had to fight with herself to stay focused. One more hug from him, one more genuine look of concern, and she would have thrown the rest of her plans out the window. Damn, he did something to her every time she saw him.

She took several slow breaths and stared into the mirror. She'd made herself look tastefully nude. Her makeup matched her skin that matched her lips, with a hint of bronze blush; only her eyes, rimmed in a smoky kohl pencil, stood out on her face. Her gown was the same color as her skin and hosted flecks of silver beading strategically dripping down the low-cut bodice. Her gown, slit up the side to the thigh, exposed her legs when she walked. Her deep-bronze heels gave them extra length. Add the fur, diamond-and-dark-topaz teardrop earrings, one heavy bracelet that looked like a handcuff, and she'd be ready. Yeah. Paxton would follow her home.

" 'Welcome to my parlor,' said the spider to the fly," she whispered. He had to be the one who did it. Momentum was at full velocity. It wasn't about brass balls; the steel balls were in play. This had to go down smooth—to close the book on everything—then she was out.

Once again Broad Street, now dubbed the Avenue of the Arts, was loaded with dignitaries. She was so tired of the game. Her thoughts went to the Caribbean. Blue water, white sands, the simple life, and warmth were calling her name. That's where she'd go first. The islands, mon. Maybe she'd promote Najira, give her a fat bonus with increased salary, send her on vacation for a month, and tell her cousin to claim that she'd come down with a nervous condition for a year while she toured the resort scene. Najira could run that shop—and had her whole life in front of her.

Laura looked at the huge all-glass-and-chrome doors of one of Philadelphia's newest construction jewels. A three-story-high wall of important names etched in muted marble, wrapped around the entire lobby inner sanctum beyond the doors, stared back at her. Old money had built this place, and interesting liaisons had created the nearly five-hundred-million-dollar multipurpose entertainment complex, whose plush burgundy seating, cherry and mahogany wood, and acoustic superiority alone had cost ten mil. Her reflection in the tinted glass gave her pause.

Did she want to be on this circuit all her life? One day, as she walked upon marble floors and mingled under cathedral ceilings, would she become like Elizabeth Haines, hungering for the impact of making an entrance? Even in her sable coat the thought was chilling. How much was enough?

Just one more little detail to wrap up, and she was out. Hell, Najira could practically run the office better than she could, and there were enough staff consultants and secretaries to keep the paperwork flowing. But who would work the magic?

The moment dollars hit the water, fund-raising piranhas, real estate barons, and industry mavens went after it. Post-election promises became contracts or hefty grants and were doled out based upon one's *investment* in the right political candidate up front. It was like going to the casinos and hedging a bet. The wise kept a little on black and a little on red. That's why Najira's father had been moved out of the way, like her own father had. He'd fucked with the wrong people and hadn't properly hedged his bets. That was something that couldn't be taught from a textbook.

One had to watch and learn. Still, Najira could manage the logistics while learning the basics from the less senior consultants, and it wasn't necessary to turn over the reins completely. Under normal circumstances, much of what had to be addressed could be handled from a laptop and a cell phone. Laura smiled sadly. Yeah . . . a cell phone could change a life.

What she had to school Najira on was learning how each event brought her closer to her targets, and how being in the mix opened up new opportunities. The way business was conducted was as standard as an architect's blueprint. Money, big money, would be at the gala. On the surface, philanthropic supporters would buy expensive tickets, and the moneys collected would go to help a charitable or political cause. But the real deals were made behind the scenes. That's where pacts were formed, where people talked in code and were given the opportunity to rub elbows with the deep pockets. Which organizations got funded began with the politics of the game—not with the merit of whatever was written in a grant proposal. Basic.

She handed the valet her keys, got a ticket for her Jag, and blended into the promenade of who's who entering the Kimmel Center.

But then she put her hand in her pocket, and her fingers came in contact with rubber. She didn't need to pull it out to know it was the unused condom abandoned from her earlier brush with Paxton. It was an overlooked, minor detail, yet the fact that she'd slipped like this made her heart race. Her mind locked on every detail she had employed. What if she'd slipped somewhere else? What if there was one little loose thread? Laura swallowed away the taste of worry and kept walking.

Yeah. She had to be cool. It was all worth it. There was private foundation money to be acquired, as well as coveted government funds. The private money always tracked the same course as federal initiatives. In the government sector, the first money stone got cast from the federal level—the big boulder. Then that influx of money fanned out and widened in concentric circles of dominance, hitting the state level, then trickling down to the city—the Main Line blue bloods were at the farthest reaches of the city and county lines but held the widest power radius and span of control over available contract funding after any election dust settled. But every one of Darien Price's cronies who were waiting for a return on their campaign investments were gonna be shit out of luck this time. The blue bloods would distance themselves from the rest of his rat pack, too. Self-preservation was always a good imperative. It was instinct.

For a moment, Laura just hovered by the door, dreading going into the event. She could feel bile rising in her throat just from the thought of how much had not changed since dirt. After the blue bloods fed with impunity, the newer white money and non–blue-blood ethnicities had a span of control, along with minority politicians. Then came the holders of dirty money, racketeers, who had power and were feared but not respected. After them, the athletes were in line; they had no power, earned no serious respect, ate from the hands of old wealth, but were invited everywhere because of their marquee value. Only a few entertainers in the limelight had realized this sad truth and fought back by using their moral authority and platform of fame to create significant change.

Laura took in a slow, cleansing breath. She could respect those people, those who stood for something even though they had a lot to lose. But it grated on her no end that the black elite in general didn't seem to realize that they were only one ring away from the poor, minority, inner-city center of gravity. Fools. And, yet, they had enough power and influence to make a difference in some struggling soul's life. In her mind, not to act was a crime of office. However, all of that was about to change. What just went down in the media was going to kick this whole thing off and create riptides. It had to, this time. Too many had ridden the backs of the people, poor people.

She forced herself to walk up to the wide, double glass doors, remembering those days of wanting to be on the inside so badly that she had employed every device, even dressing the part of the environment, like a chameleon, to get in. Then she'd realized that dressing like the environment didn't mean matching the vibe of the decor; it meant dressing like those who had power over her. God bless Najira. Been there, seen it, done it—now Laura owned it. The last time she'd naively attempted to become one of them, however, the color was green.

As she took off her coat, and spoke in pleasant tones, she kept her eyes moving, scanning the crowd. Before she'd arrived, she'd made a note to try to avoid any of the underground buzz. To be next to it now would send very wrong messages. The joint was hot with gossip; everyone, men and women alike, was breaking off into small threesomes and murmuring.

She always had to steel her nerves to do the wine-and-cheese circuit. Her cousin thought it was glamorous to mingle with the beautiful people and laugh at them, but it was strictly business, nothing glamorous or fun about it—especially not now. And it was all theater, from the way one walked into the room, claimed it, marked off territory within it, circled it, and picked off fattened calves within the herd one by one. Laura stood taller, summoning the confidence to go through with the last phase of her plan.

The pros knew that the initial entry point was essential for maximum impact. Where one stood, positioning oneself next to the prominent, was essential. Packaging. It was all packaging and performance. Money was in thc Kimmel Center, lots of it, and she'd come away with the lion's share for her anointed organizations, her firm and its clients—Paxton and his flunkies would be none the wiser. All she had to do was blend in and make her move. There was no way to force a hopeful kid like Najira to understand that you never became one of them unless you were one by birth, but like her grandmother had once said, "You can show 'em better than you can tell 'em."

But as she spotted Paxton, her internal alarm bells went off. He was in a too-cozy conversation with Elizabeth Haines. That was *not* good, especially given what she'd learned from her own brush with the woman and from Carter at her kitchen table. Paxton's back was to her; he hadn't spotted her yet. Excellent. Laura glanced around fast for Donald Haines and moved toward him. Paxton had to be doing damage control, hedging his bets in case she welshed.

Interestingly enough, as she spotted Donald Haines, he dispensed with formality, looked up at her, smiled, and crossed the room to her. Oh, now, *that* was very different.

"Laura," he said fast, smiled, giving any possible onlookers the impression that things were just fine. "There's a new variable."

"Talk to me," she said with a polite smile, but he understood her tone.

"Elizabeth has been a busy bee. Seems that she found the paper you gave me—with the new slate on it. It is now in Paxton's possession. She thought she was spiting me. This had nothing to do with you, as she has no understanding that this was your proposed slate, and ironically, she is quite fond of you. This is an old personal war between her and me. However, I'm sure Paxton will immediately know this came from you."

For a moment, all Laura could do was stare at the man. He'd told her so much in so little time. Acceleration was at maximum speed. Oh, yes, the ball was rolling now.

"I hear you."

"Good."

He'd nodded, but it was still blowing her mind that he'd let on just how much he knew of what she was doing—and that was definitely not good. How much did he really know? On the flip side, however, he was still on her side. Her answer was a simple nod as she processed the new data.

"Decide how to play this, quickly, Laura. He's coming your way. I'll do the media drop tonight; this way I'll be the culprit, and your nose stays clean."

"No," she murmured. "Stay the course. This is a game of chicken." She smiled at Paxton as he crossed the room. His expression was tense behind his false smile. She glanced at Haines. "Let's wait until after the funeral and the formal indictments; thus, you can stay out of this and not look callous." Their gazes met, and she held his. "This is between me and Paxton."

Donald Haines nodded and began to move away from her. "Do not sting the wrong frog and drown, love." His gaze was kind.

She watched Haines meld into another section of the

crowd. His last comment stilled her. It sounded so much like what Brother Akhan would have told her. But she didn't have time to process the statement. Paxton was now only two feet away.

"You look lovely," he said, his tone strained. "Glad you made it. I would have escorted you, had you let me."

"I was at the salon," she said with a smile, "and knew you couldn't be late on my account."

He paused, reading her expression, but his eyes were hard. "You will sit next to me?"

His question sounded more like a command than a request. She didn't like the tone, but it was time to play for keeps. She hated having to go to these affairs that required her to appear to play nice with the types of people she despised. Her internal response was always visceral. All she had to do was think back.

The past fought for space within her mind as she sent her gaze out the window, toward the perfection of the dark sky. Fall was her time of the year; spring brought back too many memories. At least the leaves were changing. So was the old guard. She could do this. Over the years she'd learned to don a game face and swallow away the surge of disgust like a pro. But just like in spring, the significant color to blend into was always green. That same color was also the one that exposed.

"Well?" he asked, his tone rigid like his spine.

The sound of his voice jarred her back from the past, back to her living nightmare. Laura pulled her gaze away from the window and reached for his forearm.

"Of course," she said, creasing her brow. "Why wouldn't I?"

"Because you may be nervous that I might wring your neck," he said, leaning in to send the threat into her ear.

She touched his shoulder and chuckled. "Oh . . . Elizabeth. I see she found my mock slate, did she?" Laura sighed and shook her head. "Haines will never approve that."

Paxton backed up, his eyes searching her face. "Then why the hell would you give it to him?"

She looked out the wide glass windows, acting bored, then dropped her voice to speak through her teeth. "Because every one of the networked families just hit the newspapers. I wanted the man to trust my judgment implicitly. So I offered him alternatives that he'll reject after he studies them for a few days . . . It bought me time—and you time, to give me better places to send that goddamned twelve-point-five." She touched his arm, smiled prettily, and pulled back, watching his expression slowly change. "Now, if you will stop fucking with me, honey, I'm going to work the room. Let me know where you're sitting."

Before he could answer her, she sashayed away from him. She didn't look over her shoulder at him. She didn't have to. She knew what his expression would be. Totally stunned. Then she was pretty sure that Paxton's face would go to a sly smile as he appreciated the brilliant logic of what she'd said. Then he'd relax. That's when she'd have his ass, because workin' it like that would definitely turn him on. At her house, she'd get a full confession. Sure she'd sit next to him during two and a half hours of classical music, calmly making him tremble in his chair as the orchestra gave them Beethoven's Fifth or whatever the hell they'd be serving onstage tonight.

It was so easy to dispense with pleasantries as she flitted around to talk to people she knew. In no time she'd be on an island, sipping a piña colada. Yeah, that's right. She would intermittently come over to Paxton to stroke his ego while she floated in and out of now meaningless conversation. What was there to talk about with the other competing firms? The legislators were a lock, courtesy of Senator Scott. The major campaign contributors were sewn up now, courtesy of Gentleman Haines. And the old regime of black power brokers was scramblin'.

The hunt was over, and she'd come away from the black

forest with 12.5 million worth of program bucks tied to the roof of her car. What nobody but she and Haines knew was, she was pulling over a hundred mil in moose hitched to a trailer, too. She'd gotten her hundred and twenty-some million with a single precision shot. Shit, Paxton didn't know who he was dealing with. The room had been picked white-bone clean before his ass even got there. Twelve-five? Honey, that was peanuts. And the beauty was, she'd taken it from people who'd done her people wrong.

A pure victory in her grasp, Laura relaxed and kept flowing within the room. In her mind she was so close to turquoise-blue water that she could almost feel the warmth of it lapping against her shins. When the lights dimmed and came back up to signal showtime, Paxton found her. But he was in a much more relaxed mood. His vibe almost seemed mellow. She had to keep glancing at him from the corner of her eye to be sure she was sitting next to the right man.

Clapping after each boring legislative posture and proclamation—which was a necessary evil from the podium draped in Democratic banners—she finally settled down and began to unwind. Two hours of music with nobody saying a word would do her good. She almost closed her eyes, finally feeling just how tired she was. But she didn't. It was never prudent to close your eyes in the dark while seated beside a target—or a predator.

Sheer force of will kept her alert. She monitored Paxton's body language. There was still a bit of tension in it—not sexual, not business; something else was coursing through him that she couldn't put her finger on. That definitely kept her sharp.

"We should do this one-on-one soon," he murmured near her ear once the lights went down.

His cologne wafted toward her. The richness of his voice was almost soothing. The solid male mass of his presence next to her almost felt protective. Under different circumstances, were he a different kind of human being, this thing might have worked. Shame. What a waste. Laura sighed.

She could feel him fight to keep from taking her hand in his own. For a moment she almost felt sorry for him. In her peripheral vision she studied his fine profile and dignified stature. What would a little love and acceptance have brought out from this brilliant mind and flawless body? Who would this person have been, were it not for a tragic detour?

She tried with all her might to cast away the awareness that at one time, Michael Paxton was somebody's child.

The thought was dangerous, though, because it took root and began to grow in her overactive imagination. But she couldn't help it. What must this man, who was once a beautiful little boy, have endured to make him the way he was now?

Something very peculiar began to erode the hard edges of her soul. For all her loss, for all her grief, at least she had something to grieve; he didn't. While her parents were alive, before all this went down, she was loved. Deeply, profoundly, unconditionally loved. She was Daddy's girl and Momma's joy; she had sisters whom she adored and who adored her; her family unit was never in question . . . Howard Scott came to her mind, as did the old senator.

They were horribly grief-stricken. It was written all over the old man's face when he tried to paste on the politician's smile and couldn't keep up his facade. Darien Price's siblings were grieving. From the little bit of gossip she'd overheard, Martin Ramsey's wife was in hysterics. Brad Crawford was probably on the verge of suicide. Don Edward and Jim Thompson were nearly prostrate. That was the buzz she'd avoided all night, had needed to avoid but had to hear nonetheless—and it was her handiwork. This was all these people had. *Oh, God . . .*

Laura glanced at Paxton's strong jaw, which was tilted up in defiance of the world, and wanted to touch his face. She'd want to touch anyone's face that had been denied love like that. A child pushed away from an arrogant, hard father. A child, a young black boy, unable ever to get the approval he needed so much. A mother so committed to ambition and revenge that the effects on her child went unnoticed. And in that delicate moment, between the string section's mournful wail, the French horns, and the flutes, she knew: she should have listened to Aunt Maude, let go and let God.

The music sent a sad chord of knowing through her. What had she done, all in the name of revenge? She had to keep looking at the stage, which was producing a symphonic rendition as though Heaven had opened a door. God forgive her—please, even though they weren't on speaking terms. And although she didn't have anything to do with the sordid affairs of grown people, each one of those families had children . . . and each set of children grew up with a hollow in their heart that paled hers by comparison, truth be told. Yet she'd invested so much in hating these people that the cyberterrorism used to blow up their world seemed appropriate then. The end justified the means . . . but did it ever?

For the first time since he'd been telling her this, she finally understood what Brother Akhan had meant when he'd said, "The universe is efficient. Let it be." Oddly, the kids of today said it in a way that was more direct but no less profound: don't hate. They were right.

She closed her eyes. If she ever had a child, wouldn't she do all that was necessary to ensure that part of her would live on, would do better, would excel beyond the barriers she hadn't been able to hurdle . . . out of love for that being, made and carried within her womb? Detours . . . people had simply taken very human detours and had crashed and burned in their own high-speed momentums, devoid of brakes, devoid of values to slow their roll—and somehow she'd become one of them. She wondered if Brother Akhan was right. What if the ancestors could see? What if her mother and father and aunt up in Heaven could see? What would they advise? Vengeance at this level? Not likely. But the die had been cast.

"Beautiful, isn't it?"

Michael's question made her sadder. She nodded. She wished he hadn't done what he had all those years ago. Then she wouldn't have to do what she had to do now.

"Yes," she whispered, but she didn't open her eyes. She could only think about Haines's comment about not stinging the wrong frog.

Carter closed his cell phone and looked at Steve. "Captain patched a call through from Donald Haines."

"Haines?"

"Yeah," Carter said slowly, staring at the phone. "Haines called him at home from a fund-raiser at the Kimmel. Said he was concerned about Laura Caldwell."

"Why?" Steve set down his beer and glanced around the bar.

"Said she'd left with Paxton . . . after Paxton took a couple of calls that made the blood drain from his face."

"And?"

"He was concerned for her physical safety."

Steve stared at him for a moment. "Haines doesn't strike me as a man to call the cops, especially not high up in the department on some routine bullshit gossip. Not while he's wearing a tux in a money room."

"I hear you."

"Wanna flip a coin?" Steve said. "You think Paxton took Laura to her house or his?"

Carter hesitated, then downed his beer and stood. His partner's question was eating a hole in his stomach lining. "His."

She took her time punching in the house alarm code to deactivate it. Michael's presence loomed behind her. She hated what she had to do. He followed her upstairs to the first-floor hallway and, unlike before, helped her out of her coat. He stood in the semidarkness, backlit by the moon and the streetlights, and gently placed her coat over the newel post. He drew a deep breath and let it out real slow, then looked down at the floor. She waited, not quite sure of his new, strange mood. He hadn't taken off his coat.

"Laura," he murmured, "you are the one who came closest—do you know that?"

She did. But she couldn't go there, not now. "I don't understand."

"Jim Thompson called me on my cell in the lobby after the concert, while we were all mingling and getting ready to leave. . . . His call was followed by one from Martin Ramsey. They knew I'd be there at the fund-raiser, and wanted to drop their little bomb while I was standing in a crowd—a crowd that will probably shun them *for life.*"

She froze as his gaze slowly leveled to meet hers.

"Their call was for pure spite—to let me know that they'd played one trump card: immunity." He shook his head and sighed. "I underestimated them. They told me that they were taking me with them if they went down. They'd gone to the police, had told the authorities everything from the past, even down to how Darien kept your photo from the prom. Stupidity is dangerous, as is desperation, Laura."

Adrenaline shot through her as she slowly moved back and deposited her clutch beside the hatbox on the secretary. "I don't understand."

"Yes, you do," he said evenly. "Don Edward, who is out on his own recognizance, rode by here this afternoon. His goal was to try to plead for your support—just like Monica did. Howard told them about your meeting with her, which is why you're on the inside with them these days, and Martin and Jim told me in the lobby, during the context of their spite call, that Don saw Detective Carter standing on your steps with a wrapped sandwich." His voice was vacant as he spoke. "Did he bring you a cheese steak or a hoagie, Laura, when he came for a booty call?"

For a second, she couldn't breathe. Her mind flashed back to what she'd always known, information clicking in milliseconds: Philly was a big city but had a small-town grapevine, no matter where you lived. The boys in the network always told. In their sly, bitter conversations, they rubbed each other's noses in shit for sport. And no cop brings lunch, unless it's personal.

"It was a cheese steak," she said as calmly as possible, holding the line of vision of the man who had murder in his eyes. You didn't make any sudden moves when a Doberman was snarling and blocking your path.

In two long steps, he was on her. The backhand strike he delivered was so swift and so hard, it took a few seconds for her to feel it as her head snapped back.

"You bitch!"

She was still within his swing range, but she needed to hold her ground. The salty taste of her own blood in her mouth brought her fingers to her split lip, and they came away moist and warm. "I wanted to know who did my father. That's my right, Counselor. Carter probably knows."

"Do you have any idea what I was prepared to do for you?" He stalked away from her and paced back. His voice was low, seething with rage, his motion to and fro, dizzying. "I've never let *any* woman get this close to me in my fucking life! Did you fuck him, so you could fuck me in the pocket?"

She still didn't move. Half of it was paralysis; the other half was determination to hold the line in her house. This was *her* house, damn it. He'd been the one who'd committed the first act to start this vendetta. When he reached for her throat, she pivoted, grabbed his arm, and flipped him, sprawling him on the floor.

"Fuck you," she said through her teeth. "I know you were behind some of this shit—and I told you before, I can fight."

He gathered himself up slowly; the look in his eyes as he stood was surreal. Pure evil lanced her with a glare. When he reached in his coat breast pocket, she was the definition of motion. They drew at the same time—her hatbox-stashed Magnum to his Glock nine-millimeter. It was a standoff, Southwest Philly–style.

Laura wiped her mouth with the back of her left hand,

gun cocked, her voice quiet rage. "And check it out: in my house, mine is bigger than yours, motherfucker. Don't you ever threaten me."

They were both breathing hard, arms extended, trembling more from the urge to kill each other quickly than anything else.

"How'd you do it?"

"Do what?"

"The cell phone transfers?"

"I didn't do that." She spit blood on the floor. "How'd you move the cop's body?"

"It was simple," he hissed. "At least I take credit for my work."

"Like you don't hide, and—"

"I don't have to. I have *slaves* do my damned work—except for the important shit."

"You shot him, didn't you?"

"My father was a drunk and too inept—went to sloppy Italians. One clean shot, they fled. The cop went down, the papers went with me, and in plastic, he went into his own trunk . . . and I drove him to a convenient spot and dumped him. Then got a convenient ride home." Paxton smiled. "You don't think I'll do you, Laura. Is that it? You took a few little self-defense classes and have some old-style ghetto gangster gun, probably your daddy's, and think you're getting out of here without working out something with me?"

She didn't answer, just kept her eyes trained to the center of his chest, where her gun barrel was pointed.

He shook his head. "You've never shot a soul in your life, baby. Didn't they tell you in your classes—never pull a gun unless you're prepared to use it?"

"You won't shoot me—you've got too much to lose." Her heartbeat was racing so fast, it was difficult to breathe. The ringing that the elevated blood pressure produced in her ears made it hard to hear him. But the look in his eyes instilled something in her that went beyond terror. It definitely wasn't supposed to go down like this.

He sighed, his cool winding the tension within her tighter. This bastard was for-real crazy. She hadn't banked on that. A fight, maybe. But a Glock, no.

"Laura, I had too much to lose," he said quietly. *"Had."*

She brought her other hand up to share the weight of the too-heavy weapon.

"Your arm is gonna get tired. You fire first, and you'd better make it a good shot and kill me. And then you'll need another lawyer." He laughed, the sound of it mad and shrill.

"This thing doesn't require accuracy—just point and shoot, and she'll take out the broadside of a barn. That's why I like her. She's sloppy but effective, and very ghetto."

"I'm trying to decide if I should shoot you or do you like Juanita Price. I hated that bitch, too, and until now I didn't think I could hate any woman more. I've grown." He laughed harder, delighting in his own wit.

She blinked twice. He smirked as his laughter abated.

"If we don't do this now, oh, trust me, we will do this again. There are a lot of ways to make someone go away, Laura."

"Mrs. Price? Why the hell . . . ?"

"That was Darien's mother. She was going to take away everything owed to me by inheritance, to give it to Darien, after my father married her; then she was going to try to still do so after old Pax died. I couldn't let that happen, just like I can't let this happen. Meds to add to her drinking habit was not sloppy, and was very effective—just like my father did to my mother. I learned from the old man . . . which was why he revised his original will, once he saw things my way. Only she didn't know it until she took the last sip of her drink." He sighed. "That's the only reason my father's entire estate didn't go to Darien."

"Then let's work a deal," Laura said quickly. She had to get him to put down the gun, even if they had to fight throughout the house.

"You don't have shit to bargain with, Laura." The deranged smile on his face ebbed into a cold, tight line. "Or do you?"

"How about a hundred and twenty-two million?"

He stared at her. She made herself smile.

"Bullshit."

"Really? Ask Haines."

His gaze narrowed. "Did you do Haines, too?"

She moved a pawn position on the board without admitting to anything or implicating anyone. "Did you do Liz?"

Paxton pointed his gun to the ceiling. She matched his action and pointed hers up, taking it off his chest.

"Did you get a good look at the paper that a little birdie gave you at the concert?"

He didn't answer but reached into his tux pocket, his eyes still on her, then glanced at it quickly.

"I didn't think so," she said coolly. "She had to give it to you fast at the event, and all you read were the names, before Haines might see the handoff—but if you study the brilliance of my work, you'll see buildings, factories, storefronts . . . real estate, brother. The ante just went up and got another zero added to it." Laura shook her head in disgust. "And you come in here asking me bullshit about whether or not I fucked a cop?"

He stared at her. She moved another pawn.

"You let male ego get in the way. Like some cop would tell me—for what?—about the intricacies of his case. Are you mad? He came over here with a stupid cheese steak, because I'd been uncooperative and he'd been a hard-ass. So today, he came back playing good cop, Mr. Nice Guy, trying to interview me at my own kitchen table with no legal representation." She scoffed and sucked her teeth. "Like I was born yesterday—or even eat that high-cholesterol shit."

She watched a cold smile come out on Paxton's face, and a low chuckle issued from his throat.

"I don't suppose you would eat that shit anymore."

An opening presented itself, and she took it. "Michael, I've scrapped like a yard dog to get myself out of the ghetto. I've worked hard, kept my nose clean, so why would I ever want to go back? Look around. And from the little bit you've learned about me, do I seem like a woman who is foolish and wants to go to jail, or die?"

He didn't answer, but his eyes held uncertainty.

"Put the fucking gun away, Michael. You're stressed out, acting crazy, albeit you throw a pretty good punch."

For a moment he didn't say a word, and then he suddenly laughed. "Oh, shit, Laura."

She took another chance as the safety went on his weapon, and lowered hers, but she never put it down. He still held his, too.

"Darien said you could fight," Paxton murmured, his gaze now undressing her. "I was the only one he told the truth. And I can't tell you what the image does to me."

"Did he tell you I kicked his ass?"

"Yes . . ." Paxton's voice had dipped to a low, sensual tone. "That's the image that keeps playing back in my mind—now I've seen it and have an updated mental video of what you can do." He took a deep breath in through his nose. "Laura Caldwell, you are an incredible woman. You kicked *his* ass, but not mine. Remember that. I am not Darien, by any stretch of your imagination."

She nodded. It was irrelevant. Darien Price was dead, the situation with him had happened twenty some years ago, and Michael Paxton Jr. was out of his damned mind—she was *way* over it. This bastard standing in the hallway before her was sick. She watched him. He stepped closer. Her grip on her gun tightened. He reached out to touch her split lip, and she jerked her head away.

"You made me do that," he said quietly. "Don't ever make me go there with you again. Understood?"

She just stared at him.

"You don't know how long I've fantasized about acquiring you . . . thought you were off the market; then, two years ago, you show up on radar in Philly—after being gone to build your empire for twenty years." His fingers trembled as they touched her cheek. "God, you're beautiful."

No matter what the plan was, no matter what she'd originally thought she could do, this was not it. She'd finally found her line.

When he stepped closer, she backed up.

"Don't tell me you're afraid of me, now." He smiled, triumphant. "That makes it even better, baby."

"No. I'm not afraid of you. I'm disgusted."

"But I thought you liked it rough." He chuckled and moved forward.

The muscles in her forefinger contracted against the trigger, but she forced herself to fight the urge to fire the weapon. He was missing the point and definitely going to make her drop her first body. He'd just confessed to killing two people!

The doorbell rang. She jerked her head to look at the door. Paxton immediately clicked off the safety on his weapon and dropped his gun barrel to aim at her before she could get hers into position.

"Walk ahead of me, answer it, and tell whoever it is to leavc. My car is in your driveway, so we cannot act like we aren't here—especially since you seem to have a lot of cop drive-bys these days."

She had no choice, at least none at the moment. Damn. Played. Fucked-up timing. She let out her breath hard and rounded Paxton to walk before him. He stayed right behind her, his gun nuzzling her kidney. A brief wave of relief washed through her to see James and his partner on her front steps, while another part of her was totally freaked. That they both had come was good—it might throw Paxton off the truth. But seeing two cops, now, in his state of mind, was too volatile.

In all Paxton's madness, he'd forgotten about her split lip—so had she. As soon as she opened the door, the look in Carter's eyes said it all. It all happened so fast.

Carter glanced at her mouth, then to Paxton; Steve looked at her, looked down and saw her gun—then saw Paxton's. Carter never saw Paxton's weapon as he hurled a punch over her shoulder to land square on Paxton's jaw. Paxton went down, falling backward, away from her, firing as he fell. She made herself small against the frame of the door, her gun pointed up, both hands at the sides of her head, a scream frozen in her throat, then renting the air as Steve took the first bullet—then the second one ripped through Carter's thigh. It all happened so fast, as Carter drew going down, and unloaded an entire clip for twenty-six years of history, his partner, and her.

Epilogue

On a hill in the park at Valley Green, she wore a black cinched-waist Ellen Tracy coatdress, spike-heel black pumps, a wide-brim black hat with a tulle veil to camouflage her damaged lip, and dark glasses to hide her regret. There, amid the mourners, she numbly watched the swirling fall winds blow white ashes in a sweeping dance . . . the cell phones forever concealed and commingled within scattered human remains. Tears stood in her eyes, but no one saw them. Just as no one could ever fathom the depth of her involvement.

This was not how it was supposed to go down, though.

Laura swallowed hard and followed the black-clad crowd, this time last in line, holding her wide brim against the wind and adjusting her barrel purse on her shoulder. So much waste. St. Luke's Church had been packed to capacity in the hundred-year-old Episcopalian bastion. Germantown Avenue had been clogged for blocks as the endless stream of limos and sedans claimed it with their lights on during the day. She was glad that Najira had opted not to attend, not to witness this.

In the distance, she saw Donald Haines through the delicate dotted pattern of her veil. Brother Akhan was in the throng; his face was stoic, his nods thoughtful and wise. Yet somehow, the anvil of weight on her chest simply would not go away. Breathing was difficult—she needed blue water and warm air.

"Laura," Senator Scott murmured. "Thank you so much for coming, sweetheart."

"I wouldn't have missed Monica's funeral for the world," she told him as they embraced and parted.

He swallowed hard and didn't seem ashamed to wipe at his eyes. This was about more than politics or positioning—this was family. Laura touched his arm.

"Thank you for putting the music box in with her before we had to . . ." His voice broke, and he cleared his throat. "I'm just glad that she had good friends while she was here."

"I wanted to give her back something I should have never taken from her in the first place," Laura said in a quiet voice. "What was in it was way too valuable and should have stayed in the family. Now it's been released and set free, just like her."

"That was too kind. Bless you for all that you've done for us," he said, patting her arm and moving away as Donald Haines found her.

Haines kissed her cheek, laced her arm through his, and patted her hand. "So, dear Laura, where to now?"

"Blue water," she said in a soft, faraway voice. "My nerves are simply shattered. I'll be back in time to organize things, though. Don't worry."

He nodded. "We understand. And I have never worried about your capabilities."

They walked for a while and said nothing. She spied Brother Akhan, wishing she could hold his arm now, too.

"I have everything in place," Haines finally said, his tone reverent. "The tapes you provided—and under such stress—will work to move things quickly through the judicial process. The wheels of justice do not always have to grind slowly."

They stopped walking, and he stared at her now.

"Thank you, for choosing your words very, very wisely indeed on those recordings. Both Elizabeth and I appreciate your level of discretion." Donald Haines cleared his throat and looked off in the distance. "The media has been duly advised to be favorable to you, as well. You were simply a victim, who had the presence of mind to have your home wired for security purposes, sensing a potential threat. You were not involved. But I don't believe they will be kind at all, posthumously, to the person who shall remain nameless . . . rest his soul in peace."

She smiled a half smile and urged Haines to walk, with a gentle tug. "I have a gift for you and Brother Akhan."

Donald Haines chuckled as they approached the man who wore a bright, electric-blue African robe trimmed in gold with a matching square kufi cap.

"You stung the right frog, my dear—he turned out not to be a prince. I am more than pleased with that gift alone," Donald Haines said as he held her in a warm hug for a moment, then released her.

"For swiftness in the courts, media protection, and one hundred and twenty-two million going to my community on my slate—oh, no, I have one more gift, but it is to be shared." She smiled.

"Ashé," Brother Akhan said as he joined them and overheard part of what she'd told Haines. "But a gift?"

"To be shared," she murmured, touching both of their arms. "Peace, and for unique alliances."

Both men smiled.

"In the evidence that was collected from Paxton's home, tell Captain Bennett to look into his history. Feminine intuition . . . or maybe an ancestor's guidance, but go with it."

Quizzical expressions slowly dawned on both elderly men's faces.

"This all began inside a slave ship," she murmured. "Open it up, look down in the gore within its hull, and I believe you will understand why there's been such a longstanding vendetta.

Use the papers wisely—there's a police officer's blood on them."

She kissed their cheeks and made her way back to her black Jaguar. Some things hadn't changed since dirt.

"Yo, partner, how you hanging this morning?" Carter looked down at Steve and gripped his hand, balancing his weight on his uninjured leg while trying to get used to maneuvering with a cane.

"Pretty fucked up, but at least I'll live," Steve grumbled, wincing. "You know, if you hadn't thrown that punch, all three of us might not be here."

Carter chuckled. "I lost perspective, brother—didn't even see the damned weapon. All I saw was Laura's busted lip, and flipped out."

Steve coughed and tried not to laugh as he held the place on his abdomen where he'd been shot. "Trying to fight a man with a Glock nine with your bare hands—you're nuts."

"But damn if baby didn't get the tapes, huh?"

Steve's smile widened. "You know she's guilty, right?"

Carter chuckled. "Guilty as sin."

"You feel like investigating her angle to find out how she pulled it off?"

Carter's smile faded until Steve winked. "Naaaah."

"Yeah, me neither," Steve said, chuckling till he coughed. "But aren't you curious, man? I mean, when did you figure it out?"

Carter glanced toward the window. He and his partner both knew he'd never tell that. "Like you told me once, some things ya gotta just let go. Justice has been served—*lovely.*"

Steve nodded, then motioned to the door. "Here's Mata Hari now, doing black to the bone."

Laura smiled and sauntered into the hospital room, delivering a kiss on Steve's forehead and then one on James Carter's cheek. "How're you guys doing?"

"We're alive; that's a start," Steve fussed.

Carter looked at her, wondering how she knew how to make all those moves. Everything was so perfect, so clean . . . and even coming from a funeral, Laura Caldwell was to die for. "Take a short walk with me," he said, then turned to his partner. "Don't worry, I'll be back in a minute—I can't go that far."

"Hey, I'm here for the duration . . . go handle your business." Steve blew Laura a kiss and grabbed the TV remote by his side and shook his head.

"Go easy on an old man," Carter teased as Laura threaded her arm through his, helping him hop-walk with the heavy cast.

Feeling her warmth at his side radiate through him made him know for sure that he'd been one lucky SOB. The bullet got thigh muscle, not bone, and had left him a working limb without pins. Still, the minor exertion was kicking his ass, and he leaned against the wall as he talked to Laura in the hall.

"I hear you're going away for a little while before all the trial madness starts."

"Yeah," she said quietly. "Holiday time with my sisters, plus I could use some blue water to help me think and clear my head—I'm a Scorp." She smiled. "Water does me good."

"Black does you good . . . ," he said, the memory of being with her permanently branded inside his skull. "Bronze does you good . . . tan does you good. Yeah . . . you take a well-deserved break, and I'll see you as soon as you get back, when my leg is a hundred percent." No lie, this was definitely a Scorpio woman—fine, even with a busted lip.

She smiled wider and looked away. "You might decide to join me one of these days, maybe?"

"On my salary, baby, I can't half get to Atlantic City."

She nodded and looked at him. "You've got enough years to retire. If you could, and money was no object, what would you do with the rest of your life?"

He laughed. "If I hit the lottery, you mean?" He swept his palm over his jaw and leaned on his cane. "Damn . . . that's such a fantasy, I don't dwell on it. But, I might pick up where I'd left off before I joined the force."

"Which was . . . ?"

There was something about the way she was looking at him, a quiet excitement in her eyes, but searching his for honesty. All the laughter stopped. It was as though her gaze had siphoned it away.

"I joined the force to try to make up for things I'd never said to my dad when he was alive. Also wanted to find out who'd shot him. Now that I've dealt with that, I really don't know where I'm headed."

"What did you want to do before you started this mission?"

He shrugged. "Had some crazy notion to take my urban studies degree to the next level, maybe write, make changes." He chuckled and looked away. "I was an educated revolutionary—was gonna change the world with words. Never thought I'd have to use a gun as my change agent."

She touched his arm and brushed his mouth with a soft kiss. "Think about what you want to do, and let me know. Where there's a will, there's a way."

He chuckled and pushed away from the wall. "Yeah, but reality is reality, too."

"If a lottery ticket, like a cruise pass, lands in your mailbox, get on that ship that debarks out of Philadelphia." She looked at him hard. "I never want to see you shot, or have to drape a flag over your casket. We're getting too old for this shit, Jim. There's gotta be another way."

He nodded and watched her walk down the hall . . . somehow knowing that if Laura Caldwell was involved, another way was sure to be made.

She sat on the side of the tub and shook her head, glancing out the bathroom toward her packed suitcases on the bed. How did she get caught like this? By a cop, no less. All these years of dodging, being smooth, and Joe-regular is the one to slow her roll? Deep.

Laura stood and threw the bright-pink plastic pregnancy-test stick in the trash. The ancestors had to have a hand in this—along with a cosmically efficient sense of humor.

"What did it say, girl?"

"I'm cool," Laura announced through the bathroom door. "You got all your stuff? Ready for some white sand and blue water?"

"Ready? Pullease!" Najira hollered back.

"You check your bank account and credit report?"

Najira appeared at the bathroom door, hovering in the entrance. "No. Why? Girl, around your smooth-criminal ass, nobody is safe. Talk to me, Laura."

Laura shrugged.

"Damn, whatchu do now, girl?" Najira's eyes darted nervously between her cousin and the wastebasket.

"You should always check your accounts regularly, and always keep your mind on your money . . . might find a little something in there to allow you to more fully enjoy your vacation."

Najira covered her mouth.

"It's all good."

"Whose account did you tap, Laura?" Najira whispered.

"Aw, relax," Laura chuckled. "He won't miss it. Trust me. Brother owed you for a bitch slap—and since he was the education czar, you don't have any more bogus student loans from that bullshit program that never readied you to get a job, any ole way. Chill."

"What!" Najira slowly came into the bathroom and glanced down at the trash. "Oh, shit . . . You're crazy *and* you're busted. Whose is it?" she asked, pointing toward the pink-stained stick and also referring to her sudden inheritance. "Now whatchu gonna do?"

Laura laughed. "What I always do. Call James Carter, later, and hedge my bets."

* * *

She didn't even struggle against the inevitable as the blue water around her became cloudy and pink. She knew what was happening. She'd been waiting for the universe to come into balance, as it always did. She pulled herself toward the side of the pool as a harsh cramp doubled her over. Laura looked up at the dawn filtering in through the clouds, each ray of bright light making her squint with pain. There was always a price. She knew that going in, but had hoped to defer it this one time.

An eerie calm befell her as she held on to the rail and walked up three flat steps in the shallow end of the pool. Stumbling across the terrace, her sopping footfalls slapped against the slate. Another sharp pain nearly made her retch as she felt a clot pass out of her body and into her bikini. Hot tears filled her eyes. She'd only been pregnant for a month, her womb a host to new life that was now being siphoned out of her to repay a cosmic debt.

Laura covered her mouth and tried not to wail aloud. Rippling chills swept through her as she neared the telephone. Najira was asleep, and it was best that she stay that way. Instead, she'd wake the doctor at his home and get someone to send a car. Her soul hurt worse than her body, anyway, and there was no cure for that. The only person she wanted to be there to hold her hand through the ordeal didn't even know she was pregnant. He was many miles away in the states. Poetic justice, perhaps cosmic retribution. It didn't matter. She was losing the baby. Monica's children flashed through her mind. Orphaned.

Laura gripped the edge of the small breakfast-nook table, her eyes shut tight but her body yielding to fate.

"You all right, miss?" a soft voice asked as the day maid entered the kitchen.

Laura could only look up. Her voice caught in her throat upon a hard contraction. She watched the older woman's eyes rove down her body and remain fixed on the warm, dark puddle at her feet. "Just call the doctor," Laura breathed out through her teeth when the maid gasped and covered her mouth with her hand. "Don't wake Jira. I was too old, anyway."

Without a word, the maid went for the telephone and quickly punched in a number. "I'll pray for you, girl. It'll be all right."

"Don't pray for me," Laura whispered. "I don't deserve it."

The older woman looked up, the lines in her ebony face seeming to deepen with worry as Laura swayed and grimaced again. "No, chile," she murmured. "That's where you wrong. We all deserve a prayer. We all human . . . no matter whatchu tink you did."

Laura closed her eyes, tears streaming down her face as she nodded. Yes, the elders had been right. She should have let the ancestors handle it all.

The following is an excerpt from
BLIND TRUST
by Leslie Esdaile-Banks,
available in September 2005
wherever books are sold.
ENJOY!

Chapter 1

Grand Cayman Island . . .
Present day, after the storms . . .

He hadn't called. She hadn't asked him to come. Detective James Carter hadn't even sent a postcard or birthday card. Her birthday was in November, his was in April, and neither had made contact. But hadn't that been the way she'd wanted it? Almost one full calendar year had passed. The lies she'd told herself had worn thin. She'd stopped checking the mail and running for the telephone months ago. She'd survived a miscarriage alone, while he'd apparently dealt with a miscarriage of justice by himself.

It seemed they both quietly understood that they had to do what they had to do. Everything in her life had been decimated. Her parents were dead. His parents were dead. She'd lost the baby to an early miscarriage. Although she'd survived, layers of her life had splintered and peeled away like the wood from her villa. Her faith . . . What was that these days? It seemed like the good died young and those who were evil lingered indefinitely to do more injustice—unless helped to a timely demise. None of it was fair. None of it was right. But it was what it was . . . and there wasn't a soul on the planet who could understand the depth of her losses, or who she could fully share the pain with, not without revealing too much. Laura had to take care of Laura.

With everything else that had been washed away, why wouldn't what she'd briefly shared with James Carter have been as well? They hadn't been together long enough to cement anything between them. Then again, had they been together for years, the cracks and fissures in any old mortar they might have shared would have surely given way.

Her island home was now mere rubble after a category five hurricane. Vengeance also apparently gave as good as she got. There was no sanctuary from any of it.

"Miss Caldwell," her manservant said, "please consider coming back, once all of this is behind us. It will take at least six to eight months, they're saying, before all of this is sorted out." He looked around at what had been a palatial villa in despair. "But we should get you to the airport soon. The roads are still questionable, at best." His wife simply sighed and walked away with tears in her eyes.

Laura nodded toward the graying couple, not really looking in their direction. Yes, Mr. And Mrs. Melville understood, just like she also intimately understood the emotions that underscored loss. Things should have been different, but they weren't. What was supposed to just be a tropical storm had become something so much worse.

James should have seen this place before it was destroyed. They should have had breathless nights here, his thick, six foot five, chocolate frame enveloping hers . . . their child sleeping peacefully in her crib. But their relationship never stood a chance and she'd never carried his child to term. Just like the devastating storm, the loss had been an act of God. She remembered James's eyes, though. A year away from him couldn't erase that.

All of it crowded into her soul so quickly that she couldn't speak as she picked her way around the perimeter of what had been her villa, knowing true disaster would never be fully behind her. The past was a specter, it was a living and violently haunting thing. Just like they named hurricanes, old deeds also had enough velocity and force to shatter and take lives. Perhaps those things seemingly past needed to be given a name, too. But it was probably best that no one did.

Splinters of pink wood lay strewn along the sparkling white sand . . . like flesh of the house torn away from the frame, bones. It was all gone. The sun had the nerve to be out strutting her stuff, stunning in the aftermath. Laura wondered if that was how she'd appeared to others when she'd showed up at the funeral in a designer ensemble, her black hat elegantly tipped to the side with a dramatic veil? Flaunting, like the sun, without censure or shame . . . a contributor to a murder, much in the same way the sun's warm air masses had collided with a cold front to create a force of nature to be reckoned with.

What did Senator Scott do in the aftermath of his niece's death? Did he walk around in a daze, wondering about all his past deeds that led up to the shamble of his life? Although she wasn't a direct contributor, Laura had to admit that she'd provided the heat in the system, and Monica Price was dead. *That,* she'd take to her grave.

Turquoise blue waters lapped against the beach, returning sodden deck furniture with its attention. Ruins were washing up on the shore. Laura wondered as she stared down at the waterlogged personal effects, what battered part of her life might one day wash up on a beautiful coast?

Shards of stained glass mingled with coral, seaweed, and downed silver thatch palm branches on what had once been her front steps. Dead birds, that had once been gorgeous jewel-green-hued parrots, were ugly, bloated, sand covered, and gray. Like her furniture, the birds were hardly recognizable as they lay in nature's open morgue beside dead shellfish and injured turtles that had simply become part of the sewage now taking up the center of the road. No power, water only in sporadic, rationed quantities, fuel was almost nonexistent.

Yes, it was time to go back to Philly.

* * *

A full year, almost, and not a call from her. She'd dropped off the face of the earth, just like she'd promised she would.

But despite the court cases, the grand jury indictments, and trials that he and his partner, Steve, had to endure testimony at as cops . . . and despite knowing in his soul that she was as guilty as sin, he couldn't get Laura Caldwell out of his mind. Tall, cinnamon-skinned, curvaceous, crazy . . . with short, dark, velvety hair and legs that could stop traffic on Broad Street. Unforgettable. Dangerous as hell. Sexy enough to make a man reconsider his badge. Lethal.

James held the twisted hunks of metal in his fist. The moment the funeral director had quietly summoned him from the hospital, he knew what the melted fragments were—the cell phones she'd used to set up and take down a family empire. Being a detective had its advantages. Favors were always being curried. The good senator had obviously forewarned his man to give anything to the cop who could be trusted.

The irony was profound; the senator worried that an old Blackberry or Palm Pilot stashed in a cremation-destined coffin by Monica's friend, Laura, might indict him—but Laura had hidden evidence that would have taken them both down and cleared the Price-Scott family name.

That was the problem with double-dealing. Sometimes you played yourself. This time, unwittingly, the senator had given away the keys to his kingdom. He now owed a mortician. The senator probably thought he also owed a cop, big time. Maybe he did. It might buy Laura more amnesty, if the good senator thought she was protecting his family interests to the very end. In any event, it was an excellent marker to have out there in the streets to call in one day. The woman had brass balls.

James rubbed his tender thigh that still ached in certain weather. He still walked with a slight limp. The cycles of bullshit never ceased. Where was his woman, and who was she with?

He leaned against the stern rail of the cruise ship and

waited, allowing the sharp fall breeze to cut at his face. Raw winds took up residence in the old gunshot wound in his thigh, making the muscles begin to knot. Over forty was no joke. But she wore it well . . . last time he saw her, at forty-four, Laura Caldwell was drop dead fine. He'd always envisioned taking a cruise with her, versus a cruise to nowhere to simply cover her tracks. But he had to let the past go while in international waters . . . just like it was time to let Laura go. It was over. She hadn't called for him. Hadn't remembered the hot nights that were still burned into his skull forever. James opened his hand and watched the charred remains of her many lies fall from his palm and disappear beneath the churning water's dark surface.

Maybe it was better that way.

Laura put the key into the front door of her Pennsylvania Avenue home in Philadelphia and turned off the alarm as she crossed the threshold. There were no suitcases to set down. Her handbag was the only weight on her shoulder—that and her conscience. It was so quiet that her shallow breaths echoed throughout the immaculately kept space.

She glanced around. The maid had been diligent. Nothing seemed out of place, except her. This wasn't home, it was a place to crash and burn. She'd never owned a real home; everything in her name was simply real estate.

Weary beyond imagination, she moved throughout the sand-colored environment. Her mind still had the beach within it; salt water and surf still stung her nose. The fall was beautiful back East, the colors profound. But there was no sun like Caribbean sun, no water so blue on the planet. No ebony sculpted body like James's. Yet, paradise had ousted her. Cosmic justice.

Johnny Walker Black was calling her name. James used to drink that, she remembered, as she dropped her barrel Coach purse on the crescent shaped secretary and hung up her Burberry raincoat. A lot of things were calling her name.

She hadn't been in a man's arms in a year. Hadn't really laughed, except when her sisters and her cousin, Najira, came to visit. But that was different. There were things they couldn't discuss, things that they couldn't comprehend through a mere glance. Suddenly, being within her own space felt hollow.

He nursed a Grand Marnier from the observation deck, wondering why he'd chosen her old drink instead of his. Nostalgia had him in a headlock. He saluted the wide-open sea with his brandy snifter. Good riddance to a bad woman. A Scorpio woman could be poison. She'd been trouble since the day he'd laid eyes on her, worse from the moment he'd put his hands on her. Now what was he going to do?

Going back to life on the force was out of the question. Early retirement, then what? Now that the trials were over, Steve had suggested that they open a PI agency, but hunting for criminals, even for way better pay, had lost its appeal. Although he and that crazy, roughneck white boy would make one helluva team. Still. The thing with Laura had been a mission. She'd helped him solve his father's murder, and put the past behind him. Justice got served, even though it wasn't legal. James raised his glass to the sky; may the dead rest in peace. Mission accomplished. Anything else was just something to do. Just like jumping on this ship was something to do, all the amenities of being here felt like something critical was missing. Laura.

She stared at the telephone, willing it to ring and then laughed out loud at her own insanity, snatched it, and punched in the number she knew by heart.

His hip vibrated and he let out a long, annoyed breath. But when he stared at the number, his thumb hit the receive button so fast that he almost disconnected the call.

"Hey," her voice said, coming through the line like a silk noose.

He pressed the phone closer to his ear and shut his eyes—instantly hung. "Where you been at, girl?"

"Home . . . Detective. Why?"

"So now I'm just 'Detective' again?"

She laughed. He was slightly pissed. Where had she been and why hadn't she called?

"No, James, you're more than that." She chuckled. "Why so testy, though? Hello, baby, would've been nicer."

"Ain't heard from you in a long time. A man might have a few questions."

"And I haven't heard from you . . . in, like, a year, James."

He could hear a tinge of annoyance in her voice that was comforting.

"Lotta trials. A lot of things had to be made neat."

She smiled and closed her eyes. Of, course, that made sense. Wise move. "Yeah. True. On both ends."

"Cool."

Silence rippled between them.

"You busy?" she asked carefully.

He could tell she was listening to his environment, as though sensing his whereabouts. He liked that. "I'll have to get back to you in a few days."

"Oh," she murmured. "So, it's like that, now. I understand."

He stared at the horizon. She'd never understand, just like he'd never tell her that he hadn't been with anybody while waiting for her call like a fool. He didn't want to know if she hadn't. That would fuck him up worse than he already was now. "You hear, but you don't hear," he said, his tone distant.

She hesitated. "What don't I hear, James?"

"That I'm somewhere that won't allow me to get back tonight."

She chuckled. "Tell her I said—"

"Her name is *Sea Farer's Mist,* and she's about as long as a football field—"

"What! *You* took a cruise and didn't come see me? Why?"

Laughter filled his ear and coated his insides with her warmth. He took a sip of his drink and winced. "Yeah, I took a cruise, alone. All right? And the ship just crossed into international waters about an hour ago."

A long silence numbed the line.

"I had to put some *heavy* things to rest. Hear me?"

Another long pause greeted him, and he could hear her swallow.

"Thank you for the belated birthday present." She stirred the liquor in her short rocks glass with her finger. The lack of calls and correspondence made so much sense. James was a practical man; that was one of the things she loved most about him. His mind.

"Don't mention it," he finally murmured. How did a man forget a Scorpio woman? Especially when the nature of their relationship needed to remain off all radar. "What are you drinking?"

"Johnny Walker. Black. For old times' sake."

He smiled.

"I said thank you," she said, her tone growing gentler.

"Yeah," he said quietly, thinking of how to catch a plane the moment he hit landfall. "You can do that later."

"Was on my agenda anyway, baby."

Donald Haines drove slowly as he came off the Schuylkill Expressway and tried to remember which way to turn to access the Girard Avenue Bridge. From there he'd have to make a left, or was it a right, to go by the park to meet his friend, Mr. Akhan. Good thing he'd allowed extra time in case he got lost. But the very fact that he had to mentally struggle at the directions he should have known in his sleep, told him all he needed to know. It was time to end the game.

Finally bringing his silver-gray Mercedes to a rest at the curb, he remembered how Akhan liked things done. Neat. He would get out, walk to a bench, sit quietly and wait for his aged, fatigue-wearing comrade, who often donned African robes and sandals under his ragged combat gear. Akhan would pass him with a nod to signal that they might walk a bit together and talk where there were no walls with ears. Then they would sit like two obscure old men on the benches. One from the Main Line, one from North Philadelphia, one an Anglo aristocrat, the other a dignified black activist . . . and they would see eye to eye, before returning to their very private, powerful lives.

A shudder ran through Donald Haines as he smoothed the velvet lapels on his herringbone tweed chesterfield, grabbed a large manila envelope off the passenger's seat, and got out of his sedan. Brisk winds cut through the warmth of his coat. It was raw outside, just like his nerves had become.

He found a bench quickly and sat down, glancing over his shoulder. What if it was the wrong park, or the wrong day? Mild panic began to seize his breath and it made him stand and glance around with added purpose, his motions jerky as perspiration began to cover his skin. Hot tears of frustration rose to his eyes, blurring the dangerous-looking images around him. Shadows of humanity seemed to be everywhere. The park had predators, drug addicts and dealers, all lying in wait for an unarmed white stranger from a neighborhood far from here.

As a thick-bodied man approached, bearing a face he didn't recognize, Donald clutched his manila envelope tighter. He had a right to be in a public park. "Get back," he said through his teeth. "Get away from me."

"Old friend," Akhan said, his tone soothing. "Let us sit today and watch the birds. A stroll may be too taxing."

Donald Haines relaxed as his mind grappled with the dark image before him. The man's face was vaguely familiar. Ruddy skin, wise old eyes. His bald head shielded beneath a crocheted knit cap. A bright orange dashiki peeking out from under a weathered, military green army jacket. Brown corduroy pants that ended at dingy white socks and sandals. He let his breath out in relief. "Mr. Akhan. You came."

Akhan nodded and sat first, peering up at Donald Haines. His once steel blue eyes seemed clouded by fear. His normally immaculate, barbered blond hair was out of place, as though someone had been chasing him. Although he wore an expensive coat, he still had the appearance of being slightly disheveled. "Why wouldn't I?"

"I don't know . . . one can never be sure how things will turn out." Donald Haines glanced around and then sat slowly beside Akhan.

"We go way back, you and I," Akhan said calmly, trying to stem the alarm coursing through him. Haines didn't look well. "The hour of the call, the sound of your voice, I knew it was important."

Nodding quickly, Donald Haines thrust the manila envelope toward Akhan. "I changed this right after Laura left town—so it should hold up."

Akhan accepted the package but studied his ally's face. "Talk to me, Donald. We are too old to play cat and mouse."

Haines leaned in and then shut his eyes. "I'm losing my mind," he whispered and then sat back and studied the sky.

Neither man spoke as Donald collected his emotions and tucked them away. Akhan was a patient man, always had been.

"Alzheimer's, is what they're saying," Donald Haines finally murmured. "For a man with as many secrets as I have . . . I cannot start babbling, or begin speaking to the wrong person at the wrong time. Cancer I could have accepted—but not this." He balled his fists tightly and then opened his hands slowly as he stared at them. "My medical records are in there as well . . . should I say something incriminating, it can be chalked up to the insane ranting of an old man with a diagnosed condition. You might need to have that as a defense one day. My will is in there, too, with a notarized alteration to it that was done long before I became less than myself. Guard these records well, my friend."

Akhan nodded as he addressed the brilliant blue fall sky. "Ashé," he said quietly. "Ashé."

"I have too much personal dignity to be held hostage in my own home by a wife who despises me, or be sequestered to a bedroom, drooling on myself, with a fucking day nurse to wipe my face and my ass." Haines spun on Akhan, holding his line of vision with rage glittering in his eyes. "After all you and I have been through, this final indignity cannot be!"

Akhan nodded and closed his eyes. "And you have come for a last favor."

"Between friends."

Akhan nodded. "Between friends." He looked down at the manila envelope. "I would have done it for free, you know. We have history."

"Yes, and because we have history, I want you to be sure that everyone who is supposed to get what they deserve, does."

Again, neither man spoke as the far-off sounds of street traffic filled the void.

"They will be hiring a nurse?" Akhan asked quietly, not looking at Haines.

"Yes. Soon I won't be allowed to go out alone or drive, and my telephones at home are already compromised." Haines looked toward the tree line. "Please make sure she's skilled so I don't choke to death on my own vomit."

"It will be quiet and in your sleep," Akhan said, standing slowly. "You are owed that much."

"Thank you," Haines whispered as he stood. "But . . . I don't suppose we could just walk one last time, you and I? I will miss our collusion as we strolled." He gazed up at the sky and then at the dilapidated mansions that rimmed the park. "There just wasn't enough time to fix all the wrongs."

"No," Akhan said, as they began to stroll. "We fixed so much and then had to tear down so much . . ."

Donald Haines let out a long, weary breath. "That's why I had to concede to the gaming industry coming to this state. It's the cycle of political life—you itch, I scratch, then vice versa." He searched the sky for words as sentences began to elude him. "It was out of my hands," Haines said with another weary sigh. "For a hundred twenty-five million in city program funds routed the way I wanted, I had to give the state level a pint of blood."

Akhan clasped his hands behind his back as they continued their lazy stroll across what had become park badlands. "Legislators are allowed to enter into blind trusts . . . one percent personal equity in each of fourteen slot charters, which means they could own up to fourteen percent at any one time without having to ever make the public aware of their interests. They don't have to show a paper trail on any lobbyist forms; only the blind trust has to be named."

Haines chuckled, but the sound was laced with pain. "See, my friend. I was already becoming senile, then. Insane."

"Crazy like a fox," Akhan said with a knowing smile. "Oh, no, Donald, I am sure you had a plan."

When Donald Haines didn't answer, but only smiled in return, Akhan pressed his point. But the tone of his voice was not accusatory, just a bland statement of fact. "The casino industry will descend upon the region like vultures, and will also bring the rest of their more unsavory businesses and colleagues with them." He stopped walking and looked at Haines hard. "Donald, they made you give up more than a pint. Under any circumstances, that is not like you to get cheated."

"For a man who has run out of time to use his mind . . . where his influence is dwindling and health failing as his son begins to realign his assets, I decided to offer them my head on a silver platter rather than lovely Laura's. It was only a pint," he said with a sad smile. "I'm already dying and can do without the transfusion of more assets. Let it rest."

They began walking again. For a long time neither man spoke.

"I had to allow my Italian friends to bring their casino interests here," Haines said casually after a while. "I owed them for the Paxton situation, even though I paid in cash—we know that cash is merely the down payment. Until a favor is bestowed, a solid one, it doesn't count. Besides, who will ever keep my busy little bee, Elizabeth, from unraveling all our good work?"

"Ashé," Akhan said deep in thought. "Your wife could be very . . . It could get complicated."

"If I begin talking in my sleep or begin to forget how much she hates me?" Haines nodded. "Yes. Now you really understand. So rather than also have her sudden, yet timely, demise on my soul when I die, why don't we simply take my piece off the board. I'm only sparing her for my son's sake. That's the least I can do for him after she ruined him." He stopped walking and held Akhan's shoulder. "The king is finally down, even thought the queen is still alive. But it was a good game. Checkmate."

"But it was a good game indeed," Akhan said, placing a firm hand on Haines's shoulder to match his stance. "And I shall miss our walks."

Donald Haines nodded, and then glanced around. New tears suddenly rose to his eyes and then burned away. "Show me to my car, old friend. I cannot remember where I've parked it."

She heard a heavy motor enter her street, stop, and back up. Laura quickly got up from the sofa, closed her cream silk robe and tied it hard, and then walked to the front bay window. She stared out at a vehicle that she didn't recognize. Frozen, she watched the black Sequoia with tinted windows pull into her driveway. She immediately cut the lights and moved toward the closet to retrieve her father's peacekeeper from the hatbox perched high on the top shelf. At five A.M. this wasn't a pop call from friends and family, it was most likely a hit. If so, she had an old .357 Magnum to address it.

She slid against the wall and glimpsed out of the window without moving the butter-hued sheer curtains, and then smiled.